LILLIANA HAZEL

Beneath the Light of the Moon

First edition

ISBN: 979-8-9995602-1-6

Cover art by Sage & Fable

This book was professionally typeset on Reedsy.
Find out more at reedsy.com

For all the people who felt like reading and writing was their only escape—the only place they were allowed to be heard—this is for you.

Contents

Author's Note

Hello there! *Beneath the Light of the Moon* is a darker romance book, so before you continue on, please read the following content warnings. Your mental health matters, and if any of these give you pause, please do *not* read. If you have any questions, or would like to know anything in more detail before you read, feel free to email me at lillianahazel9 49@gmail.com. I'd be more than happy to clear anything up for you.

Also, the characters' actions in this book are toxic and should not be used as a baseline for a healthy relationship. What I write fictionally is not what I support in real life.

So, without further ado, here are topics and triggers BTLOTM covers:

- Autopsies/viewing dead bodies
- Blood and gore
- Cancer
- Childhood trauma
- Death of a parent
- Dubious Consent
- Gentrification
- Guns/knives/weapons
- Kidnapping
- Masturbation
- Mental health challenges
- Mild alcohol and substance abuse

- Mild torture
- Mutilation of a corpse
- Non-consensual drugging
- Non-consensual pictures
- Referenced misogyny
- Sexually explicit content/texts
- Somnophilia
- Stalking
- Threats
- Violence
- Voyeurism

Playlist

Scan to immerse yourself fully into the gritty world of Mikko and Anika.

I

Falsifications

1

Nightmares

Mikko

The Truth Behind Portland's Night Scene

"**S**afe nights out on the town? A thing of the past apparently," reports Steve, one of The Portland Social's most dedicated journalists. After some digging, we were appalled to discover Bubblegum, a notorious nightclub in downtown Portland, may not be as safe and carefree as the owners would have you believe.

From the trendy pink neon sign hanging above the entrance, Bubblegum entices visitors to slip inside for a night of dancing and drinking. But after multiple reports from partygoers, the club might be in a sticky situation. And not the kind found under your dance shoes.

One woman said the drinks were watered down while still gouging her bank account. Another stated the space was cramped and in need of a deep, deep cleaning. A man even told us someone had stolen his wallet right out of his back pocket while he was dancing.

While most of those mishaps may seem ordinary and a consequence of many night clubs, that's not where these perils end.

A few evenings ago, someone anonymously confirmed the murmurings surrounding the apparent gambling dens located in the basement of the club. Many lower levels of businesses hold boilers and mildewy storage space. It seems Bubblegum *is not one of those places. We can't help but wonder where this money is coming from and going off to? Who would participate in such heinous activities?*

And most importantly, why have the police not stepped in?

Great.

As his eyes skimmed over the article—which was written like a cheesy reality TV script—Mikko found the urge to drown himself in liquor creeping in. It was wrong, he knew, but it was so, so much *easier* that way. The bite would erase the acidic taste accumulating in his mouth.

His finger twitched involuntarily.

Instead, he picked up his cellphone from the corner of his work desk and called the only person he could at this early hour. The time displayed on his phone was a little after two in the morning, but he knew Cristiano would pick up.

Sure enough—

"Something better be on fire," Cristiano answered on the third ring, "because I had *just* gotten my pillow fluffed right to fall asleep."

Mikko snorted. "You and that damn pillow. You know when you start seriously dating, you're going to have to hide that ratty thing."

"Hush, let me worry about that," muffled rustling could be heard in the background as his friend no doubt stuffed the pillow behind his head, "now, please tell me why you've interrupted my beauty sleep."

"Didn't know you had a set bedtime," Mikko said, a sly grin on his face. He crossed a leg, his ankle resting leisurely on his knee waiting for his friend's response.

"Well, I would, but crime never sleeps," Cristiano countered, "so,

4

neither can I."

"Remind me to rectify that for you, yeah?"

"Of course, of course," he said, "but remember, I only accept your ploys via—"

"Cash," both men stated in unison.

"Ah, so you *do* pay attention," Cristiano teased.

"I find you stop repeating yourself when I do."

"Hey, I told you to go to the doctor's to get your ears checked…I was starting to think they were *clogged*." Mikko could almost hear the way his friend lifted his arms in faux surrender, his own smile widening. Cristiano always knew how to yank him back from the dangerous abyss in his head.

"I did," Mikko replied, "and they said I'm *fine*."

"A second opinion never hurt anyone—"

"*Cristiano*."

That shut him up. "Yes?"

"Have you checked the books recently because it seems a certain someone has been missing their payments."

A brief pause, then, "No, I haven't."

"Well, Ivan Morovich is spending his rent in other ways."

"Oh, god," Cristiano groaned, "I told him to knock that shit off or you'd be chewin' his ass out. I see he didn't listen. Seems like *he* needs his ears cleaned."

Mikko would've laughed if not for the stupid article sucking all the fun out of his evening. "Not only did he not listen, but journalists have latched onto *Bubblegum's* problems due to his negligence."

"Don't they have other people to harass besides us?"

"Apparently not."

A dramatic sigh echoed through the phone's speaker. "Send me the article," Cristiano finally said.

"Get your glasses ready, the small text might give you a migraine."

"I fear the content will do that all on its own, but thanks for the concern."

A few tense seconds passed while Mikko waited patiently for his friend to read through the same brain melting words he had moments before. An antique clock, one his mom loved, ticked away on the wall across from his desk.

"They're really gonna use a gum joke in this damn article," Cristiano finally said, disbelief evident in his tone. "If this man hadn't already been warned, I'd find this shit funny, but now…"

"Yeah," Mikko drawled, "the watered down drinks and stolen wallet are all typical, but the fact that someone spilled about the gambling? That tells me Ivan's got a rat in his midst."

"And we're sadly pest control."

"Since the police are mostly in our pockets, I'm not too concerned about them, but the fact the article practically states that has me slightly worried," Mikko finally answered. "Looks like we need to pay Ivan a visit."

"Indeed. When will you be back in town?"

Looking at the multiple tabs pulled up on his computer screen— blatantly ignoring the news article still lingering there—Mikko contemplated the best approach.

"Tomorrow," Mikko said, "I have a meeting with some investors in the city in the afternoon."'

"Oh, he finally returns from his brooding castle."

"That's not why I came out here—"

"Sure, whatever you say. Did you at least run through the halls in a princess gown?"

"—and it's hardly a castle." Mikko talked over Cristiano.

"The square footage says differently. You of all people should know that."

Sighing, Mikko knew there was no changing his friend's mind.

"Friday night it is then."

"Works for me." The sound of Cristiano tapping on his phone, likely inputting the meeting in his calendar, filled the small moment of silence. "Although, that's a busy night for the club. You sure you wanna go then?"

"We have no choice."

"As you wish, boss."

With a playful eye roll, he hung up as Cristiano's laugh resonated in his home office.

Crazy bastard, he thought, uncrossing his legs before standing and walking toward the inky panes of glass framing the last vestiges of night.

Mikko had chosen this plot of land for its views and ability to frame every sunset. It amazed him how dusk fell into night's embrace. A reverent turning of the sky as the colors darkened—soft pinks and lavenders giving way to fathomless indigo until finally...black nothingness.

Earlier, before the article and talking with Cristiano, his mind had been mostly at peace while he browsed through upcoming meeting agendas and multi-million dollar properties he managed or leased. Romanov Real Estate was known for partnering with privately funded organizations predominantly focused in healthcare and technology. WELL USA and Tech7 being some of the most notorious. The properties he showed and managed ranged from industrial warehouses to empty plots of land with potential or posh high rise headquarters. Government was another sector they dabbled in. It was a "you scratch my back, I'll scratch yours" mentality. The work was tedious, his sharp eyes unable to miss any details lest it cost him a future contract.

Or in tonight's case, a rowdy tenant that made him want to pull his hair out. At this time of night, the day hung on him like a wet blanket, exhaustion marring the skin beneath his eyes. While he might be good at what he did, it didn't make it any easier. Donning a charismatic persona could be draining. It was a piece of him that only came out when he wanted something.

And with his lifestyle, there wasn't much left for him to yearn for. Anything he'd ever wanted had been available to him at his fingertips—perhaps some things came with more blood, sweat, and *bullets,* but regardless, they came to him.

He had luxurious cars, a wardrobe boasting designer names, and a house he'd explicitly designed himself. Cristiano had called him a control freak—still did, actually—but his discipline had lent itself to his wealth.

Well, that, and his dead father's restless spirit.

Despite the abhorrent man being gone for nearly six years, Mikko found himself unable to escape the lessons Alek Romanov had so tediously bestowed upon him. Running a business was more than it seemed, and Alek had made sure Mikko knew that at a young age.

"There's no other life for us—for you moy syn," Alek had gritted through crooked teeth, spittle threatening to land on Mikko's young, tear stained face. *"This is who we are, and the sooner you accept that, the better."*

Who we are.

It was an honorable thing to say, a supposed tender moment between father and son, but the blood staining Mikko's hands at his father's behest made sure those traumatic influences were *never* misconstrued. Alek had been a selfish man, ensuring his son had no other choice but to move in the direction he was told.

No matter what.

Mikko's left hand twinged, an old and familiar ache blossoming there as he thought about the documents and necessary notes for tomorrow's meeting with WELL USA and a new potential client who sold sneakers. A swath of land had come available near the riverfront, and it was prime real estate. It might be small, but with some tweaking and design, his soon-to-be clients would reap decadent rewards. When in doubt, always build up.

And Mikko, well, he profited both in the eyes of his government—God rest his tax paying soul—and under the table. One thing Alek had been correct on was when you pretend for long enough, become who they want you to be for long enough, then people stop asking questions.

It appeared businesses were the same way.

Outwardly, Mikko and his "family owned" business were prestigious, offering the best experience along the upper west coast, but look closer and organized crime would rear its ugly head. Real estate and development were the perfect cover ups for money laundering.

"Necessary evils," or whatever his father had convinced himself of to let him sleep at night.

It was a shame Mikko had begun soothing himself with the same bullshit devotions when the nightmares persisted. While his Russian ancestors were turning over in their frosted graves oceans away at his rejection of religion, he wasn't below an occasional prayer.

Whoever said the past stayed dead had never experienced a short life with his father.

With tired eyes, Mikko loosened his tie and unbuttoned his cuffs before rolling them up. The glittering decanter across his sleek home office tempted him, the clear liquid inside the only solution yielding near immediate results, but he resisted. While he may be a questionable man, he tried to refrain from getting drunk on the job...most of the time.

Would tonight be one of those nights?

Tick. Tick. Tick.

His mother's clock was always there to remind him time was

passing him by whether he wanted it to or not. His eyes watered from lack of blinking. Mikko scrubbed his face, shutting out the walls of his office momentarily. Cristiano had called his taste cold and calculating, lifeless, but Mikko disagreed. Every piece had a place, a reason for being there. When the rest of his life was in disarray and veering off the tracks, he could count on his sanctuary being neat and clean.

Wood grain was imprinted into the concrete, the formwork from when the house had been built a couple years ago a faded memory. Every element of the room had been accounted for, every niche serving a purpose. Mikko used those voids to display small art pieces he'd collected and to store books—the titles ranging anywhere from real estate how-tos to self-help books. The latter were courteous of Cristiano, and therefore, untouched by Mikko.

The insufferable bastard liked to think he had jokes, Mikko thought, a sardonic smile almost breaking through the weariness of his fatigue.

Plush rugs lined the concrete floor, the moody rust hue of them softening the utilitarian feel of his office. Leather and wood furniture were arranged artfully throughout, encouraging conversation. Though, if Mikko was being honest, no one ever stayed here long enough to engage in such activities with him.

From his vantage point, foam capped waves sloshed against one another below, the depth of them unfathomable as nighttime rendered them into something closer to a void than a body of water.

Expensive trinkets lined his desk, pens and paper there for his thoughts and scribbles. A lone plant occupied the corner of his desk— the only one he could keep alive. A small snake plant, a specimen he couldn't kill even if he tried. And he had, his long stints away from his oceanside house promised droughts for the plant, yet it *still* thrived.

If he was honest with himself, this office had the bones of a creative, albeit a stifled one. It was a physical representation of his life; the beauty of art captivated him, but that piece of him had long since died. Now the only way for him to cope was through his blatant acts of control.

Like father, like son.

The vodka-filled crystal decanter was no different. A piece within the larger picture of his life. His fingers itched for it, his tongue watered for the smooth burn that was sure to erase the buzzing growing in his head.

No, no, no—

His eyes flicked over to the self-help books on his shelf. Maybe he should read those instead, hoping to God that they'd save him. But before he could stop himself, his feet had carried him over to the decanter, the liquid sloshing into a clear cut tumbler. Without even taking a sip, his nerves had already settled.

2

An Enticing Dusk

Mikko

L ate summer sun warmed his back as Mikko sped toward the glimmering skyline dotting the horizon ahead of him. His meeting was in a couple hours, his clothes sure to be wind blown and hair askew, but he didn't mind. At this point in his career, anything outside the mind-numbing repetitions proved exciting. Stuffy suits ruled his life, one moment without them wouldn't kill him.

Although, leaving his oceanside house behind—its monolithic architecture sunken into the cliffside a safe haven for him—felt bittersweet. He'd left the city last week, the seclusion and fresh air much needed after multiple return clients, one being Tech7, grew fed up with his unorthodox ways of running the business.

His reign was ever slipping, Alek's firm grasp on people still evident all these years later. It tired Mikko. Times had changed, people had changed, so why was it so hard to keep things running smoothly?

Memories of his childhood and of blood stained floors sent him to his oceanside house. Cristiano hadn't asked questions since he also had his own demons from Alek instilled inside of him. Instead, he let his friend leave, content to look after things until he got back.

Time healed all, but for Mikko it appeared time was crushing him.

Now he was recuperated and ready to take on the tasks set before him. Alas, his city penthouse would suffice, even if the city was too loud; too much. At least until the ordeal with Ivan blew over.

Until then, these moments on his motorcycle would help him cope. The engine roared below him as his body was bent over the tank, pliant from endorphins. Finally, he could think; finally he was free. The wind whipping at his clothes plucked all other thoughts from his mind.

As the dashed lines blurred beneath him, he let his mind wander. The ghosts of his past clung to him despite the speeds he traveled, an image of his mom flashing across his mind. It'd been twenty-two years since she'd been gone, but it never got any easier. Not a day passed where he didn't think of her.

Or more so, what she'd think of me, her once precious and gentle son forming alliances with monsters.

Mikko had grown up into something terrible despite all his best efforts. Blood coated his hands, the mistakes of her past forever in his mind. Since his mom was no longer alive to encourage his true self, he'd buried it along with her. He'd transformed into the man his father had wanted instead. It was easier that way.

It was kill or be killed, and Mikko had chosen the lesser of the two evils.

Although now, he wished he hadn't.

And maybe traces of her still lingered in him. Evident in the ways he would escape to his seaside estate, much the same way his mother would flee his father's wrath and find seclusion elsewhere if only for a while.

It was too late now, his fate determined long ago, and his body struggling to keep up. Regardless, his spite fueled him, along with the tingling in his fingers as his eyes scanned the road before him. Excitement dulled his sense of sadness and self-preservation, his mind snapping back to the present moment.

But that was the point of these solo trysts with his motorcycle.

To think. To move on. *To forget.*

If only he knew how difficult that would soon become.

MOLTEN ORANGE SHIMMERED against the harsh line of the cityscape, an inevitable marriage of man-made structures and nature.

While his back had faced the sun on the way into the city, he was now able to catch a glimpse of it between the looming silhouettes of the buildings. The precipice of the moment was palatable, the burst of colors glaring as the sun kissed the horizon. The clouds were stained a hue reminding him of marmalade before cascading into rosy pinks, and at its edges, it was violaceous, a coolness settling above him.

He'd seen a sunset a hundred times before, but the uniqueness of each one called for him to stop and appreciate the moment.

My little daydreamer, his mom used to murmur.

Sighing inside his helmet, Mikko wished to capture it. The familiar shutter of his camera cementing the view before him into a picture, but deep down, he knew it wasn't worth it. The beauty before him was ephemeral, no picture could hope to seize it and contain the colors inside a screen or piece of photo paper.

Instead, he'd tuck—

"What's that saying?" a voice interrupted his daydream. "Take a picture, it'll last longer?"

Rolling his eyes, Mikko turned to the source of the voice, perturbed that his friend had somehow read his mind, yet mocked him.

Typical.

Cristiano had pulled up behind him along the curb, his gray Mercedes sleek in the fading light of the sunset that had *just* consumed his mind. While they'd talked on the phone a night prior, Mikko was still glad to see his friend in person. Sarcasm and all.

Flipping up his visor, Mikko met Cristiano's humorous gaze. "And here I was going to say how much I missed you."

"A lie if I've ever heard one." Cristiano stood on the edge of the curb beside where Mikko had maneuvered his Yamaha R6 motorcycle into a parking spot, a grin plastered on his face.

Shaking his head, Mikko swept his kickstand down as the sounds of the city filtered in around him. He grimaced as cars sped by, faster than was necessary in the heart of the city and distant sirens grew into a cacophonous swell around them, reaching a crescendo grating on his nerves.

Oh, Portland, how I've missed you, he internally scoffed.

But that wasn't what held his attention.

It was the shade of Cristiano's hair—a light powdery *blue.*

His friend noticed the infinitesimal flick of Mikko's eyes, his mouth already opening, "If you say *one* mean thing about my hair," Cristiano started, "I'll make you take care of Ivan by yourself."

Closing his mouth beneath his helmet, Mikko swallowed his words and swung his leg over his bike.

Cristiano clicked the fob in his hand, and the Mercedes' headlights flashed amber, glinting off his white smile. "Didn't think that would actually work."

He spun the keys around his pointer finger. The streetlights around them would soon flicker on, nighttime blanketing the city once the sun set the rest of the way.

"Fuck off," Mikko mumbled, tugging the gloves off his hands and tucking them into the pockets of his riding jacket.

"I would if I could, but *you* have a tendency of scaring any prospects away," Cristiano teased, "but here I am, still trying. Obviously." He gestured to *Bubblegum* behind him. The infuriating shade of pink on the sign glinted off the glass buildings nearby, but all Mikko could think about was *The Portland Social's* article. A headache was building behind his eyes.

A line was forming outside the door, opening time almost upon them. It was one of the many establishments Mikko owned, his real estate development business renting out dozens of properties within city limits.

Regardless of how this night would end, he suspected it would begin as an evening of Cristiano blowing off some steam.

"Although, if you're giving me permission to kill two birds with one stone…" his friend continued, words trailing off before he punctuated them with a devious wiggle of his brows.

Socking Cristiano in the arm, he walked by him with a tired sigh. "I'm going to demote you."

"Personally or professionally? Because the former is impossible; I'm afraid you're stuck with me forever, sweetheart."

A small smile threatened to spread across Mikko's lips. His friend's nicknames were always cringy and appalling, but he wouldn't have it any other way. "I'll find a way to make you disappear, *darling.*"

"Oh, sounds ominous." He fell into step with Mikko. "But consider me interested."

"Let's get this night over with, yeah?" Mikko hated coming here, and any other place like it. The music was always too loud and the stifling weight of bodies pressed around him made nausea churn in his gut. So many people in one room was *asking* for trouble.

It made him anxious.

If the deviants he employed and paid knew that, he'd be in trouble.

And if Cristiano knew, he would laugh his ass off until he fucking cried.

"Whatever ya say, boss."

Cristiano dodged Mikko's second playful punch.

"Since when did this place get so busy?" Mikko asked as he finally slipped his helmet off, relishing in the cool air brushing across his cheeks.

"Since forever, you just don't get out. *Ever.*"

Mikko's hand gripped his helmet tighter, his companion's words stinging with truth. His mind wandered back to last night, the crisp taste of vodka erasing his lonely, shut-in evening.

Cristiano continued, unaware of the other man's thoughts. "But I agree, we should hurry before the line gets any longer."

"You act like we don't own the place—like we can't *cut* the line," Mikko countered.

Cristiano shook his head as if Mikko was missing some obvious point. "Sometimes I like to pretend I'm a regular person."

"By waiting in line?"

Cristiano nodded.

"While I commend you and your patience, you'll never be normal with that shade of hair."

"What did I say about making fun of me?" Cristiano chided before surging forward, and flipping Mikko off over his shoulder as he was left to stare at the atrocious color adorning his friend's buzz cut. "It's called being *spontaneous,* you should try it sometime."

Rolling his eyes, Mikko slipped through the door, the bouncer letting them pass easily. Both his and Cristiano's faces were recognizable to many—a perk and a curse. Before the dimness of the club's interior consumed him, a flash in his peripherals forced his ever watchful gaze to linger.

There, in line, was a woman; her tan skin glowed in the fading colors of the sunset, the city skyline unable to keep it from kissing along every exposed surface of her flesh. And even from this far, it looked soft and supple, a delicious place to set his rough hands.

Dark ink was etched across her shoulders, most of it hidden by the people she waited behind in line. Her ebony hair was styled, cascading over her shoulders in silky waves and a small section of it was blonde. It framed her face, the brightness against the onyx making him squint.

Like the colorful stripe on a poisonous creature, the contrast was meant to entice—to draw him in and force his eyes to pause.

But that wasn't all.

Her eyes, pools of honeyed amber reminiscent of sunlight dappled whiskey, met his icy perusal.

And something dark slithered in his gut.

The bouncer ushered him along before he could dwell on it further, his intuition prickling in his stomach.

Why did it feel like her gaze had met his intentionally? And why did that pique his interest?

Cristiano *was* right, he didn't get out.

3

Just a Touch

Mikko

The cool surface of the bar top kept Mikko grounded as people filed into *Bubblegum*. After leaving his helmet and jacket at the coat and purse check-in booth, both men had walked deeper into the club. Mikko had been intent on finding Ivan and starting the night off immediately, but just as he'd suspected, Cristiano had other plans. A friend had waved him over, his parting words to Mikko being something along the lines of, "I'll be right back, don't have too much fun without me, yeah?"

His silhouette had faded into the crowd before Mikko could protest.

Now, a snifter of vodka was clutched in his hand, the harsh burn of each sip keeping his anger at bay. *For now.* The bartenders here, or anywhere really, knew to give him something cheaper to make him grimace. It was a willing sacrifice he made to keep his wits about him in a setting such as this. In reality, he shouldn't be drinking at all, but his hands needed something to do.

While Mikko envied his friend's ability to let loose, he also valued it. He was unable to ever unclench his jaw unless he resorted to substances to soften the razored edges life had given him.

We all have our vices, he supposed.

Speaking of which, somewhere below him, in the pits of *Bubblegum,* a certain someone was awaiting his unorthodox trial. Those rooms, dark and stuffy in their own right, were predominantly used for gambling as the news article had said, but Mikko's men had retrofitted one in preparation for tonight's activities.

Ivan was one of many people Mikko's business dealt with. While they may appear as a savvy corporation, they spent their nights moonlighting and shuffling large sums of money around under the guise of real estate. Most months, Ivan flew under the radar, paying his dues as needed and keeping his nefarious habits out of the spotlight.

Until recently.

When the city news channels started circling like vultures, Mikko's hair had prickled in irritation.

Staying out of the spotlight was the number one rule.

Or rather, the *only* rule.

If people started poking, they'd discover more than Mikko and his "employees" would ever want them to see. It was a position that had its perks, but Mikko still had to be wary of the consequences. He used his power illegally, so when shit started falling apart, he was forced to act quickly. If he didn't make an example out of Ivan, Portland would be up in arms. Besides, the city couldn't run on *nothing,* organized crime needed hierarchy and organization too.

Nonetheless, Ivan's vaults had dried up entirely if Mikko had to guess, and his rent was in the red. And the only red Mikko liked to see was on the hands of his men.

Although Mikko was sequestered in the quieter—if one could consider that possible—sections of *Bubblegum,* it still allowed for him to observe the onslaught of people filling the space as the minutes ticked by. The seats at the bar near him were occupied, well, except the ones right next to his standing form. People tended to steer clear of his harsh gaze, a look Cristiano said he needed to break, but old habits died hard.

Speaking of which…where *was* that man?

Scanning the bodies beginning to dance beneath the lights, and the ones lingering along the sides of the club, Mikko searched for his friend.

And came up empty.

Another sip to quell the fire igniting in his chest. This would be the last time his friend talked him into—

"If you're searching for a dance partner, your sour mood isn't gonna do you any favors." The feminine voice had his eyes cutting down to his side, thoughts interrupted. Dark hair with a blonde money piece had his heart stuttering.

It was the woman from outside.

His teeth clenched, a blunt reply on his tongue when she continued, making herself at home despite his obvious coldness toward strangers. "You should've stuck around to hear the vitriol the others outside were calling you." His eyebrow raised. "Seems like line skippers aren't appreciated around here."

"Good thing I don't care what others have to say about me."

"Still," she huffed, "jumping the line doesn't earn you any brownie points, no matter how good you look."

Mikko slowly blinked.

"If I didn't know better, you sound jealous," he countered, eyes observing the casual way she held herself. It was as if no one could touch her—or her ego.

Her deep eyes looked him up and down before she said, "Perhaps. So, are you going to tell me who the lucky lady is?" Her gaze turned back out toward the rest of the club as if searching for who he'd been looking at.

"Who said I'm looking for someone?"

"You're telling me you're *not* on the hunt?"

"I'm not," he gritted out.

"Hmm, weird." She leaned leisurely against the bar, close enough that her body heat whispered across his skin. "Suits like you never deny the accusations pumping your ego as surely as you pump your cock at night."

His eyes widened at her boldness, jaw loosening for once in his life. "I—"

"Don't worry, I won't tell anyone." She patted his arm, the crisp black button down rustling beneath her soft touch. Suddenly, he wished for his riding jacket, needing the extra layer to ward himself against her charms.

Underneath the tingling discomfort, Mikko felt a warmth stirring. There was an easiness between them making him think they'd met before, but he'd remember someone as mouthy as her. While he may hate to be perceived as anything other than untouchable, this might be an exception.

Her audacity was refreshing, and paired with the shadowed lights of the club, he allowed himself to let go. *Slightly.* No longer did he worry about her looking for a chink in his metaphorical armor, but instead he sunk into his other side. The side that got him what he wanted.

"Apologies for giving you the wrong idea," he crooned, "but I *rarely* have to smile since my name does all the talking for me."

"Lucky for me that means *nothing* since I don't know who you are, *line skipper.*"

"I think you're a liar."

He assessed her reaction, lashes fluttering against her cheek as she glanced down at his drink.

"And I think you're egotistical."

"What're you gonna do about that?" he taunted.

His usual quiet demeanor was gone. In its place was a rare version of himself. Mikko noted the sharpness of her features, liner darkening the edges of her intoxicating eyes. Her lack of rebuttal annoyed him, her confidence digging beneath his skin—

Snatching his drink from his clenched fingers, she knocked it back. The emptiness was undeniable in his hand as he watched her throat bob as she swallowed. Her nose wrinkled at the burn tracing a path down her throat and to her chest, but that was the only indication she gave of her discomfort as she set the glass atop the bar with a *clink*. Well, that and a skeptical side eye.

"Find you something better to drink than *that*," she mumbled before pushing the empty snifter to the edge of the bar top. He realized a beat too late that she'd technically answered his last question. Irritation simmered in his veins.

"Maybe your palette isn't as refined as mine," he quipped. It was rude, but his sharp tongue couldn't help itself, and he had a feeling she liked a little bite.

The woman laughed, her teeth glinting in the lowlight, and Mikko suddenly wanted to know what they felt like biting into his skin—

"While I'm sure most women let you believe whatever you want, I can't let you go through life thinking *that*"—she nodded to his empty glass—"is 'refined' taste."

Chuckling darkly, he shook his head once. "And what do *you* think is good quality liquor?"

Ignoring him, she flagged down the bartender. Her lithe body leaned over the counter, momentarily distracting him, as she motioned for the man to get something else for them to drink. Whatever it was, Mikko wasn't interested. She was purposefully toying with him, and he wouldn't rise to the bait.

Except, when a fresh tumbler slid across the bar, he caught it in his awaiting hand.

So much for that plan.

He waited to drink it, mind wholly set on observing the woman before him, curiosity piqued in a way it hadn't been in years.

Fuck.

That feeling was exacerbated when Mikko watched her pull a crisp one hundred dollar bill from the inside of her dress. The movement had his gaze lingering on the swell of her breasts, an enticing swath of amber skin that had his mind wandering yet again.

And he wondered if the bill she'd produced was still warm; if it smelt like her. A soft, alluring scent wafted off her hair and skin every time she moved, something that was reminiscent of vanilla. At its base, though, there was a richness he could almost discern—a dark tobacco, laced in pepper and spiced with rum.

Just one little touch won't hurt, right? he internally reasoned. *One little taste.*

"My eyes are up here," she chastised with a sweet smile—one that grew when he obeyed and fixed his eyes back on hers, "and you're still acting so mysterious hmm? Clinging to what little bravado you can muster up?"

"I don't know what you're talking about," he said gruffly.

Reaching out, she touched the starched material of his button down, eyebrow cocking in question. The warmth of her fingers sent a jolt up his arm, his spine stiffening. "See, you're barely giving me anything to work with here."

Her hand now rested in the crook of his elbow. The layered fabric from his rolled up sleeve shielded him from most of her heat, but not enough.

"I'm here on business," his fingers clenched the tumbler, still untouched by his *lesser refined* palette. Her brazen touch was making it hard to think, the faint whisper of her wandering fingertips scattering his thoughts.

Mikko felt the way her gaze assessed him, eyes lingering on the exposed blackout ink covering his forearms before slowly trailing up his front and settling on a smaller tattoo that had to be peeking out above his unbuttoned collar. *CTRL.* Or control. There'd been a time where he thought tattooing it into his skin would serve as a reminder, but the direction of tonight was proving his theory wrong. Most of the time, he hid his tattoos, but he'd gotten comfortable. Cristiano's relaxed ways were rubbing off on him, and he feared it'd get him in trouble tonight.

A new song began playing out above the dance floor, the reverb of it rattling through his chest, but the woman leaned in, determined to make her point heard. "Business, huh? Well, lucky for you, I *like* mysteries."

His eyes, which had been scanning for Cristiano over her shoulder dismissively, now flicked back down to her. She met his gaze, unafraid at whatever emotion flashed across his countenance.

Dangerous, this is so very dangerous.

Her formerly sunlit whiskey eyes were now colorless in the nearby flashing lights, but he could still read the sinful glint in them. Her pointer finger traced the edge of one of the flower tattoos on his forearm. Biting the inside of his cheek, the taste of blood was the only thing keeping a shiver from racing up his spine.

"But unfortunately for you, I have business of my own to take care of—have fun finding a new target, *Mikko.*"

He cocked his head, a predatory move she cataloged, but still appeared unbothered. Questions gathered on his tongue, especially the one demanding how she knew his name when she'd explicitly stated prior that she *didn't* know him.

A liar indeed.

And what's her *name?*

With one final smirk and squeeze of his arm, she was off. His eyes dipped down the length of her back, heated gaze lingering a moment too long on the swaying of her hips before the dancing bodies around them swallowed her up.

He growled, grabbing the drink she'd bought him and downed it, choking on the *tequila.*

What the hell?

A meager cough escaped past his lips as he set the tumbler back down—an action the bartender noticed with a grin, quirking a brow when he teasingly held up a lime wedge with a pair of tongs.

Fuck all these people.

Glancing at his watch, he prayed for his friend to appear and whisk him away from such annoyances before he did something rash. Until then, he'd be staring at the dark lipstick stain the mysterious and infuriating woman had left on the rim of his other glass.

4

Wicked Theatrics

Mikko

The unusual encounter with the woman set his teeth on edge. Even as Cristiano led them deeper into *Bubblegum's* basement, her words resonated in his mind.

Have fun finding a new target, Mikko.

While he'd initially been confused when she'd called him by name, it was now obvious she'd been lying. He was a notable figure in Portland society. Albeit against his will. A day didn't pass when someone didn't recognize him. If he could remain as a recluse—Cristiano's words, of course—Mikko would.

He'd seen the way women flocked to him and Cristiano, drawn in by the former's money and status, and the latter for his easy-going smile. Mikko had been naive before, but not anymore.

"No such thing as coincidences, Mikko," his father's voice echoed in his head. His whole life had prepared him for moments like this; he wouldn't let an attractive woman derail him. Until proven innocent, she was guilty in Mikko's eyes.

Regardless, his brain was preoccupied, mind mentally tracing the edge of her shadowed silhouette. Her tattoos had been on full display, tempting him to reach out and touch them as she'd done to him. Soft lines depicted flora and fauna across her arms; anything ranging from flowers to ferns carved into her skin, perfectly complimenting her body. And how could he have forgotten about the line of text running down her spine as she walked away. He had no idea what it said, but he'd find out.

Something dark tugged at his stomach.

Lust? Curiosity? Cristiano is definitely *right, I do need to get out more. Dip my dick into something—or someone.*

He killed the thought before it got out of hand, annoyance already coating his tongue at the fact he had business to attend to in the club and none of it included watching *her* from the darkened booths lining the corners of *Bubblegum's* main lounge and dance floor.

Instead, Mikko was shackled to the ruse of his job. The empire his father had built decades ago was now left in his possession, its blackness seeping onto his already dirty hands.

Corporations weren't built on good people and virtuous standards anymore. Instead, they were created by those who were strong enough to evade the rules.

By blood, money...

And fear.

Acquiring land to grow his territory and meeting with clients was the tip of the iceberg. Below the surface of the icy water—under the rot and decay of an illustrious surface image—laid an expansive network of immoral exchanges.

It was what made Alek successful. And what kept Mikko in power over many of those within the city still to this day.

So, this new interaction stirred something unique inside him. Pursuing a random stranger was stupid and dangerous, and Mikko knew he needed to stop thinking with the wrong goddamn head. No one else would do this; they'd leave it as it was—a harmless crossing of paths.

But Mikko wasn't like everyone else. And it'd been a long time since he'd been approached so callously by a woman. It excited him. It became a new fixation for his brain to ruminate on. Just when his everyday life became monotonous, this new woman tempted him with an escape.

Wickedness slithered from his deepest parts, encouraging him to do unthinkable things.

"I had our men secure Ivan before we got here." Cristiano's relaxed voice startled Mikko from his brief reverie. "We should be all set to...interrogate when we get down there."

A smirk was evident in his friend's tone.

Before Mikko could respond, Cristiano stepped ahead, determined to open the ebony door before them at the foot of the steps. It was the second one he'd rushed ahead to get, and it made Mikko's eyebrows scrunch in annoyance.

"Do I look incapable of opening my own doors?" Mikko eyed his friend.

Cristiano shook his head playfully, thoroughly aware of all the ways to taunt Mikko. "After you, princess."

Once Alek had passed, many people Mikko thought he could count on showed their true colors. People despised him for his role within the business and wanted to take over what he'd inherited. They thought he was too young, not passionate enough for the job—himself included, truthfully—and wanted him gone. Many of the scars he bore were a testament to the hatred of those he used to call family.

"No, *boss,* I just don't want you to waste all your energy," Cristiano supplied cheerfully, "You've got a human punching bag waitin' on ya, after all."

"You already know how I feel about you calling me that," Mikko scolded.

That earned him a laugh. "That's why I do it...boss."

Dodging the swat Mikko aimed at Cristiano's shoulder, he let the metal door *snick* shut behind them. Ahead laid a mundane hall, charcoal walls made everything feel claustrophobic. Perhaps that was the intent since Ivan had always craved power and instilling hierarchy into people as soon as they stepped below the public realm.

Where the name *Bubblegum* came from then, Mikko would never know...

Doors lined each side of the corridor, individual rooms laying beyond which usually hosted gambling sessions, small meetings, and private events. It appeared Ivan enjoyed his pastimes more than his wallet could maintain.

And tonight, the soundproofed rooms would serve Mikko's purpose. Using them against Ivan felt like an amusing twist of fate, one that made Mikko smile. Ivan had gone on without consequence for too long. Hell, the article he'd read had been icing on the fucking cake.

A familiar feeling of undeniable restlessness settled into his bones as he came to a stop in front of the room holding the man in question. Usually, Mikko didn't feel this off kilter, but his sips of vodka and entire three finger poured glass of tequila lit something inside of him.

His reserved mask was slipping.

A guard stood by the door, one of Mikko's men, waiting. His arms were loosely clasped in front of his belt in a casual but alert stance. With a single nod, the man swung the door open for Mikko and Cristiano. As they crossed the threshold into the room, Mikko found himself nailing the coffin shut over his curiosity, firmly affixing his mask right where it needed to be; it was time to begin.

One harsh overhead light illuminated the space, and Mikko

squinted as he approached the center of the small room. The usual furniture had been moved aside to line the perimeter of this non-porous hellscape; the table was pushed up against the far wall, its chairs accompanying it.

All but *one.*

Ivan's form was tied to the single chair, a piece of duct tape covering his mouth. Mikko fought the twitch tugging at his mouth at the sight—Cristiano liked his theatrics and played into stereotypical tropes when he could.

Two more men stood in the room, magnifying the cramped feeling Mikko was experiencing. How Ivan held groups of men down in these rooms without grinding his teeth into dust, he wasn't sure.

Looking him over, Mikko noticed the swelling present on Ivan's face along with deep lacerations. Cristiano had made sure their men *weren't* gentle about restraining Ivan when they'd brought him down here.

Anger that Mikko usually kept on a tight leash lashed at his mind and his muscles, commanding him to let it out in the only way he preferred. While Alek's teachings may not have aligned with Mikko's ethics, he still knew how to play this game. A true predator learned all the different methods of extracting information—violence needed or not.

Straining against it, he let it build inside him all while maintaining a stoic facade. He was in control. Of his body. Of Ivan. And of his urges. It was imperative since all other aspects of his life were steeped in impotency—

The feeling of soft fingertips grazing along his arm, exploring higher, interrupted his ritualistic preparations. Her face popped into his head unannounced, again, silky onyx hair framing her beautiful face.

A different kind of anger, one composed of spearing shards of ice cut through his gut at the intrusive thought. He'd told himself on the walk down that he would stop thinking of her, that he'd stop letting her erratic behavior plague his thoughts. He was above this.

But despite his best efforts, his brain had other ideas. Disregarding the walls he'd erected in his mind to keep her out, she'd somehow crept through the small mental cracks. Years of discipline slipped through his fingers, shattered by one thought—one person. That was why he stayed away from women; they either used him or distracted him.

"It's refreshing to see these rooms used for something other than your *activities*," Mikko started, revealing nothing of his warring thoughts. He made sure to take note of the room, before letting his gaze linger on Ivan's battered form.

"Remind me why I gave you a piece of my empire when I have others who'd *kill* for your position?" Mikko stood outside the ring of light. "Or should I keep you down here for a few weeks so we can both watch what your absence attracts in these bloody waters?"

Ivan's mouth wiggled under the duct tape, a smart response most likely on his lips.

"You're disposable, Ivan. Replaceable, even. A fact you certainly know by now, so what happened?" Mikko stepped closer. "Did the title get to you? The money?"

Ivan mumbled something unintelligible, face reddening in frustration as Mikko smiled coldly at his squirming. "No need to struggle so, it's a simple yes or no question."

The bound man nodded his head enthusiastically.

Taking his eyes off of Ivan for a moment, he inclined his head to the rest of his men in the room. If he was truly his father's son, the men would've been dismissed for Mikko to handle Ivan on his own, but nights like this, he hated getting his hands dirty all alone. Instead, this was a gesture of solidarity.

"I wish I could say I'm surprised, but you've always had a knack for disappointing me. Since I can't be caught with your blood under my nails at my next client meeting, I brought some help with me. Small mercies," Mikko shrugged, hearing Cristiano cough out a laugh behind him, "for me, but *certainly* not for you."

His men readied themselves at Mikko's words, ready for his next signal, but for now, they waited. Stoic and trained like rogue soldiers, their menacing silhouettes were cut from the shadows themselves. To some, using manpower to accomplish his goals was weak, but not to him.

It was efficient.

And it keeps me from turning into my father completely.

Ivan's perspiration dripped down his temple, his struggles and nerves visible on his glistening skin. The promise of suspense gave Mikko a feeling of authority.

"Father always warned me against those who became money hungry, although I suppose he should've taken his own advice," Mikko broke the tense moment, ice coating every word. "And to think, I was going to let these transgressions slide…until your carelessness bled out onto the public."

The chair squeaked as Ivan wiggled. He *knew.*

"Care to explain why journalists are gnawing on the clues you're throwing at them like bones?"

Cristiano took that moment to throw a printed copy of the article Mikko found at Ivan.

More fidgeting like a goddamn rat.

He knew Ivan couldn't tell him with the tape over his mouth, but he didn't care. Mikko wanted to watch the man struggle. After a few more seconds of watching the man writhe under the light, Mikko looked at Cristiano, motioning for him to remove the tape.

And he did—harshly.

Mikko smiled at the noise erupting out of the bound man. Pain was the ultimate sovereignty, a steady constant throughout life no matter how hard one tried to avoid it. It was always there, its blistering kiss brushing across the fragile surface of one's body—one's heart.

"Persistence is as much a virtue as patience, son." The words slithered across his skull, his father's voice inciting the ever constant ache across the scarred flesh of his left hand. Memories from another time flared in the back of his mind.

Now is not *the time.*

Cristiano slipped into view before walking behind Ivan. Roughly, he grasped the man's thinning hair, tugging his head back. "Enough screamin', my boss has a question for ya."

The men's actions reinforced the discomfort Ivan was feeling, but he still spoke. "You know I don't have the money." A shaky inhale. "I need more time!"

"I *have* given you more time, and you've done nothing with it. Except rack up an even larger debt to me *and* draw unwanted attention. You know how much the paparazzi are frowned upon, Ivan."

"And you know how they are, like wolves circling their prey." Ivan's cheeks reddened as he spoke, bruised skin mottled.

Mikko smiled, and it didn't reach his eyes. "Wolves are known for finding the weak link."

"Your father was never like this," Ivan spat, a small amount of blood tinged spittle flew out of his mouth, landing somewhere on his pants. "He realized he couldn't command every piece of his city, but *you*... you've got a chip on your shoulder."

Mikko's will, which was already bending from the stress of the day, broke at those words. "You're right, my father *buried* those he couldn't command, Ivan."

Ivan's lips pressed into a thin line.

Mikko continued. "God, I'm glad my father isn't here. All this talk of him after he's been dead for six years would inflate his already huge ego." Mikko paced the concrete floor in front of Ivan. "While I knew change would be slow within this line of work, your ability to ass kiss this long is impressive."

Red clouded Mikko's vision, thoughts of the woman at the bar gone for now. How many times did he have to tell people he didn't *want* to do things the way his father did. Little did they know, it was because it was his last form of rebellion. A sickeningly sweet action he hoped made his father roll over in his grave.

Aloud, he said, "Though, if you're so keen on it, I can ensure you can become his neighbor in short enough order."

Behind him, Cristiano snorted before mumbling something sounding suspiciously like, "Same day delivery, even."

Ivan paled slightly at the threat, but pushed on, "If speaking the truth paints me in the wrong light, then so be it. Your father would've understood; he knew what it took to run a business—"

"Ah yes, of course, because you know how to run a business *so well.*" The predicament Ivan found himself in showcased his own poor business endeavors all on their own.

"At least I'm loyal," he panted. "The same can't be said about the rest of you. You're a watered down version of him; you'll always be overshadowed by Alek no matter how hard you try, *malen'kiy yagnenok.*"

Little lamb.

The nickname made Mikko's teeth grit together. "Last time I checked, you're taped to a chair *I* gave you when I leased the place. You're in a room *I* designed and built. You may think you own this building and everything in it, but I do." A sharp grin spread across Mikko's face. "And I own *you.*"

"Otvali." Fuck off.

Cristiano stepped back, already sensing the direction of this conversation.

"Since you claim my father did such an outstanding job on running his business, you'll already know how he handled situations like this," Mikko drawled, stalking closer.

The light above him cast severe shadows on his body, showing every plane of hard muscle through his crisp button down. Mikko had spent hours honing his physique for moments like this. It'd become obsessive the way he routinely worked out.

And Ivan knew that, realization settling into his eyes. "I-I don't think that's necessary."

"Honestly, I think it's overdue. My father did worse for far less. As his son, I would know."

Silence.

"I wish I could say I'm surprised, but you always did run back to your master when times got tough." Mikko enjoyed the way Ivan's throat worked nervously. "And who *is* your master, Ivan?"

"You?" the man hurriedly muttered, hoping more ass kissing would save him.

"No," Mikko tsked, "although, it should be, but that can be... corrected."

"W-what do you mean? Then–who?"

"A dead man. One who left the stains of his sins all over this disgusting city. One who didn't care about men like you despite his sweet words, so why stand by him now? Why stand by Alek who isn't even here to see your weak submission?"

"He-he's all I know."

And for a second, Mikko could relate.

Hands clapped down on Ivan's shoulders, the motion nearly knocking the wind out of him. Mikko's clean skin clutched the soiled fabric of the man's shirt, emotions spilling from his actions despite his hatred for such displays of sentiment.

"It's sad that the man you chose to cling to couldn't even remember which one of my hands he'd *burned*."

His rough hold slipped away, wrinkles left in the fabric of Ivan's shirt.

Straightening, Mikko stifled his inner emotions as he focused on the task before him. Inwardly, he longed to wipe the grime off his hands, but he suppressed that. "Last chance, Ivan. Care to wire a hundred thousand dollars to my account while also paying off those you attracted the attention of?"

Although Mikko expected it, it was still disappointing to be proven right when Ivan remained soundless. He had a faraway look in his eyes, his begging long since flushed out of his system.

Good, that makes this easier, Mikko thought darkly.

"No?" A cracking of Mikko's knuckles. "Well, it'll be a pleasure doing *business* with you, then."

"Always hiding behind your men," Ivan spat as Mikko signaled to those standing in shadow. "Can't stand to torture me yourself? Hands too soft and pretty to—"

Thwack!

A fist cut off Ivan's taunts, the interruption welcomed by Mikko as he slipped into a spot next to Cristiano standing along the edge of the small room. As the rest of Mikko's employees descended upon Ivan's prone form, the words spoken pricked at his toughened exterior. He'd never live up to his father's legacy—infamy or otherwise. Mikko wouldn't want it any other way, but it still irked him.

Smack!

Another punch landed on the man's jaw, the force of the motion almost sending him flying backward if not for another man already there, holding him in place. Caught by his collar, Ivan was helpless to the onslaught of punches. The metal chair scraped below him from the assault, its legs struggling to stay upright. It was a gory orchestra, the men working in flawless tandem to deliver the retribution Mikko had grown to live by.

He might let people think what they want, but at the end of the day, they obeyed him whether they liked it or not. The weight was ineffable, but there was no turning back now. The horrid smacking of skin upon skin and wet splattering proved that.

As Ivan's teeth clacked together audibly, Mikko found his solitude in the show of violence. Deep down, he knew it was a terrible act of justice, but it was better than the alternative.

Doing the punishments myself.

That made him feel more like his father, his skin stretched tight over a dead man's cursed bones. So, he stood back, letting his men handle it. What fun would his job be if he didn't take advantage of the perks?

Another man's fist connected with Ivan's nose. Cartilage broke, unable to withstand the force applied in the men's relentless assault.

To anyone else, this was a moment of insanity as the shell of Mikko's body slipped over the metaphorical edge of the deep end. It didn't matter. He was a husk of a person going through the motions. Times like this were the only pardon; the only time he felt alive. After all, Alek had made sure he'd been desensitized to it long ago.

A copper tang permeated the air, its sharpness undeniable. Familiar, yet sickening.

Blood sprayed forth from Ivan's injuries, Mikko's knuckles tightening at his sides as he watched his men's fists cut easily through the fragile flesh of his face. The crimson splattered onto every surface close enough: Ivan's clothes, the trained assailants arms and hands glimmering in gore, and fittingly enough, the printed article Cristiano had thrown earlier. It was a macabre painting detailing the atonement occurring.

Cristiano was nothing but another silent watcher, steadfast in all the usual business matters they found themselves a part of. He understood the agony living beneath Mikko's facade—understood it needed to be satiated.

Ivan's groans filled the air as both men observed. If they wouldn't get money from him, they'd make sure he *would* give something else in return.

An offering.

While life loved its pain, it also craved sacrifice.

Losing track of time, completely consumed by the act of his own men erasing every single piece of his father, Mikko didn't tell them to stop until their hands were tired and aching and split open.

Beneath it all, Ivan was covered in his own viscera. Alive and breathing, but probably wishing he wasn't. More of it was smeared across the skin of the men surrounding him, their clothes speckled with crimson.

The hate and rejection that had created Mikko fueled him now and released a monster beyond saving.

Besides, Mikko didn't want salvation; he wanted justice.

Or even a simple life to call his own...

But *this* was what he'd been raised to do, groomed to inherit.

In this world, being a slave to anything or anyone was a dangerous game, so Mikko chose wisely. After his father, he refused to let anyone reign over him, only letting one thing have authoritative power over him.

Blood.

It was the ultimate compensation—the ultimate control.

And it was the only thing he would ever bow his head to.

5

Sleuthing

Mikko

Mikko's office overlooked the cityscape opening up before his window, providing the ultimate view of the skyline. And he *loathed* it.

Being in that office, his *father's* office, was stifling and confining and inescapable. He had no idea how Alek had done it for so long. If Mikko could avoid these four walls, he would, but today that proved to be difficult. The tasks with his name marked beside them piled up, refusing to let him go.

With an internal groan, Mikko wished the windows opened this high up so he could throw himself out.

His office was spacious, situated in the corner of the building which maximized the window space. The seams between each pane of glass were nearly undetectable. Whoever had designed it, made sure to erase the line keeping him in and the elements out. On the surface, it was beautiful, but beneath it all, this place held memories.

Long nights sequestered on the couch while his father took phone call

40

after phone call. Early mornings resulting in red welts on the backs of his hands after Alek had repeatedly smacked them with each task Mikko did wrong...

His eyes slid to the wet bar lining one wall.

A sip of vodka wouldn't hurt, he thought momentarily before shaking it off.

No, he didn't drink here. That activity was reserved for his alone time at home. The expensive drinks and snacks at the bar were for clients. Everything was always meticulously stocked, his assistant Emma, taking inventory of what was running low and replenishing it promptly. Glass decanters and tumblers were arranged neatly on a tray, waiting to be touched.

The only time it was ever used was when clients visited him—something he tried to avoid. He preferred to meet people in more casual settings, or better yet, have Cristiano woo the public. He was so good at it that it was a crime to *not* have him do it. Regardless, Mikko didn't like the stuffy personas people donned inside this sleek skyscraper. People put on their best performances here, dresses and suits ironed to perfection, their faces sculpted into flawless masks of coolness.

But Mikko didn't want to see that.

He wanted to see people's true side—their vulnerability. *That* was when he learned the most about them. Alek had taught him that, taught him everything he would need to know to take over one day. And that day had come much sooner than he'd wanted.

With his large, stately desk positioned just right, Mikko was able to have the sightlines he required to work semi-comfortably. He was still stuck in this dreadful building after all; he might as well make the best of it.

His finger traced the edge of stacked papers on his desk, playing with the notion of getting cut. Teetering on the edge of stinging pain, his mind wandered to Ivan and the state of his henchman's hands after they doled out their punishments. Cuts and bruises had marred their skin from the work they'd done. It was fascinating to Mikko how the body was so resilient, yet so fragile all in the same breath.

And in a sick, twisted turn of events his brain recalled the moments before the basement—before Ivan and his glaring disrespect. His eyesight blurred, thoughts shifting and settling on the phantom feeling of *her* fingertips burning a treacherous path along his skin as she traced the ink along his forearm.

Glancing down, his vision returning, Mikko peered at his suit jacket's sleeve. Even though he covered the flowers and blackout ink on his arms, a vulnerability in his eyes—a piece of him he rarely shared with others—she'd managed to find and exploit it. Here he was at work letting her worm her way into his head.

He didn't even know her name, yet...

Have fun finding a new target.

Those six words had haunted him, *tormented* him.

She's an admirer, someone who knows your status, he'd chanted internally, hoping eventually the incessant repeating of the words would make them stick.

It didn't.

He'd encountered and entertained women who were chasing after his money and status and they'd never acted this way. Something was off, and if he was smart, he'd keep his guard up when it came to her.

But one word erased every second of his hard work.

Mikko. Mikko. Mikko.

He still couldn't get over how she wielded his name like a weapon, all while previously feigning ignorance.

Oh, she's wicked, a temptress I should be wary of.

Mikko considered himself...orderly, trying to never let his emotions get the better of him. But that wasn't out of choice, it was out of necessity. He had a habit of feeling things too viscerally, obsessing over a looming notion leading him to dark places in the past.

There'd been women before this, ones his father had scared off, ones who'd taken advantage of him, or others that had simply thought him too much.

At first it would begin innocently, his mind fixated until sleep began evading him, his emotions unpredictable. Then self-loathing, doubt, and isolation crept in, eager to sink their nasty claws into him. It always ended with Cristiano calling or finding him like this, then dragging him up out of bed, tossing him in the shower, and nursing him back to health. He couldn't have this again—couldn't be consumed so fully with something, *someone,* such as this. A woman he hardly knew.

Yet, here he was, spiraling.

And to make matters worse, the note he'd found on his motorcycle after the events at *Bubblegum* felt like an omen. Or a secret message she'd left for him.

After reemerging from the depths of the club, Cristiano not far behind, Mikko had been surprised to find a fluttering receipt tacked to his bike's windshield.

"Did you get a ticket?" Cristiano had asked, a smirk evident in his tone. Amber lights flashed as he unlocked his Mercedes. "Looks like they missed me." His friend's windshield was devoid of paper.

Walking closer, Mikko noted it wasn't a parking ticket at all, but instead a note. Loopy scrawl, not yet legible from this distance, mocked him.

"Well, what's the damage?" his friend asked from afar, one leg already inside his car.

"Why do you care? You gonna pay it for me?" Mikko's voice was teasing despite his eyes scanning over the piece of paper warily.

The words he read made his heart stutter.

I've waited a long time to devour you.

That was it. No signature, no indication as to who could've left it, but Mikko's brain was already picturing whiskey eyes and dark lips and tequila.

"I would...but that doesn't really make sense now does it, boss," Cristiano's voice cut through the whirring in his head. "Last I checked, *you're* the one who writes my paychecks. So, you'd just be giving it back to yourself."

"Maybe I should take it out of your paycheck all together," Mikko mused instead. He desperately tried to keep his emotions locked away. The note felt both like a threat, but also intimate. He would never hear the end of it from Cristiano if he found out. He was sure of it.

"What'd they even get ya for? If it's sad enough, who knows, maybe I'll be nice and let you take a chunk of my salary to make yourself feel better."

"How *sweet* of you."

Plopping down into the driver's seat of his Mercedes, Cristiano shrugged as if his act of kindness was the nicest thing he'd done in a while. Maybe after the night they'd had, it was. While they might've cleaned up in the club's bathroom and changed clothes, the scent of copper still clung to their skin.

Intuition clenched in his gut, a soft voice murmuring in the back of his mind to do more research on this mystery woman as soon as he could. If she'd left this note, he had plenty of questions to ask her.

And maybe I want to see her again too.

"It was probably one of Ivan's men trying to get back at you," Cristiano said, rolling his window down so he could still chat with Mikko with his car door closed. Thunder rumbled nearby, small droplets of rain falling from the clouds forming up above. Shit, he'd have to hightail it back to his penthouse to avoid getting completely soaked.

"Probably…" was all Mikko could say. Ripping the note free, he realized it was tacked to his motorcycle with *gum*. That piece of evidence made him certain it was—

A soft knock drew him from his reverie, the surroundings of his dismal high end office coming back into focus around him.

There, framed within the spotless glass of his office door, was Emma. Waving her in, Mikko leaned back in his office chair, trying to portray his usual cold exterior even though heat was rushing through his veins at the thought of *her* leaving a note *and* chewing gum on his bike. He was both offended and intrigued.

Mostly the latter since he'd saved the piece of gum.

For evidence, his mind reasoned.

Emma stepped through the doorway, her navy pantsuit crisp. Most would find her attractive, but Mikko merely found her mundane. It was how he saw most work-related items. She was someone his father would've tried to set him up with years ago. She was a woman who came from money and matched his professional physical appearance with one of her own.

"Mr. Romanov," Emma said, greeting him with a stiff nod. She advanced farther into his office as the door closed behind her, her heels muffled on the carpet. Mikko dipped his chin back in response, content to do as little talking as possible. "The funds you've requested from Ivan have been wired over to us this morning."

A cold smile slipped over Mikko's face.

I wonder what he had to do to pull that *off.* Out loud he said, "This is great news. Let's hope he stays on track from now on."

"That would make my job easier," Emma said, her own knowing grin barely morphing the rest of her face. "Also, between our efforts and Ivan's, the news articles and reports have been expunged from the media. No one should bother us now, sir."

"Perfect, thank you." Sitting up, Mikko straightened the already pristine papers lining his desk. "I don't think we should have any more troubles concerning him now."

"Glad to hear it."

Glancing at his watch, he asked, "Am I still meeting with my two o'clock?"

Emma nodded. "Yes, I'll come by soon to collect you. Based on the number of people they're bringing with them, I've reserved the main conference room, both for space and first impressions."

"Thank you," was all he said, grateful Emma knew what he needed without him saying. Despite her being newer—Alek's old assistant intolerable and quickly fired when Mikko came of age—she understood the ways of his mind.

Most of the time, real estate was about making connections and impressing those with the most money or sway. The high end Romanov office never failed to influence people and distract them from other inner workings happening after dark.

Unless that was what they were interested in themselves.

But those were secrets for later. Right now, Mikko would plan accordingly and let a certain *someone* occupy his mind for the time being. He already had her handwriting and a chewed piece of gum in his possession.

What could go wrong?

When Emma returned a few minutes later, signaling to him his new clients had arrived, Mikko decided to use his power for devious things. The world was at his fingertips; he'd be foolish not to use that to his advantage. Besides, this little game was a welcome distraction to his usual repetitive lifestyle.

Walking the expanse of the office leading toward the main con- ference room—more large swathes of glass visible from where he was and an extravagant light fixture hanging in the middle of the room—Mikko found himself smiling. For the first time in a while, he felt *excited* about something.

There was an underlying caution, a reservation he'd keep in place until he learned that this woman wasn't up to no good.

But until then…

Gripping the conference room door handle, Mikko cleared his thoughts and fixed the metaphorical mask over his face. Stepping inside, six pairs of eyes greeted him, and in that moment he felt the power his father had chased.

"Gentleman," he crooned, voice low and rich, "what brings you in today?"

* * *

CLICK. CLICK. CLICK.

The sharp sound of his computer mouse amid the silence of his office made the act even more furtive and scandalous. His meeting had ended a couple hours ago, and he'd been sequestered back in his office, mind hungry for more information ever since.

If only Cristiano could see what I'm using our money and technology for.

On the monitor before him, security footage played. To most, it was an uneventful scene, partygoers filling the dancefloor and surrounding the bar to eagerly order their drinks. Everyone had filed in to forget their weeks—to dance and drink and fuck away their sorrows.

But Mikko didn't care about them.

Instead, his sharp eyes had lasered in on a specific timestamp.

Seven thirteen.

The moment he'd glanced at his watch last Friday, and his brain was unable to unsee it. Even now, as he'd fast forwarded through the footage, he'd had an end goal in mind.

On the monitor, he stared at the proof that his interaction with the unknown woman was true and *not* a dream. Multiple cameras had captured the moment, the shift in time that he was beginning to think was the inception of something new.

There, currently in view of one of the cameras, he leaned against the bar top as he remembered. A snifter glass of vodka was keeping his hands busy, the look on his face pained as people swarmed around him.

He already knew the woman wasn't in frame yet, the time stamp a couple seconds too soon, but he couldn't help himself, couldn't keep his eyes focused on one spot. He'd wondered if she'd seen him long before he'd noticed her, her predatory gaze latching onto him before proceeding to approach him. Or had she simply invaded his space for the fun of it, no other introduction needed.

Counting down the seconds, Mikko watched as she strode into view, her form lithe and slipping between the bodies along the outskirts of the camera angle. Even now, he could seemingly *feel* the devious intent behind her movements, the sultry prowess she exuded.

Not stopping until she was almost pressed against him—a memory making him shudder in delight—he realized how close she'd been to him. No one ever dared to cross such a blatant boundary, especially with him, but she didn't care. It was obvious she thought Mikko was beneath her.

A fact that both angered and pulled him in.

In the past, everyone treated him as if he was a bomb ready to explode. Men either feared or revered him, his reputation well known. Women usually shied away, concerned with getting mixed up in the grimy underworld. Or they clung to him like a lost puppy, eager for whatever he could provide them. Anika was none of those options.

Leaning in close, she assessed him like an animal would a piece of meat; she was on the hunt long before he'd even realized it. Another certainty that'd become obvious to him after watching this footage over and over.

More than thirty times to be exact...

Pausing the video again, Mikko inclined his head toward the monitor. Her face was nearly completely obscured by Mikko's shoulder, but he could still see how her lovely mouth parted while she spoke to him.

And as he remembered—as if his brain could ever let him forget—her hair cascaded over her shoulders in a silky wave of night, all except for *one* piece. Bright and glowing in the strobe lights, Mikko found himself enraptured again.

Pressing play, he continued to watch the rest of the interaction from this angle, unable to see the way she'd touched him—stoked a fire within his chest. In the moment, he'd thought it'd been his drink, the alcohol burning his throat and making him perceive things differently.

But...

Her gaze flicked to another camera, one Mikko had also combed through, her fuzzy eyes hard to discern, but he *knew* she'd found his camera. She'd staked them out, gestured to them and given them small, secretive smiles. As if she knew he'd be here now, watching this all back.

Fuck.

He observed her flag down the bartender, the crisp hundred sliding across the bar top, and the smug look on her face as the glass of tequila was pushed his way.

All of it was too much. Mikko's senses were short circuiting, brain whirring in desperation to uncover the true meaning behind all of this. He had a feeling this woman had ripped a hole in his safeguards, eager to crawl inside his mind and rot.

And he'd done most of the work for her, obsessively watching the footage of their meeting, walking on eggshells at the thought of her turning up at his work or while he walked the busy streets of Portland.

Gritting his teeth, Mikko was annoyed he'd let her in this far, but at the same time, twisted notions were forming in his own mind. Maybe it was because something about her reminded him of someone else long ago, only this time he'd have a second chance to prove himself. Or maybe it was the emotional trauma he'd endured all those years ago shoving him toward this woman, his fixations clawing their way out of his chest.

He was going to find out who she was, even if he had to do questionable things to obtain the answer.

It was only right.

She'd done this, *she'd* poked at him like a human would a bear. Now it was time for him to examine her.

Clutching the leather armrests of his office chair, he realized he was torn between two sides of himself: the logical side and the emotional side.

Logically, Mikko should be wary of this woman, not knowing her intentions. His family business had been profitable over the years, but not without making enemies along the way. She could be someone looking to get back at him for his father's endeavors. While it hadn't been Mikko's doing, or desire for that matter, Alek had destroyed neighborhoods to build a new empire. Cultures and groups of people had been gentrified, erased all for the sake of raising value and rents and money.

Those kinds of actions were bound to create enemies.

But the emotional side...

Switching to the other camera, Mikko rewatched the entire scene again, her profile clear and her sly smile at the camera lens noticeable. This one was angled at the side of both of them, tucked away behind the bar above the highest shelf displaying alcohol.

This time, he could see the way she touched him.

This time he noticed the way her glossy lips tipped up mischievously.

And he recounted how every time her touch passed over his skin, his hand gripped the new glass of tequila tighter. It was a miracle it hadn't shattered.

But there was something else Mikko couldn't place, a deeper provocation in her mannerisms.

A danger.

His line of work had revealed corruption was rooted deep within the despicable, and he knew the signs—like called to like, certain people able to detect the atrocities flowing in the blood of others. It was like a mirror, shattered and demented. And whatever horrid things consumed those he worked with, he realized they *also* devoured her.

His eyes burned from lack of blinking, not wanting to miss a single thing.

You may have waited a long time for me, he internally recalled, *but this game has just begun, and my patience is formidable.*

Rewinding, Mikko was unable to escape the way she touched him. As if reliving it each time, he could recall the softness of her hands, adorned with rings and her black nail polish impeccable. He remembered the way her eyes glittered at his blatant discomfort. She was enjoying his displeasure, pushing the boundaries to see how far he'd let her go. And he let her cross too many lines.

Cristiano would claim he was being paranoid and delusional. Perhaps he was, but something was off about this woman. And Mikko wasn't sure if it pissed him off or turned him on. Electricity tainted his blood along with the bitter tang of angst as he kept replaying the security footage.

Who is she? What does she want? Where does she live?

With all these questions piling in his head, her voice and lips forming around his name—one he dreaded because of his father—Mikko was unable to keep his thoughts from plummeting. A deep carnal hunger, not the kind that could be satiated with food, but something *more,* flooded his senses while he sat behind his desk.

Something darker.

His cock stiffened, pressing against the zipper of his trousers. All alone, he let his hand drift, palming his erection while watching Anika's pert figure all but harassed him on screen.

The sun warmed his back as it set behind him, the city skyline swathed in vibrant hues of clementine and scarlet. While he was stuck in his office, the endless frames of the woman in front of him covering his screen made the space tolerable.

Maybe *this* was how his father had endured it all those years.

He'd found an obsession and let it swallow him whole.

While space and time separated them in this moment, her visage only but a pixelated image, Mikko wanted to be near her again. He wanted to know why she'd stormed into his life and left him questioning things.

It was *torturous.*

But he was determined to figure it out, to figure *her* out.

Closing out of the windows he had pulled open, Mikko pushed away from his desk and grabbed his helmet.

While the unnamed woman was too busy taunting him, she'd failed to realize what kind of person he was—what kind of man he could be behind all the stuffy business schemes. Where he lacked, he made up for it in other areas—other fixations. The empire his father built may be a terrible weight Mikko had to carry, but it'd shaped him into the man he was now.

For better or worse.

Mikko was going to find her and question her motives. In his world, trust didn't come easily, so until then, he'd expect the worst.

Unless his possessive nature consumed him first.

Work could wait. Slipping from his office and cloaked in the fading sunset, he patted his jacket pocket to make sure the small bag with the piece of gum was still there. He had a favor to call in, even if it did make him a bit crazy.

Or rather, a *predator* on the hunt.

6

Signatures

Mikko

Mikko's R6 roared beneath him as he sped across the expanse of highways looping through the city. After leaving his office, Mikko was halfway to his destination when he called in his favor.

The phone rang a couple times before Dr. Layla Žofia finally picked up. "I'm almost scared to ask what you need, Mikko." Her greeting was blunt yet warm.

"Who says I need anything," he responded, the Bluetooth device in his helmet making it easier to talk and ride.

"Anytime I see your name on the caller ID, I know."

"Ouch, I thought we were friends."

Her laugh rent through the small space inside his helmet. "Oh, Mikko, we both know our professions don't allow us to have those. But all jokes aside, I do believe I told you I owed you one after taking care of my ex."

"He was a big guy…" Mikko said.

"I know, I know, and he took a lot of your men to lift his dead weight," she joked. "Hurry up and ask your favor though, I'm between appointments right now."

Downshifting, Mikko carefully formulated his question. "How soon would you be able to get DNA results back on a piece of gum?"

"Hmm, how old is it?"

"A couple days."

"Shouldn't be too hard, bring it in and I'll see what I can do."

"Are you available in"—Mikko checked the clock on his bike's dash—"seventeen minutes?"

"Only for you."

"Good, I'll be there in fifteen."

With a friendly scoff, Dr. Žofia hung up, not one to question his demands.

GRIPPING HIS HELMET, balaclava, and the bag containing the chewed gum, Mikko waited in the too small seats at Dr. Žofia's office. She primarily worked for the police department, running tests and analyses for them, but occasionally Mikko could sway her to work for him. Tonight was one of those nights.

Like she'd mentioned, her ex-boyfriend had been a dipshit, giving her trouble when all she'd wanted was for him to leave her alone, so Mikko and his men took care of it. He was also notorious for cheating at a couple of Mikko's establishments, so it benefited both parties.

Just taking the trash out, he'd told her once it was done. That was the only time he'd seen the doctor get emotional.

The hour was growing late, but Dr. Žofia liked to stay after hours, catching up on work and letting her mind relax as she lost herself in her tasks. Mikko could relate in some ways.

After buzzing him in, he waited for her to appear, fidgeting in the quiet space, mind loud. Any minute, one of the wooden doors lining the room would open and the doctor would lead him back to her lab.

A buzz came from his phone.

Cristiano: *Where are you*

Of course he'd be the one to notice his absence.

Cristiano: *And don't lie, I have your location*

A fact he'd been pressured into giving up for the sake of safety. But now, Mikko wondered if that'd been a ruse so his friend could spy on him.

*Calling in a favor :***Mikko**

Cristiano: *Care to loop me in*

*No :***Mikko**

Cristiano: *You're such an ass*

Cristiano: *I also have favors I can call in and find out*

*I'll tell you later, it might be nothing :***Mikko**

As he sent the message, a door opened and Dr. Žofia stood there. Her brunette hair was graying prematurely near her temples, the color noticeable from the tight bun she kept her hair in. This job hadn't been easy on her body. She was short and fiery—a fact Mikko had discovered accidentally one evening when trying to push her for an expedited forensic analysis. Her eyes were dark, damn near black, as she watched him.

Tucking his phone away, he rose from his seat and walked forward.

"Thanks for takin' me in this late doc," he said, brushing past her.

"I would say 'anytime,' but I wouldn't mean it," she replied, a slight smile evident in her tone as she stepped into rhythm beside him. "You remember the way back?"

"Yeah."

Taking a couple turns, Mikko ended up in the sterile lab, the room devoid of colors and filled with equipment he had no idea the names of.

"Let's see the sample," Žofia said while donning gloves.

Pulling it from his jacket pocket, he wished to suddenly hide his face. Layla didn't know what this was about, but he did and it made him skittish. This little game he was playing was for his eyes only, but he was desperate. The internet could've helped him with his sleuthing, but that'd take too long. This testing would still take some time, but it'd be accurate. And that was what Mikko wanted at the end of the day. No guessing or fumbling through social media. He wanted concrete facts.

"Do I want to know what this is about?" Layla asked, prepping her equipment and eyeing the plastic bag.

"Uh, probably not."

"I figured. Well, this will take a while," the plastic bag crinkled as she opened it, "so you can either wait here and get comfortable, or I'll call you when it's ready."

Holding up his helmet, Mikko made his decision. "I'll be running some other errands. You know where to find me."

"Of course."

Before crossing through the lab's door, he glanced over his shoulder.

"Thanks again, Layla."

Her nod was the only affirmation she gave, and he was on his way.

Little did he know the name flashing across his phone screen a couple hours later, nighttime at its peak, would change everything.

* * *

Anika

Anika Simmons.

Her signature was scrawled across one of the many documents passed across her desk. As a financial analyst, every day contained similar tasks letting her brain settle and focus. An attribute she didn't usually have outside of these four walls. Most of the time, her mind was always running, thinking, and scheming.

It was the nature of her inner workings—her personality. It boiled down to her innate need to always be ten steps ahead, or the smartest in the room. If she could understand her environment, threats and deviations could be neutralized.

But each time she wrote her name, a piece of her withered away, a burning hate simmering beneath her skin. There had been a time when she was Anika Naidu, her family's surname indicating her culture, her identity, and her unwavering love for her parents who'd given her the world.

And she'd thrown it all away.

In the name of safety, she internally reminded herself.

The erasure of herself and her heritage had been a necessary evil, even if it did make a piece of herself wither away. It was too late to ruminate on that now, she had tasks set before her to complete.

Gray lined the walls of her office, the drab color seemingly everywhere. In her attempt to alleviate the color, she'd brought in some plants from home. Foliage always had a way of softening the edges of a room and bringing a calming tranquility to Anika's racing mind. Gardening was one of her favorite pastimes, so the small amount of plants she had here spoke of her love for them.

Her coworkers had described her space to be more akin to a forest than an office, but Anika hardly constituted the twenty various potted plants anywhere near comparable to the dense underbrush of a woodland.

Her leather chair squeaked as she settled in, crossing her legs and rearranging the stationary on her desk between assignments. To an outsider, things might look scattered, but to her everything was in its place.

Sighing, she picked up the stack of papers and straightened them, the edges *clacking* against the top of her desk. Setting those aside, she realized she had a few moments before her next meeting and decided to use her time wisely.

Clicking through multiple real estate listings, Anika searched for something specific to her needs. She already owned a house, but a small piece of her yearned to test the waters when it came to owning more real estate around the city.

Deep down, Anika didn't care what property she obtained as long as it was one with the name *Romanov Real Estate* emblazoned across the listing. She might be a little vindictive and a little curious, but after meeting Mikko at the club the other night, she realized all her preconceived notions about him were correct.

Arrogant, wealthy, stoic, and closed off to name a few.

But of course she was right, she'd taken her time observing and analyzing until she'd reached her final decision. As always. Now it was time to approach Mikko Romanov, an untouchable real estate mogul.

He was someone she loathed by association.

Everything he and his company stood for disgusted her. She wasn't the only one either, the city of Portland feeling his effects as prices increased at his behest. But beneath that, his ugly interior lurked. As everyone knew he—well, his father—was the source of climbing rents, they also murmured about the abominable business deals happening after dark.

As if stealing people's livelihoods wasn't enough.

Or in her case, *lives.*

Looking back, Anika should have been nervous, but her insightfulness and precautionary research had eliminated all doubt in her mind. She knew him as well as he knew himself, if she had to guess.

Maybe even better...

And that was how she liked it.

Her day job was more analytical and data based, but the same tactics could be applied elsewhere. Her sure fingers and smug smile were evidence of that.

If I can't have Alek, then his son will have to do.

Beyond her cunning plans, Anika was also fueled by rage. What was there to be afraid of when anger had burnt through every fiber of her being? She had nothing to lose.

Mikko's reputation proceeded him just like all the ways he liked to torture and interrogate men. He was known for being ruthless, outgrowing his father's shadow, but Anika saw him for who he really was: a man desperately trying to find his purpose. Someone who had never met someone like her: a self-assured business woman who didn't want him for money or status. No, she yearned to entice him into a larger game, starting with...

Selecting a remote warehouse on the outskirts of town, near the river, Anika infilled all the necessary fields to request a tour of the property for tomorrow after she got off work. While she had no intentions of buying the run down building—its land and location more valuable than its structure—she wanted to see if *he* would show up.

Anika couldn't picture him, a stuffy suit fitted to his frame, meeting with her out there, rusty nails and broken windows a backdrop behind his cleanliness.

But a girl could wish now couldn't she?

The thought made her chuckle, his designer shoes stepping into a puddle of stagnant water and splashing up onto his expensive slacks. Maybe, if anything, it would lift her spirits all while letting her see inside his head.

Settling back into her office chair, the midday sun blinded her as it streamed in through the glass, but it did little to deter her daydreams. When Anika saw something she wanted, she fucking got it.

7

A Showing

Mikko

The manila folder Dr. Layla supplied Mikko with after he called in the favor currently sat in front of him, minimal information on a certain Anika Simmons staring up at him. Any *normal* person would feel guilty for prying, but Mikko considered himself to be above that. And this wasn't the first, or last, time he'd used his power to get information on someone. It was a habit he'd grown used to, the access his last name granted him undeniable. Besides, he only had Žofia gather the readily available information about his mystery woman—nothing too scandalous.

Name, height and weight, date of birth. *Address.*

The last one tempted him beyond anything else, but he averted his eyes. For now. A small picture of her accompanied the information in the folder. It was clipped from one of the security cameras, but it still set Mikko's heart racing. Almost as much as the real life visage of her did.

While he'd tried to keep himself and his thoughts far away from her, his brain couldn't let her go—not without a little investigation. There'd been nights the folder he currently held had burned a hole in the locked desk drawer he'd left it in, in hopes the thought of her would go away.

But it was futile.

The more Mikko resisted looking into the folder—into *her*—the more his mind screamed at him.

When his fingers finally brushed along the edge of the papers a couple nights ago, the lamplight his only witness, he'd justified his actions. *It's for the safety of my business.*

A lie. He didn't care about his father's business, if anything he wanted out. Anika was steadily becoming an outlet, one he'd been using to escape the dull afternoons at work. When she was in his thoughts, the day flew by. When he contemplated stopping by her house to antagonize her, his life suddenly felt whole.

It was the same feeling he got when a beautiful painting captured his attention or a picture's composition struck awe into him. His creative self was forever chasing captivating things.

The well-being of Romanov Real Estate only mattered to him partly, and that was because of Cristiano. The business motivated his friend, kept him busy and doing things he enjoyed—minus the torturing, but even then he found the positives. If Anika was plotting against the company, Mikko wanted to be the first to know.

After all, she'd come up to him, wants and desires unknown. In Mikko's world, that was a dangerous place to be, but everyone could be bought and persuaded, he just needed to find out what Anika's weaknesses were.

Despite these circumstances impacting Cristiano, Mikko kept this close to his chest, unwilling to admit to his...

What even is this?

Regardless of its name, Mikko wanted to keep Cristiano from

prying, his friend always poking his nose where it didn't belong. If he'd sensed Mikko's curiosity, he never would've let him live it down.

But now he wasn't even sure that was a truthful reasoning.

His inquisitiveness had grown, percolated into a bitter tonic Mikko was beginning to crave. He was addicted to the idea of her and what she stood for, grasping for something he couldn't have—someone he couldn't catch.

And now he didn't want to stop. He didn't even know *how* to. The fantasy was too delectable to give up.

In a few short days, his sanity had slipped through his fingertips. The control he usually prided himself on vanished when his thoughts strayed to her, which was more often than not these days. It was miraculous how a small interaction and his compulsive thinking had consumed his thoughts.

He'd been here before, with three other women and it ended in flames...

This time is different, he thought, damn near pleading insanity.

All those other times outside factors had squashed his chances, but this time he was in control of his fate.

Mikko wanted another chance with Anika—wanted her to touch him again. It'd been so long since he'd felt a connection like that. People steered clear of his looming form, knowing his presence meant trouble. But not her. Maybe she was unwise approaching him, ignoring every red flag he usually displayed to others: his stern looks, his unbecoming small talk, and his blasted infamous last name. As foolish as it sounded, there was no denying her intrigue. And if anyone asked, it was for the welfare of the real estate business. At least, that was what he'd been repeating internally until his laptop *pinged.*

A new notification in his email inbox indicated someone was

interested in one of the properties he'd listed for lease. Clicking on it, his surprise was hardly masked.

First, the property was one he imagined wouldn't get much traction, its location prime, but the work needing to be done to it scared most buyers off. Mikko knew there would be a bit of finagling to get it to sell, but now he was eating his words.

And the second part made his stomach drop.

The words entered into the *name* field of the contact form was one he'd seen before—one he'd recently learned and was currently daydreaming about.

Anika Simmons.

The world was becoming an increasingly small place, and he wasn't sure if he liked it or despised it. She *had* to be baiting him.

His thoughts raced for a different reason. Again, his name was an advertisement all on its own, but his picture never accompanied his listings. If he really wanted to paste a face up somewhere, Cristiano usually took on that role. The cocky bastard enjoyed the free attention.

Should I send him out to this property?

There was no way in hell Mikko was going himself. While he may be constantly thinking about Anika, he couldn't face her in person again. Not yet. It was too soon, his mind convoluted. The last thing he needed was to see her and say or do something stupid. Once he had his logic watertight, he'd meet her. If the transaction even went that far.

She might see the property tomorrow and run the other direction. She'd be smart to do that honestly. Quickly, he texted Levi who was one of his more trustworthy employees with the real estate firm. The idea of even using Cristiano in this situation hit too close to home. Levi could handle it and be far enough removed that Mikko wouldn't chew his inner cheek tissue completely off in the time being.

Are you free tomorrow evening at 5:30? :*Mikko*

A few minutes later, his colleague responded.

Levi: Yeah, what's up?

I need you to go to this showing :*Mikko*

Here's the address :*Mikko*

Levi: Sure, I'll put it into my calendar

Before he could lose his nerve, or even think about what he was doing, Mikko forwarded the email containing the rest of the listing's information.

8

An Unsettling Curiosity

Anika

To both her disappointment and predetermined expectations, Mikko was *not* the one who stepped out of the glaringly white BMW the next day. Instead, a man with blond hair and a navy button down greeted her.

In the softening dusk light, his blue eyes were striking, maybe even disarming to some, but Anika kept her guard up. While this wasn't how her original plan had been, she could make due.

What's the saying? When life gives you lemons...

Brushing her hair over her shoulder, Anika extended a hand, introductions already rolling off her tongue. "Anika, and you must be..."

"Levi," he said as his warm hand slid over hers, a loose shake completing the social dance.

"Ahh, and here I thought Mr. Romanov himself would come to greet me for one of his properties"—a lie—"but I assume that's because he's a busy man."

"Indeed he is, but I can assure you, you're in good hands with me."

His lowered tone made her think he was referring to something *else* too, but she ignored it, pasting a pretty smile on her face. "I have no doubt."

"Well, let's take a closer look, and see if this place is the right fit for you," he said while they walked. "You said you started a leather goods business?"

Another deception, but what fun was life without a little *spice.*

"Yes, I started off in my home studio, making small wallets, book marks, and purses. Now it's grown into something I need a few more people for and a place to store goods. My house is a mess because of it."

Nodding, he took it all in, ever the keen listener. "Good to know, if anything, this warehouse might even be one you can grow into as you expand your items."

"That's the plan." *Among other things...*

"Right this way, Ms. Anika." Levi gestured ahead of him politely like a pseudo-gentleman.

Anika stepped forward, her sensible heels *clicking* against the filth surrounding them.

"I've noticed this property has been on the market for a couple weeks now," Anika began as she waited for Levi to unlock the entrance door. "Is something terribly wrong with it?"

Looking up, she traced over the historic brick with perceptive eyes, noting some spalling and cracking marring the bricks. But more than that, she saw Levi's attention turn to her. Her neck was elongated as she peered up, hair effortlessly tossed over her shoulder, and in a moment when he thought she wasn't looking, he drank her in.

Typical.

Is it bad I'm wishing for Mikko right now instead of this prick?

Too late to abandon her task now.

Quickly, turning back, she caught Levi still staring at her, his grin slimy. "Nothing is wrong with it per say, it just needs some TLC."

"I feel like that's a line you're *obligated* to tell me," she teased.

He chuckled and motioned for her to step into the warehouse. A tingling sensation skittered up her spine, and she couldn't tell if it was from turning her back to a stranger or something else. There was no time to dissect it since Levi was already closing in on her heels and blabbing in her ear.

"I'm on your side here," he said, "at the end of the day, our clients' satisfaction means the most to us." Another regurgitated line if she'd ever heard one. "I think it's important to look past the superficial and see what the space could be."

"I'm trying…" she started, feigning ignorance. "It's a bit difficult though."

Water pooled on the cracked concrete slab throughout the open space, the roof compromised in many areas. Large wooden beams held up the overhead structure, the craftsmanship evident despite the wear on the material. The large industrial windows let in diffused light, their hazy quality due to the grime coating the panes. Oil stains marred the hard floor as well, the previous owner uncaring for the mess left behind along with rusted equipment.

"We can always produce renderings of the space if necessary," Levi answered, his eyes following hers across the squalid space. "Many of our clients have found those helpful when it comes to properties in this condition."

"I'm assuming those are an added cost?"

Levi smiled as if that would make her forget about the dollar signs he wanted her to spend. "We can have it budgeted into our service agreement."

Internally, she sighed. Externally, "I'll have to think about it. I feel I can get a pretty good idea what the space can be like already."

She stepped away, trying to put some distance between them while pretending to inspect one of the closest columns, but he was as persistent as her shadow.

"Of course," he said, "I can give you my business card in case you change your mind."

"Perfect, thank you."

He swiftly procured a crisp white piece of cardstock, letting his fingers brush over hers as he handed it off. She bit back a retort, wishing to verbally lash out at him for his stupidity. Instead, she played the game.

Levi Lantsov.

His face was emblazoned across half of the card. Anika stifled her laughter at the sheer audacity of the photo, but that wasn't what she was looking for. There, displayed beneath his name, was an address. She noted it was different from the Romanov's Headquarters downtown.

"Did your office move locations?" she asked innocently.

"Oh, no, that's my personal address."

"On a business card?"

He winked. "Yep, you never know when connections are going to be made or when clients might need to stop by."

Oh, gods the way she wished she could punt this slimy man across the warehouse. "Of course…makes perfect sense." Lying became easy when she was around people like Levi.

"Do you have a card?" he asked.

"Yeah, hang on," she rifled through her purse while he watched her, his eyes leaving a burning trail across her exposed skin. Or a rash more like. "Here you go."

She handed it to him, the cream paper and dark text much classier than his, but she kept her opinions to herself.

His eyes narrowed at her title. "A financial data analyst, huh? So the leather goods really is just a hobby?"

"You could say that."

Levi pocketed her card before placing a hand between her shoulder blades and leading her out. "I do love a business savvy woman."

She fought to shake him off.

This shit better be worth it...

* * *

Mikko

Fuck.

He was in so much trouble.

Despite telling himself he wasn't ready to face Anika, he'd still found his way to the property.

So much for *not* doing anything stupid.

Mikko had ridden his motorcycle to work that morning, and so he'd donned his gear once more and headed out. Since the exhaust was loud and conspicuous, he'd been forced to cut the engine and coast up the side alley leading to the warehouse. His tires crunched over the small pieces of gravel littering the road, but that was the only sound he made.

He tucked himself away into a space diagonally opposite of the property before locking the handlebars of his bike and walking the rest of the short distance. He crept closer, his identity hidden beneath his helmet while he focused on keeping his breathing calm and his mind semi-clear. All things he was discovering to be nearly impossible when Anika was involved.

Slinking between the historic brick walls, he honed in on the side entrance of the warehouse Anika had requested to view. The neighboring facilities looked similar and were also vacant. Soon, this area would be revitalized, sporting shops and cafés and living spaces for those eager for a taste of what it was like in the industrial part of the city.

Until then, the area was quiet as if holding its breath. The ghosts of its past were silent for now.

Rounding a corner, he heard Levi's muffled talking. Striding closer, he remained concealed, but popped his visor up to let in a breeze along with a clearer version of Levi's voice.

"—just needs some TLC," Levi stated. His charm was turned on, forever embodying a salesperson. Mikko also assumed talking to a beautiful woman inflated his ego farther, his chest puffed out to impress.

"I feel like that's a line you're *obligated* to tell me." Her voice was as he remembered it, enticing and dangerous. Although now, it seemed as though she'd lightened it, her own business facade slipping into place.

Pressed against the brick of a nearby building, he listened as they walked closer toward the entrance. Caution flared in his gut.

Levi chuckled at her words, and Mikko gritted his teeth. "I'm on your side here. At the end of the day, our clients' satisfaction means the most to us." The way he said it made Mikko's gloved fists tighten. He could only imagine the way Levi's eyes roved over Anika.

Yet here he was, hiding out like a scared child, forced to listen to Levi—a shameless flirt—while he talked with Anika. Maybe Mikko should've known this was the direction his employee would've taken things, but he'd been too preoccupied with avoiding her altogether.

The *creak* of metal hinges snapped him back to the present, his hairline prickling with sweat. After a few moments filled with his deep breaths, he finally peeked around the corner. With them now inside, he knew he wouldn't be spotted. There, parked in the drive was Levi's shiny BMW and behind it was what he assumed was Anika's car. Her black sedan, a Kia K5, glinted in the evening sun.

Mikko added her car make, model, the color black, and her tags to his ever-growing mental list.

He strode toward her car, confident the dilapidated interior of the warehouse would keep them preoccupied. Peeking into the passenger window of her vehicle, he made to find out more about her. The tint made it difficult, but he managed to see a stack of papers laid on the seat held together by binder clips. A water bottle and coffee cup littered her cup holders. Cherry Chapstick and what appeared to be a perfume roller—the brand name mentally noted as well—rested on the middle console. Clean and mundane. No indications could be seen as to who she was. She didn't even have anything dangling from her rearview mirror. There was nothing here to give him any clues to her personality or her passions.

With a deep sigh, he rounded the car, putting it between him and the warehouse in case she, or Levi, glanced out one of the tall, dirty windows.

Crouching down to better conceal his tall frame, he stripped off a glove and wrote a note of his own on the back of the warehouse real estate listing he'd tucked into his jacket pocket.

To devour me, you must have teeth.

He smiled, tucking the paper under her windshield wiper. Time to fight fire with fire. Now if only he had a stick of gum to chew on and use it to adhere his note...

With one last glance, he crossed the alley and returned to the location of his motorcycle. He'd be able to see a sliver of her when she came back out, but the evening shadows were lengthening and his own lurking form would be indistinguishable.

Minutes ticked by, allowing his brain to roam.

He could suddenly picture Levi and Anika making small talk while she looked at the property. Levi complimenting her and asking if they should meet up sometime, *"For business, of course,"* he would assure her. And like the infuriating woman she was, she'd agree. He'd seen his employee's attempts at flirting before, his charm sickly sweet and somehow always working to draw in those of the opposite sex.

Or maybe they wouldn't even make it that far, their clothes hastily pushed aside as want and pure attraction flowed through their veins. It'd be the perfect spot, the warehouse's decrepit walls their only witness to their sexual acts.

Mikko's leather gloves squeaked as his fists tightened.

Stop, stop, stop.

He'd been watching too many reality TV shows with Cristiano lately, and they were clearly rotting his brain.

The telltale sound of the door opening again, its hinges rusty and squealing horrifically, had Mikko's head snapping up to look at the gap between the buildings in front of him.

First, he spotted Anika as she walked into view while Levi locked up behind them. Their chatter continued, but it was indiscernible. The early autumn breeze whipped her hair around, pieces of it blowing across her face and lips as she smiled at something Levi said.

When is that bastard ever funny?

Her work attire consisted of dark slacks hugging her hips and thighs before straightening out at her ankles. A deep forest hued blouse was tucked into her pants, the material appearing to be soft as it pressed against her skin in the wind.

Mikko's lips twitched.

Like this, she looked nothing like the temptress she'd been the night they met—her skin on display, her tattoos attractive against her skin,

74

and the outfit she'd worn then...

"Thanks again," she called to Levi as she rounded the front of her car, "I'll be in touch!"

Oh?

Maybe he could take the sale over from here, and completely kick Levi out of the picture—

"Of course! You have my direct number, so give me a call when you've decided." Levi stepped closer, his slacks and crisp button down visible from where Mikko was observing.

The man was conventionally attractive—lean build, short blond hair he kept styled and trim by attending a nearby barber every three weeks, and a face conveying his approachability. But his sudden enthusiasm pissed Mikko off. There'd been many sales before this one where Mikko had to damn near pull teeth to get that man to work.

"And if I don't hear from you, I'll reach out to check in," he continued, hand running through his hair. Mikko rolled his eyes.

She nodded, but her spine stiffened.

The note.

Mikko was positive she noticed it tucked neatly where he'd left it, his scrawl taunting her.

Without indicating what it was or that she saw anything, Anika slipped it out from under her wiper and climbed into her car. A smile was still plastered on her face, but it looked like it hurt her to maintain it.

Inwardly, Mikko was laughing. It felt good to return the favor she so *kindly* took upon herself almost a week ago.

Throwing his leg over his bike, Mikko turned the key, letting the razor thin headlights of his R6 shine in the dimness. She'd pass him to leave and he hoped she would notice him.

Another small parting gift, if you will.

A little something to scare her. It was all fun and games until he started showing up at places she least expected it.

Turning on her headlights, Anika pulled away, content to leave Levi waving at her like a schoolboy with a crush. But the moment Mikko's headlights lit up the side of her car as she drove by, he saw her head whip to the side. He revved his bike, unable to stop the impulsive thought. Ever observant, she pinpointed his form in the dark atop his motorcycle. Mikko coyly waved before she sped away.

Her tail lights faded into the distance, but still Mikko waited. A painful amount of time passed before he allowed himself to make his decision. He knew work was most likely piling up on his desk but...maybe one little detour wouldn't hurt?

Mikko turned the key the rest of the way letting the machine beneath him rumble to life as his Bluetooth headset connected.

"Starting route guidance..."

9

Seeing Green

Mikko

Like he had when he'd arrived at the warehouse, Mikko was sure to cut his motorcycle's engine and headlights to avoid being spotted by Anika. He'd already tempted fate once by letting her see him at the riverside property, if she saw him again here it'd be too much of a coincidence for her to ignore. There would come a time for that but…

Right now, he wanted to sit in the dark, the street lights spaced far enough apart he could remain mostly unseen. His all black attire, helmet, and bike also kept him in shadow—shadows she should stay far away from for her safety and his sanity.

But he feared she never would, always walking the gray and enticing Mikko to come closer.

Peering up at the massive white oak trees lining the street in front of her house, he waited for her while she pulled in around the back of her house through an alleyway. He thought about creeping closer, positioning himself *just* right to see inside her ground level windows or catch a glimpse of the decor inside her house. Anything would be helpful to add to his ever-growing list of facts he had about her. The thought of viewing her lifestyle so intimately made his pulse pound in his ears.

While she made her way to her house, Mikko glanced around, curious to see what kind of neighborhood she found pleasing enough to buy a home in. It was a smaller, historic suburb of the city, a place he didn't visit often since many of his clients lived closer to his headquarters, but he could change that.

Old homes sat like soldiers on their lawns, well-groomed and evenly spaced. Currently, they were indistinguishable, but in the daylight Mikko was sure their facades were painted in various colors. Each portrayed a piece of the owner inside, and judging from the glowing porch light at Anika's, hers was dark green.

Neighboring windows glowed with soft light from lamps and only the sound of insects chirping could be heard. The subtle hum of the highway was far enough away that his brain hardly registered it.

Propping a foot up on one of his motorcycle's pegs, his eyes focused in on the front of her house, waiting with bated breath for a light to turn on. A thin sidewalk led to her porch, dark foliage softening the edges of the man-made structure. In the dark, it bordered on overgrown and unkempt, but Mikko wondered if that was really the case. Everything he'd learned about her screamed the opposite.

Maybe organized chaos...

A light flicked on.

Mikko's jaw clenched, his body freezing.

It was the large picture window to the left of her porch.

Sheer cream curtains framed the glass, allowing for him to see inside. It appeared to be her living room, the tops of rusty orange velvet chairs and a worn leather couch were visible. He could barely see a knitted throw blanket draped over the sofa. A lamp was positioned in front of the window, but Anika had yet to turn it on. Currently, the light was coming from a taller one positioned behind the couch.

Botanical wall paper lined one wall and a subtle green color covered the others from what he could see from his vantage point. Frames hung on the walls, the pictures indiscernible, and half of a bookshelf stuffed full with tomes caught his eye.

So much to see, so much to catalog.

Stepping into view, Anika's form halted his thoughts. She was still in the same outfit as earlier, her skin aglow with the lamplight, but she held her phone up to her ear.

Resisting the urge to leave his motorcycle unattended and stalk up to the sill of her living room window, Mikko tried to read her body language; hell, even her lips, but it was impossible. Popping his helmet's visor up, he strained his ears for the sound of her voice through the panes of glass, but again, it was futile.

With a sigh, he tried to reign in his frustrations, contemplating taking what he'd learned and heading back to his penthouse. He'd gathered enough information for one night, he could afford—

His phone buzzed, the screen lighting up from where it was mounted near the small dash of his motorcycle. Tearing his eyes away from Anika, who was still on the phone, Mikko expected to see Cristiano's name appearing on the screen.

Levi.

Mikko's brow rose and he swiped to unlock his phone.

Levi: *We might have the warehouse property sold*

A bold statement.

To who? ***:Mikko***

Levi: The woman who toured it today

And you know this how? **:Mikko**

Levi: I'm on the phone with her right now and she sounds giddy

Mikko glanced back up at Anika and *giddy* was not the word he'd use to describe her. She seemed focused, rearranging something in her living room before disappearing out of sight. If she was excited about purchasing the industrial property, she had a unique way of showing it.

Great **:Mikko**

Keep her talking **:Mikko**

And he knew Levi would.

Locking his phone, Mikko searched for signs of Anika again only to see she'd made her way upstairs and was currently standing in front of an upper window. Her phone was tucked between her ear and shoulder as she unbuttoned her blouse.

Mikko tasted copper as his teeth sunk into the flesh of his cheek.

Slowly, she undid another button as blood continued to flood his mouth.

Is this a trick?

And as he was about to hop off his motorcycle—

The curtains closed. Mikko swallowed.

And the fantasy that was beginning to bloom in his mind turned to ash.

What the fuck am I thinking?

He wasn't, simple as that.

And he certainly wasn't using his head—well, the right one—when he yanked his key out of the ignition and slipped into the vegetation lining the edge of her yard.

Maybe I can catch a glimpse of her if I sneak in closer.

As he was about to open the gate leading into her front yard, a second window upstairs illuminated.

And there she was, in all her glory.

Somewhere along the way, she'd pulled her hair up into a messy bun and lost her blouse entirely. Standing in front of the window without a care in the world, Mikko could damn near see the lace of her bra.

Blood raced south; his mouth watered.

Why had she chosen him to antagonize? And why was he letting her get under his skin?

A demented form of escapism, perhaps? It was the only thing he could rationally think of, and even then, that didn't deter him. He wanted her to touch him again, trace his tattoos and damn near spit in his face—anything as long as she distracted him from the responsibilities weighing on his shoulders.

A sliver of envy weaved through his chest. He longed to be normal, to break free of the duties holding him captive, but there was nothing he could do. People were counting on him. This infatuation had to go away.

Or else.

Instead, he was forced to be a Romanov; a man resigned to real estate and money laundering.

And long ago, he'd discovered just how dangerous women could be. Especially for men like him—*obsessive* ones. But there was no one to be mad at, to blame. He'd chosen this, he'd put himself in this situation. All those years ago when he should've retaliated against his father, he'd chosen to grit his teeth and stay silent.

Now he was paying for it, but it didn't mean he couldn't taunt her in other ways.

Together they could play this game.

And play he did.

With every piece of clothing she dropped, he unraveled a little more.

10

Picked Lock(et)s

Unknown

You knew every action had consequences.

Forgotten keys led to being late for work; befriending strangers led to memories you might've originally missed out on; dried blood beneath your fingernails pointed to the moment your anger got the best of you.

But it was all an illusion of choice. *Fate.*

Fate, the ever present puppet master, pulled the strings connected to every outcome before laughing at us for believing there was anything greater than our own minds.

Perhaps that was what erased the feeling of adrenaline mounting in your gut as the locked door before you *clicked* free. If the universe hadn't wanted you here, then the door to *his* penthouse wouldn't be swinging open and beckoning you in.

Or maybe...if Fate existed, it was *you.*

Who else could reign over you so wholly? Who else would you let control your life so thoroughly?

Maybe long ago, there'd been a time when someone held power over you, making you wish for a different life, but now?

No.

Never again.

Never again would you suffer at the hands of someone else. It was your turn to wreak havoc on those who deserved it. Revenge licked at the tips of your fingers, craving retribution, itching to show the world why you were to be feared.

Not yet, you softly chided.

The restlessness was almost unbearable, but you'd made it this far. A little longer wouldn't kill you.

Play the game, a muscle in your jaw twitched, *always play the game.*

Until then, you'd never cease to terrorize those who sought to end you. After all, you were beyond saving, the vileness in your heart eating away at the tender flesh around it. Gone was the young child who had stared at the world with wide-eyed wonder, and in their place...

No. No. Not now.

Snapping back to the present, you cleared those thoughts away. You had a task to complete, preferably before the owner of the penthouse came back. Stepping over the threshold, a shadowed darkness and faint twinkling city lights enticed you to walk closer. Trailing a gloved finger over the closest table, you noted its contents. The glass top was devoid of dust and clutter and contained only a sleek lamp and a decorative bowl for keys. One item rested in it.

A key fob with a locket attached.

Among the flashes of sterility in the space you'd gathered thus far, this seemed like a deviation—a clue.

Your fingers closed around the keys, silently picking them up and cracking open the locket. Curiosity flared in your gut; this was a private moment, a sliver within time that would've made anyone else feel guilt, but not you. This glitch had been constructed for you, *by* you, and you'd be damned if you wasted it.

And the little faces staring up at you, the locket's contents barely revealed, made your teeth clench.

Searching for the light switch, you quickly flipped it on, uncaring if the flash of warm light drew attention to you. You needed to be certain of what you were looking at. Whatever digital footprint you were creating at this moment could be deleted, your knowledge in the matter unparalleled. Despite living in a technology centered world, *everything* could be erased. Especially with the right tools.

With narrowed eyes, you confirmed it. The woman and young boy staring up at you had your chest constricting.

You'd come here to ravage this man's home, to leave a message in your wake, but this...

This was too delicious to pass up.

This would hit them right where it hurt.

Tucking the locket and key fob into your pants pocket, you rummaged through the rest of the penthouse; you left papers scattered on the countertops, chairs moved slightly to the right of their original position, and couch cushions on the floor.

The first step was supposed to be the hardest, but you felt like you were free falling, whipping past all the barriers deeming someone's character as good or evil. Being in someone else's space felt like a twisted sense of home, of solitude. Or maybe that was residual from knowing how pissed this specific person would be when they finally returned.

Did someone know when their soul was irredeemable? *Yes.* Did they know when it was too late to go back—to expunge their past of all the horrendous wrongdoings littering their memories? *Yes.*

It started as a small whisper, only a piece of your mind that was afflicted and diseased, but it grew. The inky black spread and corrupted every fiber within you until you found yourself consumed with rage. Until you discovered yourself standing in a place you didn't remember walking to. And until bits of your memories faded away.

Fate had chosen you, molded *you* into a weapon, one that had to suffer and *bleed* first before retribution could be had. A necessary means to an end; you'd have it, no matter what it took, forsaking the parts of you that you lost along the way. In the end, if the only thing left standing was a shell of you filled with vengeance, then your job was complete.

Only then could your soul finally *rest*.

The endless whispers forever tormented you. Yet, one thought remained louder than the rest. One notion. *Bloodshed.*

A wicked smile carved itself across your face.

A pleasant promise was evident in the air, eager to wrap itself around your weary, yet determined frame.

Let the games begin.

11

A Tasteful Gift

Mikko

Aknock on the clear pane of glass leading to Mikko's office startled him as his eyes caught sight of blond hair and a pressed blue shirt.

Glancing up, the stray strands from his relentless hair pulling tickled his forehead. While it was a little after noon, it'd been a rollercoaster of a morning. Despite multiple deals falling through, his mind still lingered on Anika, and the way he drove past her house two nights before. His curiosity had gotten the better of him, the thought of her skin on display on a constant loop in his mind.

Waving Levi in, he hoped the other man would have information he secretly wanted.

"How'd it go?" Mikko asked. "Were you able to get the client to commit to the property?"

Sinking into the couch, Levi sighed. "It went well. She was really interested in the space, even called me as you know." Something akin to jealousy crawled up the back of Mikko's throat as the other man continued. "Despite the amount of work it needs, she doesn't seem deterred."

"And the listing price? Is she agreeable to that?"

"Mostly," Levi fidgeted with his cuff, a tell of his, "but I'm thinking that might be her only reservation."

"Convince her otherwise." The words hurt leaving his mouth, but he donned his CEO persona so Levi wouldn't think twice about the rhythmic tapping Mikko was doing against the top of his desk. One of *his* tells.

"I'll see what I can do. She has all my personal information, so I'm hoping that eliminates any barriers."

Unable to stop himself, Mikko retorted, "Perfect. It's a good sign the client can see the potential in things."

Levi chuckled. "Y'know, I think she said something similar, but it seems like a good fit for her."

Tap. Tap. Tap. Tap.

"What's she planning?"

"She started a small, leather goods business, and now that it's growing, she needs more space, material, and people." Mikko nodded, moving his hands to his lap. He clasped them tightly to keep his fiddling to a minimum. Levi couldn't see they were white. He hadn't known about this little tidbit. "She gave me her business card…well, for her day job since the leather business is a hobby right now."

As if needed to prove his victory, Levi fished the small rectangle of paper from his pocket, flipping it over his fingers as his other arm stretched out over the back of the couch.

Why does it feel like he's gloating?

Mikko was losing it, his mind largely dramatic with any and all things to do with her. It was nothing; he was reading into Levi's actions. "I'm assuming it has all her info on there for you to follow back up if phone calls don't cut it?"

"Yep, although I'm already planning a dinner event, and she's at the top of the invite list." His teeth flashed, his grin mischievous. It irked Mikko.

"Wonderful, clients like to feel special," Mikko bit out, the words containing a double meaning in his own mind.

"Of course," Levi looked at her card one more time before pocketing it. "While most of our transactions are discrete for legalities, I still remember how to be a true realtor."

"That's why you always were my favorite—a quick learner." The lie burned Mikko's tongue.

"Gotta earn my keep around here someway, boss." The use of *boss* made Mikko cringe. "Regardless, she appears to be a harmless woman to do business with. I could see the brightness in her eyes at the idea of expanding her business and making it into something of her own."

Mikko knew Anika was far from harmless, but kept his thoughts to himself. Aloud he said, "That's what this business is all about: making dreams come true."

"In more ways than one."

Levi stood, walking over to the wet bar along the wall, his fingers running over the glass decanters. Mikko wanted to scold him, to tell him to stop touching his stuff and to get out. He got the information he wanted—all of it damn near worthless—but he kept calm. Leaning back in his chair, he watched his employee peruse the untouched alcohol selection.

"Is this one new?" Levi asked suddenly, his hand halting near a bottle Mikko couldn't see clearly from his vantage point.

"I hardly pay attention," Mikko replied. "Which one is it?"

"This one." Holding up a dark amber bottle, its neck long and slender, he let Mikko take a look at it. "I don't remember it being in here last time I was in your office."

"You sneak in here often?"

Levi grinned and set the bottle back down. "Maybe."

His own curiosity winning out over his annoyance, Mikko stood and met Levi at the small bar. Sure enough, the bottle's color and silhouette was out of place among the rest of his collection. While he wasn't lying when he said he didn't touch these, his memories served him well.

This one was new.

And its label indicated it was tequila. His mind wandered to one person specifically.

"I'll have to ask Emma if someone sent it while I was away," Mikko said.

"Secret admirer maybe?"

Mikko's heart stuttered. "If you think all the gruff ass men we work with are romantic types, sure."

Levi laughed, "You got me there. Well, that was all I needed. I'll be in touch with both you and Anika in hopes of closing out that sale."

Nodding, Mikko kept his eyes on the bottle as Levi walked out. Slipping his phone from his pocket when he was alone once more, he dialed Emma's direct line.

"What can I do for you Mr. Romanov?" she inquired after the second ring.

Cocking his head at the amber glass, he asked, "Did someone deliver a nice bottle of alcohol here for me?"

"Oh, yes! I forgot to tell you since you were busy with meetings all morning, but a local delivery service stopped by with it earlier. They told me it was for you and there was a note attached explaining the sender's gratitude." She shuffled papers around on her desk before she spoke again. "I didn't read it since it was a sealed note, but it's on your desk. Top corner under the base of your desk lamp."

"Thank you, Emma."

"Of course. Hope it's from a pleased client, you deserve the recognition."

"One can only hope."

After she updated him on another upcoming meeting, they hung up. His feet already carried him to the corner of his desk, her directions succinct and stirring his anxiety.

He tried to think back through all the deals he'd closed the past few weeks, but nothing came to mind. At least none warranting an expensive bottle of liquor to appear with a note.

His calloused fingers pulled the stiff cardstock from under the lamp, the seal untouched. Ripping into it, his patience was nearly gone as his thoughts of Anika resurfaced while he read the typed words on the thick paper.

Pleasure doing business with you. Although if we're to work together, I fear you'll need to refine your palate...

Mikko scoffed, his mind flashing back to similar words falling from her plush lips a week ago. But there was more:

Also, maybe this will loosen you up, gods know you need it

Well, he'd be damned. Even if it wasn't signed by her, he *knew* it was Anika's doing. The letter's wording reeked of her humor and smugness. The timing of it was too perfect; his refusal of showing her the property himself and Levi swearing he was closing in on the deal at the forefront of his mind.

And Mikko would be lying if he said her words didn't make him smile.

Maybe it *was* time for him to refine his palette—time for him to dip his tongue into something a bit more...fiery.

* * *

MIKKO INSERTED HIS key into the lock. His penthouse front door was the last barrier standing in his way to solace after a long day. A weird feeling had been needling him all afternoon ever since Levi had damn near gloated about his time with Anika at the industrial property. It was stupid and silly, and if it were any other client, he wouldn't care, but this time it irritated him. Turning it, he waited to hear the telltale click of the mechanism springing free, but...

Nothing.

Twisting it again, the sound he was searching for came. That was when he realized his front door was unlocked, and he'd just *locked* it.

Fury along with adrenaline bubbled in his veins. After everything, he'd wanted to come home and slip into bed—clothes and shoes still on if he was really lazy, but someone else had a different idea.

Unlocking the door, Mikko quickly pocketed the keys and withdrew the gun he had concealed under his suit jacket. The hall outside his penthouse was empty, only one other person living on this floor. Besides, if anyone saw him, he could *make* them forget.

Nudging the door open, his eyes caught on the way the light from the hall spilled into the darkness inside. Slipping through the opening once it was large enough for him to pass through, he let the door *snick* shut behind him. Slowly, his eyes adjusted to the shadows as his back pressed into the cool surface of the door. If whoever had left his door unlocked was still inside, he'd make them wish they'd left before he got back.

The silhouettes of his furniture sharpened as the seconds passed, softly backlit by the skyline beyond. Light pollution stained the sky a dusty gray with a splash of warmth. Buildings glittered in the floor to ceiling windows lining his residence, and Mikko let them guide him as he continued on.

This unit had been designed to use as little walls as necessary so the view would be unhindered which also proved advantageous for sightlines. There were only a handful of places to hide since the closets and bathroom were the only rooms to have walls and doors.

Muscle memory steered him around the sharp edges of his kitchen island, charcoal finishes an endless void in the minimal lighting. Before him, his couch cushions littered the floor along with papers that had been pulled out of drawers and left to decorate his space. His furniture had shifted almost infinitesimally, but his keen eyes caught it. Clearing the living room, his dress shoes padded noiselessly across the polished concrete floor and area rug all while missing the mess strewn about.

His night trained eyes snagged on the bathroom door—it was open, its maw yawning wider and beckoning him closer. Gun trained straight ahead, finger hovering over the trigger, Mikko prepared for the worst—a bloodstain on his floors. His penthouse was one place he *tried* to keep the violence out. He had expensive furniture to protect after all.

Closing one eye, Mikko stepped into the room, flipping the light switch on quickly to stun anyone who may be lingering. The brightness made his one open eye squint, but he was greeted with nothing. The usual bathroom accessories met his eyes.

Leaving the light on and turning away from the small room, Mikko opened his closed eye. Since that one had maintained its night sight, his other one quickly adjusted back.

Wrapping the corner, colorful city lights illuminated his figure as he crept around his own damn apartment. Around every turn, he found nothing. No one lurked in the deepest shadows for him.

After he cleared his bedroom—finally determining no one was there—he walked around and turned on a few floor lamps. The warm glow was harsh, but welcome after the stress of expecting an intruder. It still didn't erase the violating feeling blossoming in his chest.

Someone had been in here, in my space, and slipped out undetected.

Re-holstering his gun, Mikko strode back to his kitchen. The cool feeling of his glass decanters underneath his fingertips comforting. A portion of his kitchen had been converted to storing liquor, just as one might designate a coffee area. Letting his mood guide him, each bottle more extravagant than the last, he finally settled on a bourbon. A deviation from his usual drink of choice, but he was feeling agitated.

Forgoing ice, Mikko poured two fingers into a crystal tumbler. The color reminded him of Anika's eyes. His annoyance flare brighter.

The first sip burned.

The second one warmed.

And the third loosened the tension between his shoulder blades.

With his glass hanging from his fingertips precariously, Mikko sat at his desk, content to check his security cameras now that he knew no one was lurking around. His system was robust and nothing would be able to get past his surveillance.

Paranoia had its perks.

After combing through the last couple hours on the digital footage, Mikko deigned no one had been inside his penthouse. Which was impossible. There was physical evidence of someone touching his things, so had they tampered with his security cameras?

Abruptly standing, Mikko shuffled around his residence, searching for anything that could be missing. He was feeling slightly tipsy, the amber hued liquid on an empty stomach making him sloppy as he ran through his mental catalog.

Nothing appeared to be amiss besides the disarray left behind.

With his thoughts hazy, he remembered one last place to check:

the small dish near his front door. In his haste to clear the space, he'd forgone checking to make sure his spare keys were there, but now a sinking feeling unfurled in his gut.

Creeping closer, he blinked rapidly, his eyesight blurry, but there was no denying it.

His keys were missing along with a piece of his mom: a locket with her photo in it.

His molars squeaked as they clenched together; there would be hell to pay when he found out who did this.

12

Droplets

Unknown

It was *too* easy to follow them.

The way they tried to slink amongst the shadows as if they could hide and cloak their wrong doings was laughable. Nonetheless, you sought them out, delighting in the chase.

People were creatures of habit, following their routines—clinging to them as if their life depended on it, and maybe they did—but it made stalking that much easier.

Somewhere nearby, water dropped steadily, a timekeeper of its own as you lurked in the inky corners of a warehouse. A city as large as Portland made it easy to come and go as you pleased within the industrial districts. Long haul trucks continuously came in to pick up their wares before leaving. Trains stopped with ear piercing screeches, but never stayed long enough to memorize your face.

The constant buzz of activity dimmed at this hour, but even still, those who lingered had jobs to complete, other worries lining their faces. They wouldn't notice a few weird occurrences in the area.

Or screaming.

The freight trains desensitized even the most skeptical.

It'd been too easy, following the man now dead before you, leaking blood onto the dirty concrete floor. One bright hole in the center of his forehead told the story of his death, a slowing stream of crimson pooling beneath him the closing remarks to his life.

Men like him portrayed themselves as powerful, untouchable, but in the end, they all died the same. Some of them even begged, which never made a difference. If anything it made your black heart swell.

A train's horn blared nearby, its harsh sound covering anything else, which had been in your favor earlier. The man's incessant babbles forever seared into your head.

I don't think that's necessary.

Please, d-don't do this.

I already paid what was owed.

I don't have what you want.

On and on he went, talking through the motions of you screwing a silencer onto the end of your gun until the bullets quieted him, permanently. It had been in beautiful harmony with the clamor of the factory plots all around.

A poetic ending for a vile man.

But your work was far from over. While he may have paid his money, he still owed *you* a great deal. He was a pawn in a larger game—his death serving an end goal. A smile stretched across your shadow darkened features. This man's death was accomplishing more than his life ever had.

Creeping closer, eyes flicking back and forth from the body to the shadows, you made sure you were still alone. Although you'd done your research, knowing this warehouse was between tenants, being caught this early wouldn't do any good. The plans you'd made for yourself would abruptly end.

No. No, you couldn't have that.

Besides, the right people would eventually hear of you. Word of mouth spread differently in these hellish circles, where even the dead had things to say when their mouths no longer could.

And so, placing your gun back in its ankle holster and slipping a knife free from another, its blade glinting, you went to work. There was much to be done after all.

Closing the eyes of the deceased was a practice of respect, but that emotion had long left your body. You longed for the opposite effect. He deserved *worse;* he earned the right to have his eyes wide open, baiting whoever stumbled across his corpse to *know* what it felt like to suffer.

Sharp steel met the tissue of his eye, slicing through like butter with a stomach turning *squelch.*

* * *

A LITTLE WHILE later, his cool skin seeped through your gloved fingers, the dead body a perfect host for your next clue.

Deftly, your hands slipped the key fob from a clear plastic bag to its final resting place. An idea you'd decided on long ago, your mind feeling a bit devious. A small incision in the man's stomach—made by your own hand—barely leaked any crimson since his heart was still. Steady fingers probed the handmade wound, prying it open wide enough for you to push the key fob in. A faint sucking noise told you it'd reached the inner layers of muscle and fat.

A gentle pat on Ivan's stomach calmed the inner racing of your heart. Everything was coming to fruition, like you wanted.

Now, the dull sawing of thread feeding itself through flesh kept you company.

Stitch after stitch.
Suture after suture.

13

Eyes Everywhere

Mikko

"Look at this," Mikko said, his hand running anxiously through his hair while Cristiano peered over his shoulder. "You can't tell me this hasn't been edited?"

"I mean the timestamp skipping thirteen minutes is...telling." Cristiano leaned in, eyes squinting at the security footage of Mikko's penthouse.

"It takes time and skill to do this, to splice it this clean." While technology wasn't his strong suit—he paid others for that—there was no denying the evidence in front of the two men. Sitting at his desk, he watched the surveillance back again and again, searching for clues or shadows or a hint of something the intruder left behind.

Nothing.

Heat flashed up his neck, his anger fresh despite the incident occurring yesterday. After discovering his keys and locket to be missing, he'd been fidgety and decided to put the energy to good use.

Which lead him to finding *this.*

Mikko tolerated a lot but, this...this was crossing a line. Once he found the perpetrator, they'd face the wrath he and his men were known for.

"And you said the only thing missing was the locket and your keys despite the mess they left behind?" Cristiano asked.

Mikko nodded, unable to voice his emotions.

"Weird. Out of all the enemies we've made, that isn't something I'd think they'd go for."

"It's more personal than the work we do..." Mikko trailed off.

"Which is concerning," Cristiano filled in.

Mikko's fingers had drummed the wooden surface of his desk, contemplating if he should call the security company again. They'd already told him there was nothing they could do. While they supplied the equipment, storage and deletion was in the owner's domain, therefore, they had no access to it. He'd been sure to tell them how ridiculous that was before promptly hanging up.

Now one of his few safe havens felt tainted. Someone had been here, let themselves in, and became acquainted with his security measures enough to manipulate them to their advantage. If only his list of enemies wasn't the length of the city's population...

Cristiano straightened as a tired sigh slipped past Mikko's lips. His back felt strained and ached from sitting at his desk all day again. The hour was getting late, and the screen was too bright compared to the rest of his room, but work had to be done.

"Well, no time to dwell on it now," Mikko said, shuffling papers around on his desk, "these land acquisitions won't win themselves."

"Maybe not, but you look like you could use a night off...boss."

Mikko waved his friend away, glaring at him for using that blasted word. "I'll get a day off when I'm dead, yeah?" He couldn't let these projects slip through his fingertips, the money and resources were too precious. Besides, a business—no matter how corrupt—had to run efficiently like all the others.

"Still, I have a feeling you need to get laid, you've been awfully—"

"My sex life is *not* up for discussion tonight." Mikko clicked out of the security footage, his annoyance flaring up each time he looked at it.

"Because it's nonexistent," Cristiano taunted as he walked away toward the liquor bar in Mikko's kitchen.

"Just because I don't share all the details of my intimate activities, like you do, doesn't mean I'm not partaking."

His friend chuckled as he poured himself a splash of bourbon into a tumbler. "Even so, the signs are all there, Mikko. You can't fool me."

Mikko didn't say anything; his insufferable friend was right. "What signs?" he said aloud instead.

But the answer never came.

Looking up, Mikko saw Cristiano with the tumbler poised between the counter and his lips, frozen. In his other hand was his phone.

"What's wrong?" Mikko asked, abruptly standing. A sinking feeling, one that went past the basic emotions of violation, started creeping in.

"I–uh...Devon texted me..." Cristiano trailed off, setting his glass back down. His hand scrubbed over his face. "He said Ivan's been found dead."

The world narrowed to a point, all sound around Mikko fading out before it rushed back in again.

"What?" When Mikko had last seen Ivan, he'd been very much *alive*—battered and beaten but still breathing. Besides, Emma had confirmed Ivan had paid his dues and kept *Bubblegum* out of the journalism spotlight. Mikko's message had been clearly received by the dimwitted man. For the time being, their feud and debt was cleared.

"Yeah, um, he said his body was found inside one of the warehouses along the waterways," Cristiano answered. Death was common in his line of work, forever trailing a few steps behind him his whole life, but that didn't make this news any less surprising. Or less infuriating.

After the past couple days, this was icing on the cake.

"One of ours?" Mikko asked out loud.

"Yes, and it seems he went out *gruesomely.*"

Mikko's hand fidgeted with a pen sitting on his desk. "Which property?"

"The one Levi showed the other day."

"That listing is never going to sell now with this kind of history attached to it," Mikko lamented.

Cristiano finally took a sip of his alcohol, most likely needing the burn to keep himself centered. His phone pinged again as he asked, "Who did he show it to? Someone we have history with?"

Silky black hair and whiskey hued eyes flashed across his mind. "No one important," Mikko said.

"You're positive?" Cristiano asked. His thumb brushed across his phone screen, reading more texts pouring in.

No. "Yes," Mikko continued, uncertainty cloaking his already weary shoulders. "But you said it was gruesome..."

"Yeah, Devon said the scene was a mess," his friend cleared his throat, "and that he was mutilated."

Mikko's eyebrows raised. "And how was he killed?"

"A gunshot wound to the head."

"And the mutilation?"

"Well, that's the weird thing," Cristiano hesitated, "the mutilation was done post-mortem."

"A message then, for whoever would find the body and not for torture purposes," Mikko said.

"It would appear that way, yes." He continued mumbling under his breath as though Mikko wasn't there, "at least I hope it was done post-mortem because *damn*—"

"Where was it, Cristiano?" The use of his friend's name snapped him back into the present.

"Uh…his face."

"Where on his face?"

Cristiano locked his phone and tucked it into his pocket as if locking a metaphorical door and throwing away the key. "I'm not sure you wanna know, it's giving *me* a headache just thinkin' about it—"

"*Cristiano,*" Mikko was stern, "you know I hate when you do this."

A tense beat of silence passed as Cristiano knocked back the alcohol.

"His eyes," he finally answered, voice tight. "His eyes were messed with, and let's just say…they're not there anymore."

Something about the way Cristiano described the information from Devon made this death feel different. It was something fueled by anger. A personal vendetta.

"Does Devon know of anyone who could've done this?" Mikko mused. He knew *he* did, but he wanted to see what the other man said.

Cristiano laughed, his momentary disgust vanishing. "I fear we may have a longer list of enemies than most."

"True." *God, now my head hurts.* "I'll start combing through people who've made moves against us in the past and create a list. Hopefully it leads us somewhere. I'll also call in some favors that are owed."

"I'll do the same. I'll probably drive out there tomorrow and talk with Devon personally. He said he's handling the cops now along with any evidence they take."

"Get a new phone since he shared that info with you. We can't have people tracking this—tracking us. The less the public knows the better, and I'll be sure to up the Portland's Police Department budget to keep them happy."

"And silent," Cristiano tacked on.

"Exactly."

Both men stood in silence for a bit longer, the weight of the world inching in with each breath. Finally Mikko spoke, "You're more than welcome to stay here tonight, it's getting late."

His friend smiled, the planes of his face dull and tired. This job took so much from both of them. "I appreciate the offer, but my bed is a hell of a lot cozier than your expensive couch."

"You can take the bed."

"You snore I'm afraid." Cristiano slipped his shoes on with a grin. Mikko walked closer, ready to usher his friend out. "No, I don't."

"How would you know? You're asleep."

"Get out, I rescind my offer."

A genuine laugh slipped past Cristiano's lips and for a moment everything was normal. "Well, I'll update you tomorrow," he opened the door, "so until then, keep the doors locked."

"Looking forward to it," Mikko scoffed and waved at him as he closed the door behind his friend.

After he'd made sure the door was locked and his security system was armed, Mikko shucked off his shoes and threw his clothes in the hamper in his bedroom. The quiet of his penthouse surrounded him, and the thoughts in his head grew louder with each passing second.

There was never a dull moment.

And while Mikko hadn't been lying when he said no one important had toured the warehouse, he still felt guilty for keeping his friend in the dark.

Soon. I'll tell him soon, Mikko thought, but only after he had more answers to the questions Cristiano would surely ask. On top of that, he had his work cut out for him. Most of the time he only trusted his men as far as he could throw them, but this incident *really* had him questioning everything.

Especially Anika.

The occurrence happening in the same warehouse Levi showed her had a weird feeling brewing in the pit of his stomach.

Sighing, Mikko sat back down in front of his computer, the screen illuminating his features as he opened a new tab and prepared himself for what he might find as he sunk into the clutches of the dark web.

If there was a will, there was a *price*.

14

Ride or Die

Mikko - 15 Years Ago

Blood ran down the length of his fingers before slowing along the flesh of his palm. The sticky liquid soaked into the knees of his pants as he knelt there, dumbfounded. It was the first time he'd had to follow through with his father's threats. It was the first time such a color stained his hands. This violence was abhorrent, a gritty means to an end that Mikko didn't understand.

Why not strategize in other ways? Why crush people in hopes they'd fear you enough to respect you?

None of it made sense. Only the loud thrum of blood rushing in his ears and the racing of his heart kept him grounded. And even then, his body felt light. He wasn't sure he was really here. Black spots crept into the corners of his vision, the adrenaline taking over and shutting down his organs in an attempt to survive.

"It had to be this way son," his father murmured, standing nearby with the gun still clutched in his hand. Truthfully, he'd forgotten Alek was there, his brain tired and overwhelmed. "This is the only way for you to learn."

Dead eyes stared back at Mikko, a single hole framed between the eyebrows of the man before him. Only a few moments ago he'd seen his father interrogating him, and now...

Now his life had been snuffed out without a second thought. Heartlessly.

"I don't understand why I'm here," was all Mikko could manage, his tongue thick with emotion. He was trying and failing to not show weakness even as acid bubbled up in the back of his throat. Alek hated it when he cried, blamed it on his mom for raising him to be weak. But Mikko knew his father didn't mean it—remembered a time where Alek was also gentler. Now those days were long gone.

Alek spoke. "Mutts that disobey get put down. No exceptions."

Squeezing the blood-soaked rag in frustration, Mikko finally looked up. "This is *your* mess, not mine. Why should I—"

Smack!

Alek's palm struck the back of Mikkos' head, clipping him in a manner that wasn't meant to be painful. It was a warning. "Everything I do in the name of this company is for you too. We went over this already."

"We did."

"And are you deaf?"

"No."

"Dense then? Your brain too stuffed full with pretty things and the sweet nothings your mother whispered to you as a child for you to realize life isn't like that? Look at what it did to her. After all she gave—all the good deeds she did—cancer still sucked everything away."

A tear formed in Mikko's eye. His father was right.

His mom had embodied life, what it meant to be unique and unapologetically yourself, and it'd only sent her to an early grave.

"You drained her, took everything from her." It was the wrong thing to say, but it slipped from Mikko's mouth regardless.

"And this is why we're here," Alek gritted. "You say the stupidest shit and expect people to go along with you."

Mikko's resolve hardened. "Learning from the best, you could say—"

Before the last of his sentence had left his mouth, Alek was on him. Gripping the short hair at the nape of Mikko's neck, his father pushed him to the dirty floor. The dead man's ring of blood seeped out, the uneven surface letting it pool nearby. Alek's heavy weight landed on his back, his hot breath at his ear. Blood and cooling crimson splattered across Mikko's face. His cheek agonizingly ground against the hard floor until his jaw ached, droplets of copper and grime slipping into his mouth as his father pressed harder. Sputtering, Mikko bucked and thrashed, desperate to be let up.

This was too much—

And in a twisted moment of fate, Mikko's eyes locked with the dead man's across the mirrored pool of his cooling life source. There they were, two people who were not so dissimilar. Faces pressed to the floor, eyes wide with fear, and Alek—a man who reigned over the city—looming above them.

The tears in Mikko's eyes fell, the salt mixing in with red.

"This was supposed to be a simple day," Alek chided. "A moment where I could've shown you the ropes, made you into a real man, but you're too squeamish. I can't believe you're my son." His fingers gripped tighter at the back of Mikko's neck. Cool wetness was absorbed into Mikko's clothing, the entire front of his shirt and pants ruined from the blood. "I'll beat this weakness, this *disease*, from you if I have to."

Mikko cried out as his father put more pressure on his head, the floor beneath him unforgiving. His nerve endings felt like they were on fire, hairline cracks seemingly racing across his stained face, his skull moments from shattering. The other man's bodily fluids coated Mikko's lashes, clumping the short hairs together. Each blink fragmented the picture unfolding before him, the blood marring his vision. The pressure behind his eyes became unbearable, his gasps loud and muffled all at once. Time slowed until—

"I'm starting to think you're a bastard. No son of mine would act this pathetic—this feeble. *Ty mne protiven.*" *You disgust me.*

And in that moment, something shattered in Mikko.

* * *

Present Day

The scent of blood clung to Mikko's skin even though he'd showered and changed his clothes as soon as he'd returned to his residence. After watching his men damn near decimate another loose-lipped employee, he couldn't get the smell out of his nose. It brought back with it unbearable memories.

Between him and Cristiano, they'd interrogated a dozen men today, their efforts revealing little. No one seemed to know why or how or who would kill Ivan. Most responses boiled down to his cheating habits during games or his wife being fed up with his behavior and hiring a hit man. All plausible, which meant nothing could necessarily be eliminated.

His head fucking hurt, and his eyes ached inside his own skull. The lick of vodka tempted him once again, but a new idea had unfurled in his brain.

Standing in front of his full-length mirror, its size ostentatious even for his tastes, he adjusted the long sleeve compression shirt fitted to his body. It was slightly uncomfortable, but it would protect his skin from the body armor he needed to slip on. He wasn't one to forgo his motorcycle gear.

My tattoos cost too damn much, he thought.

Once his armor was strapped on and secure, he pulled a thick, black hoodie over it, the size large and able to conceal his gear and figure. And for tonight, *that* was important. Remaining unknown in the shadows was imperative.

A dark balaclava covered his face, only his vibrant eyes visible. Grabbing his gloves and helmet on the way out of his penthouse, Mikko took note of the space. Ever since Anika had found him, she'd plagued his thoughts, but it was more than that. Everywhere he went, there was always the telltale prickle on the back of his neck as if he was being watched.

Perhaps I'm just as paranoid as my father.

That notion stung, but it allowed him to move on, flicking the lights off and locking his door behind him.

On the elevator ride down he studied his reflection mirrored in the glass lining the car while his mind recited the encounter at *Bubblegum* again—the way Anika found him, approached him, *and* talked to him. The way he found her undressing in front of her home's windows…

He thought having a name to know her by would suffice—would curb the growing curiosity in his gut—but it didn't. Instead, he'd snuck around to see her interaction with Levi, had driven by her house, and knew her basic information like the back of his hand.

Cristiano would've called him crazy and stupid and other words the English dictionary probably didn't even know of. Which was fair. Mikko *was* all those things. That was why he'd kept this all a secret, a nasty little piece of himself he hid from the light. Anika was his to figure out and solve. His to torment once he discovered her motives.

With a tired sigh, even though his evening was just beginning, Mikko stepped out into the lobby of the lower level of the parking garage connected to his building. Gloomy concrete walls surrounded him as he strode across the empty parking spots toward his reserved corner.

There, under the sterile lights, his Audi RS 6 and motorcycle glinted—both dark as night. While the color appealed to him for many reasons, tonight's activities would showcase his preferences.

Stealth.

With his smug smirk hidden beneath his balaclava, he pulled his helmet on and swung a leg over his bike.

Time to forget about his troubles for a moment and pay his latest obsession another visit.

* * *

AFTER SPENDING *WAY* too much time combing through Anika's digital footprint—a pastime quickly forming into a habit abusing all of the power at his fingertips—Mikko knew exactly where she was tonight. He knew she got off work around five-thirty or six depending on her work load before grabbing a quick dinner. Her meals were small, a prequel to her actual dinner hours later, consisting of fruit, a protein shake, and a granola bar.

It was then that she headed to a stylish gym a couple blocks away from her office building. Once there, she'd spend exactly two hours training cardio and lifting weights. And if he timed it right, he'd be pulling into the small parking lot just as she would be finishing up.

With the loud roar of his engine and music playing softly in his ears from the Bluetooth device connected to his helmet, Mikko wove through the city streets.

With his identity hidden, he could be whoever he wanted. And after the day he'd had, anonymity and shedding the Romanov name sounded heavenly. Who he'd be when he got there, he wasn't sure, but he knew she was smart enough to most likely recognize him from the warehouse showing a couple nights ago.

Until then, he kept his composure and turned into the small parking lot. Most of the spaces were full, the evening routine of most city-goers lining up with Anika's. But on his bike, it didn't matter. Slipping between cars, he found her Kia and maneuvered his motorcycle beside it. It was a tight fit, but he managed.

Anika's car was farther from the closest streetlight than he would've chosen for himself, but the shadows allowed for a place to lurk. He killed the engine and remained astride his bike, feet firmly planted.

Minimal foliage allowed for him to see across the street and into the large panes of glass fronting the gym. Searching for her, Mikko tapped his gloved fingers on his gas tank impatiently. Evening air brushed past him, his body hardly noticing it beneath all his layers. Risking a portion of his face being exposed, he popped his visor open about an inch.

Ah, much better.

Chilly October air grazed across his heated face, providing momentary relief.

Pressing the button on his Bluetooth, he stopped his music all together. His senses prickled on high alert, his eyes scanning for Anika when—

"Have a good night!" a feminine voice called out, her tone light as it echoed off the hardscape around them. *Anika.*

"You too, I'll see you next week," another woman answered back. Mikko craned his neck to see her over the tops of the cars in the parking lot. He caught the back of a woman's head, a blonde ponytail swinging as she walked away. "Don't even *think* about canceling!"

Anika's head shook playfully before she crossed the street. Her own hair was pulled back to reveal the angles of her face and the lethal set of her brows and nose.

His heart fluttered.

Fuck, I'm acting worse than I did in grade school.

Although, he never stalked anyone then...

Despite the steadily cooling wind blowing off the nearby river, Anika's workout outfit didn't reflect that. Deep emerald green leggings hugged her muscular legs and a matching tank top showed a sliver of her skin. A skintight shrug hugged her shoulders, ensuring her toned arms were on display even if her skin was hidden behind a layer of fabric.

And the closer she walked, the more Mikko's mouth dried up.

Glancing over her shoulder, she noted her surroundings before cutting through the gap between the nearest car and heading straight for him.

He should've slouched, leaned into the inky depths around her car—anything really—but he was frozen. Why was it that every time he saw her, in person or through a screen, his body glitched.

He was in deep, *deep* shit.

A smart aleck comment tried to form on his tongue, but nothing. Mikko's words were suddenly failing him and—

"I hope you didn't scratch my paint," Anika stated, voice dark as her keen eyes spotted his hulking form. It sounded nothing like her friendly goodbye moments before. "Since you deemed *that* an adequate parking spot."

Clicking his visor into place with his gloved hand, he reminded himself she didn't know it was him. With a smirk, he spoke. "Have a lil' faith in me, yeah?"

"Last time I trusted a man, it didn't end well"—she looked him up and down while walking closer—*"for him."*

Mikko's grin turned into a full blown smile. So devious. Out loud he said, "I think I can hold my own against you."

"Well, let's hope we don't have to test that," she said, stopping by the hood of her car, keeping the hunk of metal between them. "Until then, I'll wait," she gestured for him to move.

"If you're expecting me to move, I just got here..."

"Shame, I needed to put these things in my passenger seat." She held up her empty protein shake bottle and small duffle bag.

He nodded to the back of her car. "Trunk's still an option."

"For my things? Or you?" Anika cocked her hip, defiance written all over her glistening face. From this distance, he could see the thin layer of sweat coating her skin. The frizzy flyaways framing her countenance made him picture her with a dark, wicked halo.

Fitting, he thought.

Turning his handlebars and putting his kickstand down—the distance between their vehicles closing even more—Mikko got off his bike. Maybe his height would be more persuasive...

But even from where he now stood, he'd forgotten Anika was much taller than most women. Her strong and lithe figure still reached his jawline.

Ignoring her insinuation, Mikko slipped past his motorcycle and closed in on her. Even though she should've seceded, she didn't. Her sneakers remained firmly planted on the asphalt, resistance etched into her alluring features.

And that fucking money piece—a sliver of light amongst the darkness. A drop of salvation. It was reminiscent of the slash of a crescent moon hanging low in the sky

My little moon.

The nickname fell into place before he could stop himself.

"You're quite *bold* for being out here all alone," he said, voice low from beneath his helmet.

115

"Are you threatening me?"

He leaned against the ebony paint of her vehicle like it was his—like he was right where he needed to be. Little did she know, he *was.* A soft breeze whispered across the lot, the evening wind carving through the tall buildings around them. And for a split second, he *swore* he smelled her.

Beneath the perspiration, a faint fragrance transported him back to that fateful night at the club. Sultry sweetness, whiskey steeped vanilla beans melting into a light and spicy pink pepper scent. Mikko licked his lips, hunger gnawing at his gut—one he was sure food wouldn't cure.

"Weren't you literally just threatening me by saying you'd put me in your trunk?" he finally responded, letting the air hang heavy between them.

Scoffing, she dropped her gym bag and tossed her bottle on top of it. "It wasn't a threat," she stepped closer, her anger palpable, but Mikko couldn't find it in himself to care, "more like a promise, *Suit.*"

The nickname struck a cord in his chest. He'd been discovered.

Of course.

Anika was too clever for her own good. Leaning back, his gloved palms flat against her car's hood, he chuckled. "Do you call everyone Suit, or is that nickname reserved just for me?"

"Just you." Anika stepped closer, unaware of the monster she was slowly provoking. "You might not be in your typical costume, but I recognize you."

"How sweet." His hands formed a heart which she promptly swatted away. "But what if I'm not the Suit you think I am?"

"Oh, you are. Your voice and height give you away." *Shit.* "And my gym is a *women's only* gym, so unless there's something you want to tell me, you're not welcome here."

Double shit.

In all his excitement, he hadn't thought to look into the details of her gym. He'd been more focused on her and trying to masturbate his way out of this infatuation.

"It's not nice to make assumptions."

Her eye roll nearly made him laugh, until, "Get the fuck off my car."

He snatched her wrist, the heat of her skin seeping through his glove, when she gestured at him. It almost made the ever-present ache in his left hand fade. With a harsh yank, she fell into him, his legs bracketing either side of her hips. She barely caught herself, somehow preventing the rest of her body from pressing against him.

"Although, are you sayin' you've been checking me out? That you know *my* body? *My* motorcycle?" He chuckled. "Careful now, you might inflate my ego if you keep doing that." He couldn't resist taunting her more.

"I think it's big enough as is," she mumbled.

"You could say that about my di—"

Her glare was enough to end his words, but he chuckled regardless.

Mikko continued, "Such mixed signals, Anika. First, you degrade me only to follow it up with a compliment." Mikko's grip tightened if only to watch her struggle—to see the fire in her eyes blaze hotter. Saying her name relinquished some of his leverage, the flash of curiosity in her eyes evident. It seemed she was figuring out that he *also* had his ways of gaining information. "It's no wonder I followed you here regardless of the consequences."

"Let. Me. Go," she hissed.

"Oh, now you don't want to play games?"

"No."

"A shame honestly," he crooned, eyes catching on the bead of sweat rolling down her neck and settling into the hollow of her throat. The urge to lick it overwhelmed him. "I thought we were going to have fun, me and you."

"As if." Anika tried to knee him in the crotch, but his other hand blocked it.

"Tsk, tsk, tsk, that wasn't very nice."

"I'm never described as nice."

Mikko cocked his head. "Really? Because I remember you being *very* nice the night we met."

"Mikko." It was one word, but he couldn't help but relish in the way she said his name, her lips forming around the syllables. "I won't ask again; let me go."

"I'm afraid I can't do that, Anika." Her brows scrunched. "While you've been out here living your life, I've been unable to scrub that moment in the club from my mind."

Pulling against his hold, he released her this time, not wanting to cause too much of a scene. And it was satisfying to see her stumble backwards, her eyes wide for a moment before settling into their telltale annoyance.

"Obsessed much?" She flicked her ponytail over her shoulder, the muscles in her arms catching in the distant street lamp light.

"I consider myself more...diligent than anything." Standing again, Mikko looked down at her. "Besides, I'm protecting what's mine."

"What?"

"My company, my friends, me."

"You don't get out much, do you?"

Did she and Cristiano hang out? Pick from the same vocab?

He ignored her. "If you fuck with me, Anika, I hope you're prepared for what's to come."

A muscle in her jaw clenched, her teeth holding back whatever retort was resting on her tongue. He used her moment of indecision to walk back to his bike, heart racing and blood thrumming in his ears. He needed to leave before he did something he regretted. Before he let her in more than he already had. Her claws were sharp, and he hated how he found himself enjoying the sting.

Swinging his leg over his motorcycle, he spoke one last time. "I'll see you around," his kickstand clicked up into place. "Consider it a *precaution.*"

Anika reached for him as the roar of his engine echoed throughout the city block, drowning out whatever she tried to say. It didn't matter anyway. He'd be in the shadows regardless.

Obsession or precaution—it mattered not for him.

15

A Life Worth Living

Anika

Anika had spent the rest of the weekend gardening, anything to get her mind off Mikko's random appearance outside of her gym. As autumn fully settled in around her, the last of her produce blossomed. It'd been a good year, her gourds the last thing left to harvest.

Many of her flowers had bloomed and returned to their leafy states in preparation for fall. A few weeks ago she'd collected the last dregs of her violets, drying them out and saving them for garnishes and drinks.

But even the solace her plants usually brought her wasn't enough.

Mikko loomed in the back of her mind, her eyes wandering over her shoulder every so often in hopes of catching him driving by or strolling through her yard like he owned it. She knew this game of cat and mouse was dangerous; she'd provoked a beast—a man with endless resources and a traumatic background—but it'd be worth it.

Besides, it was nothing her feminine rage and handgun couldn't handle.

Packing up her things, Anika noticed it was almost time for her to leave. Like clockwork, every two weeks she paid a visit to Evergrove, and this week it was no different.

* * *

THE JARRING SOUND of the front door's buzzer beneath her fingertips brought back memories Anika wasn't sure she was grateful for.

The antiquated facade of Evergrove Assisted Living sprawled out in each direction of her peripheral vision. The facility boasted historic building construction, but all she felt while looking at it was cold. Ivy clung to the stones, somehow brave enough to grow, thrive even, this close to death. While everyone inside may be alive, their minds were elsewhere. *Tortured.*

"Name, and reason for visiting?" a voice cut through on the intercom, scratchy from interference.

"Um, hey, it's Anika, and I'm here to visit my mom, Ira Naidu," she answered stiffly.

A pattern had fallen into place over the years, eight to be exact, but it never got any easier. She was never content to see her mom in the declining state she was in. As a child, it was normal to assume parents would die before their children, but this...

Anika's circumstances were different. A fact she held close to her heart, letting it warm her on lonely nights. And there were too many of those.

The door mechanism unlocked quickly, the operator within the building content with Anika's answer. Reaching out, her hand gripped the cold metal before pulling open the heavy door and slipping inside.

A yellow tinted vestibule greeted her, its age not a reflection of the exterior, but still a dated era nonetheless. It was a conglomerate of years mushed together, miscellaneous renovations overlapping and creating the current space. Anika wasn't sure if it was hideous because it *was,* or if her bias was influenced by the memories attached to this place. Regardless, she never lingered long.

The old door slammed on creaky hinges behind her, triggering another memory of how the noise had startled her for weeks when she'd first started coming here.

So much has changed, she thought.

"Anika," the woman behind the desk said, "good to see you back."

The wires embedded in the glass warped her face, but Anika knew who she was. With her routine visits, they'd formed an acquaintance.

"Hi Barbara, good to see you."

Grabbing a clipboard, the dark haired woman stood and exited the small office she was confined to in the entry. Opening the door to the vestibule, she waved Anika the rest of the way in as a warm rush of air trickled in from the furnace, making her shiver. It was an unusually cold day even for the beginning of October.

Maybe the universe knows where I'm heading and decided to set the mood.

Brushing the thought away, Anika followed Barbara silently.

Originally, Ira had wanted to come here on her own since she required physical therapy and a nurse who was on standby. Years ago, Anika had fought her mom on that, trying to care for her on her own. But between school and working to provide an income for both of them, it became too much to bear alone. Ira needed constant monitoring, the ghosts of their past haunting her every waking moment.

Anika had her own demons to deal with, but she hid them—buried them beneath all the dark layers of her heart—to care for her mom. They'd already lost so much; the secrets within Anika's heart needed to remain as such so her mom could embrace the peaceful life she deserved. Sanity was a fleeting attribute, and Anika didn't want to risk it.

Not only did memories ail her mom, but also her physical scars. Phantom pains from the bullet wounds she'd sustained that day still radiated throughout her torso and legs, causing her to groan and wail.

It was horrendous.

Now, Anika walked the halls of Evergrove, a place boasting quality care. Well, as quality as Anika could find within her budget. It'd been a miracle when her mother was accepted in—a weight lifting off both their shoulders. But now, looking at the peeling wallpaper, Anika wondered if she did the right thing.

Confinement was relative Anika supposed, knowing some people enjoyed the structure it brought. Many were content living inside a cage as long as they were sheltered from the ways of the harsh world.

Ira was one of those people. Her mom didn't mind the yellow lights and the worn furniture. Anika tolerated it too, knowing it was necessary for their survival. It was the other patients, the ones who roamed and searched the halls for an escape, that Anika watched closely.

Their soft sneakers squeaked on the waxed floor as Barbara led Anika down familiar passages. Among the pauses of silence, small talk ensued among them; Anika commenting on her work, and Barbara updating her on her daughter's progress in school.

Stopping in front of a cherry stained wood door, Barbara entered a passcode and pushed it open.

"You know the drill, ring the bell when you're done, or if you need anything." With that, Anika was left alone with her mom. Or the shell of her.

A beep and the sound of the lock sliding into place behind her hardly stood out as unusual. It kept her mother safe unlike all those years ago when a poorly cloaked excuse of a real estate business broke into their family home and took her father before he could see his daughter grow up. It kept the people they didn't trust out, so they could live as though they didn't carry the weight of those terrible echoes.

"Hi, mom," Anika said, pulling up the chair beside Ira's bed. Most days, her mom was awake, eager to attend the activities the staff had planned for her and other people within the facility. But some days her mom slept, erasing the hurt with medication and unconsciousness.

Today was one of those days.

Reaching out and taking her mom's warm hand nestled within the blankets, she sat there, content to listen to her breaths. Anika hardly ever did anything during her visits, just soaked up these moments. They weren't ideal or picturesque, but it was enough.

And it was a reminder of what had been stolen from them—what needed to be taken back. The note she'd found on her car flashed across her mind again.

To devour me, you must have teeth.

Indeed; good thing Anika had been sharpening hers for *years*.

"I'm getting closer to finding out who did this, mom," was all she said, letting her words fill the space around them. "And once I get close enough to take a shot, I will."

* * *

Anika - 18 Years Ago

Thirteen.

That was how old she'd been when her life had changed. It was at that moment that Anika decided the world was cruel, uncaring for its inhabitants, and so, she too would become cruel and unforgiving.

Heat from the stove permeated the air, the scent of food inescapable. Soft humming filled the quiet din of her mother moving around the kitchen. Utensils clacked together and vegetables sizzled, a harmonic melody lulling her deeper into concentration.

Laid out before Anika were scribble-filled papers, each containing lines and lines of equations. She preferred math above other subjects, enjoying its reliability and patterns. There were formulas she could follow—a stark division between where she was right and where she had gone wrong.

Even now, her homework was completed, but she wanted to experiment and try to find other ways to solve the problems set before her. It was in her blood to be an endless debater. Puzzles and other intellectual challenges fueled her, mind racing to discover something most would overlook. Her mother, while she didn't always understand, still encouraged Anika, forever enthralled with her skills.

But her father, well, he was exactly like her. That was one of the many reasons he was a successful businessman. Numbers came to him just as easily as understanding people did. His small shop near the city thrived, people eager to buy his wares. Her father had started out as a small, humble entrepreneur, but Anika saw the growth, the excitement in his eyes when he came home in the evenings. Anika's observant eye also didn't miss the new pieces of jewelry her mother sported.

One day, if she wanted, her father's store could become hers. He'd said as much to her a year earlier when she'd tag along with him.

It made her heart swell despite the whispers of her father being delusional, passing off a business to a young woman. He ignored them, winking at Anika every time.

"They don't know the sharpness of your mind, dear, but I do," he'd encouraged weeks ago.

So, she worked hard, writing until her hands cramped and her eyes blurred.

But tonight was different.

While soothed by her equations, something in the air was off. An anxiousness not even her mother's cooking could erase; a lingering in her bones.

The telltale click of the front door opening stopped Anika's pencil in its place.

Her father was home.

Her sock clad feet pressed into the linoleum, eager to see him after a long day, but another sound stopped her.

Hushed whispers.

And they didn't belong to her father.

Looking at her mother, Anika's eyebrows raised in an unspoken question. *Who's here?*

Her mother set her own utensils down, turning the stove off before abandoning the food there. Curiosity was also evident in her features as the crinkles around her eyes became more prominent. Gesturing for Anika to stay put, she watched as her mother's frame hovered in the doorway. Her time worn fingers gripped the wood as her mom tilted her head in the direction of the sounds.

Anika opened her mouth to ask who it was but—

Bang!

The harsh sound ripped through the small house, decimating Anika's ears. Her mother jumped back into the kitchen, away from the source of the sound as Anika clasped her hands over her ringing ears.

Squeezing her eyes shut, she swore she heard groaning...mumbled pleas, but another shot rang out through the house.

Hands gripped her shoulders, jostling her. Anika's eyes snapped open, the brightness of the kitchen light blinding, but the worry etched into her mother's face was worse. It was a look that would haunt her forever, she was sure of it.

Her mom's lips moved, but Anika's mind struggled to hear what she was saying.

Anika.

It was as if she was underwater, voice dim and faraway.

Anika.

Another desperate shake.

"Anika"—her hands fell from her ears—"you need to hide."

"W-why?"

"Now." Her mother didn't answer, too busy pushing her toward the darkened hall behind them leading to the bedrooms. "Hide and don't come out for anyone." Ira's hair tickled Anika's nose at their closeness before her worried-filled eyes flicked across Anika's own shocked face.

"I—"

"Did you hear me, Anika? Hide, now."

Without another word, Anika ran.

16

Shadowed Interruptions

Mikko

Waiting in his Audi, engine off and enveloped in shadow outside of Anika's house, the minutes dragged on. He was restless, the blood roaring in his ears while he passed the time. At least these excursions helped him avoid work—specifically the mystery and roiling unrest whispering through the business at Ivan's death. Men had already questioned Mikko's plans of action, stating he was too calm in the face of trouble, but he brushed off the words.

"Death is our only constant," Alek would say, and seasoned men like them should realize this by now. Yet, they still blabbed and bred distrust among the darkened streets. Besides, Mikko *was* investigating; he had questions he felt could only be answered by a certain woman.

Now sitting outside her house, he realized what a nasty habit this was becoming, but it was a necessary evil if he wanted to stay one step ahead of her.

The sun had set and Mikko knew the dinner plans Anika had scheduled with a business partner were well underway. He'd have all evening to do as he pleased and immerse himself into the thoughts swirling around in his head every time he pictured Anika. It'd only been a little over a week and a half since they'd had their fateful meeting at *Bubblegum*, but so much had happened.

And the only common denominator was Anika.

Despite his own conflicting emotions, he swore to put his theories to rest by shedding light on whatever she was hiding. He'd modified his own work schedule to accommodate her routines. Wherever she went, he wasn't far behind. A day didn't go by where he didn't see her, even if it was from afar.

Although tonight was different. Instead of trailing behind her, sitting at a table across the restaurant she was currently in, he stayed behind. Following her around had proved to be an entertaining distraction, but time was a valuable thing. Ivan's death meant Mikko needed to turn up the heat. And he was left with no other choice: go straight to the source by *selectively* breaking and entering. A man of his was dead and he needed to chase down every lead. Even if the excitement flooding his veins was a new emotion.

No, not new. Buried.

Being in her personal space felt like sin, something dirty a corporate man like him should be above, yet this was where he flourished.

With a deep breath—the aroma of leather prominent inside his car—he readjusted his balaclava and made sure his hood was firmly in place. The only sliver of skin visible was around his eyes. He quickly donned the pair of leather gloves sitting on the passenger seat. Even if someone did see him, he was nothing but a darkened smudge, unremarkable and untraceable.

As Mikko was about to slip from his car, bright headlights approaching from behind made him pause. With bated breath, he waited, but he expelled a sigh when the car continued on, its pace leisurely. The unknown driver passed without a second thought to whoever could be lurking in the dark. *Someone like him.*

It seemed her quiet neighborhood would never know of the monster slinking in its depths tonight.

Without a second thought or moment to change his mind, he stepped into the cool evening air. The tree's leaves rustled above, whispering as the autumn wind breezed through them, their color shifting from lush verdant to soft orange. He smiled to himself as the season's shorter days offered a refuge for his stalking.

Sleuthing, his brain corrected annoyingly.

Closing his car door softly, his eyes swept the surrounding land-scape once more, adequately acquainted with it. It'd become a familiar sight, his visits to this area frequent.

Silently, he made his way to the wrought iron fence separating her lawn from the sidewalk and her neighbors. The flared finials of the pickets were weather-worn, but well maintained from what he could see. Most of the flora was well-kept, albeit overwhelming since Anika seemed to believe having any open space was a sin.

The flowerbeds lining the fence were overflowing with native plants. A couple large trees sprawled overhead, blocking out the moonlight.

An avid gardener, good to know, he mentally noted. *I wonder if that's where she got the inspiration for her arm tattoos?*

Pretending as though he belonged, Mikko walked right up to the gate in hopes of avoiding any suspicious, nosy neighbors. Although, eye witness accounts were hardly admissible. There had been *many* times fate had been in his favor in a court of law throughout his business years—

A loud *screech* rent the night air, chilling his blood.

The damn gate wasn't as well-maintained as he'd assumed.

"Fuck," he muttered, feet rooted to the spot. Of all the times he'd been here, why hadn't he noticed this?

Because you've been preoccupied, his mind countered, the voice sounding suspiciously like Alek.

No time to ruminate on it now as his tall frame hovered at the gate, in a potentially conspicuous position. Closing the gate once more—its hinges refusing to be silenced—Mikko stepped back, confident he could scale the fence and avoid it altogether.

Four soft breaths and a couple furious heartbeats filled the silence.

And before he could think better of it, he vaulted himself over it. It was easy since the finials only came up to his mid-thigh. Still he held his breath; the last thing he needed was to become impaled by one and live through the embarrassment of Cristiano having to come pick him up.

Landing softly on the other side, Mikko took a couple seconds to calm his erratic breathing. While he was in excellent shape, the excitement pulsing through his body made it difficult to keep himself under control.

Get in, find the evidence you need, and get out.

This act was nothing more than business.

Business.

A word he'd used with Anika and she'd thrown it back in his face. The universe had a funny sense of humor, one Mikko didn't find himself enjoying.

A concrete sidewalk cut through her front yard, its narrow path light against the darkened grass. A decorative covered porch loomed ahead of him, swathed mostly in shadow despite the porch light shining next to her front door. More flowerbeds overflowed with plants nearby, all of which were still green, but the incoming autumn chill would soon change everything. Creeping closer, he took his phone out, snapping a couple pictures of the vegetation. He'd look up what the species were later.

Maybe if I send a bouquet of flowers to her office containing similar plants, she'll be rethinking our dance?

An image of her out there in the summer sun, tending to her plants, teased him. Dirt on her hands, knees in the soil, and sweat dripping down her neck as it followed a trail he wanted to suck and kiss.

Her head tipped back, cinnamon whiskey eyes peering up at him, her lips stretched around his—

A dog barking down the street snapped him out of his reverie, and he scrubbed at his covered face.

Fuck.

His mind was operating without his command, taking him into the deep, depraved recesses existing there. He was in so much trouble if he didn't shape the *fuck* up. He allowed himself a few more deep breaths to slow his heart before he pushed onward.

Over the past couple days, he'd been toying with different ways to get into her house, carefully considering the advantages to each entrance. In the end, the problem had solved itself. A couple days ago, while Mikko had been watching her house for anything unusual, someone had shown up.

A blonde-haired woman around Anika's age parked in front of her house, mere car lengths away from where he was, and walked through the open gate. A detail Mikko now realized attributed to him not knowing about its squeaky nature. Regardless, her familiarity with the house let him know she was someone Anika knew and trusted. That meant Mikko could also trust her to show him what he needed.

Walking to the side door, the vines from surrounding plants reached for her as she bent down and peeled up a door mat. Straightening, Mikko had noticed she'd retrieved something shiny.

A key.

And anyone with that kind of information could let themselves in...

It'd been fate beckoning him closer, and now he stood at the same side door, black mat at the toes of his boots. Looking around, he confirmed no one was watching before crouching down to retrieve the key. It had been etched into his memory since that moment.

Now it glinted up at him in invitation.

Quickly, he shoved it into the lock and turned the mechanism.

How many times did I stand outside, contemplating how to do this?

Now, he could finally put those thoughts to rest.

Slipping inside, blackness welcomed him as the door softly closed behind him. Briefly, he let his eyes adjust, his ears attuning to the sounds of her house—the way the wind made the branches of nearby trees brush up against it or the settling creaks that came with the old structure. He heard the humming of equipment nearby, but he was more focused on listening for animal movements. Mikko was almost positive Anika didn't have pets, but if they were small, they might've slipped under his radar.

But no hisses or meows; no toenails clicking on the nearby floors or telltale barks to warn intruders.

Perfect.

Entering onto a landing, a set of steps led up to the right and another set led deeper into what he assumed to be her basement. While *Bubblegum's* basement may hold secrets, Mikko was certain Anika's was dark and dank. He was more interested in the rest of her house.

So up he went.

The short length of stairs protested beneath his weight, but no one was around to hear the noises. Instead, he backtracked and walked up the steps again, memorizing which ones gave him feedback and which ones didn't. Sweat began prickling along the nape of his neck while he worked, the fabric of his balaclava and hoodie trapping his body heat in.

Satisfied with his findings, Mikko's boot planted itself onto the tile floor at the top of the steps. Excitement buzzed in his veins; the scent of her was everywhere. It brought back the memories of her fingertips grazing across his forearm.

This is definitely an unhealthy way of thinking.

A dimly lit kitchen unfolded before him. She'd left the light on over the stove, it's spotlight drawing his attention to the pots and pans left on the stovetop. His head tilted in curiosity. If she was going out to eat, why cook food beforehand?

Walking closer across the black and white mosaic tile floor, the aroma of herbs in the air told him it may not be food she'd prepped. Sure enough, as he peered into one of the pots, he saw it contained bits of apples, oranges, and cinnamon sticks. It looked inedible, but it made her home smell delicious.

A small dining table was pushed against the far wall underneath a window. There were only two chairs and two placemats, and a vase full of fresh flowers arranged neatly in the middle. More plants were clustered on either side of the table, ready to soak up the sunlight during the day. Creeping closer, he traced a gloved finger over the nearest leaf.

How cute, she's a plant enthusiast. A small smile graced his hidden mouth.

Dried flowers and herbs hung in bundles along her walls, the scent of them cloying. Opening a few cabinets, he noticed a collection of deep brown plates and cups. Her pantry was filled with Mason jars holding pickled vegetables, jams, and other preserved fruits he had no idea the names of.

Pulling one out, he read the date on top, confirming his suspicions of her canning hobby. His brow raised; another piece of information about her to store away in his mind. Mikko took more photos as he went along, ensuring they'd be added to her personal file once he returned home.

Moving on, Mikko slipped into the main hall leading to the front door. Each boot fall soothed his adrenalized muscles, a single thought comforting him along the way: this must be done to lay my own demons to rest. Besides, he'd done this before. Anika's house wasn't the first or the last house he'd gotten access to. The only reason he'd been nervous this time was because of the damn emotions swirling in his gut.

After this, I'm going out, he thought, *being this desperate and touch-starved is way too embarrassing.*

Once he blew off some steam and tracked down the true events of Ivan's death, he could let Anika go.

Lies, a soft voice whispered, but Mikko ignored it. He was determined to find the rat and deal with them, no matter the cost. He might hate his father's company, but he also couldn't stand to be outdone when it came to dismantling everything Alek had meticulously built.

Rugs overlapped one another, their patterns dizzying in the soft light streaming in from the porch light outside the front door ahead of him. Pictures lined the walls of the corridor along with filigree wall paper, the pattern barely distinguishable. Stopping to look at the photos, he was careful not to brush against the frames. Their mismatched outlines varied in proportions and detail. Many of the pictures behind the glass held art prints instead of photos of people. Only a few contained friends and family.

Anika stood out to him as always. A darkness glittered in her eyes, evident in a few of the photos. The ones where her carefree smiles failed to reach the honey hazel depths of her piercing gaze.

His gloved fingers itched to capture the essence he saw within her, his own love of photography a way for him to express his creativity. Mikko was forever an artist no matter how hard his father tried to rend it from his head. Currently, his day job sucked most of his energy, but when he was at his lowest, photography, painting, and design were always there for him.

An older couple, likely her parents, were also in some photos, but they were from long ago. Anika was smaller, younger, in these. The mature bone structure defining her exquisite face now was softer and disguised by childhood.

But her caramel eyes were the same.

There were more pictures of Anika with her parents, but they never changed, never grew older.

An eerie feeling settled into Mikko's gut.

And the longer he looked, the more uneasy he became. He couldn't determine if her parents looked familiar because he had studied Anika's features so closely—ones they'd passed down to their daughter—or if it was because he'd met them before. It wasn't unlikely, his business allowing him connections all over the city of Portland, but if Anika and him were almost the same age, then he would've been too young to be running the business. But it wasn't impossible. Alek's own persistence back then could've landed a young Mikko in the vicinity of them years ago...

The scent of her simmer pot faded as he stepped into her living room, the same one he'd seen multiple times through the open window, but actually being inside the space was different. Exhilarating. The sheer curtains and botanical wall paper greeted him as always. Again, he could smell the addicting undertones of bergamot and a sugary musk—sweet and innocent with sultry notes to ground. It was explicitly Anika.

And damn him if his mouth didn't water.

He'd smelled it on her outside of the gym and at *Bubblegum*.

Suddenly, a wave of lust washed over him as the memory of her warm fingers tracing his skin assaulted him. The fire in her eyes outside of her gym as he leaned on her car like he owned it lit a simmering desire deep within his chest.

And now, inside her personal space, he lost himself in a fantasy.

Her soft body pressed against his—against the nearby door, its cool surface making her gasp.

Rain pitting against the roof of her house, drowning out the world outside.

Her skin flushed with the same inexplicable emotions building in his chest as he trailed a fingertip over her tattoos leisurely. Anika's breath quickened, her chest heaving. He was simply repaying the favor from the club.

His mind deviously wondered about all the other ways he could elicit lovely little sounds from her mouth—

Knock! Knock! Knock!

Knuckles rapping on the front door mere feet away halted his thoughts.

His heart dropped into the darkest pits of his stomach. While his identity was hidden by his outfit, his eyes still scanned for a place to hide. Mikko was confident Anika wouldn't knock at her own house, but it didn't prevent a cold sweat from breaking out along his skin.

Frozen, he waited for the person to either knock again or go away. The time indicated it was too late for it to be a delivery or a solicitor, but Mikko didn't like the idea of it being someone more personal.

Someone with a key, perhaps...

As if reading his mind, a female voice called out through the door.

"Anika?" Her words were unworried, casual. That made Mikko relax *slightly*. "Anika, are you in there? I couldn't remember if it was tonight or tomorrow that you're free."

Slipping deeper into the shadows of Anika's living room, Mikko tried to get close enough to see the woman while simultaneously remaining silent. Anika's old house made it more challenging than he'd like to admit.

"Why am I talking through the door"—the woman continued, unaware of the man inside her friend's house—"I have your number."

Her shuffling could be heard on the wood planks as she presumably dialed Anika and waited for her to answer. All the while, Mikko's posture was ramrod straight, his adrenaline flowing freely. His simple night of snooping was hindered.

"Hey, where are you?" the woman asked from outside once Anika picked up. A couple beats later, "Ahh, I should've guessed." A faint laugh filled the space while Anika said something Mikko couldn't hear.

"Well, I came by your house to drop off the huge Monstera I found." *Just my fuckin' luck,* he thought. If Anika came back now, Mikko would have to slip out the side door and loop around the block to avoid being spotted by the women. It was a feasible plan, but he *hated* to be interrupted.

Anika had her routines, he had his.

"Oh, shit," the female voice stated, "of course I mixed up the dates. Do you want me to leave it on your porch or bring it with me tomorrow? It's in my car, and I don't think it's too cold out–oh no, goodness, no need to come back here for my sake. You know I don't live far."

A slow exhale from Mikko.

Farther away now, the woman responded again, shoes *clunking* on the porch steps. "I'll bring it tomorrow. Be safe, and call me when you're back home…"

The rest of the conversation trailed off as she walked away. The telltale squeak of the iron gate opening and closing was the last piece of confirmation Mikko needed.

He was in the clear.

Exiting the living room, pulse racing from the close call, Mikko started up the steps leading up to the rest of the house.

The old stairs groaned under his weight, echoing all the years the house had endured—all the people. He trailed his gloved hand along the sturdy railing, imagining her doing the same, retracing her movements. An image of her walking up the steps ahead of him, grazing her fingers along the rail like he was and beckoning for him to follow almost sent him to his knees.

Fuck.

Quickly, he built a wall in his mind to keep from losing sight of his mission. His jaw clenched, his teeth threatening to crack at the pressure. He pressed forward, knowing her bedroom was somewhere up here, and that thought alone propelled him onward.

It kept him from hiding, from waiting for her to get home so he could have a *taste*.

Another breath, another wall built.

A hallway greeted him at the top of the steps along with more picture frames lining it. Four doors waited for him to venture further and open them to reveal whatever was inside.

He conceded.

The farthest one on his left was a guest bedroom so he moved on, uninterested. Next was another bedroom, only it didn't have a bed. Instead it was filled with a couple boxes and unused items. Situated in the corner was a small desk with a monitor. All of these details built a better image of her in his mind, but one thing stood out.

Hadn't Levi said Anika had started a leather goods business?

Combing back through both rooms, he saw nothing that spoke of such activities. If his colleague had stated she needed a facility for hydroponics, he wouldn't have thought twice. But leather? Anika was lying, but why?

Perhaps a game truly was underway, a thread of fate pulling them together. It frustrated the *hell* out of Mikko. He couldn't imagine she'd been the one to kill Ivan, but at this point all the signs were pointing to her guilt.

Quickly, he shot off a text to Levi.

Did Anika see you enter the lockbox code at the warehouse? **:Mikko**

A few seconds later:

Levi: *No, why?*

Mikko didn't have time to explain right now, especially over text, so he left him on read. When he got back, they'd reconvene.

Back out in the hallway he tried another door. It was a bathroom filled with white tile up to his chest. The smell of shampoos and lotions hung in the air, but they weren't hers; this was fresher, a scent fit for visiting guests.

The fourth and final door loomed before him: Anika's bedroom. A place he hoped would tell him everything he needed to know about her.

The door gave way to him on quiet hinges. Stepping inside, Mikko immediately noted the rumbled bed sheets and open curtains. The nearby city's light pollution and the moon provided him with enough light to see by. Two windows faced her backyard with another large tree visible from his vantage point. A couple articles of clothing were on the floor, scattered like she'd hurriedly gotten ready, unable to decide what she wanted to wear. His boot nudged some pieces out of his way.

A large part of him hoped she noticed the change. He knew he would if the roles were reversed, and his mind flashed back to the night of his penthouse being in disarray.

Even if that was a dark spot on his memory, Mikko didn't let it distract him from this moment. While he couldn't put his emotions into words, he was content to stand there relishing in whatever feelings swept through his bloodstream.

He couldn't stop it from surging in his throat—winding his muscles tight.

He'd been trained to be desensitized to these kinds of nefarious actions. In the past, if he were to get caught, it would end in bloodshed. Now, if he got caught it wouldn't be about retribution, it'd be about the *chase*. It would promise something more wicked than murder…

Lust fueled by intrigue.

And hatred.

A dangerous concoction even for a mafia man like him.

Still, a different kind of hunger crawled beneath his skin. Mikko didn't care if Anika hated him because he knew he could convince her to see him as he was. An equal. Desire and loathing ran hand in hand in his mind; what harm would this little fire between them result in? All he needed was *time*.

And I'm a patient man. Mostly.

His eyes snagged on her bed again, noting that beneath the rumpled green duvet lay soft, satin bed sheets. They were also wrinkled and slept in and covered in *her*. His outstretched hand hovered in midair above her bed, chest aching. Mikko had the sudden urge to touch them.

Fuck, I want to do more than touch them.

He yearned to climb in, intertwine himself with her musky scent—the same one currently polluting her whole damn house and preventing him from thinking straight—until they were one, indistinguishable from the other. His mouth watered at the idea, blood flowing lower as his erection strained behind his zipper.

Before he could stop himself, he fell to his knees at her bedside. Primal instinct took over, controlling him like a master would his beast. Leaning impossibly close, his nose skimmed the sheets, and even though his balaclava prevented him from touching it freely, he still groaned at the scent she left behind. He could only describe it as a soft touch of cashmere woods and milky sweet marshmallows. It was barely there, the hints of tonka bean and deep, silky caramel, but it was enough to make Mikko crave more.

It was *intoxicating*.

He palmed himself through his jeans, unable to keep his desire under control. His cock ached and throbbed, his year long celibacy suddenly feeling like a fatal mistake. Just when he'd decided to give up on women, one had singled him out and made him question everything.

He wanted to take her on this bed, on the floor, and on every goddamn surface of her house until he was satisfied. He yearned to have her wetness dripping down his chin and coating his cock as he rutted into her like a madman. What sounds would she make as he stretched her tight little cunt out—made her pay for all the times she'd taunted him?

Mikko's fist pressed against his mouth to stifle a groan building in the back of his throat. He feared he'd *never* be able to get enough of her; he'd never be satiated. His days as a CEO would be reduced to worshiping her until she screamed his name and begged for him to stop—begged for him to make her come. Again and again and again...

Fuck, I'm losing it.

Mikko fought to build another wall in his mind, but he was struggling. He struggled with every fiber in his being for control over his body once more. But while she may tempt him, her guilty actions were still at the forefront of his mind. *Mostly.*

So, he locked away the unruly side he'd let slip out. Tonight was not the night to entertain the thoughts formulating in his head. The ones where he lurked within the shadows before pouncing on her when she returned home and making her plead for mercy he would not give.

Frustration coated his tongue, his mind addled by emotions he'd dealt with in the past, but had no idea how to manage. Anger came easily to him, an almost comforting emotion, but these others…they were more troublesome. Harder to control and to understand.

This was why people always ran away from him; he never did anything half-assed.

Hating the uncertainty lining his gut, he craved the fresh air that came with riding his motorcycle—the distraction of the wind and speed ripping at him as he tore down the ribboned highways.

It's the only way to escape her.

Pale numbers on the clock on her nightstand ticked away as he knelt there, torn. It continued to count, moving forward in time, all too willing to leave him behind. He had approximately thirty minutes before she was to return home and again, he fought against the idea of letting her find him and interrogating her for answers he desperately needed.

Shaking his head, he cleared his thoughts before regretfully standing. The absence of her scent left a void in his chest, something like regret twinging there.

His father would be disgusted at the man he'd become.

A quick glance in the drawers of her nightstands revealed nothing earth shattering. There was hand cream, lip balm, and medicine—the first two items he pocketed as trophies. Until he went to close the last drawer.

There, something unusual caught his attention. Shoved underneath a stack of gardening magazines, he spotted something pink. He'd almost missed it, but his eyes honed in on her vibrator.

Well, well, well, he thought deviously, lips twitching at the image playfully crossing his mind.

He yearned to take off his glove and touch it with his bare hand. The idea of rolling up his mask so he could lick the silicone replayed in his mind over and over again.

Did it taste like her, even if she cleaned it? What did she look like when she was up here all alone and needy, using it to get off? Who did she think of when she came undone?

The last question made his teeth grit together in jealousy. He wanted her to think of *him*. It was unreasonable; he knew this. His hold over her was damn near inconsequential—for now—but his mind still wanted it. No one else deserved her attention; no one else would sate the hunger he sensed within her like he could.

Abruptly, he slammed the drawer shut.

If he didn't stop now, there would be no going back. And he was wasting precious seconds daydreaming when he should be searching through her things for clues about Ivan...one of his own *dead* employees.

With a sigh, he stood and assessed the rest of her room. A dresser with jewelry and perfume bottles lined on the top were glinting in the moonlight. Peering closer, he memorized the names and fragrance notes. Since she'd been kind enough to send him tequila, maybe he could send her a gift of his own, one that let her know he'd been here.

A vintage chair sat in the corner of her room with a quilted blanket draped over the back and armrest. Other than a few stray pieces of clothing and her unmade bed, Anika's room was well organized. Mikko didn't expect anything less. The poise she held herself with spoke to that.

Business clothes lined her closet, all the colors dark and moody. Casual clothes were folded in the drawers of her dresser along with underwear and socks. He'd be lying if he said he hadn't clutched onto a pair of underwear for a solid two minutes, wrestling with himself on if he should take them.

In the end, he didn't.

Maybe I can take something else...

A vision of her standing where he was, trying on different clothes, intruded his thoughts. Her onyx hair cascading over her shoulders, trickling down her back and tickling against her skin, was vivid in his mind. He could *almost* feel her, the sensation of her disarming honeyed eyes on him, unfreezing the ever-present chill in his heart.

A shiver coursed down his spine at the thought.

Crossing the room, Mikko opened the final door. It led to a small ensuite bathroom which tempted him to step in farther. He did.

A window provided him with enough light to see by, her toiletries and cosmetics scattered over every flat surface in the room. Mikko smiled to himself. She represented a piece of him he wished he could have. Spontaneity. Freedom.

His own city penthouse was spotless, a cleaning company coming every week even though it was hardly dirty when they did come. Everything had its place, and he enjoyed the cleanliness of it. *The control.*

Dark gray towels hung on hooks and a botanical themed shower curtain caught his attention.

Of course it's plant related.

While he may not be getting any additional leads on Ivan, he *was* learning that Anika, plants, and the color green all went hand in hand.

Small wins, he thought, closing her bathroom and bedroom door behind him as he slipped out. While he didn't want this night to end and the game to ebb, Mikko knew there were other responsibilities piling up in his computer's inbox. Tonight might not have shown him explicitly how Ivan and Anika were connected, but it showed Mikko how invincible he was.

Time would force the truth to come out, and he'd be waiting.

Until then...

His restless fingers couldn't help themselves. He'd slipped one of her soft scarfs from a coat hook in her foyer on his way out.

An excuse to come back, he thought as he left the spare key where he found it and disappeared into the night.

17

A Nuisance

Anika

The familiar buzz of her phone drew her out of the small reprieve she'd managed to cocoon herself in at a local coffee shop. It was only lunch time, the work day dragging on as constant paperwork—both digital and physical—piled up on her desk. Anika had barely had a moment to take a breath, mind constantly whirring and working.

Escaping the confines of her office, she'd tucked herself away for a quick lunch, but the constant string of notifications on her phone prevented complete solace. Setting her coffee cup down, she unlocked her phone to find the usual suspect flooding her messages.

Levi.

Ever since the warehouse showing, he'd been texting her. At first, it'd been harmless, an occasional check in about her thoughts on the property—she'd passed it up, unable to get over the sense of dirtiness clinging to it—and if she was interested in others. She wasn't. Yet it never deterred him. If anything, he fought harder, eager to weasel his way into her life.

While her interest in him was waning, she couldn't help but soak up the attention and pathetic nature he exuded around her. It had a small smirk spreading across her face.

Men are so utterly pitiful, she thought while messaging him back.

Somewhere along the way, he'd gotten more personal, more focused on her and her life. Levi was rapt when it came to her job, her lifestyle—since she was somehow still a single thirty-one year old— and anything else he even remotely discovered about her. In all her years away from grade school, she'd forgotten what it was like to have a clingy man around.

Especially these days. Most men veered out of her path, the coldness settling into her eyes forcing them to steer clear of her. It was a side effect of her tragic upbringing, but she preferred it this way. It allowed her to think and focus on herself.

Until now...

Levi: Are you free to grab lunch right now?

Rolling her eyes, she hit send on her own text.

Sadly, no. Work has me running a three person job. Alone **:Anika**

Levi: Boo

Levi: How about later? Dinner?

You're not going to take no for an answer, are you? **:Anika**

Levi: I will but I'll be sad :(

Anika stifled her derisive snort, taking a sip of her hot coffee. The strength of the beans made the corners of her eyes crinkle.

*You don't even know me, how can you be sad :**Anika***

Levi: *I know that I love talking with you, no matter the occasion*

A few seconds passed, the dots dancing across the bottom of her screen while she waited for him to double text, *again.*

Levi: *C'mon, just one date and if you don't like me, I'll leave you alone*

*Oh, so it's a date now...not dinner? :**Anika***

She really didn't give a fuck what he labeled it, she was only giving him a hard time because she was bored.

Levi: *It can be whatever you want it to be*

*Do you do this to everyone you give showings to? :**Anika***

Levi: *No only you*

She scoffed. Sure.

*Does your boss know? :**Anika***

Levi: *No, he's too busy to care about what I'm doing*

Anika felt her brow arch in interest; duly noted.

And if we have dinner and I hate you, you'll delete my number? :Anika

Levi: Whatever you want

Dangerous words to say to a stranger :Anika

Levi: You're hardly a stranger

Levi: So, is that a yes?

Persuasive little twat. She'd admit that Levi was attractive, someone most women would fawn over, but she found him to be slimy. Besides, her life wasn't meant for finding love. It was forged for revenge.

Which had an idea popping into her head.

She was certain Mikko had her in his crosshairs, their interaction outside her gym all she needed to know. While it'd been unexpected, she knew it was only a matter of time before he let his compulsive tendencies win. From her own personal research and experience, Anika knew he tried to remain unfeeling and unreadable in the face of others, but there were telltale signs of his facade cracking.

She'd heard rumors and murmurs of his men spreading their dissent. Comments of him "being too young" or "too emotional for the ruthless family business" or "he's nothing at all like his father." The last one had piqued her interest a couple weeks ago. How could Alek's spawn *not* be like him?

It was an impossible feat, one Anika wanted to discover for herself.

Levi: Man, you're playing hard to get with me right now, aren't you?

His persistence reminded her of her own. Maybe fate had a reason for allowing her to meet Levi. Another sip of her coffee had the feelings in her chest settling as another layer of her mind unraveled itself.

I'll only agree if you take me to my favorite restaurant :Anika

Levi: *Done*

* * *

A FAINT KNOCK sounded on the frame of her office door. Expecting a fellow coworker heading out for the day, she glanced up—

What the fuck.

There, standing with his hands behind his back, was Levi. His icy gaze tracked her movements, something coy laying in wait there. Anger pooled in her gut; she'd never given him her work address.

"Didn't expect you to be tucked all the way back here in your own office," he began, voice easygoing like she'd invited him here.

Keeping her fury in check, she cocked her head. "Not sure what you mean by that"—she glanced at her watch—"and you're early."

"Nervous habit." *Doubtful.* "You've got a nice view though," he continued, stepping into her space. She noted the exquisite detailing of his suit, the price of it more than her mortgage payment if she had to guess. And as soon as she was about to counter, his hands unveiled what had been hiding behind his back.

A bouquet of flowers.

A romantic gesture to most, but her extensive plant knowledge couldn't help but force her to linger on what kind of flowers he'd brought.

Leafy ferns were the backdrop to golden columbines and vibrant purple snapdragons.

Fascination, foolishness, and deception.

151

Did he know what this meant? Surely he had to, but Anika wasn't entirely sure his brain functioned so acutely.

Her teeth gritted. Through text, he seemed eager like she was his first ever date, but now he was off-putting. Even last week when she'd walked through the warehouse with him, he'd been lighter. Maybe he'd set his sights on trying to persuade her to buy from Romanov Real Estate. Most people were either too scared to work with them or too scared to turn them down. She had a feeling Levi was hardly ever told no.

Glancing over her shoulder, the act of taking her eyes off him hopefully giving him false hope of her faux comfortability, she said, "Worked hard for this office. How does it compare to the one in your tall tower over at Romanov Real Estate?"

"It's close." His grin widened as he ran a hand through his short, blond hair.

"Guess real estate pays well."

"It has its pros."

"Like picking up female clients?"

Levi's smile might've reached his eyes, but there was something weird about it. She knew he was playing with her, watching her reactions and cataloging everything. There wasn't much to notice, most of it hidden behind the facade she *wanted* him to see, but it annoyed her all the same.

Is he going to report back to Mikko? Or does he have his own motives?

Men had a habit of trying to thaw her exterior, claiming she needed to "smile more," but the only connection she craved was the wicked promise of retribution. Levi would do well to learn that quickly.

"I swear this is the first time I've done this," he answered.

"Of course, it's rude of me to assume. It's as they say, 'innocent until proven guilty.'"

"Innocent isn't the word I'd use, but..." he trailed off, his words painful to hear.

"And there's *plenty* I'd use, but we'll start with 'I still have thirty minutes left of work.'"

He leaned forward, setting the flowers down on her desk. Their scent was pungent and made her head spin. Unaware of her internal battle, Levi picked up a stray pen off her desk before twirling it between his fingers. "Do you really have to stay?"

"Yes," she said dryly.

Anika knew she was being rude, but she wanted to let him stew in his own misery for a moment. She never claimed to be a *good* person. All her life, she'd considered niceties as subjective, especially when it came to those involved with Romanov Real Estate.

Turning her attention back to her computer, she resumed her last few tasks of the day. There were emails awaiting her response, ones she wanted to get out before going on this *date*.

"Have you given any other properties some thought?" he asked, unable to not be the center of her attention.

"No, I've put that endeavor on hold since my day job has picked up." Her voice was cordial, but there was underlying sarcasm. The man before her missed it. While she usually knew how to read people, their true colors showing no matter how much they tried to shield them, Levi didn't have the same ability.

Plucking one of the snapdragons free from the bouquet, Levi leaned over her desk. His height invaded her personal space, but she forced herself to sit still. Gently, he tucked the petals behind Anika's ear. Frozen and unable to process this man's audacity, she sat there with a painful smile on her face.

Of course it had to be the fucking snapdragon too, she thought.

Her instincts were screaming, encouraging her to smack his hand away, but she refrained. Anika's game was with Mikko; Levi was a stepping stone to get there. She'd known what she'd signed up for when she agreed to his stupid dinner.

"That's a shame, I was looking forward to celebrating a sale with you." Annoyance flared in her gut.

"Never say never," she muttered as she continued to type. Louder she said, "Besides, I wouldn't want to look at too many properties at once and overwhelm you.

"It takes a lot to overwhelm me, I can assure you."

Anika made a mental note to check his background, mind suddenly curious to know who he *truly* was.

Why does he work for Romanov Real Estate? What does he hope to gain with me? And why is he so damn insufferable?

The last one felt rhetorical.

Flicking her gaze over to him, reminding herself to play along, she teased. "Good to know." *Ugh.* "Do you always talk this much?" Her honeyed voice softened the underlying edge of her question. Again, Levi missed it.

Levi's laugh was an unexpected reaction; Anika's sharp edges usually resulted in others being short with her, not this.

"Are you always this reserved?" he countered playfully.

"Depends."

"Well, the same can be said for me too," he said. "But I think once you get to know me, once you give me a chance, you'll like what you find."

Resisting the urge to shake her head, Anika forced a grin. "Of course, but as much as I enjoy your company, I need to finish up a few things. If you wait in the lobby, I'll meet you when I'm done."

His good guy facade flickered, then righted. "Ever the business woman, I see," he teased. "Don't leave me hangin' now, yeah?"

"I wouldn't *dream* of it."

As soon as he left, Anika snatched the snapdragon stem from her hair and threw it in the trash along with the whole damn bouquet.

18

It's Not A Crush

Cristiano

"While I know you hate being in the office, did you think I wouldn't notice your absence?" Cristiano teased.

Mikko leveled him with a look that would've sent most running, but Cristiano wasn't most people. Emerald eyes flicked from Cristiano's face to his hair. "And you thought I wouldn't notice *that* color?"

Cristiano's hand rubbed across his short hair. "*That* color is green, and don't try to change the subject on me—"

"Neon green," Mikko countered over Cristiano. Now, it was time for him to glare at Mikko. "You look radioactive."

"Okay, *fine*, it's neon green, but not much would cover the blue, so…" A shrug was all he could give Mikko as he ignored the latter half of his friend's comment. "Your turn."

"I don't know what you're talking about."

"If you think you can lie to me of all people, try again."

"Fine," Mikko carded his hands through his hair four times which

155

Cristiano knew to be one of his tells, "I *may* be a little more absent because I'm trying to get to the bottom of whoever targeted Ivan, and in turn, targeted us."

Nodding, Cristiano waited for him to reveal more, even if it was like pulling fuckin' teeth. Mikko continued, "If you're looking for more of an update, that's all I have unfortunately."

"While I believe you on that topic, that doesn't mean you get off easy on this." Before Mikko could protest, Cristiano pulled out a plastic bag containing a note and what appeared to be remnants of a chewed piece of gum. He tried not to look at it for too long, the sight grossing him out.

"Where'd you find that?" Mikko's tone was sharp.

"Laying in an *unlocked* drawer in your desk." The plastic crinkled as Cristiano shook the bag. "Gonna tell me what it's all about? Especially the ominous note?"

Mikko's jaw clenched and unclenched. Another tell. If Mikko had it his way, nothing of importance would be revealed, but Cristiano could be annoyingly persuasive.

"Ominous is a bit bold—"

Cristiano cleared his throat and smoothed the plastic out over the note inside. "*'I've waited a long time to devour you,'*" he quoted. "Sounds pretty ominous to me. Or kinky..."

Another sigh from his friend-turned-boss. There was no escaping Cristiano's interrogation methods.

"If you must know, I found it stuck to my motorcycle the night after we interrogated Ivan."

"If this has to do with Ivan, I think I should know. But also ew. Is that what the gum is doing in here?" Cristiano side eyed it before he flicked his gaze back to his friend, a light bulb going off in his head. "So that *wasn't* a fucking ticket you liar."

"Yes, it was used to adhere the note." *Ew again.* "But it's also partially responsible for my absence." Mikko's fingertips pinched the bridge of his nose. "I'm trying to find out if it's a threat or something left in jest."

"Tell me you've at least figured that out." The tilt of Cristiano's green head had Mikko's mouth pinching into a line. "Did you send the gum out to get tested at one of our labs? We have so many connections and people who owe us, you'd be *dumb* not to." Cristiano paused, something like regret lining his voice as he added on, "And please, for the love of God, tell me you didn't chew—"

A sharp slap of papers on Mikko's desk halted the rest of Cristiano's words. "Yes, I had Dr. Žofia run tests on it, which is why there's only a small portion of the sample left."

Cristiano looked at the papers currently under Mikko's protective palm. It was a thick manila folder. *"And?"*

"And nothing."

"One of our men has died suspiciously, Mikko, you don't think sharing any info you have is important?"

Mikko huffed. "I don't want you getting involved."

"I work for you, I have to get involved. It's actually part of my job description."

"And you will, once I get the details sorted. Just keep pushing on the leads you're chasing down with Devon."

"There's nothing to tell." The sarcasm was hard to miss in Cristiano's tone. "I'm not sharing my leads unless you share yours, so…care to divulge what you know?"

"Not really."

"I see why women avoid you—you're a ball of *tense* energy. It's a turn-off."

"Some people like tense," Mikko replied.

"Yeah, massage therapists. You keep them in business."

"Who said it was massage therapists?" He shook his head. "But *tense* and *hard* are two very different things."

"Stop," Cristiano held up a hand before walking closer to Mikko's desk, dropping the bag near the manila folder, "I don't need to think about what I *think* you're referring to."

Mikko chuckled softly. His faint smile erased some of the tension resting on his friend's countenance. At the end of the day, Cristiano knew he taunted Mikko until the point of annoyance, but he did it as a distraction. Whatever he had to do to see his friend smile, he'd do it. It was the least they could do for themselves—two men who'd been forced to grow up too fast.

There'd been many times Cristiano had stayed on the phone with Mikko years ago when Alek would come home drunk and searching for a reason to explode.

The sounds of screaming and a crackling fire still haunted him—

"Seriously, though, you know where to find me if you need help sorting out information." The offer conveyed more than both men were willing to say, but they understood it all the same.

"Even if I didn't, your hair would point me in the right direction."

"Hey, you're just mad you can't pull this off." Cristiano gestured from his face to his outfit. He was dressed more casually today, business attire something he tended to stay away from; unless it was a soft sweater and comfortable slacks with his favorite Italian loafers.

Now neutral colors adorned his body—an oversized sweater providing warmth on an October day along with baggy cargo pants. A single gold chain dangled from around his neck and clean sneakers brought his outfit together.

"Maybe so," was all Mikko said, his crisp suit a stark comparison to Cristiano's attire.

Cristiano made to leave, knowing Mikko wouldn't give him much more unless it was absolutely necessary, but he paused. "Actually, I have one more question."

Mikko shuffled some papers around on his desk, pointedly avoiding looking at the plastic bag. "Of course you do. Will you go away if I answer?"

"Maybe," Cristiano smirked. Mikko motioned for him to go on. "The handwriting on the note, it looks *feminine.*"

"And?"

"Are you sure you don't have a secret admirer?"

Mikko's swallow was audible. "I don't think that's what this is."

"I don't know, man, you're a pretty big name now."

That made something glimmer in Mikko's eyes, and Cristiano couldn't place it, but it made him want to press a little harder. So he did. "Do you have a crush? Someone you're sneaking out to meet, Mikko? I won't tell if you—"

"No."

"Are you sure?" he stepped closer. "You can tell me. Hell, I might be able to even give you some pretty good advice."

"I don't need your advice."

"Oh, so you *do* have a secret little lover—"

"No," Mikko cut in. "I don't *need* your advice because there is no admirer, crush, whatever you want to label it as!"

Cris smiled. Mikko was lying his ass off right now. Usually work never got him this fired up which meant it wasn't work related at all. The only other time he'd seen him like this was with Samantha and Ellie; two of his serious relationships that had gone wrong years ago. "I don't know, you're getting pretty flustered about this. It's nothing to be ashamed of, Mikko. Who is she?"

"Cristiano."

Oh, fuck, he thought, *I know that tone.* While he could push his friend more than most, he still had a limit.

"There isn't anyone, and even if there *was,* I wouldn't be coming to you for dating advice."

159

Mikko's stern look made Cristiano hesitate, but his brain was unable to stop the words falling from his mouth. "I think the reviews I've gotten from some past lovers might change your mind, besides who said anything about dating? I was going to—"

"*Cristiano.*"

"Yes?"

"Get out."

The way Mikko was sitting there, his discomfort palpable, had a grin threatening to stretch across his face. Stifling it, he nodded and slowly backed out of Mikko's office with his hands up in mock surrender. *Someone* had gotten under his friend's skin, and Cristiano wasn't sure if he was excited or terrified.

Maybe both.

"My offer still stands," Cristiano tacked on as he slipped through the door. The only response he got was Mikko flipping him off. As he closed the door, a chuckle burst free from his lips, and he didn't stop laughing until he got all the way back downstairs to his Mercedes parked along the curb.

* * *

LATER THAT EVENING, Cristiano was debating between going out with a few acquaintances or staying in.

My couch does look awfully *comfy...*

Unlike Mikko, who was a natural born recluse—a surprising fact to many since he was the CEO of Romanov Real Estate—Cristiano tried to fill his time with noise. Being alone wasn't an issue, it was the thoughts plaguing him that were. He'd learned that the hard way growing up.

So now, as an adult, he liked to use what little free time he had for himself. And that meant mingling with whoever was available. No one would understand him like Mikko, that was a once in a lifetime friendship, but on nights like these, that didn't matter. Cristiano needed a distraction. Both from Ivan's case and whatever Mikko wasn't telling him. He knew he'd come around eventually, but it still stung to be kept in the dark. Cris told himself it was a by-product of Mikko being Alek's son.

His fingertip brushed across the clothing in his closet as his mind weighed his options for each outfit idea—

Ring!

"Speaking of distractions," he muttered as he turned back to his bed, phone screen alight with Mikko's photo and number.

"Finally cave and decide to ask me for relationship advice?" Cristiano said, unable to help himself.

"Sometimes I could slap you." Mikko's voice was humorous, but there was an underlying shortness; something was wrong.

"Hey, *sometimes* violence isn't the answer. Remember how you gave me this job because you liked me and wanted me close and needed an extrovert to help you through all your clumsy interactions—"

"Cristiano." It was the third time in one day he'd been scolded by Mikko. He was toeing a dangerous line.

"Sorry, boss." He wasn't, but he was more concerned with Mikko's unusual tone than joking anymore. "What'd ya call me for?"

"How long have you known that Levi has been texting one of our clients?"

"Umm, I didn't know. Why? Is there a problem?" It wasn't unheard of for realtors and other employees at Romanov to text clients.

"It hasn't been work related."

Oh. "Well, that's not unusual for him. I find him to be quite...what's the word...uncouth."

"And you didn't think to mention this before I let him attend a showing with a woman?"

A woman, huh? "I feel like there's no right answer here, boss. I know just as much as you do, probably less honestly. I didn't even know he'd been messaging someone." A thought clicked into his head. "Speaking of which, how do *you* know he's been talking to a client?"

Mikko huffed. "That's not important."

"Oh, but I think it is," Cristiano's neck was prickling. He knew his friend. "It's the same woman who left the note on your motorcycle, isn't it?"

"No, that's not—"

"Don't be coy with me, half the city owes you favors, and the other half you could buy," Cristiano countered, knowing he was onto something. "And that thick ass manila folder on your desk had to contain something. What were the lab results?"

"While that may be true, I wouldn't—"

"Oh, you *so* would," Cristiano practically shouted, his intuition screaming at him. "I *knew* you had a crush. So, tell me, who is she? Levi is a twat, and you can probably impress her *way* more than that dud of an agent could."

"She's not a crush, she's a *client*," Mikko corrected.

"Perhaps, but if you're two consenting adults…"

"Stop, it's not going to happen. Besides, the company is consuming most of my time, especially now that Ivan is dead."

"If you say so, boss. I won't stop you, but when you're ready to admit your feelings, I'll be here." Cristiano grinned. "I won't even tell you 'I told you so.'"

Mikko's voice sounded farther away, like he'd stepped away to get something. "How generous of you."

"Hey, my generosity is what gets me ahead in life. It's what brought me to you after all." It was meant to be a playful jab, but the way the words fell from his mouth felt more like an admission.

Shaking his head, Cristiano continued, "Regardless, if you change your mind, or want me to put itching powder in Levi's underwear, I'll do it. Just say the word."

"I don't want to even know how you thought of that, or why, but thank you...I think."

Cristiano turned back to his closet. "Anytime."

"I'm going to go for a ride to clear my head"—the telltale sound of his voice echoing in a parking garage confirmed his location—"but until I can completely clear her, Anika is dangerous and all of us should stay away from her."

"Anika, huh?" Cristiano caught Mikko's slip up. "So she has a name now?" It was a shame no one but his clothes could see his eyebrows wiggle.

"Forget about it," Mikko's motorcycle's exhaust rumbled to life in the background, "just steer clear."

"Of course, boss, wouldn't want her meeting me before you now, would we? Might ruin your chances with her."

He yearned to annoy Mikko farther, but the line went dead. "And people say *I'm* the dramatic one."

19

Hopeful

Anika

Like a nasty case of toenail fungus, Levi wouldn't go away.

She'd entered the lobby, a hopeful expression on her face when she didn't see him at first. Maybe he'd gotten tired of waiting for her—it'd been almost an hour—and left. But she could never be so lucky. Just as she was about to rejoice, his lean frame materialized. He'd been sitting behind another group of employees in the lobby, but as he strode over to her, there was no denying his intent.

Levi was here for her, and he wouldn't be deterred. Despite her previous unsavory attempts at persuading him to give up, Levi still clung to her like she was his lifeline. It didn't matter if she was nice or mean or long winded with her answers or short. She even divulged gross personal details she'd hoped would deter him, but if anything it made him sidle closer.

Men were *tenacious*, if anything.

"I was starting to worry about you," he replied as soon as she was

164

in earshot. A soft brush of his lips across her temple as he swept her into a hug made her spine stiffen.

"I…had more emails come in after you stepped out," she replied, body short circuiting at the unwanted touch. "I should've texted you."

"No need," he pulled away, hands still gripping her shoulders. "I called and moved our reservation back."

Great. "Thank you," she said aloud instead.

"Anything for you." She winced, but he didn't notice, too busy offering her his elbow as if she needed to be chauffeured out of work on a Friday evening. If anyone asked her about this slimy man next week, she'd set the building on fire. "Although I'm sad to see you without the flowers in your hair."

"I'm sorry," she wasn't, "but I didn't think they were formal enough for our dinner."

He chuckled, holding the door open for her, "Anything you wear, Anika, would be appropriate for our dinner date."

Ugh, there was that word again. "Of course, I should've known."

"It's okay, maybe just ask me next time."

The gun strapped to her ankle currently pulsed with promise. It would be so easy to slip it free and push it into his ribs, anything to get him to shut up.

"While I appreciate your gestures, I'm not really the type of woman to ask for permission first," she said. It was blunt, but it was better than her former thoughts. Levi didn't answer her for a moment, guiding her to his telltale white BMW at the curb in front of her office building. Opening the car door for her as well, she didn't miss the way his eyes roved over her figure as she sat down into his awaiting passenger seat.

Thank goodness she wasn't wearing a skirt.

She bit back a shiver as his azure eyes twinkled with mischief. "I can see why they gave you your own office."

"What's that—"

He closed her door, silencing the rest of her words.

"That was rude," she muttered while watching him walk around the front of his car. He should count his lucky stars she couldn't reach over and press the accelerator and run him over.

"Apologies," Levi said immediately when he got back in. "I don't want to be late for our reservation."

She glared at his side profile, unafraid to make him uncomfortable with her gruffness. "For a dinner you never asked me if I wanted, mind you."

He pulled away from the curb, soft jazz playing from the car speakers. "I did, and you agreed."

"I'd call that harassment more like." Anika's arms were crossed.

"It's more like persuasion," he shook his head playfully before his free hand settled on her thigh. "Sometimes women need a little push, then they realize what you mean to them." He squeezed her leg to punctuate his meaning.

Her mouth popped open. "That's a telling detail."

"What? I'm just being honest." His voice was so at odds with the poison slipping from his mouth. His appearance was honeyed and innocent, his features schooled into the perfect look of placation. Anika was beginning to wonder if she was hallucinating.

"Honesty doesn't suit you," she said, "hence why you're in real estate."

Now it was his turn to glance over at her, mouth ajar. "Well, aren't you just a little firecracker?" The nickname had her fingers twitching for her gun again. She longed to flash it at him and show him what a pathetic ass he was. But she refrained. "I like how unapologetic you are."

"Men never apologize, so why should I?"

"A fair point." He thankfully turned onto the street the restaurant was on. She had to keep up this charade for a bit longer, then she could be free. All the while, her plan solidified in her mind; Mikko had found her note and it was stoking an internal flame inside of him if her missing scarf was any indication. It was a shame Alek was long gone, or else Anika might've found herself having fun toying with Mikko while trying to derank his father. But alas, life had a different plan for them.

"Also, don't expect that flowers and a dinner will get me into bed with you," Anika said, the sign for *The Stuffed Pepper* appearing. While appalled by his behavior, she wasn't surprised. He wasn't the first man to act this way with her and wouldn't be the last. She twisted the rings around her fingers in muscle memory. A gesture he'd most likely read as anxiety.

Set the trap...

Levi's eyes had flicked from her fingers and back to her eyes, like she wanted.

And catch the prey.

He feigned being wounded by her words as he pulled his car up to the valet. "I would never, but what kind of compliments or gifts *would* you like?"

"You're playing with fire by asking a woman that."

His grin had widened at her words, pure male arrogance sweeping across his countenance. "What can I say, I'm here to serve."

Anika's eyebrow raised. "I'm listening."

"Name your price and consider it done."

Oh, she had a price, one even *he* wasn't ready for.

Let's see how long it takes for jealousy and intrigue to draw my other suitor out from the shadows...

Procuring her deep crimson lipstick from her purse, she reapplied before answering. "I'll think about it and let you know."

"Oh, so mysterious."

Stepping out of the car, he handed the valet attendant his keys before rounding the vehicle to get Anika. Levi thought he was getting what he wanted: a woman he'd deemed unattainable. Another notch in his bedpost was all she was, and that was fine. Levi meant nothing to her either. He was another piece within her puzzle, his own lust and want making him the perfect bait.

He just didn't know it.

* * *

SEATED IN A booth across from Levi, Anika pretended to scour the menu.

"Get anything you want," Levi spoke, interrupting her thoughts as usual, "my treat."

Fighting the instinct to roll her eyes, Anika nodded demurely. "Of course, it *is* a date after all."

She met his eyes through her lashes, expressing something she knew looked flirtatious. In reality, heat threaded itself into her muscle fibers, her hands itching to smack the sly grin off the man's face.

Pleased when he shut up, Anika's eyes caught on the highest number on the menu. *Perfect.* If Levi thought she was someone he could parade around—bragging all the while about trying to fuck his client—then he had another thing coming.

"I thought the name of this restaurant sounded familiar," Levi said, glancing around the lavish interior.

"Have you been here before?" She already knew the answer. Previously, she'd caught wind that Mikko frequented this establishment and hoped tonight would be one of those nights.

"Yes, a couple of my real estate buddies like to bring clients here."

"What a small world," she supplied, eyes back on the menu, "I remember when I found it about a year ago. A slew of good reviews finally made me cave and try it. Can't go anywhere else now." *Lie.*

Levi set his menu aside, "Ah, I love a woman who does her research."

"Which is exactly why you should be thanking me for agreeing to this."

"Why?" he grinned, "did you do your *research* on me too?"

"Maybe."

"Like what?"

His annoying persistence had her deciding on the most expensive vegetarian entree as she set her menu aside.

"I can't quite tell you that," she said, eyes watching him and the mirror slightly above his left shoulder which reflected the entry door they'd come in through moments earlier.

"Oh, don't be like that. I wanna know; what does the vast internet say about me?"

Licking her upper teeth in contemplation, Anika decided between playing dumb or intimidating Levi. The latter won.

"Well, you live alone," she started and Levi wiggled his eyebrows suggestively, "preferring to explore the city instead of being holed up in your apartment. You're well traveled, and judging on the timestamps of your last several years on social media you prefer flexing in front of a mirror more than showing up to work.

"You've only been working at Romanov Real Estate for about ten years from what I can find…" Anika trailed off, yearning to unleash more, but trying to strike a balance between tormenting him and playing the game for a little longer. "And yet you've been traveling before then which leads me to believe you have an inheritance or wealthy family. Especially since you like to spend most nights at local clubs spending money and harassing bottle girls."

That erased his stupid grin.

"You sure know how to *woo* your dates," he replied, sarcasm below the surface of his words.

"You asked."

"True…" Levi flagged the waiter down, eager for a break in the conversation. Anika barely managed to cover her smile as the man stopped to take their drink order. While alcohol was something she tried not to divulge in frequently, tonight was an exception. She needed *something* to power through this date.

After she'd picked a Malbec from the menu—also enjoying the market price next to it—she waited for Levi to lead the conversation. She wasn't going to do all the talking, this date was *his* idea after all.

And I'm here for other reasons, she thought mischievously, eyes still straying to the mirror above Levi.

"Where were we?" he prompted once the waiter had left, his words indicating he knew but didn't want to return to the topic of himself. Well, that was a lie, all men liked to talk about themselves, but Levi wasn't fond of the information she'd gleaned in the span of a week and some spare time. No, he'd wanted to paint himself in a different light, a *better* one.

Sigh.

"I'm sorry if I came on too strong," Anika supplied finally. "It's a habit I'm trying to break." The lie rolled off her tongue easily. If people thought her to be too much, then they could leave.

Levi chuckled, fiddling with his cuffed button down sleeves. The cerulean fabric made his eyes shine, and in the warm amber lighting of the restaurant, they *almost* looked like someone else's.

Emerald pools holding secrets I want to rip *free.*

"No, no, it's alright," he continued, "that's why I asked you out. You're different from a lot of women I've met and tried to date." *Wow, I've never heard that before.* "It's what drew me to you in the first place."

"Is that so?" Anika's fingernail tapped rhythmically on the tabletop, her eyes pinning him to the spot. Levi was caught somewhere between enjoying her attention and also squirming under it. And that was *just* how she liked it. "Finally get tired of the bottle girls and dancers?"

"Yeah, it's been, uh, it's been hard to find women I connect with these days."

"And you connect with me?"

There was an infinitesimal pause from him that Anika caught before, "Yes."

Something was amiss. It was like a prickle in the back of her mind, incessant now that she discovered it, but the harder she tried to pinpoint it, the more it seemed to escape her. It was as if one minute he enjoyed her conversation, then the next he was in dire need of escaping.

Had Mikko put him up to spying?

It felt that way.

Too bad Mr. Romanov couldn't do his own research by himself. Instead he had to resort to grunt workers.

"That's interesting," she started, waiting to continue since the waiter had returned with their drinks. Levi took a sip of his whiskey and soda while she resumed her thoughts, "I've also had some...difficulties in the dating department." Not a lie, but it wasn't for the reason she was about to divulge.

"Really?"

His surprise was on par with most people's reactions.

"Yes, men have a hard time realizing my job is significant to me."

"I could see that being an issue."

Anika smiled as if this was her first time hearing his words. "I always thought I hid it better, but as I grow into myself, I realize that I don't. But, in any case, work tends to come before my friends and family—a by-product of my independence, if you will—and it rubs potential *suitors* the wrong way."

171

"Sometimes men can't handle independent, smart women," Levi said before taking another swig of his drink. He was looking for something to take the edge off, to occupy his hands.

"Indeed. They want a pretty little trophy wife, but what they don't know is that I'll take the fucking trophy *myself*." Taking a sip of her wine, Anika paused, eager to let him speak, curious as to what bullshit he would spew this time.

"I admire that about you"—she nearly choked on the crimson liquid settling over her taste buds—"it's not often that you can find someone who cares for their job in that way. Dedication is a rare trait these days."

A bold statement coming from him since he seemed lazy in every meaning of the word, but oh, if only he knew the lengths she'd go to.

"I'm glad to share this with you. Maybe this is exactly what we need. A fresh start, of sorts." Anika knew her words were feeding into his fantasy, but she couldn't help herself. A little indulgence never hurt anyone. Well, most of the time.

Levi smiled. "That's what I'm hoping for."

In the mirror she'd been watching, she caught sight of movement. The door to the restaurant had opened, revealing dark hair, a crisp suit, and green eyes she couldn't get out of her head.

He really can't stay away, can he?

Lifting her delicate glass, wine sloshing gently inside, she *clinked* it against Levi's tumbler of whiskey. "Here's to hoping."

And she swore she saw Mikko's grip on his helmet tighten in the reflection.

20

Wine Stained Voyeurism

Mikko

Cristiano's questions from earlier had taken root in his head, the words refusing to leave his mind. While Anika was far from a lover or crush, the way the words had pricked at his chest made him question everything. His need to protect his business was morphing into something else.

And it didn't help that Levi, someone he trusted as far as he could throw him, was weaseling his way into her inbox. It'd make his own sleuthing harder since there would be two witnesses to his prowling. But this was a consequence of his own actions; maybe he could play it off to his benefit. A faux gentleman pushing Anika right into Mikko's arms.

Her stolen scarf sprawled across his bed in his penthouse spoke volumes...

In an attempt to clear his head, Mikko had left his residence after calling Cristiano, enjoying the cooler air as evening rolled in over the city.

And now, his motorcycle rumbled beneath him, the feeling of the wind erasing some of the doubt sprouting in his head. Mikko had lost track of time, the minutes slipping by until dusk settled itself above him and the wind he braced against became too cold to bear.

Downshifting, Mikko focused on the gas station up ahead, his evening rides draining his tank. If only it depleted the thoughts in his head just as fast.

The bright lights in the overhang made him squint even though his tinted visor dulled the illumination greatly. Pulling up to a pump, Mikko tried to keep his thoughts on the task in front of him. If he didn't, his mind would return to the place he didn't want.

Anika. Her house, her scent, her scarf. Her friend interrupting my search. Levi...

He'd do anything to prove Cristiano wrong, starting with forgetting about Anika, but it was clear she was a threat. So, he needed to cut her open and see what spilled out.

I won't be distracted, he vowed.

Mikko's father always taught him to keep his head clear and his anger restricted behind an internal wall. And most days he succeeded, careful while he worked and callous to most horrors.

"Rational thought is your best weapon. A clear head is a sharp tool, one that will flay angry men from their bones," his father articulated in a past memory.

Lately, though, that control had been slipping. An emotion akin to curiosity simmered beneath the surface of his skin, fueled by whatever Mikko saw in her. It was something he hadn't felt in a long time. A diversion, something to occupy his mind when the weight of work became too much.

An anomaly. Someone who might want to dismantle everything Romanov Real Estate stood for if the clues Mikko was collecting spoke to her end goals.

His mind ran through ideas and schemes, each one darker than the last. There were many twisted routes they could go, all of them spurred on by the idea of proving her wrong.

Proving Cristiano and Levi wrong.

And proving to himself he was above such temptations.

He wasn't obsessed with Anika, he was *annoyed.*

* * *

THE BLINKING RED dot on the map on his phone indicated Levi was at one of their usual restaurants: *The Stuffed Pepper.*

Treating our clients well, no doubt, he thought.

Despite the anger in his chest, Mikko encouraged Levi to grow closer to Anika, to persuade her into buying one of their other properties. There were other places her hoax of a leather goods manufacturing job could occupy. He'd spew just about anything that would keep her nearby.

Either way, walking into the restaurant—the warm glow of the interior doing little to thaw his growing ire—became difficult the closer he got. Clutching his helmet with frozen hands he peered through the glass. Mikko could see Levi, his elbows casually propped on the table as he listened to Anika. And even though her back was to him, he *knew* her silhouette as much as he loathed to admit it.

Shaking his head clear of the thoughts, he gripped the sleek handle of the entry door and slipped in. The soft din of cutlery and the faint conversations bleeding into one another greeted him. The light was comfortable inside, bright enough to see by, but still dim to cultivate an elevated yet intimate atmosphere. Deep leather booths framed the outer edges of the eatery, people in various stages of their meals and unwinding after a day at work.

175

Again, his eyes found Anika's back. Even though her dress covered her skin, he could picture it regardless. Everything about her was becoming second nature to him. He could faintly recall the ink etched there along her spine, and the way her toned muscles contracted when she walked away that night in *Bubblegum.*

"Good evening, sir," the hostess said, bringing his attention back to the front of the restaurant. "The usual?"

Nodding, he let her lead him to one of his favorite tables, his chilled hands finally warming after his evening ride. This place was a frequent stop of his, the food consistent and the color palette relaxing. Pendant lights accented certain tables while others were lit only by candle votives clustered in the center. Tall ferns fluttered in the furnace's breeze, the verdant color softening the harsh edges of the rich colors throughout.

Adjusting his hold on his helmet, he desperately tried to avert his gaze from Anika's lithe back. Instead, it landed on Levi, honing in on how he was talking to Anika, eyes sly and hands inching closer to her folded ones.

The sight should've pleased him, Levi taking his role seriously. It wasn't uncommon for Mikko and his business partners to wine and dine clients, but this was more personal.

In the end, Mikko did what he did best: sat back and let the events unfold before him. Long ago he'd worked through the ranks and done the dirty work. Sometimes the stench of a bloated body rolling around in the back of his getaway vehicle still haunted him. Or the times he'd had to shower multiple times to get all the blood and viscera off his body and out of his hair.

Now, Levi and his other men handled those occurrences.

It was unwise of him to creep much closer; she couldn't discover his curiosity before he had her pinned right where he wanted her.

But, *damn,* envy was one hell of a bitch.

176

His eyes flicked to the way she grasped the dainty stem of her wine glass, fingernails painted a deep scarlet to match her dress. One lipstick print already littered the rim, giving him a visual of the color painted on her lips without him even having to see her face. Clenching his jaw, he tore his eyes from her and Levi, determined to play his own part—a devoted eavesdropper.

To his delight, Levi didn't even look at him as he passed, pretending Mikko was just another patron. For tonight, he was, but oh, how he yearned to see if Anika's gaze snapped to him. A small part of him hoped his cologne wafted to her nose, inviting her into a game of his own.

It hadn't hurt his case when he'd texted Levi beforehand, warning him to remain focused on Anika. No additional questions had been asked, his employee content to drown in her aura.

"Here you go," the hostess stated, motioning for him to sit. With no other choice, he nodded politely and settled in for the evening. A couple rows of tables separated him from Anika, but he could still see her.

God, this is dangerous.

And he loved it.

* * *

TWO LONG HOURS went by. The moments of Anika and Levi settling into their own manicured comfortability burned into his mind.

Sipping on vodka, Mikko's eyes tracked Levi's playful grins and touches. The flirtatious laughter and flushed faces made Mikko's blood boil. Sometime over the course of their dinner, Levi had waved Anika over, persuading her to sit next to him on the same side of the booth. It annoyed Mikko, but it allowed him to look at Anika unobstructed. She was tucked into the side closest to the wall, sheltered from the outside world.

As if she needed that.

Mikko was getting the sense she could flay men alive with their own words and actions if needed.

The whole night was a double edged sword, proving to reaffirm his notions of staying home and refusing to linger in public for longer than necessary. It reminded him how alone he was, forever an outsider.

Levi was good at what he did, his stereotypical attractive appearance appealing to many women—Anika included from the look of it—and it was why Mikko had let him to weave his way into Anika's life so they could learn more about her.

She played with the rings on her fingers, nail polish glinting in the low light. Occasionally, she tucked fallen strands of ebony hair back behind her ear, sharp eyeliner matching her observant eyes.

Although, she hadn't so much as even looked over at his dark corner.

Shifting in his seat, another wave of anger washed over Mikko. No longer was he upset about Levi's advances—a small lie, perhaps—but he was triggered by her blatant disregard of him. Attempting to leash his sporadic emotions, Mikko forced himself to sit and watch. This was an interaction he'd designed nonetheless; time to suck it up and deal with the consequences.

But while Levi entwined himself with Anika, Mikko found himself wishing it was him. It should be *him* learning more about her, baiting her into revealing more about herself than she originally intended.

Not Levi.

She'd chosen *him*.

An inexplicable need to carve a place for himself into her life overcame him, an obsessive thought linked to his need for control.

Mikko wanted to be all she thought about, a haunting apparition preventing her from sleeping, from living as though he didn't exist after she'd taunted him. He wanted to be the one afflicting her mind as she talked and kissed Levi. The hot and cold treatment she'd given him was confusing, *tempting,* and he wanted answers.

Tapping on his cell phone, Mikko abused his power.

It was too easy *not* to.

Pulling up Anika's cellphone number, he let his fingers hover over the keyboard. Entering her number was a simple and easy act a week ago. Spelling out her name was like second nature, the letters making a permanent home behind his eyelids.

Typing a message out to her right now? Now, that was difficult.

*I wonder if he can tell how bored you are, little moon :***unknown**

Okay, maybe not *that* hard, but he'd been simmering in his angst for too long and needed to blow off some steam. Watching, he took a sip of vodka as his muscles tingled with anticipation. Licking a stray drop from his lip, Mikko knew when she received the text. Anika's eyes quickly flicked to her phone, which she kept on the table, the screen lighting up. Her mouth moved as she explained to Levi what the interruption was as she picked up her phone.

A grin spread across Mikko's face.

With a quick response of his own, Levi stood and excused himself. They shared a knowing look as he glanced over at Mikko's darkened spot on his way to the bathrooms.

Perfect.

Humor replaced the general intrigue that had been evident on her delicate features. He found himself torn between looking at his own phone in anticipation of her text and meeting her head on as she looked around the restaurant. Scanning the dimly lit interior, she tried to find *him.*

The small piece of power he'd gained through his reckless act was what he needed to erase the sickly feeling growing in his chest from Levi's work. Her honeyed eyes were almost indistinguishable from this distance as they roved over each table and booth until finally landing on him. And against his better judgment, he didn't avert his gaze.

The pounding in his chest stopped, seemingly commanded by her. While the distance between them and his shadowed nook prevented her from seeing him fully, he could still discern the recognition passing over her countenance. And he *swore* the edges of her lips tipped up in a smile.

Schooling her features back to disinterest, Anika tore her eyes away from his and looked back at her phone. Three little ellipses danced on his own phone screen while he waited. Impatiently.

Anika: He can't tell his asshole from a hole in the ground

Mikko stifled a snort.

*Sounds like he makes a great first impression :**unknown***

Anika: You would know, you sent him after me...

*I don't think I understand what you mean :**unknown***

Anika: Playing stupid isn't a good look on you, Mikko

He froze; she sent another text.

Anika: Does that mean you're still sipping vodka over there?

180

*And if I am :**unknown***

Anika: *I guess the bottle I sent you was a waste then*

Anika: *I'm sure Levi will drink it for you*

She had already pieced together that it was him who was texting her. Of fucking course she did. Mikko's hand shook as he gripped the phone. Every time he tried to be in control, she managed to throw him off. A different kind of rage settled over his bones, one cooling the previous emotion running through him. It focused him in the way he needed.

*Maybe I was saving it for a special occasion :**unknown***

Anika: *That's exactly something a cuck would say*

*That's quite the assumption :**unknown***

Anika: *Says you, sitting in a dark corner watching my dinner date*

Oh, what an evil little minx.

His stomach dropped, but he also couldn't help the small laugh slipping past his lips. She was playing his game and not being meek about it. Her double texts were purposeful, meant to distract him. He hated to admit it *did.*

And that he *liked* it.

When was the last time he'd had fun like this?

*If that's the kinda stuff you're into, the guy you're with isn't the one for the job :**unknown***

Anika: And how would you know? Have you slept with him?

Mikko huffed and took another sip from his snifter.

He left a woman upon finding out about her OnlyFans account :unknown

I, on the other hand, don't shame people :unknown

Anika: Just harass them?

Our definitions of harassment are vastly different :unknown

Anika: Does following someone to their gym count?

That was a coincidence :unknown

Anika: Riiiight

Quickly, before Levi came back and diverted her attention, Mikko typed out one last message.

Don't say I didn't warn you, though :unknown

He doesn't know how to find the clit :unknown

Slipping his phone into his pant's pocket, Mikko left money for his drink and a tip on the table before quietly standing. Without another thought, he walked out the back door, Anika's eyes on his back the whole time.

Hopefully, Levi could handle the rest.

*** *

THE DARK CONFINES of his penthouse consoled him while Mikko's heart beat wildly against his ribcage. His body was in sync with the storm opening up overhead, dousing the city in rainwater. He'd made it back to his penthouse before it'd begun. Luck was on his side sometimes. Just not when it came to Anika...

Anika: *Sent an image*

Anika: *Looks like he might find it*

It'd been an hour, but his brain was still in shambles. The picture she'd sent burned into his mind; even when he wasn't looking at it, he could still *see* it. Which might've been a worse fate.

There, each pixel clear as day on his phone screen, was Anika. Well, her toned and tattooed legs. On one thigh, there was the head of a wolf inked there bordered in roses. It appeared she was sitting down somewhere—in her house if the wood floors and eclectic rugs were any indication to him—while Levi was kneeling in front of her. Mikko had never seen his employee in such a compromising position before. And even though nothing scandalous was happening in the photo, the way it was angled, and her words, made it feel naughty. Her intent no doubt.

Upon closer inspection, he noticed Levi's hands were undoing her shoes. The picture had been taken while he'd been in the middle of slipping them from her feet. A dainty vine tattoo wrapped itself around the same ankle.

Shaking his head with an incredulous huff, Mikko closed out of the photo and resumed trying to type up a snarky response. He'd tried

183

many times throughout the course of the night since he received it, but everything he typed felt desperate.

Maybe because I am? he thought sullenly.

But he couldn't let her have the last word.

You might need to brush up on your anatomy knowledge... :unknown

Wow, an award winning response, for sure. Mikko rolled his eyes, pressing send anyway. Nothing would suffice; it was best to message her and get it out of the way.

Expecting her to take a while to text back, for reasons he tried to ignore, Mikko paced around his darkened penthouse.

Why was he letting Anika bother him so much? How had she clawed beneath his skin so thoroughly? Maybe this was his karma for all the years of living a life riddled with crime and wrongdoings. With his father gone, someone had to step into the dark reign, but it made Mikko's skin itch. He avoided the nefarious dealings the best he could, but it was inevitable.

People had lived and died by his hand, and now at his command.

The thoughts of it kept him up at night. All the lives he'd taken or changed all for the name of development expansion or money. Portland's landscape had changed over the last couple decades, prices of land and real estate increasing all while pushing thousands out who could no longer afford the rent. It was a terrible occurrence, one Alek had deemed necessary for the city's resurgence.

It made Mikko's stomach turn.

Small communities and cultures were erased all for the sake of dollar signs. Maybe one day, Mikko could speak up and change everything, but such radicalities took time. So he'd wait—

His phone rang in his pocket and cut through his spiraling. Groaning, his head fell forward to press against the cool glass overlooking the city.

Let it go to voicemail.

But it continued to ring as if sensing his lack of action. The sound grated on his nerves, or maybe that was apprehension creeping in from sending Anika a text. Regardless, he looked down and saw the name *Cristiano* glaring back up at him. His friend had a bad habit of calling Mikko when he was the most inconvenienced.

"I swear, if you're calling me to tell me that Levi went out on a date, I already know," Mikko said immediately. His annoyance was palpable, but he couldn't hold it in. "Besides, you know I like my evenings quiet."

"If that doesn't sound like a guilty conscience, I don't know what does," Cristiano huffed in his ear. "Especially, since I *wasn't* calling about that. Good to know though; Anika and Levi: a touchy subject."

"I'm sorry, the stress of it all must be getting to me."

"We both know you're not actually sorry *but* you don't have to go through all this alone, y'know." Cristiano waited a couple seconds before continuing, changing the subject thankfully. "Besides, your quiet evenings can still consist of you walking around naked and flexing in the reflection of your big windows. I would *never* stand in the way of your self-care, but"—his friend drew out the last word— "I've got a development on Ivan."

Mikko's mouth opened to counter Cristiano's idea of what he did at night when he shook his head and decided against it. "Go on."

"Oh, all business despite my dig, unless what I said is true which I could've done *without* that mental image—"

"Cristiano," Mikko interrupted with a small smile on his face, "you're the one who planted that image in your own head. Now, tell me about Ivan."

"Right, right. The morgue called about an hour ago to tell me about Ivan's autopsy. I'm heading there now."

"I hope you told them the excessive amount of drugs in his system wouldn't be unusual." It was common knowledge Ivan—and others in his circle—struggled with substance abuse. An unavoidable side effect of the job.

"They didn't even mention it, but they *did* say they found something...unique."

"Please tell me they told you more than that," Mikko said, mind racing to uncover the answers to Cristiano's cryptic sentences. "Unique how?"

"Uh..." his friend cleared his throat, "they found something *inside* his body, something that was, erm, placed there intentionally."

"Like a clue?"

"All the mortician would say was it wasn't organic material."

Mikko's eyebrows raised in surprise.

A foreign object?

He opened his mouth to speak, but Cristiano took his silence as an answer all on its own. "I think it'd be best if you came by the morgue too and saw for yourself." Cristiano accelerated on the other end of the line, his destination the same.

"Let me change my clothes and I'll head that way," Mikko said.

"Okay, I'll send you the address. See you when you get there."

With that, they both hung up, leaving Mikko with more questions than answers.

While Ivan's reputation wasn't the best, it wasn't any worse than most of the men Mikko worked with. Mikko's associates usually remained within their own sectors of the city. It prevented internal conflict, for the most part. And what couldn't be prevented, Mikko and his men squashed, snuffing out the root of the problem before it became a bigger one.

But with Ivan, he thought he'd done that.

"Should've killed him like I taught you," his father's voice echoed in

his head. Pressing his palms against the cool panes of glass, Mikko pushed off. The frigid temperature irritated the burn scars on his left hand, but now was not the time to dwell on old wounds.

Turning and heading toward his bedroom, Mikko checked his phone for the address Cristiano sent. He already had an idea where it was, but he wanted to make sure. Before he got that far another message caught his attention.

Ah, fuck, about that...

It was from Anika, her response coming in only a couple minutes after he'd sent his.

Anika: *Haven't you heard of foreplay?*

Anika: *Besides, the foot IS an erogenous zone*

The thought of kissing her instep flashed across his mind—

With a sigh, he closed their message thread and changed his clothes so he could meet up with his friend. Her, and her schemes, would have to wait.

21

Vigilance is Key

Mikko

The ever persistent rain plaguing the Pacific Northwest had stopped, leaving the night sky clear and devoid of any clouds. Only half of the moon was illuminated, leaving the other side to be swathed in shadow, hiding its pockmarked surface from the rest of the world for a couple more nights.

Mikko relished in the wind blowing across his body. With the rain gone, he'd opted to ride his motorcycle again. He longed for another moment of quietude before meeting up with Cristiano. It was risky since the weather was unpredictable this time of year, but he'd chance it anyway. Only God knew what was about to be unveiled to them both. Although he had a sneaky suspicion it had to do with his missing car keys and spliced security footage.

The cool night air allowed him to *finally* get Anika's scent out of his nose and off his skin. Despite multiple feet separating them at the restaurant, it didn't stop his keen nose from detecting it. He'd been in her house for fuck's sake; he knew everything about her.

City traffic dwindled as the clock ticked closer to midnight, his bike's engine roaring along the empty highways. Mist still faintly coated the asphalt. It stuck to his leather jacket and thick sweatshirt underneath and pebbled on his visor. His quick pace prevented the droplets from lingering, the wind whisking them up and off his helmet.

Slowing slightly when his exit approached, he glanced over his shoulder, making sure no one was following him. While he was certain he could handle whatever Anika was planning behind the scenes, he wouldn't be caught unaware. Nothing but the mundane street lights glowed back at him.

After exiting the interstate, Mikko rode a couple of blocks into an area of the city consisting mainly of one story businesses, historic homes, and tree-lined roads. The streets blurred as he rode by, each facade morphing into the next. All brick or stone, all eerily quiet because of the late night hour.

Some of the buildings thinned out as empty swaths of asphalt parking lots popped up all while he pushed on. Among the uncanny silence, Mikko's motorcycle roared. His conspicuous presence was a small price to pay to feel the night air threading through his clothes.

At Cristiano's directions, Mikko pulled into the next lot he came across, and was relieved to spot his friend's gray Mercedes glinting underneath the street lights. They were far and few between, but his friend had managed to find one to park under. Mikko did the same.

As his foot swept the motorcycle's kickstand down into place, a wave of annoyance rippled through him. Things had spiraled out of control so quickly, and he felt like he was still playing catch up. Hopefully this visit cleared up some of his incessant questions.

"I told you that you weren't good enough." Mikko shook off his father's voice, the faded memory resurfacing at the worst time. The thought enraged him, and suddenly he was eleven again. Powerless. Helpless.

Ripping his helmet off angrily—gloves fighting for purchase on the rain-slicked material—Mikko proceeded toward the darkened doorway of the mortuary. Cristiano was inside, and he didn't want to keep him waiting.

Dew clung to him, a dampness settling into his bones, and already he was dreaming of a shower. He'd turn it as hot as it'd go, the scalding water sure to erase the chill. And the illusion of Anika's touches that he could still fucking feel all these weeks later.

Pocketing his keys, he freed up his hands to hold his helmet. Mikko observed the weathered brick lining the one-story building. Its texture was evident in the low light as he walked in. A worn awning flapped in the small gusts of wind, only a few pieces of the business's name remained on the canvas.

Miller's Mortuary.

As he neared the threshold of shadows before him, he realized why it was so dark. One of the exterior wall sconces had burnt out completely while the other had been shattered. There were jagged pieces still protruding from the light socket. His eyebrow raised. Exterior maintenance wasn't a priority here and something about that triggered him.

"Let's hope they maintain the interior better than out here," he grumbled to himself. His irritation grew since the thought of looking at a dead body didn't stir his insides with joy.

Armored gloves still covered his hands—another weapon added to his arsenal—as he reached for the door handle. It opened on silent hinges, cool air rushing out to greet him.

Stepping across the threshold, Mikko's displeasure intensified as the door *snicked* shut behind him. A chill settled onto his damp clothes and skin making a shiver race up his spine.

A dimly lit lobby greeted him with a sickly pale green glow reflecting off the linoleum floors. With a squeak of his boot, he looked over his shoulder, his head on a swivel to avoid any surprises. While his relation to organized crime meant he dealt with unsavory tasks and people, something about being surrounded by dead, *preserved* bodies put him more on edge. The door he'd stepped through had a film on it, now bubbling and peeling away, to prevent the outside from looking in.

"God, this place is depressing." He even hated the way his mumbled words echoed in the space.

Facing forward, he noticed two halls branching off from the lobby, mirroring one another.

Where's Cristiano?

As if summoned by his thoughts, footsteps echoed from the left corridor, and seconds later his friend appeared.

"Ah, you're here finally," he said, coming up to Mikko and briskly clapping him on his back. It was more reserved than their usual greeting which wordlessly told Mikko something was amiss. Not far behind was an older man.

"Wouldn't miss it," Mikko replied sarcastically. Cristiano grinned, mood lifting slightly. He turned to the man behind him, ready to introduce everyone. The aged gentleman, presumably the mortician, beat him to it.

"Joseph," the man said, his hair ghostly white in the fluorescent light. His crisp lab coat also reflected it, and Mikko fought the urge to squint.

Mikko nodded in response, holding a hand out, all business. "Mikko."

"I assumed that already—we don't have all night," Joseph said curtly, ignoring his outstretched hand. "Follow me."

Before either of them could say a word, Joseph was already disappearing around the nearest corner. Cristiano and Mikko shared a look. He supposed working with the dead made one's social skills a little *rusty*.

Without another word, they followed Joseph. To keep up, the men had to lengthen their strides, their boots squeaking on the floor. It was a small indication the inside was indeed more maintained than the exterior. Mikko sighed in relief.

In comparison, Joseph's shoes made no noise at all, and it unsettled him. There was no need to be quiet among the dead; they didn't care what anyone did anymore.

The sound of a keycard swiping pulled Mikko's attention back. He watched as Joseph opened the door, the hallway continuing beyond with more white, sterile doors lining each side. For a modest building, the corridor continued on for forever.

Maybe that's why Joseph walks so fast.

"Almost there," the mortician said, sensing the other men's thoughts. They passed four more doors, before stopping at the fifth one on the left. A small window was placed in the door, allowing Mikko a sliver of what lay beyond: sterile surfaces and a sheet covering a body.

Ivan.

Another swipe of Joseph's access card and the door opened before the men. The overpowering scent of cleaners and other embalming liquids Mikko had no name for overwhelmed his nose. His eyes watered as the odor burned his nostrils. Although, maybe this scent was better than the alternative—rotting flesh.

Cristiano coughed, the fragrance abrasive on his airways too. "How do you work with this smell?"

Mikko glanced over, catching his friend tucking his nose into the collar of his sweatshirt, desperately trying to avoid the smell. Cristiano's displeasure was evident in the furrowing of his brows. Mikko wanted to chuckle.

"Eh, when you've been doin' this for as long as I have, well, your sense of smell starts to go," Joseph replied. "And when the masks we're supposed to wear are too restricting, you have to improvise."

Cristiano scoffed, the noise muffled beneath his shirt, "Gives a whole new meaning to 'nose blind.'"

"A perk in this line of work, no doubt," Mikko added.

"Indeed." Joseph's lips tipped up at their commentary, pleased he could endure what they could not.

All at once, the men's focus shifted to the white sheet in front of them. Ivan laid beneath it, the edges of the cloth draping over the gurney. Colorless tile below the gurney's wheels caught Mikko's attention since they were well-worn, both by time and scrubbing, but that was not why he stared. Instead, it was the black grout filling in the spaces between the tiles, no doubt stained from the constant exposure to human viscera.

Dead eyes staring back at him across a pool of blood—

"Well, without further ado, let's get right into it," Joseph said, snapping Mikko's thoughts back to the present as his hands clasped together at his beltline. "I don't want to waste your time by over-explaining, and quite frankly, I like to let the bodies do the talking"—he nodded to Ivan—"since they're easier to understand."

While he wasn't wrong, Joseph's words made Mikko's skin prickle with apprehension.

Taking Cristiano and Mikko's silence as his cue to continue, Joseph gripped the edge of the sheet before peeling it back to reveal Ivan's pale face. Even though he'd seen his fair share of deceased people, it never dulled the shock. But amongst the surprise he felt, Mikko's observant gaze caught on the fleshy hole in his forehead. Bruises littered his now gray toned face, evidence that the wounds had been exacted right before his death. Everything Mikko's men had inflicted nearly a month ago had healed. Only smaller scars remained from that exchange.

Yet a larger clue had his stomach dropping.

Where Ivan's eyes should've been were gaping holes. Cristiano hadn't been exaggerating when he said Ivan had been mutilated.

"It appears whoever plucked his eyes out, waited until he was dead," Joseph said, answering the unspoken question cloaking the entire room. "As for his fatal wounds, he was shot once in the head and twice in the chest, though I am unsure of which was the killing blow." Joseph hovered his hand right above the sheet where Mikko presumed those other two holes were located.

"I'm not sure if that's reassuring to know," Cristiano spoke up.

Dropping his hand, the mortician continued, "If I was in his shoes, I'd prefer to be dead before someone started dismantling my body."

"Good to know." Mikko's voice was quieter, contemplative.

Death was common, everyone knew that, but something about this was eerie. His mind searched for the reason, determined to prove that he was not growing weak as he aged. Other aspects of his life may be unraveling, but not this one—

Suddenly, he knew why.

Ivan was clean, devoid of blood, and lacking the grime usually coating the bodies Mikko interacted with. This, the pristine condition of Ivan's body minus the deathblows, made the experience more grotesque.

And Mikko hated it. Death was harder for his brain to process when it lacked violence. A cause. When that was all he'd known growing up, the absence of it was jarring. Joseph glanced at Mikko from the corner of his eye as he swallowed audibly. Mikko waited for the mortician to go on.

"I apologize for my crudeness, but in this field it's pertinent to look at the positives."

Mikko nodded, his mind wandering to another time—to another death that had rocked his world.

His mom.

"With a little makeup, he'll look good as new," Joseph added.

"I have no doubt." Mikko said as his hand accidentally brushed against the icy gurney making his jaw clench. *Again,* he was unwillingly transported back in time to his mom's body laying carefully within a casket. She'd been devoid of life and blood and violence even though cancer had ravaged her body. He recalled how *her* skin had been cold under his touch, and the makeup someone had slathered onto her face looked terrible.

She would've hated that, was all his younger self had thought about then.

"—victim's autopsy went well," Joseph's voice faded back in and Mikko worked to unclench his jaw. "Everything seemed conducive with him being shot three times; a robbery gone wrong perhaps since his body was found in an abandoned warehouse in the industrial district along the river. It's a well traveled thoroughfare that has new people coming and going every day." He cleared his throat before continuing, "That is, if I overlooked his eyes being removed, and when I looked deeper, excuse the pun, I determined nothing about his death was normal.

"I determined that his eyes had been removed post-mortem, an act that would take time and most likely was done to send a message. They might've even been kept as a trophy by the killer since the victim's eyes still haven't been located. A typical robbery wouldn't entail this level of detail—of blatant malice."

"I agree," Mikko said.

"Good. Do you know of anyone who might've been involved with Mr. Morovich? Anyone he owed money to, secrets, revenge? Who would've wanted to get back at him in this way?"

Mikko and Cristiano shared a look before the former spoke. "In our line of work, that list of people is far longer than would be helpful, unfortunately"

"Still, it's a place to start. Nevertheless, after I noted his injuries there, I examined a fairly clean incision starting right above his belly button and ending a few inches below his Xiphoid process." Joseph donned a disposable glove and traced where the cut would be on Ivan's torso over the sheet.

"Once I reopened the *hastily* sutured wound, I came across something abnormal."

"More than his eyes being gone and the large cut on his stomach?" Cristiano countered, untucking his chin from his shirt to speak before retracting back inside the fabric again.

Joseph's fluffy white eyebrow raised. "You tell me." The mortician reached over Ivan's unveiled face and produced a bag from a cart sitting there, keys evident in the bottom corner. "I found car keys planted in the victim's torso."

Dread swelled in Mikko's gut as he looked from Ivan's motionless body to Joseph.

"They're *yours*, I hear," the older man continued.

Silence stretched taut between them.

Mikko crept closer, the plastic's glare making it hard to discern the keys inside completely. But Mikko didn't have to see them, he already knew.

And once the glare was gone...

Mikko's jaw clamped down.

Sure enough, there inside the bag was a set of Audi car keys. The small golden locket containing a photo of him and his mother inside glinted in the lights like a taunt. At least now he knew where they went, and why they'd been stolen from his penthouse in the first place. And he knew who'd done it...now he had to corner her and prove it.

"Do you know why your keys would be *inside* the victim's body?" Joseph asked. His insinuation wasn't lost on Mikko, his own deductions pointing at him too if he'd been in an outsider's shoes witnessing this.

But, for once, Mikko hadn't committed this atrocity.

"If I did, do you think I'd be standing here letting you interrogate me like a second class citizen?" Mikko asked coldly.

The idea of someone toying with him was driving him up the wall, all while Joseph thought he knew everything because the bodies he dissected "told stories."

Undeterred by Mikko's unfriendly response, Joseph continued. "Can't blame me for askin' though, can you?"

Mikko shook his head.

"The police were also curious, but once they discovered the keys were yours, their motivation disappeared..." Not surprising since more than half of the police force were in his pockets, doing his bidding on the side. Joseph let his words, a terribly veiled threat, hang in the air while he pulled the sheet back up over Ivan's face.

Pivoting to face a line of casework along one wall in the room, Joseph placed the bag containing Mikko's Audi keys into a bin inside one of the many drawers. Stepping back, Joseph locked it before letting the key slip back amongst the others at his waist. The cheerful jingle was at odds with everything else surrounding the men.

Joseph's suspicion wasn't misdirected, Mikko understood that, but it still irked him. "If it helps at all, I'm just as perplexed as to why my keys ended up in his body," Mikko said.

"I want to believe you," Joseph responded, but he still sounded apprehensive.

Cristiano piped up. "Did this incision also occur after he died?"

"I believe so. There was little blood or bruising marring the stitches which means Ivan's heart wasn't pumping anymore. Regardless, it was a decently precise cut like the person knew what they were doing and had either sedated the victim or restrained them while performing the act."

Mikko interjected. "Or had they already killed them?"

Joseph nodded solemnly. "Perhaps, it's someone in your line of work?"

The insinuation made Mikko's gut clench, a small wave of frustration curling around his heart. "While our line of work deals with death and blood just as much as yours does, we don't deal in precision. It's cutthroat, efficiency over cleanliness. Now, your field...that's a place we could start." Mikko knew his emotions were getting the best of him, but the words slipped off his tongue before he could stop them.

He was tired of feeling out of control, but that seemed to be the only sense of structure he had left anymore—continuously grasping at the grains of sand slipping through his fingertips.

Mikko needed to find out why Anika was framing him. And *fast*.

22

Death Waits for No One

Mikko - 22 Years Ago

Small, bright sprigs of grass poked through the dirt, defying the fickle embrace of spring. Despite the temperatures remaining frigid, the seeds had managed to take root, springing up through the soil in a blatant retaliation.

Their perseverance was something Mikko envied.

Remnants of dried flower bouquets littered the ground, hiding the rest of the earth he knew was underneath. They blanketed his mom, or what was left of her.

Cold wind brushed across his tear-soaked cheeks as more threatened to spill from the corners of his eyes. He wasn't sure how there was any left given how his body was tired of crying—of grieving for someone he'd never see again. But here he stood, eyes distant and wet, lips chapped from his breathy, hiccuping gasps.

If his father caught him like this again, weeping in public, he'd be punished, but Mikko couldn't find it in himself to care. Maybe the pain of his father's discipline would erase the current agony lingering in his heart. Either way, he had to get it out or he'd implode. Besides, how *was* he supposed to react to visiting his mom's freshly covered grave? She felt so far away, swallowed up by the earth, forced to return back to the ground she came from. And while Mikko knew her soul wasn't here anymore, he still felt *uncomfortable* that she was in the ground.

All alone without her colorful paints to keep her company.

If the roles were reversed, he'd want someone to comfort him and stay nearby even in death. If only for a little while.

Hushed voices spoke rapidly in Russian behind Mikko, one of them being his father, "We'll need to tighten up our forces. They'll expect weakness from me during these times, but we must show them this doesn't impact us."

"Of course, sir. We will make sure things continue to run smoothly," another man replied—one of his father's grunt workers. Mikko couldn't remember his name, uncaring for the formalities. Small talk bored him, especially now since his mom wasn't even around to tease him for his introverted tendencies.

Another droplet threatened to slip past the rim of his spiky lashes. Mikko wanted nothing more than to vanish into the darkness of his room, the ache that came with social interactions in the wake of the worst event of his young life was too much to bear.

"Good, and he will need to be monitored," his father continued, surely nodding to Mikko's hunched frame. "His mother was every-thing to him, and he's always been emotional"—Mikko's little jaw clenched—"but he knows these tantrums are not to be tolerated."

"Yes, sir. You know where to find me if you need anything else," the other man promised. A shuffle and mumbled goodbyes were muttered while Mikko took the brunt of the wind, some of it erasing the words spoken. When it died down, another man was talking with his father.

Despite the supposed time of grieving, people continued to bombard them—pestering them with questions despite the freshly overturned soil at Mikko's feet. No one cared that his mom was dead, that they hadn't been given the adequate amount of time to grieve. Instead, everyone was rushing forward, planning and scheming, making sure things were in alignment so Alek could continue his reign without interruption. The rest of the world was content to move on with or without Mikko.

Had mom known her husband would turn into this ruthless man after her death? Mikko internally questioned.

It was hard to imagine the softness of his mom paired with the brutal edges his father boasted. Although, he hadn't always exuded such tenacity. Over the years, that sinister darkness had intertwined itself with his father's very being until it seeped out, overtaking everything in its path. Mikko feared the death of his mom would exacerbate that.

The new man brought conversations about "personal belongings" and "consolidating assets" all of which made the young boy's stomach turn. Maybe this was how death always was, sterile and transactional, but he disliked it nonetheless. His mother was more than that, more than the items she left behind. Mikko hoped his father wouldn't sell off the small collection of paintings she'd created over the years. He vowed to hide them as soon as they got home.

Stooping down, eager to distract himself, Mikko touched the semi-dried flowers fluttering in the breeze. There was no headstone for his mom's final resting place yet—a matter he'd heard his father threatening another man over—but the abundance of flowers warmed what was left of Mikko's heart. She was cared for in his mind, sheltered by beauty for a little while longer. It was how she would've wanted it.

The only difference was the color of the petals; the hues had bled away, leached out from the harsh rays of the sun, leaving only brittle, withered remains behind.

Just like his mom.

In the end, all that had remained of her was a small, fragile piece of her former self. She used to shine brighter than everyone in the room, a silent but radiant figure. She was someone Mikko would cling to and search for when he went anywhere.

And now, that light was gone, snuffed out by cancer.

Mikko couldn't recall much of those last days, but the memories of her gaunt face, bony hands, and blurred moments in between stuck with him. There were many nights he'd spent asleep in the back of his father's car as they traveled from the hospital back to their house, falling into an uncomfortable and restless slumber.

But more times than not, he pretended to be asleep so Alek would speak more freely around him during his late night phone calls. It was in those moments he learned more than an eleven year old boy should've.

In some ways, these thoughts were too much, memories Mikko wished he could forget. But forgetting wasn't an option, it was a privilege.

More tears pricked at his eyes, but a rustling behind him made him inhale and force the feeling down. He waited for his father to speak.

"Say goodbye," Alek spoke, accent thick since he'd been speaking in Russian for the past ten minutes, "we have other places to go."

Nodding, Mikko hoped the evidence of his crying had vanished. One might've thought this death would bring the father and son closer, but the opposite could be said for the two of them. Alek's wife and Mikko's mom was the glue holding them together—the light they both basked in—and now she was gone.

And so were their formalities.

Alek thought Mikko soft, had said as much to his men, and had already begun to push him into the family business despite Mikko's hatred of it.

I won't succumb, Mikko thought, *I won't let him force me into something I don't want.*

But he couldn't have been more wrong.

The anger that had festered beneath the surface of his father's skin began to bubble up until it spilled out and onto Mikko. It was a contagion that quickly ate away at whatever stood in its way, devouring someone from the inside out.

Soon, the warmth of his mom was replaced with the blaze of rage, and despite longing to be better, to *do* better, Mikko failed. He discovered the universe could be as cruel as it was rewarding, and cruelty bred a whole new kind of monster within people.

Alek was the perfect example.

Too bad he'd lose everything dear to him in the process.

II

Unraveling

23

Framed Views

Mikko

Mikko couldn't bring himself to believe in coincidences. The break in, Anika targeting him, and leaving the menacing yet intriguing note. A blatant murder in a warehouse she'd toured mere days earlier. And now this—his missing car keys turning up in a dead man's body.

It was all becoming a little too sinister.

Even if murder wasn't a part of her strategic plans, Mikko was certain she was behind some of those occurrences. And he'd be damned not to get her to confess to some of it.

Seems like I may need to pay someone a little visit, he thought darkly.

Glancing down at his phone, he eagerly awaited a text back from Levi, but nothing. Jealousy made him grip his fork tighter. Being ignored wasn't his strong suit.

His most recent message glared up at him.

*Any updates? :**Mikko***

Annoyed, he typed out a follow up message.

*I'll take that as a no :**Mikko***

As he was about to call the man, three little dots popped up. Finally.

Levi: *Nothing concrete yet*

Levi: *Also, since when do you double text?*

Mikko rolled his eyes.

*Keep it professional :**Mikko***

Levi: *Always boss...although I might have to bend that rule a little*

Something flared in his gut at that little blue message.

*With the murder at that property, we need to tread carefully; bend but don't break :**Mikko***

Levi: *Of course, but I have to make this believable, wear her down*

A tick in Mikko's jaw showed his annoyance. Cristiano—who was sitting across the table from him—noticed it. "Who are you texting?"

"A certain blond mutt," Mikko quipped. "Why?"

Cristiano laughed before saying, "Let's just say, I wouldn't want to be your phone right about now."

Mikko turned his glare onto his friend. "If only this person could read the room as well as you."

"Let's be honest, all of our lives would be easier if they could do that." Cristiano chuckled. "Do I even want to know what they're saying?"

"No."

"Of course. But I also think you're getting into a habit—a bad one might I mention—of keeping things from me."

"I'm not doing that."

"But it makes sense since your kink *is* being lonely n' all."

"That's not even real–I don't have—"

"Ah, ah, ah, never say never. You'd be surprised what's out there." Mikko huffed tiredly into his shot glass as his friend continued. "Besides, I've known you for too long not to know something is bothering you."

Another eye roll only encouraged Cristiano's behavior. "At least tell me you're texting other people...ones who *aren't* work related, "Cristiano quickly added. "Perhaps a single lady? Are you finally tryin' out dating apps like I told you too? That would explain the look of disdain that's always on your face," his friend rambled on while Mikko locked his phone and put it away, done commanding Levi for now.

"Hell, I wouldn't even care if you were chattin' it up with a man," Cristiano continued.

Pinching the bridge of his nose, Mikko didn't say anything for a moment as Cristiano trailed off.

Then, "While I appreciate your *fervor,* no, I'm not talking to a woman."

"So it's a man then?"

"Yes, but not like that. You know men aren't my preference."

"Speak for yourself, although this Ivan conspiracy is taking up precious time in my personal life. Even *I* can't get any di—"

Their waiter returned then, preventing the men from saying anything more. The man refilled their waters and took note of their dwindling alcoholic beverages before promising to return with more.

The brisk silence gave Mikko time to collect his thoughts, mind wandering to the images and news on a repeated loop in his head. Both men had decided dinner might soothe their worries, a routine they'd formed long ago. Each week, either Mikko or Cristiano, would pick a restaurant and they'd spend the whole evening eating and drinking. It was a good time to catch up and blow off some steam from the week.

God knew they needed it now.

After the waiter was gone, Cristiano continued. "Anyway, let's hope my stomach has calmed down when the food finally comes out. I've been cravin' a steak for a while now."

"You had one last week when we went out." Mikko's finger tapped the edge of his glass.

"I know"—he took a sip of his wine—"but that's too much time in between for my liking. But that's besides the point. Ivan. We got together to talk about Ivan. What the fuck is going on with all this?"

Mikko wished he had more vodka to sip on, anything to take the edge out of his voice. "You know the DNA sample I got back on the gum?" Cristiano nodded, his neon hair now faded to a light sea green. "Well, I think it's time I told you about that lead."

"I'm afraid to talk right now lest you stop, so go on..." his friend murmured.

Mikko continued on, unphased. "The profile is for a woman named Anika Simmons."

"The same Anika whose name you let slip out the other day? The one you told me wasn't a crush?" Cristiano asked.

"Yes, that's the one."

"So she *is* a crush, then?"

"No, no that's not the point of this." Cris made a face that said he didn't really believe Mikko's words, but he'd keep listening. "The point is she's the same one who approached me at *Bubblegum* and the same woman who toured the warehouse…"

"The same one Ivan ended up dead in," Cristiano finished. "Do you think she's behind it? Levi could also be a suspect. He's the one who knows the lockbox code and has motives."

"His motive is just misdirected envy and self-loathing. Everyone knows he wants my position one day—thinks I'm not good enough for it—therefore, he'd be dumb to start doing something like this." Mikko explained as he continued tapping the rim of his shot glass.

Cristiano snorted humorlessly. "Exactly, he *is* dumb. Have you forgotten?"

"No, he makes it hard to forget, but Anika could have a motive too."

"And what would hers be?"

"That's what I'm trying to figure out. I've searched her name in our databases and nothing pops up. She's never been related to our business, the mob, or any clients we've dealt with. At least on paper.

"I've followed her and searched through her house. There was and is nothing to be found to connect her to all of this outside of a gut feeling and coincidences," Mikko finished.

"Alek was never one for believing in those," Cristiano mumbled. "Wait, she approached you at *Bubblegum*? Where the fuck was I?"

Mikko sighed. "It was the night we interrogated Ivan, but you'd wandered off and she cornered me."

His friend looked him up and down. "You're hardly someone who's easy to corner. You think she's hot, don't you?"

A pause. Then, "No."

"Liar," Cristiano smacked the table. "Of course the one time I'm not by your side, you get hit on by a woman."

"Maybe it's actually *you* who's scaring them off." Mikko's tone was teasing.

"You better let me meet her, I need to know who cracked Mr.

Romanov's steely facade. I bet she could melt you in—"

"Anyway," Mikko interrupted, "the signs are pointing to her. While our men usually favor brute force—a moment to teach a lesson—this is more calculated."

Cristiano's brow raised, signally he'd let the subject change slide this time, but he'd be pressing about Anika later no doubt. "You know I stand with you no matter what. At first, I thought it was Ivan's lifestyle and debt catching up to him. I mean, it was only a matter of time. That man could hardly keep food on the table for his family." His dark eyes flicked up toward the sleek ceiling in contemplation. The soft, ambient lighting in the restaurant colored Cristiano's deep brown skin in warmth. "If not Anika, then maybe it was his wife?"

"Would his wife be able to break into my penthouse, steal the keys found in Ivan's body, and edit out her entire presence being there?"

Cristiano's eyes met Mikko's. "A scorned woman is capable of anything."

Mikko's voice was low. "Exactly, and until I know what Anika's angle is, she could be that scorned woman."

"True. Anger mixed with passion and revenge would be enough fuel for anyone to cut someone up, let alone go for the eyes; if it was money she was after, eyes do sell for a fair amount on the black market."

"Whoever it was, they knew how to make a statement. There's got to be a connection between his mutilation and making someone 'see' something." Mikko mused. Something he hadn't thought of popped into his head while talking to Cristiano. Maybe Anika's motive *did* have something to do with Romanov Real Estate, and she was trying to show him.

His friend piped up as the waiter returned with their replenished drinks, "Now there's a twisted thought." A couple seconds passed and Cristiano spoke again. "Do you think she has them in a jar somewhere?"

With a snort, Mikko could only shake his head and sip his vodka while his friend speculated about Anika's alleged science experiments.

* * *

THE REST OF dinner with Cristiano had been uneventful, his friend making him promise to not do anything stupid while he was alone when it came to Anika. She was unpredictable with a background they had no record of.

But Mikko was feeling restless. If she killed Ivan, that type of violence and precision would indicate it wasn't her first time. She should be in the system for something: petty crimes which could escalate to torture and murder. Still, every time he searched her name, nothing appeared. She was squeaky clean in every way. Although paper had a tendency of lying, and Mikko feared this was the case.

He might have to call in another favor...

Dialing Devon, Mikko waited for him to answer. He was still parked outside of the restaurant, sitting in his idling car where the valet had left it for him. The sky darkened overhead with the promise of another storm, but for now, it held off.

"Long time, no see, Mikko," the man finally responded. "What can I do for ya?"

"I know you're busy with Ivan's murder, but I have a favor to call in. I may have a lead and need someone with a bit more tech skills to chase it down," Mikko said.

"I know of someone."

"Are they trustworthy?"

Devon scoffed. "They have to be to work with me."

"Good point. How fast do they work?" Mikko checked his side

mirror before pulling out into the streets. It was getting late and most were heading home in preparation for the workday tomorrow. Mikko had other plans.

"*She* works pretty fast, but a larger payment upfront could mean same day return on info," Devon responded before a door closed softly in the background. "Up to you."

Mikko's brow rose. "Can she get me something in two business days?"

"Of course. I'll send you her bank information and you can wire the amount over."

Mikko shifted lanes, his muscle memory taking him across town. "How much will it be?"

"I don't know, she doesn't post her prices up, just tells you what she wants." The man on the other end typed something out, his keyboard clacking faintly. "But whatever you do, *don't* question her. She's great at what she does and doesn't like to continuously prove it."

"Got it." His phone buzzed with a notification.

"Tell her I sent you."

"Will she cut me a better deal?'

Devon laughed. "No, but she won't immediately turn you away."

"Great," Mikko drawled before hanging up.

And there, in the text message Devon had sent him, was a name that felt a little *too* familiar.

Rebecca Graymore.

A woman he'd taken home for one night years ago when he thought the world revolved around him until he'd woken up to his valuables stolen and a message in lipstick on his bathroom mirror reading: *thanks for the good fuck...and the $$$.*

Needless to say he never saw her again—or his missing items—but now it made sense for her to be in this line of work. She had a knack for finding things. He shook his head with an exasperated laugh; the world really was too damn small for his tastes anymore.

* * *

AFTER REACHING OUT to Rebecca and sending her all the necessary information—he bet with Cristiano on if she'd remember him or his name—Mikko found himself driving along the highway. He should've gone home, but he couldn't bring himself to do it. Instead, he let the road pacify his spiraling thoughts. Highway sign after highway sign flashed in front of him, briefly illuminated in his headlights, before fading back into the night. He wasn't sure how long he drove for, but it didn't matter. Driving always quieted his mind.

Until he realized where he'd subconsciously driven to. Anika's neighborhood.

The tree-lined street welcomed him, the changing of the leaves yawning before his car as he parked nearby out of habit. Maybe he'd known all this time that this was where he wanted to go, that this was where he'd end up. While he waited for Rebecca to dig up details about Anika's life, he might as well keep eyes on her himself.

Shutting his car off, he slipped from the leather interior, his movements nearly silent from practice. Leaves barely crunched underfoot as he wove around the clusters of them with ease. Mikko pulled his jacket closer as the wind tried to needle into his skin. These days, as soon as night fell in Portland, the temperature dropped with it.

Making the walk up her sidewalk, he leapt over the short fence before slinking into the shadowed vegetation lining her house. The scent of soil and foliage was a fragrance Mikko could get used to, and even though it was wrong to still be drawn to her, it reminded him of Anika. Everything she stood for had his heart racing, his obsessive habits satiated as he watched her, learned her, and became someone she might like.

If an outsider asked, it was all in the name of Romanov Real Estate. But to him, it was more than that.

Maybe she can be my ticket out of here.

To his delight, a couple of her windows were aglow, flooding the dark lawn around her house. It enticed him like the promise of a warm fire after enduring the cold for hours. Mikko couldn't help but imagine the heat from her skin, and could practically smell the lush, sugary notes that were wholly her. Striding closer, he peered in all while risking his pale face reflecting in the illuminance. He was curious, even if it was a bad idea.

A glass of wine was clutched in her hands, fingernails glinting in the light with her legs crossed and looking across the room at something. Her hair was pulled up and away from her face messily, pieces of it still hanging free and tickling her cheeks, neck, and exposed back. Anika's tank top was loose and casual, a sight that made his stomach tighten. The palm frond tattoos along her shoulder blades were on display as she sat sideways on her couch along with the floral pieces wrapping around each arm.

Mikko audibly swallowed.

The one on her spine was barely visible, only the first few words peeking out. Stepping out of sight, he quickly searched them up: *Dulce int...sweet something.*

It wasn't enough to yield anything useful. With a sigh, he put his phone away and glanced around to make sure he was still alone. Only the chirp of crickets and the flutter of moth wings faintly echoed back to him. He let out a sigh.

But when his gaze landed back on Anika, he realized what she'd been looking at moments before. Or more so *who*.

Levi strode across her living room, a matching glass of wine in his own hand, his mouth moving all while Anika listened. Even now, that man couldn't shut up. Mikko's fist clenched inside his coat pocket involuntarily.

Watching as the man plopped down on Anika's couch like he lived there, Mikko let unrestrained anger bubble up in the back of his throat. He'd ask Levi to keep an eye on Anika, not cozy up next to her in her own damn house.

This must be what Levi meant when he said he'd have to bend some rules...

A tired sigh whispered past his lips. It seemed the instructions hadn't been clear enough for his dimwitted employee. If he wanted something done right, he'd have to do it himself. Let these escapades only serve as a distraction for Anika, but when she met Mikko again, he'd be demanding her compliance.

With clenched teeth, he resorted to watching every little touch and interaction and laugh Anika and Levi shared. He should've gone home; he should've seen if Rebecca had any updates on Anika and her seemingly hidden past that would shed some light on a murder that *should* be front and center in Mikko's head, but instead...

His feet were rooted to the soil as if he was another one of Anika's plants—another one of her playthings she controlled. It was sickening and fascinating. When he was the one that always had to make the calls, have the hard conversations, and discipline people, it felt nice to let someone else do it for a while.

A devious thought crossed his mind.

If Anika *was* the one behind Ivan's murder, she had skills and talent he could use for himself—the company. It was a weak excuse to his brain, but maybe he could convince her and others of it. That way he could really keep an eye on her.

Among other things...

Movement out of the corner of his eye pulled him back to the present.

Levi had Anika pressed into his side, his arm slung across the back of her couch, fingertips intertwining with loose tendrils of her ebony hair. His wine glass sat abandoned on her coffee table. Levi tucked a stray piece of hair behind her face. The motion had Mikko's shoulders tensing, the exposed slope of her nose and edge of her jaw all places he wanted to explore himself.

With tongue and teeth, sucking and nipping—

Stop. Stop. Stop.

He shouldn't be having these thoughts—these longings afflicting his mind all hours of the day. But that was what happened when he let himself go, when the curiosity he was so fond of morphed into unchecked obsession.

And with his status in the city of Portland, who was there to stop him?

What had originally begun as a quest for protection and vengeance had turned into *this.* He'd been sucked into her orbit, strung along while he watched everyone else engage with her the way he wanted to.

He wanted to get to know her.

He yearned to touch her hair like Levi had, wrapping the strands around his fist.

He longed to know more about the mind she kept sheltered behind honeyed eyes and a soft, knowing smile.

But instead, he was *here,* swallowed up in the surrounding darkness.

He'd told himself this would be enough—seeing her from afar, collecting pieces of her to use for examination and motive—but he was realizing that wasn't true. He needed to be closer, his stomach in knots as he loitered outside her house.

"And that's how mistakes are made, son. When emotions guide you,

you'll always be led astray." Mikko shook his head, trying desperately to clear his father's incessant voice echoing there. His father was dead. He wasn't like Alek.

With a fist pressed into the wood siding of her house, Mikko watched as Levi took her empty wine glass and set it on a coffee table next to his. A lilting laugh from Anika had his eyes zeroing in on her, cataloging what could've elicited that reaction from her so he could do it himself. Levi's lips were pressed against her neck, the soft kisses tickling her sensitive skin.

Despite the envy flowing through his veins, Mikko's cock hardened with the promise of seeing her get off. The sheer curtains were pushed aside letting just anyone look in, so he wasn't really in the wrong. Was he?

Alek always made sure to know his enemy before swooping in for the kill. Those skills had damn near been bred into Mikko, so he would use them to his advantage now. Being a voyeur never hurt anyone...right?

Suddenly, he remembered the words she'd texted him a couple nights ago: *that's exactly something a cuck would say.*

Guess she was right about that.

Her tanned skin glowed in the lamplight, making his mouth water as he palmed his erection through his pants.

Curse this carnal hunger.

The thin panes of glass did little to disguise the sounds of Anika's breathless gasps and Levi's hums of satisfaction as their playful moment turned more intense. The soft sweep of Anika's hair falling out of its bun at Levi's deft hands and the sight of his mouth on hers happened right before he pushed her back onto her couch. The slope of Levi's back was strong while he held himself over Anika. Her dark hair was splayed out around her face. The contours and shadows from the nearby lamps accentuated her figure, and her ragged breaths made Mikko's own chest ache. Levi was kissing his way up Anika's stomach, taking his time, her back arching into his mouth.

Blood rushed in Mikko's ears, the outside world fading away until it was the three of them. This was wrong. Irrational. Everything about this was unreasonable, but logic did nothing to quell whatever was simmering inside his rib cage. And behind his pant's zipper.

Levi knelt between her bent legs, her leggings revealing the soft curve of her thigh. Fingertips brushed against heated skin and Mikko could only observe as Levi caressed her, evoking sounds of approval.

A growl built in Mikko's throat.

He wanted to sink his teeth into her flesh, marking her as *his*. No one after him would be able to erase his possession of her.

Caught between the mesmerizing draw of her skin, her noises, and the revulsion he felt, he lost track of time. Agony made a home in his bones, terrorizing his thoughts, voices screaming at him.

The man captured her lips with his own once again, his own sounds of satisfaction mixing with hers as she writhed beneath him. Mikko hoped Anika wasn't enjoying herself as much as she let on, that she was just following through with the motions.

Still, Mikko felt something snap when he thought about Anika and Levi being more than what they were right now—a fake set-up.

This obsession was out of control, and there was only one way to get it back. To rid himself of this disease.

With one last glance up at her window, he drank in the scene. Her manicured nails dug into the leather of her couch, surely leaving little crescent marks on the material. He wanted her to leave similar ones on his furniture. On his back, clawing until he bled for her.

The image of her scarf tossed across his car's passenger seat had thoughts brewing inside his head. He'd brought it with him for some odd reason, call it intuition, but now he was glad he had. While he might not be able to have her right now, he *did* have something of hers that might take the edge off. For a moment.

With her silhouette burned into his mind, Mikko stalked back toward his Audi. His cock was hard, he was frustrated, and his mind was filled with sounds and perfect pictures of her to get him off. He could edit Levi out of his head easy enough for his own fantasies.

His car door thudded shut behind him. The inky depths from his tinted windows cloaked the motion of his hand straying over to Anika's scarf, his fingers wrapping around the soft fibers.

More, more, more, a small voice whispered internally.

No one was there to see him bring it to his face, inhaling the fragrance still clinging to the fabric. A groan reverberated from his throat as his other hand drifted down to his zipper, his cock hard and aching. He hadn't realized how much energy it'd taken to deny himself something so human, so *primal.*

One little touch, one little moment of weakness...

Hastily, he opened the glove box and rummaged through the items there until his hands landed on the ones he wanted: her Chapstick and lotion he'd taken while inside her house. Smearing the cherry flavored moisturizer over his lips he imagined it was her own kissing him.

He was fucking losing his grip on reality.

Hopefully, stroking himself to the thought of her might erase the ironclad grip she had on his mind. At least that was what he told himself as his hand enveloped the hard and hot length of himself, the lotion smelling like Anika slickening his cock. Knowing that she was a stone's throw away made him delirious. It was sick, *he* was sick, but the temptation was too great to ignore. Mikko deserved this small reprieve.

And with her scent stuffed into his nose and his hand—one he imagined was hers—on his cock, he teased himself into oblivion.

24

Target Practice

Anika

Viridescent eyes dappled with sunlight formed in her mind as a weightlessness swathed around her. Her brain desperately sent signals to the rest of her body, but her muscles were unable to execute. With her senses slowed and deadened, her extremities felt like they were encased in thick honey. Tingles raced down her arms, fingertips twitching in anticipation yet...

Nothing.

She was trapped within her mind—a nightmare.

A darkened room with a single bulb above them filtered into focus. Her body was still immobile, frozen in time as Mikko's face materialized. The brutal planes of his face were at odds with the emotion she *swore* she could see glimmering in his emerald eyes.

Do it. Do it. Do it.

Her arms were outstretched, feet planted while clammy palms gripped the knurling of a cool gun. Its barrel was firmly pointed at him, this moment forever cemented in time as neither of them moved.

He didn't shake. Her hands didn't tremble.

It was always like this; Mikko standing vulnerable before her in her mind just like she wanted. Just as she'd always imagined. But when it came time to pull the trigger, the gun heavy in her hand, she couldn't do it.

Why?

She hated not being in control of her own actions—her own body betraying her.

And, in turn, disappointing her family.

WAKING WITH A start, her heart thudded against her ribcage with enough fervor that it was a miracle she hadn't jolted awake sooner. But now that her eyelids had cracked open, sleep evaded her; the warm embrace of her bed was suddenly too hot and stuffy. The blankets wrapped around her legs as sweat collected on her skin and made the feel of her satin sheets unbearable. The city lights still felt too bright even though they were dimmed from the foliage surrounding her house. And her thoughts were too loud.

In reality, she should be calm, settling into her schemes. Everything was falling into place, her diligence of collecting information on Mikko Romanov to use it against him later was coming together. Anika had her house, health, and job—a piece of stability soothing her mind when she felt she was losing everything to avenge her family. At least at the end of the day, she could still support her mom if needed.

The only wild card was Levi.

After he'd left the night before, she'd promptly thrown her clothes in the washer, scrubbed her skin raw under the scalding stream of water in her shower, and brushed her teeth more times than she could count. Even after all that, she still didn't feel entirely clean. It hadn't gone farther than making out on her couch, but it still tainted her body and her house.

His borderline harassment that he cloaked in faux chivalrous gestures had ramped up after their dinner date. While that might work on some people, Anika saw through Levi's bullshit immediately. While he fueled her ego, Anika wasn't dull; despite their differences, Mikko and Levi worked closely together, Romanov Real Estate bringing together the worst of the worst, apparently. In reality, all of this was for Mikko.

Then there were Levi's ways of showing up when she least expected it, or when she hadn't given him any clues as to where she would be making her skin prickle with unease. He was Mikko's little puppet, going where he commanded, but Anika wished Mr. Romanov would grow some balls and come to her himself.

Things would be much more fun.

It was all a necessary evil, a way to kill two birds with one stone. Draw Levi in and see what useful information he would divulge about Romanov Real Estate, and in turn its CEO. Mikko had resources to watch her, stalk her, and blackmail her. He'd already begun, exacting tasks he thought she wouldn't notice, but he was daft if he believed he could win that battle. The unknown number texting her was him, the miscellaneous beauty items he'd snatched up, and the missing scarf from her coat rack near the entry door was courtesy of him as well.

Now if only he could get close enough for her to tear apart...

Turning over and kicking off her blankets, Anika's mind wandered even more. Her previous knowledge of Mikko gave her reassurance. While Levi was still a mystery to her, Mikko was *not*. As much as he pretended to be stoic and unreadable, she'd seen the tumultuous waves of emotions in his eyes at *Bubblegum*.

And their multiple interactions after that.

She'd done enough research to write a paper about him.

Not that I'd tell anyone...

Mikko was a rich, real estate developer; eligible bachelor but allegedly refused to date; lover of nice cars and motorcycles; scarce number of friends; and a recluse despite him being his father's successor.

But at night, well, that was when the *real* Mikko emerged. On the surface, he shed the corporate clothing in favor of his motorcycle gear—something he thought protected him both physically and mentally. The night he'd shown up outside her gym resurfaced, a small smile gracing her lips. He thought he was so slick, so intimidating, but Anika only felt contempt toward him.

Let him come close, let him think he has a chance.

But beyond that, the real estate facade faded away, replaced by organized crime—a detail Anika had stumbled across years ago when she'd let her curiosity and repressed hatred loose. It was another piece to her puzzle; this city was one Alek Romanov had cultivated.

The same one that took her dad and injured her mom.

Sweat slicked hands clenched the satin pillow next to her, her anger spiking.

You're not that little girl anymore, she internally coached, *you've got knowledge and weapons at your disposal now.*

Those words did little to calm her racing heart.

Glancing at the clock, Anika determined five in the morning was the perfect time to get up and head to the gun range.

If I can't pull the trigger in my dreams, I better keep practicing.

* * *

BANG! CLANK.

Bang! Clink.

The firearm recoiled against Anika's palms as she stood with her feet firmly planted. Its force was a welcomed reminder that she was in control—that she could do what she needed to when the time came.

Right? Right.

Besides, she'd done months of research, learning the parts of a gun, how to clean and disassemble it, looked into gun safety classes, and now regularly came to the range to fine tune her aim.

Nothing but her own nerves stood in her way.

But even those were dissipating with each "good job" the people at the facility showered her with when she came in with a blank target and left with one riddled with holes.

Removing her finger from the trigger, she carefully set the gun down, content to take a breather. The padded table in front of her was littered with stray shell casings and more ammunition should she need it.

An occasional *bang* echoed in the range, a few other people occupying the lanes around her. Her ear protection prevented the sound from being overly loud. They muffled the world in a way she relished. Right now, it was her and the target in front of—

"I'd hate to be on the other end of you," a familiar voice said from behind her. The decibel was low enough that her ear protection allowed for it to register. Anika's fingers stilled, the tips of them hovering over the bullets she was currently loading into the clip.

Without turning she said, "I usually have the opposite effect."

Mikko chuckled. "Noted."

Finally shifting in the small area, Anika set her things down before turning to look at the man before her. He stood a couple feet away, arms crossed across his chest. If he thought the distance between them would convey he wasn't a threat, he was wrong.

That, or he was wary of her shooting him right then and there. *Tempting...*

He was dressed in casual clothes: dark denim jeans and a black long-sleeved Henley. Despite her dislike for him, the shirt did wonders for his physique, but she made sure not to let her gaze linger, not wanting to give him any more fuel to approach her.

And those eyes, the ones she'd dreamt about, the ones sending her *here* in the first place, were slightly hidden in the shadow of a ball cap slung low on his head. His unruly ebony locks peeked out from under the rim signaling he'd woken up and came straight here. Similar over-the-ear protection sat atop his head, blocking out the harsh gunshots, but allowed for them to talk.

"Are you following me?" she asked abruptly, needing something to distract her.

"No, you just happen to go to the same places I do."

Anika glanced down at the shooting bag near his feet, dropped there as if he owned this lane. He probably did; he had enough money to own anyone or anything in the city if he really wanted. The logo on the bag matched the one of the range which had her brow quirking.

Her teeth clenched momentarily. "I'm afraid I don't believe in coincidences."

"Funny you should say that, neither do I. Although," he glanced around, "we *are* in a public space, Anika. It isn't following if we show up at the same place."

Her brain caught on the use of her name, the invasion of privacy making her spine straighten. She'd never get used to hearing it, especially when she never gave it to him in the first place. But it was a necessary sacrifice. In order to win this game of cat and mouse, she had to invite in his attention. She'd summoned his scrutiny when she'd approached him all those weeks ago, but it still didn't soften the vulnerable feeling curling in the pit of her stomach.

"Is that what you told yourself when you laid in wait for me outside my gym, by my car?"

"I don't know what you're talking about." His grin said otherwise.

"You're a bad liar," she sneered.

"And you're a bad shot," he fired back with a nod to her hanging target behind her.

Anika propped her hands on her hips. "And *you* aren't, pretty boy?" The last words were supposed to be an insult, but as soon as they left her mouth, they felt different.

His brow cocked, noticing it too. "A man can't give up all his secrets now, can he?"

"What about the secrets concerning stolen items," she said, "from inside my house?"

"You really must have the wrong guy, Anika, because I don't know what you're talking about." The smug grin on his face said otherwise and she thought about pistol whipping it off his face. "Sounds like something you should talk to the police about, not me."

"As if you don't pay all their salaries."

His hand landed on his chest in faux hurt, "I work hard to keep this city safe. Is that such a crime?"

"It's not safe enough apparently."

"A few missing items is hardly something to be concerned about, little moon." Anika's jaw clenched at the nickname as he continued. "I never would've guessed you to be someone who accused others so freely, no evidence in sight—"

"And I didn't peg you for an early riser," a glance at the clock caged up on the wall read close to seven in the morning, "I imagined you as more of a sleep in, be lazy and annoying to *all your friends* kinda guy."

"While I'm flattered you even imagined me"—she scowled—"I value my quiet time, usually in the mornings."

"First of all, shooting isn't exactly a quiet sport," Anika muttered,

228

cocking her hip out. "And second, at this exact range?"

"Looks like it."

She refused to believe he had randomly bumped into her. This range was one she'd been coming to for weeks and there'd been no sign of him. Neither of his residences were close to here either.

Why?

She had a feeling she already knew the answer; he was investigating her like she was him.

Anika sighed. She conveyed annoyance, which was partly an act— fuel to make him stay and push—but part of it was real. Covering herself with control and the upper ground was what she did best. This...

This was seceding, giving in to tempt him to come closer. A soft smile was itching to show itself, but she resisted, needing to feign exasperation to spite him. Instead, she decided to push a little bit. "Seems like fate is telling me to ask you to be my teacher then, huh?"

She didn't miss the flicker of surprise in his eyes as they widened slightly before settling back to mischief.

"I'd hate to intrude like that," a lie most likely, "especially since apparently this is *your* gun range," he said to mock her questions from earlier.

"Don't tell me a big wig like you is nervous, Romanov." A taunt.

A vein in his neck twitched at the use of his last name, but he bit at the metaphorical lure regardless. "Charity work hardly makes me nervous."

Heat flared in her chest as she tapped her fingertips on her hip and counted out the seconds she required to reign in her ire.

Mikko noticed.

Before she could change her mind, she stepped aside and gestured for him to come closer.

Bending to retrieve his bag from where he dropped it, she unabashedly watched him. He didn't look like he belonged here, instead, his physique boasted mornings *and* nights at the gym, yet...

"Eyes on the range," he said, catching her stare before moving into her space. "Distractions leave room for mistakes."

"'Distraction' wasn't the word I was think—"

"Bring the target closer," he interrupted with a smile, slipping eye protection on.

Anika pursed her lips, but did as he asked. She pressed the button on the side, a mechanical whirring audible as the large sheet of paper came closer. The automated track had the target fluttering in the wind as it neared her station.

As soon as it was close enough to grab, Anika released the button and let it settle. Mikko's observant eyes combed over the lines of the silhouette, noting the holes she'd riddled it with.

Most were concentrated in the chest, the larger surface area appealing to most since it made it easier to hit the target, especially if they were moving and unpredictable. A few littered around the outline of the head, but too many were scattered outside the thick black outline.

Imperfections. Miscalculations.

"Better than I would've anticipated for an accountant," Mikko quipped before ripping the paper down.

"I'm *not* an accountant, I'm a financial data analyst."

"Right." He drew out the word as if accepting her response for her own benefit. As if there wasn't a difference. Maybe to him there wasn't, but it irked her that he didn't believe her rebuttal.

I should use this twat as a target.

A disgusted huff left Anika's lips as she hung up a new paper target. Once it was securely in the clips, he nodded for her to send it back out. "Put it out at about fifteen yards."

Again, she did as she was told. A rarity Mikko didn't even know he was in the presence of. Once it had settled, she glanced over at him as if to say, *"now what?"*

"Now do what you would do if I wasn't here."

"Why?"

"I want to see your technique."

"And I want you gone." A lie, but she said it anyway.

"Consider this payback for interrupting my night all those weeks ago at the club," he murmured, coming in so close that his mouth was near the outer shell of her ear protection. It was way too hot and way too small in this shooting booth for this. Anika froze.

"I can think of other ways to repay that debt," she retorted, hating the way her voice was breathier than before.

"Oh, really? Like what?" Mikko's hands came up and turned her toward the target out in front of them. They were warm and gentle despite the verbal battle, and she hated that the sensation was one she could get used to. It was reckless and electric compared to Levi's touch. With him, she went through the motions and pushed him out the door at her earliest convenience. But with Mikko, she didn't want it to stop.

Warmth crept up the base of her spine, her skin tingling with his closeness.

"Like filling you with a few rounds of lead," she finally said.

If he responded, she didn't give him any space to.

Picking up her gun, she resumed her shooting position—shoulder width stance, locked elbows, fingers tight around the grip of the firearm yet still clear of the slide, and a fingertip resting on the curve of the trigger.

Bang!

The paper didn't even shiver at the intrusion, the bullet tearing through it with no resistance.

Heat and hard muscle brushed against her back, his distracting hands repositioning her arms. "You're lucky I like threats"—his boots nudged her feet into a better position—"and charity cases." Again with that *fucking* word. "But you're going to have to do better than that to fulfill your promise."

Anika's spine stiffened. She knew he meant the words that he'd spoken, but her mind couldn't help but wander to another promise lingering in her mind; one she'd vowed to herself and her mom all those years ago.

"I don't want to show off," she gritted out.

"Of course, my bad for assuming you *chose* to be a bad shot." His fingertips pressed firmly between her shoulder blades, the pinpointed warmth almost causing her to shiver. "Shoulders back," he instructed. His hand moved down, skating over her ribs until his hand splayed over her stomach. "And don't forget to keep your core tight." He tapped her one, two, three, *four* times until she did as he said.

Each place his hands stopped, Mikko corrected something as if he were rearranging a doll. And the only reason she let him, even as fury and something more sinister lurked beneath the surface of her skin, was because she'd need these skills one day.

"I do better with a *live* target," she muttered, afraid to move and mess up her posture. Anika was certain he'd touch her all over again to make sure she was exactly where she needed to be, and she wasn't sure she could handle that right now.

Mikko snorted, hands finally coming to rest near hers on the gun. "Doubtful."

"Are you going to fess up to stealing my scarf?"

His chuckle reverberated against her back as his finger trailed over the side of her hip. "Are you going to fess up to stealing my car keys?"

Anika's mouth popped open, a motion Mikko clearly saw.

"Oh, now you have nothing to say," he commented. "Funny since those same keys wound up in a dead man's body…"

"While I'm flattered you think I'm smart enough to keep up with your delusions, you're going to have to forgive me when I say I don't know what the fuck you're talking about."

"Playing dumb isn't your thing," he crooned near her temple, mocking the words she'd typed up to him in text a couple nights ago, "but I'll bite. One of my men ended up dead with *my* spare keys inside of his body inside one of *my* warehouses."

"Real estate can be dangerous, sounds like a you problem," she said, burning eyes still focused on the target ahead, her arms growing heavy.

"I'd agree," he readjusted her arms since they'd fallen, "but I find it funny that the warehouse he was found in was the same one you toured."

Bang!

In an attempt to shift the conversation, to gain her own control back, Anika fired off a round. It missed the target completely.

"That was a shit shot, Anika." His hands settled on her hips, turning them so she was square. The heat of his fingers seared through her clothes. "Want to try again? Or should we bring the target closer...say about the same distance as Ivan was to you that night?"

Anika prayed he couldn't hear or feel the rate of her pulse.

"You're absurd. I didn't know touring Romanov properties would get you implemented into crimes," Anika retorted.

"Only when the client lies about the use of the warehouse."

"Are you saying my leather goods business is a lie?"

"I'm saying I didn't see any leather goods in your home when I visited the other night."

A chill shot up her spine, the sensation unbearable. She couldn't stifle it, letting it roll through her body as he chuckled in triumph near her head.

"Does this ruse usually work for you?" she asked, quickly changing the subject.

His body morphed around hers. The nearness of him not only blurred her vision but also the lines of places she didn't want to cross. Especially with Mikko. He was close enough that she could feel his heart steadily beating against her upper back. His height dwarfed her frame, an uncanny feeling considering she was on the taller side.

"What?"

He was too close—

"Teaching women to shoot all while feeling them up? Accusing them?"

Now he really laughed, the sound low and bright amidst the gloom of the range. "Every single one of my touches has been professional and only to enhance your posture." He was incorrect, but as her tongue formulated a scathing response, he spoke again. "Besides, *malyshka,* you'd know the difference between these touches"—his right hand left its resting place at her waist and slowly trailed up over her ribs again before faintly tracing the underside of her breast, making her forget to ask what that accented word meant—"and *these.*"

Higher and higher he went, his fingers deftly grazing over her collar bones. Anika was swept into his spell. Maybe this was how he got everyone to fall into place within his world. Maybe she was just as stupid as all those who came before her.

Fuck.

With his breath tickling the flyaway hairs lingering near her temple, Anika lost her will to focus. The sounds of gunfire and people in neighboring booths faded out, replaced only with the dull thrum of her blood rushing through her ears. Her mouth dried up as he circled her shoulder before his finger slipped between her shoulder blades and traced the divot of her spine once more. It was simple, yet too much.

"Along with these touches," he lilted, his voice deep and wicked.

The faint sweep of his lips across the nape of her neck had warmth pooling between her legs.

I should've fucked someone before this, she internally chided. *Now, I can't tell if I'm horny or...*

Or what? Enjoying herself? Fuck that.

Down, down, down he went until she couldn't tell if this was another cruel dream or reality. Until she realized her brain had free will, she could tell him to stop, and yet...she didn't. In all honesty, she *wanted* him to keep going. It'd been so long since she'd been teased and touched properly.

"I believe you owe me an apology, Anika."

"Do I?" A breathy response, but she hoped both of their ear muffs prevented him from realizing.

His hand hovered between the hem of her shirt and the waistband of her cargo pants, a sinful promise waiting to be accepted. His finger hooked onto her pants. "Mhmm, for saying you'd shoot me."

She audibly swallowed. "I was...joking."

Mikko leisurely traced the outline of her waistband. "Were you?"

Her mouth popped open, *"no"* sitting right there on her tongue when he stopped momentarily. Anika's knees trembled, both from adrenaline and fatigue.

"I think we should play a little game," he said, "and maybe we can say all is forgiven, hm?"

"I hate games," she murmured.

His response came too quick, too close. *"Too bad."* His finger notched up her spine as his mouth softly pressed against her skin above her shirt collar. Goosebumps erupted in his wake. "For every number I say, you shoot. If you get five head shots, we stop. If not, well..."

She'd be forced to go on forever no doubt. Fuck him and his games. "Deal."

"Good girl," he praised, and the throbbing between her legs responded to those two little words. "L 3." It was the only signal she got, but she fired nonetheless.

Bang!

This time, it hit the target, remarkably. It wasn't a head shot, but she could settle into this new norm, make it a routine.

"Close, but not good enough"—he began the ascent on her spine—"Th 11."

Another shot; this one clipped the jaw of the silhouette on the paper. Anika yearned to press her thighs together, to relieve the pressure building in her core, but Mikko's feet ensured her stance didn't waver.

"I'm feeling nice," he said, "I'll count that one." Up, up, up he went. "Th 7."

Anika exhaled, then—

Bang!

She let another round lose, desperately trying to keep still, but her arms were shaking with weariness, and her body was quivering from Mikko's mixed signals.

"There's two, look at you go." His fingers steadily slipped into another divot of her spine, the next vertebrae already falling from his lips. "Th 3."

"I hope you remember this next time you break into my house," Anika gritted out before shooting again. It was another chest shot, her progress taking a step backward while her underwear dampened. He rhythmically tapped on one single vertebrae.

"I will, but I also know where you keep this little gun," he countered. "Th 1."

Barely having enough time for her rebuttal, she chose to shut up and concentrate instead.

Clink!

The shell casing bounced off the floor near her feet, but all she could see was a third head shot. "Impressive. Two more to go. C 7."

Another shot echoed around them. Mikko's fingertip climbed causing her clit to throb in time with his touch.

"C 5." The feeling of his finger resting right below the nape of her neck drove her insane. She squeezed her eyes shut momentarily.

Inhale.

Exhale.

Bang!

A miss. This one didn't even land within the outline, the stray hole a painful outlier amongst the rest of her shots.

"Last chance," Mikko said, his tone unwavering despite the tension rolling off them, thick and suffocating.

"Or what—"

His hand wrapped itself around her ponytail threateningly. "C 2."

I can do this, I can do this, I can do this...

In order for her to find peace, her past would have to be avenged. And to do that, she needed to take down those who she couldn't protect herself and her family from all those years ago.

Her eyes aligned with her gun's sight, leveling it to match up with the center of the target's faux head. The trigger was already crooked against her finger, all she had to do was focus. Squeeze—

Bang!

And there, right in the middle of the head—right where she'd aimed—was a small hole. Never in her life would she have imagined making that, especially with Mikko's presence behind her.

He huffed incredulously before giving her ponytail a slight tug. It sent electricity zipping down her spine. "Seems like distractions work in your favor."

"Don't get any ideas," she responded before lowering the gun. Her arms ached and her shoulders creaked as she tried to shake the tension out. But now that her thighs could touch again, she couldn't ignore the feeling of her jean's seam rubbing just ri—

"Who said I was?"

Shaking her head, she unloaded the clip from the handgun when his hands stilled hers. "We're not done here."

"What do you mean?" Anika glanced up at him over her shoulder. "I did what you asked, your services are no longer needed, *professor.*"

And if I stay here any longer, a morning with my vibrator isn't going to cut it...

His eyes were shadowed from his hat, but they darkened at the nickname. "One good shot doesn't make you a master. Do it again."

"As much as I'd love to, I need to get home so I can shower and go to work. Not everyone can be rich like you and play pretend in an office."

"Take the day off."

She fought the urge to roll her eyes. "Now why would I do that?"

A beat of silence passed between them as he assessed her. "You look tired."

Her heart stopped. "How nice of you to notice, but in reality I'm tired of you, so if you don't mind..."

She went to step around him, but he refused to move.

"Practice makes perfect, *malyshka.*"

Running her tongue over her teeth, Anika composed her thoughts. "I agree, which is why I come here every week. Which is why I don't need *you* to teach me. Now, if you'll excuse me..."

He finally let her move past, his eyes flashing with something she couldn't decipher in the brief moment they shared. It made the arousal pooling in her underwear painfully evident.

I'm so fucked.

She was relieved he finally listened and stepped out of her space. It was getting hard to breathe, and her heart was thudding painfully against her insides.

"I hope you had fun with my lotions at least," she sneered, unable to resist one last dig.

He stiffened, and she swore his face reddened beneath his hat slightly, but, "I'll see you around," was all he said before grabbing his bag and striding away. She watched him set up a few lanes down from her.

Guilty conscience much?

Before she could think any longer on it, she packed up her own things. Work did start in a couple hours and she couldn't be late, weird gun range interactions or not.

Determined not to be cornered by him again, she quickly walked out so she could return the equipment she'd rented. The man behind the counter was smiling while she signed out. "It's not every day the owner of the range gives you a private lesson."

"What?" her brain was already hazy from Mikko.

"Romanov, the man helping you shoot, he owns the range. He usually keeps to himself, coming in early or late, but this is the first time in a while I've seen him practice with someone else."

No shit. "Uh, yeah…well, that was gracious of him."

"Truly, does my old heart good to see him come out of his shell occasionally." The man seemed genuine, his eyes glistening with kindness. Had Mikko paid this man to act? She wouldn't doubt it, but her intuition said differently. Not only did Mikko own this range—because of course he did—but it wasn't often that he was vulnerable here. Why share that moment with her?

Mind games. He *had* to be playing mind games.

"He should do it more often," she started, setting the pen back atop the sign out sheet, "he's a good teacher." It pained her to say it, but it was either that or explain to the older gentleman that Mikko and her were playing a game transcending all normal societal standards.

"I'll let him know you said that."

With a nod, Anika shakily made her way to her car. After the night she'd had, the gun range was supposed to clear her head and affirm her actions, but it looked like the opposite was happening.

In the end, it didn't matter. She'd made promises, had set goals for herself, and she'd be damned if she didn't follow through. One bullet at a time would get her closer to the control she craved no matter how much her subconscious hesitated.

Being useless wasn't an option anymore.

25

Passcodes

Anika

While her aim had gotten better, Anika's feelings toward Mikko hadn't.

Diluted pieces of their interactions haunted her, every waking moment consumed by him. Even though she was emailing consultants and clients, her mind wandered to a week ago when she'd spotted him sulking in the corner of the restaurant she'd chosen for her and Levi's date. Ever since then, that memory had propelled her through all of her bad days and nearly every unbearable moment with Levi.

And then there was the gun range. She could still hear his whispered voice and gruff touch. She'd hoped the orgasms she'd wrung from her body as soon as she'd gotten home that day would've helped. Apparently not.

She'd be lying if she said it didn't do *something* to her stomach. His phantom touches lingered days later, her chest aching. Torn completely in two, Anika admired his ability to claw his way beneath her skin despite her disdain for him, but she also wasn't blind to attraction. He might be an asshole, but her body couldn't help itself. Her mind thought back to his sinful scent of blood mandarin and addictive vetiver and patchouli. His warmth had completely enveloped her in that small shooting booth, erasing every other thought.

Except for the fact he'd accused her of killing one of his men. Those were bold words coming from a man who was known for torture and murder.

And now scarf stealing.

Adrenaline had already lined her veins, the nightmare causing her to head to the range setting her teeth on edge, but then he'd shown up—slipped past her safety mechanisms. It was in her favor regardless, but again, her body wasn't caught up with such schemes. Deep down, she had carnal desires he could sate if she let him, but the thought made her shudder.

No, I cannot go there, especially with him. *Anyone else, sure.*

Her cell phone rang, drawing her back to the present. The name flashing across the screen had her pausing with a look of disdain.

Levi.

Anika debated on if she should answer, but knew she'd agreed to plans with him this evening and answered with a sigh.

"Hey," she said as she resumed typing all while tucking her phone between her shoulder and ear.

"Hey, are you still down to get dinner tonight?" Levi asked, his voice light. He was always in one of two moods: enthusiastic or withdrawn. Tonight was the former. Either way, it didn't matter, he was nothing more than the gum on the bottom of her shoe. A nuisance and a narcissist.

"Of course, where were you thinking again?" She kept her own voice airy and bright, matching his apparent fervor. His insistence on this date had been annoying to say the least, and maybe a *little* bit endearing. Endearing in the way a dog brings its owner a chew toy covered in slobber.

"Well, I know we usually go out, but since you've invited me over to your place," it'd been a tactic she'd used to get him to let his guard down, "I thought you could come by my place?"

"Don't feel like you have to repay me for that," Anika hurried to comfort, her words only surface level, "I only want to do things you're comfortable with—"

"I know, I know, but I want to. I just wanted to make sure I'd cleaned up before you came over." Her eyebrow rose, but he continued. "And I thought we could have a relaxing night in, and I could cook for you."

"Are you a good cook, or am I to have low expectations for this?" Anika teased.

Levi chuckled. "I've been told I make a mean gnocchi soup by quite a few of my guests, so I think you'd be surprised." Who his other guests had been was none of her concern, but she found it weird he'd say it like that, especially if they were to be dating.

What a slimy little man you are, Levi.

"Sounds perfect to me," she replied breezily.

"I'll stop by your office in about"—he paused, most likely glancing at his watch—"thirty minutes."

"See you then."

And as she hung up, a small smile graced her lips. She was positive a certain *someone* would hear about this little date and investigate.

* * *

THE RIDE TO Levi's apartment was an uneventful one, so much so Anika wished she'd turned down his offer to drive. Being by herself meant she could control the atmosphere she resided in, but alas, Levi's constant chatter kept her company instead.

The elevator ride up to his floor was a quick one. Her work clothes felt out of place, a piece of the day following her into the evening. She desperately wanted to take them off, but not in the presence of her current company. Suddenly she was wishing she'd brought something a little more comfortable to change into.

Too late now.

"My soup recipe shouldn't take too long to get prepped and cooked," Levi said as the elevator dinged, stopping at the twelve floor. "Ah, here we are, go ahead," he continued, holding the elevator door back for her.

Stepping out, Anika's eyes traced over the plush carpet lining the hall in either direction. It was dark, a rich charcoal accented by the forest green paint adorning the walls. Soft, warm lighting emanated from sleek wall sconces. Levi swept by her, leading the way to his apartment. She noticed the geometric patterned relief in the wallpaper on the swaths of wall between the pilasters. As much as Levi annoyed her his apartment complex had good taste.

"We're almost there," he assured, mistaking her silence for impatience.

"Oh, no worries. Quite the lovely building you live in," she responded, eyes wandering all while following him deeper into the corridor. "Romanov Real Estate makes sure its employees are taken care of it seems."

Stopping at a glossy ebony door, his apartment number 1235, he unlocked his phone before holding it up to the escutcheon behind the door handle. "I'm glad you think so, but don't tell Mr. Romanov himself"—a faint beep and click of the mechanism inside unlocked—"his ego is big enough." *Didn't she know it.*

Anika smiled, donning her best reassuring face, and he bought it.

"After you."

Stepping inside, Anika's gaze caught on the tall, narrow windows overlooking the city in front of her. While it wasn't a wall of glass like most apartment buildings favored these days, these still allowed for impeccable views. Ornate trim outlined the panes of glass, all painted a monochromatic fresh white.

Her heels *clicked* on the polished as she walked farther inside. A simple kitchen with a wall of deep mahogany cabinets and an island sat to her right and a quaint dining table matching the wood in the kitchen was tucked up against a wall to her left.

A few of the walls had chunks of plaster missing, exposing the brick beneath it—a timeless design choice even though the building was modern.

His couch was leather and stretched out in the room in front of her, the back of it falling below the window sill. A plush rug softened all the other hard surfaces. And two doors, one on each side of the tall windows, stood open. Bedrooms if she had to guess.

"For being a bachelor, your space is quite…"

"Clean?" Levi interrupted, tucking his jacket up onto the coat rack near the door. "Stylish? Homey?"

"Organized is the word that came to mind," Anika chuckled, "but all those work too."

"Here, let me take your cardigan and you can leave your shoes wherever."

Doing as she was told, Anika shed a few articles of her clothing to appease him, and to get more comfortable. Levi strode into his kitchen slinging the refrigerator door open as he collected the necessary items for their dinner.

Curious, Anika walked over to the windows—four in total book-ended with dark curtains—eager to see the view beyond. She also needed a moment to orient herself, and let Levi settle into his cooking routine. She knew when she was in the kitchen, anyone in her way made things a disaster.

Placing her palms on the cool, wooden window sill, Anika looked out. Winking city lights glimmered all around, the surrounding areas in full swing despite the growing nighttime hour. Places like Portland truly never did sleep.

Through the slivers of empty space between the structures before her, Anika thought she could see the shimmer of lights on the river. The tips of the bridges spanning between the two halves of the city were lit up and blinking.

"Care for a drink?" Levi's voice had her turning, honeyed eyes tracing the countertop he stood behind. Atop it were all the ingredients he needed and a bottle of wine.

"How did you know what my favorite wine was?" she asked, slinking closer and letting the curtains flutter semi-closed in her absence. The label of the wine bottle was one she had stocked up in her pantry. "Am I really that easy to read?"

Mikko's doing no doubt.

The cork popped, an awaiting elegant wine glass sparkling in the kitchen pendant lights Anika now noticed. Deep, red liquid sloshed inside as Levi poured, waiting to serve her before offering an answer.

"Just a guess," he replied, pushing the glass closer to her side of the island by the foot.

She picked it up, swirled it, then inhaled. The rich plum scent of it made her mouth water, but he still hadn't answered her question from before. "So, I *am* easy to read."

His eyes were downcast, focused on the sole task of washing and prepping the vegetables he'd bought. "No, no, quite the contrary actually," a small laugh from him had her own lips quirking, "but Malbec happens to somewhat pair with the mushroom gnocchi I'm making."

That, and it was the same thing she'd ordered when they were together at *The Stuffed Pepper*, but Levi had been too self-centered to remember such a detail apparently.

"It does," she perched herself on a barstool. "Glad to see you've done your research."

"Gotta impress a pretty woman somehow," he chopped the vegetables into small chunks, "in case the meal doesn't."

Anika smiled as she glanced over what he'd laid out. "Looks promising to me."

"I present to you vegetable gnocchi soup with a rich mushroom sauce."

"Chef Levi has a bit of ring to it, no?" Anika hid her grimace with the rim of her wine glass.

"Let's see how you feel *after* you taste it."

Another swirl of her wine. "True, the pressure is on."

"So," he began, back to her as he started boiling water for the gnocchi, "what made you go into financial analytics?"

"And here I thought you had me all figured out," she teased.

"As I said, it was merely coincidence tonight, but you're always so elusive. I want to know more about you, so don't avoid my question. What got you into this field?"

A sly wink had a grin forming on her face even though it didn't reach her eyes.

Why the fuck did I come here?

To get answers on her hunch that both Mikko and Levi were up to no good. Regardless, here she was *trying* to let her armor fall away in hopes she could find a detrimental weakness of both men.

"Hmm, I don't even know where to begin with that question," Anika started, memories of her childhood—both good and bad—flashing across her mind. "I guess I've always loved puzzles and numbers. They came easily to me when I was younger, a skill I honed faster than most in my grade. It made me feel accomplished, so I clung to it and realized I could make it my career if I really wanted to.

"But more than that, I enjoy the patterns and trends found in data. Observation is…how I learn, I guess you could say."

"Observation, huh? And what have you observed about me?" he asked, hands busy pan searing the vegetables to soften them before adding them into the roux.

"I thought we already played this game," she countered.

"Oh, that was all superficial things my social media told you. Now that you know me better, what has your little analytical brain brewed up about me."

Did I mention narcissism earlier? she thought with a metaphorical eye roll.

The aroma of the seasoned vegetables sizzling and the gnocchi boiling on the stovetop filled her nose. Her stomach growled at the promise of food. Instead, she took another sip of wine, trying to be careful. On an empty stomach the Malbec would loosen her tongue.

And only gods knew what would come out if that were to happen.

"I don't think you want to know," Anika said, a smile on her face despite her seriousness.

Levi took a sip of his water from a nearby glass before, "Try me."

Great. "To most you're outgoing and charming; people can't seem to say no to you even if they wanted to since you have this way of making them feel guilty for choosing themselves. It makes sense why Romanov would want you on their team since those features make a great business person."

The words were barely softened by her already simmering annoyance, but Levi didn't seem to mind.

"Nothing gets by you, does it?" Levi said, his back muscles flexing as he transferred the drained gnocchi into the sauce. "I know you've caught things I *never* would've even known to check for."

"Good thing your boss isn't here to hear you admitting to incompetence."

"I mean…incompetence is a little harsh don't ya think?" His azure eyes flicked over his shoulder, a humorous twinkle in them.

"Your pay reflects your skills," she joked, gesturing to his nice apartment. He chuckled as his deft hands plated their food. "How about you? What persuaded you to pursue real estate, with one of the biggest moguls of all, no less?"

Watching his reaction, she noticed his spine stiffened slightly, before his throat bobbed.

"It was more a stroke of good luck than anything." His hands clutched a towel, wiping the messes he'd created off the pale granite countertops. "Do you need more wine?"

Avoiding my question now, are we?

Anika nodded even though her limit was quickly approaching. She toed the balance between feeling light and soft and being too far gone. "But only if you drink with me." *And answer my question.*

"I was planning on it now that the sharp objects are all put away." Glass rang as he set another wine glass down next to hers.

"Bold of you to assume I don't have any on me." Internally, Anika was face palming herself. Externally, the wine and promise of delicious food made her more forthcoming.

"I–well, I suppose you're right." His stutter made her feel slightly better as he set a plate in front of her. "But only if you promise not to not wield it against me. Unless your meal isn't cooked to your preference, then all bets are off."

Settling in where she sat, she avoided moving to the dining table. It was too formal for her tastes. Anika grinned as Levi raised his hands in surrender as he waited for her to take the first bite.

The creamy sauce steamed on her spoon, but she carefully sipped at it anyway. The gnocchi melted on her tongue while the rich mushrooms burst across her taste buds. The carrots, onions, and celery were soft and seasoned perfectly which made her opinion of Levi raise slightly. Chives garnished the plate, enhancing the flavor of everything, and Anika could do nothing but note her praise to the man standing across from her.

"This is actually…really good." She commended, her pretty smile enough to cause his shoulders to relax.

"I don't know if I should be flattered that you enjoyed it or offended that you thought it'd be bad." He took a sip of his drink as he grabbed his own plate. She didn't miss the slight grimace on his face as he sat next to her. He quickly schooled his features back into a look of playfulness when he realized she was watching.

"Flattered," she supplied before taking another bite. "I don't give out compliments often."

"Good to know."

"But don't think your good cooking will distract me from my original question. Why Romanov Real Estate?"

His audible swallow made her smile. "What do you want to know?"

"Anything. I've told you all about me, it's your turn now. Do you always mix business with pleasure, Levi?"

Levi coughed, his food settling wrong, but he was quick to chase it with Malbec. "I, erm, well, when I was younger, people always used to tell me I was a talker."

"Never would've guessed." She playfully bumped his arm.

With a laugh, he continued. "As a kid, I wanted the adults to notice me, and from a young age I figured out I could do that by speaking with them. Entertaining them in a way.

"I was always considered the life of any party—a fact my dad came to resent me for in college."

"I can only imagine the trouble you caused."

"I feel bad for it now, but at the time I'd told my dad that this is what he wanted for us: a college experience and education."

"Us?"

A sheepish smile formed as he chewed. "Yeah, I have an older brother."

"You both went to college then?" Her spoon scraped unpleasantly against the bowl.

"Yes...although he was the one that actually made it to graduation. I'd experienced it for two years and decided it was too overpriced and stuffy for my rebellious tastes."

Anika swallowed her food. "Can't say I'm surprised by that."

"Yeah, no one ever is," a faint chuckle holding more than humor slipped past his lips. "My brother is the rule follower, but me...I thought I had life figured out. And the life I drew up for myself did *not* include college, so I began working random retail jobs since I was a great front-facing employee. That was how I met Alek."

Anika's blood froze, but she continued eating even if her stomach felt like it was lined with lead.

"He was buying out the strip mall I worked in, but when we'd met by coincidence he deemed me as someone valuable. Despite my lack of degree and flashy work history, he hired me on at Romanov. It was a dream come true. People liked and *trusted* me to sell. Plus I was a quick learner."

"Lucky, indeed," Anika commented. "Your personality seems to be the most valuable piece of your resume."

"Truly. I'm glad Alek saw that and took me under his wing."

Internally, Anika cringed. Levi was giving praise to a man who deserved *none*.

"Does his son also value you? I know there was some restructuring once Alek passed..." Anika was fishing for information.

Dabbing at his mouth with a napkin, his blue eyes bright, Levi responded, "He has no choice *but* to value me. His father made sure

I'd have a place in the firm, my potential and experience too great to eliminate."

Interesting. "Well, I'm glad you two get along then."

"I wouldn't go that far, but whatever pays the bills, right?" Levi winked.

She held up her glass, waiting until he clinked his against it. "Right." A soft pause filled the air as they sipped. "Although, working with people you like is a large proponent of enjoying your job."

"It's moments like this that make me enjoy my job."

Anika's insides clenched abhorrently. *Ew.* "Maybe one day, you can take over Romanov. Seems you're destined for it anyway. Real estate *is* tied to good client outreach and satisfaction."

She was pushing hard, and it could backfire—

"Are you saying *you're* satisfied with my work?" he taunted.

Anika grinned into her wine, nodding.

Sure, whatever will keep you talking.

Levi smiled at her before continuing. "While that's what I deserve, I fear Mr. Romanov's love of control and dislike for me might make that, hmm, how do I say...difficult."

"Never say never," she said. "The universe has a funny way of manifesting our wants."

"I suppose you're right." He fidgeted with the cuff of his shirt.

Always am.

Levi's phone buzzed as soon as they'd finished each taking another sip of wine. Through the wavy rim of the glass, Anika watched him quickly type in his password. *2 6 4 5 2*

Her brain pictured the number pad, thoughts whirring as she placed the combination together in her head. She swallowed roughly, *her* food settling wrong this time.

"Sorry," he explained, mannerisms distracted, "I was expecting an important call tonight."

"For work?"

He glanced up at her, teeth flashing in his quick, reassuring smile. "Yes, a large deal we're trying to close has come across a couple...snags, but we're nothing if not persistent."

She tapped the stem of her glass. "I have no doubt you'll get your way." A double meaning was encased within the words, but he didn't catch it. His focus on his screen instead.

He hesitated, eyes reading over a message Anika couldn't see. "Exactly," he locked his phone and turned it over before placing it on the counter, out of reach for both of them, "besides, tonight is about us."

"Of course, no worries." Dropping the subject, they both fell into silence as they finished up the last scraps of their food.

As Anika was about to suggest either another glass of wine or a taxi home, Levi stood. "Do you need anything? I'm going to run to the restroom."

"No, I'm okay, thank you." Her words were all he needed before he disappeared through one of the open doorways. It must be his bedroom, but her gaze wasn't focused on that anymore. Instead, it latched onto his abandoned phone, still laying face down on the counter.

Does he really think I'm so naive? So trusting?

It didn't matter; she was going to snoop regardless of what he thought of her. Everything he'd told her mirrored information she'd divulged on her own. Which wouldn't be a problem to most, but it made Anika's mind uneasy. *She* had things to hide, therefore, couldn't disclose all of her secrets. Who was to say Levi wasn't doing the same thing to her.

Reaching out, she plucked his phone off the counter, swiping up and entering the passcode she'd seen him type out earlier. It worked, her blood thrumming with excitement. She kept her ears perked, ready to set his phone back where she'd gotten it from within seconds.

Unlocked phone in her hand, she recalled how he said he'd been expecting a call…

Anika tapped on the phone icon, searching through his call history and a name jumped out at her.

Mikko.

Her jaw clenched. Of course. It was from earlier in the day and lasted a couple minutes.

Pulling out her own phone, Anika compared the number to the unknown one in her phone, and it was a match. Again, when was she ever wrong. Triumph swelled in her gut.

Exiting out of Levi's phone call history, she went to his messages. There, at the top, was Mikko again. For not liking one another they sure texted like grade school girls.

Glancing up, she listened for Levi's return, but all she heard was the faint hum of his furnace and the cars on the street below. Without wasting any more time, she clicked on their thread. She scrolled up a bit, curious to see the subjects they talked about and found herself hardly surprised it was about her.

Enjoy the view? :Levi

Anika looked at the time stamp and saw it was from two nights ago when he came over to her house. The same night they made out on her couch.

Mikko: Fuck off

Did you think you could sneak off? That I wouldn't notice you? :Levi

Mikko: I thought I told you to stop sleeping with clients

And I thought I told you to keep your nose out of my business :Levi

Mikko: *It's a bit hard when you work for me*

Her brain quickly put the pieces together, the prickling sensation from that night not just from Levi and his annoying presence, but instead Mikko. He had been watching her, watching them, through her open windows.

What a naughty little thing to do...

Mikko was too predictable.

She scrolled a bit more and found messages from today.

Mikko: *Is she there?*

Yes, you told me to take her out to dinner :Levi

Mikko: *To a restaurant*

Mikko: *Not your apartment*

Mikko: *Where I can't see you*

Maybe specify that next time. I can't read your mind :Levi

Thankfully :Levi

Mikko: *Did you at least buy the things I told you to? She's vegetarian*

Yes, I got stuff for veggie gnocchi soup, and I remember you telling me she likes bitter red wine :Levi

You owe me for the wine :Levi

Mikko: *The money is already in your account*

No, not monetarily. Dry wines are gross :Levi

Mikko: *Said by someone who has a child's taste palette*

Rude :Levi

Mikko: *I'm serious, stay focused and update me on everything*

I'm starting to think you're into some freaky voyeur shit :Levi

Mikko: *Have you been talking to Cristiano?*

No, why? :Levi

Mikko had blatantly ignored Levi, never bothering to respond.

So that was how Levi knew her food and wine preference; he'd had an inside source. And it was Mikko Romanov no less. Did he always dedicate this much time to learning his clients? If so, she could see why he was bitchy and had dark circles under his eyes most days. That shit was exhausting.

While the discovery made Anika feel violated, she had to go along with it, pretending everything slipped past her sight, her brain unable to keep up.

Lies.

Confronting Levi about this was a bad idea, a way to erase all of her hard work. No, she needed to stay quiet, to do what she did best.

Observe.

Investigate.

Collect.

Until she had every piece of the puzzle where she wanted it.

Her wine stained lips curved into a smile was what greeted Levi when he returned, his phone back in its original place, and her fingerprints wiped away.

26

Slippery Slope

Mikko

Levi: *I can't make our debrief meeting tonight*

The text from his informant was not unlike Levi. Still, Mikko quickly typed a message back.

*You know our arrangements :**Mikko***

Levi: *I know, I had some stuff come up with Anika. If I break away now, she'll be suspicious of us*

*What stuff? :**Mikko***

He waited for a couple minutes, but Levi didn't respond. Concern and jealousy shot through Mikko's heart, but he quickly wrote it off, knowing Levi would be fine. He had the man's location on his phone if his situation turned dire. Besides, they'd done more dangerous tasks in the past and made it out alive. Having him get close to Anika was tame compared to that. But that didn't keep his mind from ruminating on *other* things that could be keeping him busy. Which was why he needed to keep his hands occupied.

Tucking his phone back into his pocket, he continued what he'd been doing before Levi had pinged: rummaging through Anika's house. *Again.*

While he'd vowed to stop and put some goddamn distance between them, his traitorous mind had other thoughts.

Getting to know thy enemy, or whatever the fuck Shakespeare had said.

He'd already memorized her routines and knew her schedule, so sneaking in and out was easy. Especially when she was never home. A fact he was relating to as he was spending more time at the office or *here.*

After antagonizing her at the gun range early yesterday morning, she'd seemingly won by digging a metaphorical knife in between his ribs. While he'd gone home shortly after she'd left the range—his dick way too hard for public decency—and jerked off, she remained seemingly unaffected. She'd let Levi into her home. A perfect plan on his part, but his emotional, illogical side was fucking *fuming.* Just when he thought he'd gotten under her skin, she smiled back and clawed her way deeper.

Is that all you got? she'd say in his head, her molten eyes intoxicating.

And his answer was no, hence the reason he stood at the top of her stairs, short nails biting into his palm as he clenched his fists.

Despite their game, his feelings were becoming convoluted. His need to unravel her was outweighing his logic of letting her go. He feared this infatuation was the exact reason she reached out to him in the first place. It was like she *knew* he was drawn to the beautiful and the unusual.

But now, he was wading into dangerous waters.

This compulsion was consuming him—his need to know and control her overshadowing everything else. Her emotions were hidden, an unknown variable he wanted to decipher so he could say that he did.

So that I can say I've solved a woman who thinks she's untouchable.

And below that, it was deeper.

Mikko craved being seen for who *he* truly was and not what he stood for. All his life he'd been forgotten and abused, singled out in the worst ways possible. Outwardly, his life of wealth reflected everything someone could want, but it left Mikko empty. Now, with Anika, she understood him for who he was.

A fucked up human who was handed an empire on a throne of dirty blood.

And still, she engaged.

It drove him crazy, and made him want her in the *worst* ways.

This investigation into her had led to his emotions morphing into fascination. One he had no problems giving into. He should be pissed that she was the one who'd broken into his penthouse, stolen from him, and then planted the evidence to frame him.

But…

He wasn't.

In fact, her wit turned him on, made him realize life was so much bigger than Romanov Real Estate.

Even if she hadn't blatantly admitted her crimes, he still knew it was her. It had to be. She was guilty until proven innocent and nothing about her screamed blameless. Hell, even the information he'd gotten back from Rebecca had cemented this idea farther.

Anika Simmons. Anika Naidu.

Two names, one dangerous woman.

Now why would a seemingly average woman change her name?

That answer awaited him back at the office, locked away in a drawer in yet *another* manila folder. Rebecca, while a shit lover and expensive service, knew how to get a job done.

Something Levi was struggling with.

After tonight, he'd read it, but until then Mikko wanted to live in the darkness for a little longer. He wanted to enjoy this obsession, this poison, consuming him. Later he would reap the consequences of his actions. Later he would think.

But for tonight, he'd *act*. He'd escape it all.

While standing among her possessions, feet carrying him into her bedroom, he held her scarf. The cherry on top was the fact he knew it smelled more like him than her, especially after all he'd done to it.

Stepping farther into her bedroom, his eyes caught on the chair she positioned in the corner of her room. Delicately, he folded her scarf and placed it on top of the chair. Unlike the rest of the crumpled clothes she'd discarded there, this one was neatly presented, albeit stained with his cum.

It was a bold move, but he didn't care. Mikko was no longer interested in playing things safe. Safe wasn't what got him answers; safe wasn't what drew her to him. It was time for him to go after what he wanted. All the signs were there. Every move she made, Mikko wanted to know about. She occupied his thoughts, all day every day.

Soft, inked skin and ebony hair wrapped around my fingers. Golden eyes holding more secrets than I can count.

Everything was falling apart. Or into place?

Mikko pressed the heels of his palms to his eyes, desperately trying to push her out of his head. Anika was consuming him—luring him in with her wit and beauty—and who was he to say no?

His emotions always ruled him despite what he showed to others as being perceived as an immovable facade. Mikko was losing this battle between himself, his father's legacy, and Anika.

Anika. Anika. Anika.

All because of a twisted *crush. A twisted obsession.*

An exasperated sigh echoed in her bedroom.

Lust curled around his heart. Blood rushed lower as he stood there. Why should he hold back anymore? It wasn't like it'd helped him all this time anyway. Maybe if he gave in and let himself be run by his emotions he could *finally* think. His father had been wrong when he'd conditioned Mikko to keep everything bottled up, to stifle every feeling settling into his bones.

Mikko was no longer that little boy, one craving acceptance from his father. Now, he was old enough to *take* what he wanted.

And he *wanted* Anika.

Palming himself through his jeans, unable to keep his desire under control, Mikko groaned at the relief. His cum covered scarf on her chair teased him from the corner of his eye. It'd been a scare tactic at first, a violation of her space. But now Mikko hoped she interpreted it as it truly was.

Infatuation.

Would he stay here and entertain his thoughts or leave, content to let his fantasies be just that? Logically, the latter option was safer, a smart choice, but Mikko was tired of being rational. His whole life had consisted of that, and it'd gotten him *nowhere.*

So, he'd give in this once to see where it took him, to prove his dead father wrong.

With light footsteps, he walked to her bathroom. Pushing on the wood, the door creaked open. Just as it had the first time he'd been here—and the last—her scent immediately overpowered him. He groaned aloud shamelessly.

Stopping in front of her shower curtain, he quickly stripped his shirt off. He knew he had plenty of time before she returned since Levi was wooing her with his cooking skills.

Hopefully he doesn't burn the whole block down.

Standing shirtless in her space, his heart raced. It was a violation making his lips quirk up in a grin. Dropping his shirt onto the floor, he began unbuttoning his pants only to be stopped short at the small pile of clothes near his recently discarded shirt.

It was an oversized T-shirt and underwear.

He froze; his mouth watered.

Take them home, take them home, his mind silently chanted at him.

And for a moment, he stayed strong, fingers securely on the unbuttoned waist of his pants.

Until he wasn't.

Crouching, he let his fingertips trail over the bunched up fabric. Simultaneously, his mind flashed back to the night she'd touched him—traced his arm as if she owned him. A shiver zipped up his spine, goosebumps erupting across his exposed skin.

Or to the early morning at the gun range, her ponytail smelling of shampoo and tickling his nose as he positioned her inside the shooting lane. They'd been so close, yet so far, and it'd driven him crazy. He'd pretended to touch her for the sake of lessons, but in reality they were excuses. He knew that; Anika knew that, yet she didn't swat his hands away. That realization had made him want to do more—to lick and kiss and suck every inch of her body, but he was certain she would've shot him then. Something he mostly likely would've been fine with if she'd only graced him with her touch in return, her voice like honey in his ear as he bled out.

Swallowing thickly, he withdrew and stood to his full height once more. He pushed the botanical shower curtain aside and turned on the stream of water. While waiting for it to warm up, he shed the rest of his clothes, smirking when they dropped into a bundle next to hers. He wanted to intertwine himself with her in every way that he could so she felt the same kind of desperation she'd planted inside of him.

Steam wafted out from above the shower curtain signaling the water was ready. He stepped inside.

The thrill weaving through him was one like no other. His intrusion was obvious—a blatant sin—but that was what made it so *sweet*. It was terribly wrong, yet Mikko couldn't stop himself. Once he set his mind to something, he couldn't be deterred.

She'd showered here before, right where he was standing, her lithe body wet beneath the stream of water. Enveloped in steam, Mikko's mind wandered as her scent overwhelmed him. The picture his mind conjured up had his body tensing.

Her eyelashes glimmering with water droplets as she gazed up at him in reverence. Her hair was a dark river plastered across her skin, one he wanted to dive into, tugging and pulling her closer.

And the water sluicing down her body...

He imagined his tongue there to catch every stray drop hugging her curves

A weightlessness overcame him. Levi might be able to *physically* touch her, but Mikko was going to leave his mark on her in other ways. Without a second thought, he grabbed her loofah and her body wash. Lathering up with her soap, he placed the abrasive material to his skin.

Dirty and intimate, were the only words repeating themselves in his mind.

Leisurely, he scrubbed every inch of his body knowing her scent would follow him home. His own musk would embed itself onto her things too, a private trade. A secret for them to share when Levi left her all alone. It brought a smug smile to his face.

With the water at his side and the slippery soap covering every inch of his body, Mikko's mind shifted and began picturing her as he always did: framed by her window, protected from him by the glass. He'd watch as she'd undress deliberately slow. The ink of her tattoos vivid against her tanned skin in her dimly lit bedroom.

Do hers have meaning like mine, or are they something to fill the void?

He'd have to ask her later. Right now, it didn't matter; his perverse thoughts did nothing to quell the hunger mounting in his heart. Burying his emotions might be easier, but letting them out felt *so, so good.*

A groan tore free from his mouth as he stroked his cock. His other hand rested against the bright tile lining her shower. Its cool kiss should've erased the heat building within him, but he hardly felt it. Adding a pump of her conditioner to his hand to remove any unwanted friction, Mikko slowly edged himself. Each movement, every squeeze, had the world around him blurring.

What would her mouth feel like wrapped around me? Her tight little cunt?

His pants echoed around him, his breaths short and fast to match the speed of which he touched himself. He quickly realized that jerking off with her scarf had only whetted his appetite for *more.* That watching her had only made things worse.

Fuck.

He didn't want to intimidate or interrogate her; he wanted to consume her as she had him. He'd gone weeks with her in his mind, plaguing him every chance she got. Everywhere he went, she was always conveniently there, and he was starting to wonder if she was following *him.* It didn't matter, he supposed; Mikko was going to make her pay. No one came into his life and fucked it up without sacrificing something.

Especially when they had him like this—

His hips bucked against his hand, blood rushing in his ears, and Mikko pumped his fist faster before slowing back down. It was a give and take just like he would with Anika.

Steadily, *painfully,* Mikko worked his hardened length as thoughts of tearing Anika's clothes off with his hands and teeth, impatience coating every gesture, formed in his mind. Precum leaked from the tip of his cock and dripped onto the shower floor, quickly washed away. If only his lewd thoughts could follow suit.

The water's delicious heat seared through him, mimicking what he thought Anika's nails would feel like marking his back. The thought of them stabbed into her couch flashed across his mind again. He gritted his teeth.

There was a lethal anger in her, one that was sure to consume her if she let it, but a part of Mikko wanted her to take it out on him. Everything she'd held back, he'd take. Just as he'd contained himself for so long, unable to let anyone in for the fear of being ridiculed, he would unleash on her. Tongue and teeth and nails.

And before he could stop himself, Anika was there. The steam swirled around her body, her skin appearing soft and wet and oh, so *kissable*. Her figure wavered in the haze as if she were a mirage, a temptation making an appearance when he was weakest.

Fitting, he thought.

She was right there, so close he could almost *taste* her. Water droplets clung to her flesh and strands of her ebony hair were plastered across her neck and shoulders, the swirling pattern one he wanted to follow with his fingertips. He didn't miss the way the strands hugged the swell of her breasts.

A soft blush dusted her cheeks from the temperature of the water, and her lust was evident in her amber eyes. The deviousness he knew so well manifested itself to him. He could faintly feel her fingers tracing the linework of his tattoos, following the designs and floral edges until he was shivering.

Anika stepped closer, the heat of her own body somehow palpable through the steam. Reverently she grazed over the scars littering his skin, each containing a story of their own—some earned and others given. Mikko stifled a whimper, but for once, he wasn't ashamed of his marred skin. If it meant she'd touch him, he'd uncover every layer for her to inspect.

While his first tattoo had been an act of rebellion almost two decades ago, the rest had been because Mikko thought himself ugly, his mottled skin damaged. When he coveted beautiful things, his own imperfections afflicted him.

So, he covered them up. One by one.

Her hands crept lower before slipping across his abdomen and playfully stopping right below his navel. His breath hitched as her nails bit into his skin slightly.

"Don't let me stop you," she crooned, her saccharine smile at odds with her risque touch. His resolve faded. *"I know how much you like to watch."*

She watched his throat bob as he swallowed. Her words struck a chord, but it wasn't worth denying it. It was who he was—someone always willing to observe from the shadows.

"You make it easy," he panted in response to her voice resonating in his mind.

Anika let her fingers glide back up over his slick chest and gently intertwined them in his hair. His nerve endings were on high alert, body wound so fucking tight it felt like he'd snap at any moment. His hips canted up into his hand, chasing his pleasure all while she hummed against his skin.

"What can I say? I like knowing you're always there, laying in wait." One of her hands released the nape of his neck and drifted to the closing space between them. Faintly, her touch wrapped around his, mirroring his stroking motions. *"And I like knowing that you can't help yourself—that you have to touch yourself to release the ache building here."*

"Yes, I—"

She squeezed his cock, tightening his fist in tandem to draw his pleasure out. Mikko's chest heaved and the rest of his words died out.

Pulling harshly, Anika exposed his neck to her with the hand still intertwined in his hair, nails scraping along his scalp. Groaning, Mikko let her overpower him, and his knees weakened as her lips skimmed the base of his throat. If she kept this up—if *he* kept this up—he wasn't going to be able to last long.

"Always so put together on the outside, but little does the world know..." she murmured against his wet skin, *"you're falling apart on the inside."*

Fuck, fuck, *fuck.*

"Shut. Up," he gritted out, the words falling out of his mouth in tandem with his pumping hand.

"Poor baby. Let me touch you, I can make you feel so good."

"N-no—don't." He didn't know why he bothered to answer, no one there to hear, but the trembling words fell from his lips regardless.

"Liar. You think I don't see the way you look at me, the way you send Levi after me all while wishing it was you?"

He jerked, her accusations and the friction from his hand over-stimulating him. Any other person whispering these words to him wouldn't have made it home alive, but her...well, he wanted to be abused by her only if it meant she'd pay him an *ounce* of attention. That was what he'd been chasing ever since the club.

Gravity swept out from under his feet. The only thing keeping him grounded was the single fingertip she traced up his bicep. His eyes were squeezed shut, but he knew she was tracing the snake winding around his upper arm.

"Mikko, Mikko, Mikko," she repeated, the way her lips formed his name making his heart thunder beneath his ribcage. He never wanted her to stop saying it; he yearned for it to be the only name she'd ever remember. *"Ever the snake, crawling on your belly to me..."*

She was right.

A grunt was his only response. Rhythmically, he thrusted his hips forward to meet his hand, wet *smacks* resonating in the small space as if this had always been the solution to his self-induced problems. God, if only it were that—

"How badly do you want to fuck me?" she asked, teeth latching onto his earlobe, canines scraping across the tender flesh.

Sparks erupted behind his closed eyelids, his brows furrowed in an attempt to hang on—to hold off on his release. Mikko didn't want to finish in here where his evidence would be washed away down the drain. No, he wanted her to come home and *find* his release smeared on things she loved.

Like her scarf.

Loosening his hold on his cock, he quickly turned the shower off. Anika's figure dissipated, evaporating along with the steam. Roughly, he pushed the shower curtain aside as spots crept into the corners of his vision. Stepping out, he watched as water flew off his limbs and splattered onto the floor and walls.

But that was not what held his attention.

Mikko's eyes latched onto the cosmetics at her sink.

With a sinful grin of his own, he found himself dripping wet before her makeup products. His hair dripped and hung in his eyes all while he fisted his cock again. Release coiled at the base of his spine, only a few pumps needed to get him to come. His skin shone with the residual water, but he was too busy imagining Anika discovering the mess he was about to make. And the way her lip gloss covered mouth would look wrapped around his cock, molten eyes looking up at him begging for everything he was giving. After being forever unreadable, he could finally understand what she wanted.

Fucking into his hand, Mikko yearned to make her cry, makeup streaking down her cheeks ruining her own perfect facade she kept up no matter what. He knew there was more lurking below the surface—things she never showed. And he wanted that barrier *gone*.

Blood rushed his head, cock pulsing with the impending release that was sure to explode out of him.

"Yes, yes, yes..." he chanted, his hand tightening to emulate the feeling of her pussy milking him.

The edge he'd been teetering on fell away, his climax washing over him as his eyes squeezed shut in ecstasy. Hot ropes of cum spurted out, his release splattering over the basin of her sink and cosmetics. His knees trembled with the release. Warm relief flooded his body, a weight lifted off his shoulders as he stood there wearily.

Her soft laughter filled his head. Or maybe that was his own, the sudden exhaustion washing over his body making it hard to discern reality from make believe.

Cracking open his eyes, the lights suddenly bright, Mikko glanced around.

Drip, drip, drip.

His hearing faded back in, the steady drip of water falling from his body and onto her bathroom floor grounding him. Releasing his hold on his cock, Mikko stepped back, light headed from the exertion. Even though he didn't know what time it was exactly, he had a feeling his window of opportunity was closing.

Quickly, he used her towel to mostly dry off, a few drops of water clinging to his skin as he stooped down and gathered his discarded clothes. Stepping into his pants, he looked out and saw her dresser sitting perfectly in line with the bathroom door.

An idea formed in his mind.

Blame post-nut clarity...

Once he was satisfied with his little idea and his execution of it, he tugged his shirt back on. The scent of vanilla mixing with his cologne lingering on his shirt made his blood hum. A soft smile graced his lips, content in his evening activities. Once he was gone, he'd send her the photo of himself as a little tease.

But he had one more thing to do.

Retrieving a pen from her nightstand and a discarded receipt, Mikko scribbled a note out for her to find. It was stupid and silly, but nonchalant wasn't really his thing. Feeling tired but refreshed, Mikko tried to remember the last time he'd felt this free. While his motorcycle got him close, it rarely managed to fill the ever growing void in his gut. A laugh threatened to burst out of him at the thought of what he'd done. It'd been a while she he'd done something this reckless.

His phone vibrated in his pocket, and suddenly he remembered Levi never responded to him. Mikko's eyes scanned over the message that had come through.

But it wasn't Levi.

Or Anika.

Mikko's heart sank as the words seared into his head.

Cristiano: *Have you heard from Dimitri? I can't seem to get a hold of him*

Images of Ivan's brutalized body and altered organs haunted Mikko. If this led to another murder, he was going to be furious. It seemed like he couldn't avoid Anika's file for much longer.

Typing a reply, Mikko's lighthearted mood fading, he promised to do some investigating as soon as he got home.

"See, emotions are a detriment to our business." Again, his father's lifetime of scoldings pestered him, especially since he disobeyed one of the most important rules.

And look where it got him—a missing man and no leads.

"Maybe if you hadn't been stroking your pitiful cock to her face, you could finally be useful," his father's voice echoed in his head again. The

dead always had so much to say.

Ridden with guilt and smelling like Anika, he slipped out of her house undetected.

27

Cosmetics, Among Other Things

Anika

L eaves swirled around Anika's feet as she trekked up the sidewalk to the front door of her house. Levi's car idled behind her, and she could feel his ever present gaze lingering. Despite everything, she turned and waved, hoping her face conveyed the happiness and simmering desire he wanted to see from her.

It was apparent he'd been sent to look after her by Mikko, their messages incriminating, but somewhere along the way, Levi started to obey his own rules. It was to be expected; the inability to to stay on track an attribute she associated with Romanov Real Estate.

After waving back, he rolled his tinted window up, but his smug grin was already seared into her mind. She shuddered and hoped he'd think it was from the chill in the air. As soon as her front door opened, he pulled away from the curb, only the hazy cloud from his exhaust remaining.

Closing the heavy wood door behind her, Anika leaned against it, suddenly exhausted. Upholding her controlled exterior conveying enjoyment in the presence of Levi had taken everything out of her. Fatigue wove itself into her bones, her true emotions bubbling to the surface. She never had a moment to herself these days, always on the run with work, dates with Levi, tracking down Mikko and his organization. It was never ending, and after it all, Anika wanted to lay down on the ground.

Kicking her shoes off at the door, she hung her cardigan up on the coat rack before walking up the first few steps up to her room. The old treads creaked beneath her weight, the sound familiar like an old blanket or sweater.

Fingertips trailing along the banister, she pulled herself up, ready to shower and plop into bed and sleep. But when she reached the top of the stairs, she froze in her tracks.

Her bedroom door was cracked. Moonlight shone through, its source coming from the windows in her room beyond.

I didn't leave my door like that.

Her near photographic memory had served many purposes, but this one might save her life.

Ding.

Her phone buzzed in her hand. Apprehensively she looked down, dreading the name she'd find across her screen. There were only two choices and she was tired of both men right now.

Mikko: *Sent an image*

Mikko: *To give you something to think about while you're with him*

Opening the picture, she found a darkened silhouette of Mikko. He was leaning against the door frame leading into her bathroom, his one arm outstretched above his head to grip the frame. It wasn't hard for him since his height only left a few inches between the top of the door and his head. The waistband of his pants hung low, enticing her eyes to follow the contours of his stomach lower…

Her mouth dried up.

Were those tattoos?

Droplets of water dotted his skin from what she could see—she shamelessly zoomed in—but the backlighting of her bathroom made it hard to discern the details. Saving the picture into a digital folder, Anika opened the editing tools along the bottom. She dialed up the brightness on the photo to watch in real time as Mikko's face cleared…along with the defined planes of his chest and torso.

And the tattoos inked there.

The floral blackout sleeves were ones she'd seen before, but she had no idea they covered his entire arms. The head of an inked snake rested along the space where his neck met his shoulder. Vines swirled below his neckline where a collared shirt would sit along with four little letters.

CTRL.

Anika's brow quirked. She remembered seeing that tattoo peeking above his collar at *Bubblegum*.

His hair was messy and wet, an indication of what she'd find in her bedroom and bathroom mere steps away: a wet towel and floor.

A dagger tattoo carved across his sternum, the blade narrowing to a point a couple inches above his navel.

Closing out of the image, she returned her attention to her bedroom. He was long gone by now, unable to corner her after a stunt like this. She was sure of it. Still, she silently walked forward, her stance loose but alert. Using her foot, she pushed the door open, eyes scanning the room.

Before her, all was calm. The clothes she'd left on the floor remained as is, the curtains pushed aside to let the night in along with stars. Rumpled sheets littered her bed, just as she'd left it. Spinning, she kicked the door shut, checking behind it in case someone lurked there instead. She was met with nothing, which was both a relief and an annoyance.

Something in the air *felt* different, the scent skewed—not the way she remembered it. Stepping farther into the room, her eyes scanned the shadows for something that didn't belong.

She caught sight of a folded silhouette of something atop the chair in the corner of her room.

Is that what I think it is...

Sure enough, with her eyes continuously scanning, she walked over and unfolded her missing scarf. She wasn't sure if Mikko returning it was a gentlemanly thing to do or a scare tactic. Probably both since the man couldn't seem to make up his mind. As she inspected it in the lowlight, his scent wafted off the fabric—leather and patchouli. And her fingers encountered *multiple* crusty spots.

Scoffing, Anika dropped it on the floor. "Classy."

Walking toward her bathroom took an eon, the floor stretching out before her, and the air grew thicker with each step. As soon as she stepped over the threshold, humidity assaulted her skin. It seemed like someone had helped themselves to her soaps. *Recently.*

And it was easy to figure out who it was when he'd sent her a billboard sized "look at me" picture.

Angrily flicking the light switch on, she instantly spotted the haze covering the mirror, the telltale water droplets splattered over her floor, and the damp spot on her towel hanging on a hook nearby.

That little shit.

She went to step closer, the shower curtain closed, leaving a blind spot in her exploration, but a glimmer in the basin of her sink had her stopping.

It was all over her cosmetics too.

Shower forgotten, Anika leaned closer, inspecting the mess left for her to find, and without a doubt she knew what it was.

Cum.

Fire lit beneath her skin.

Mikko had come into her house—pun intended—showered in her bathroom, and then proceeded to jerk off in front of her mirror and onto her things. That was probably the only way he could finish—by staring at himself in the mirror. Anika's teeth clenched, her sense of privacy thoroughly invaded. How many times had he broken in to prove that he could? How many times had he taunted her because she got under his skin?

Too many but she'd played timid, silent, and enduring of his stupidity.

But enough was enough.

While it had been her intent to draw him in, it didn't mean she had to just take it.

Certain Mikko was long gone, Anika looked back at the mess before her. Tucked neatly near the faucet of her sink was a note, stuck there courtesy of the viscous liquid.

Since you think I pump my cock at night...
–M

She was going to strangle him.

With purpose, she walked back through her bedroom, down the stairs, and wound up in her kitchen looking for an airtight container. After perusing the cluttered stacks of them in her cupboard, she settled on the smallest one she could find before heading back up to the *scene* in her bathroom.

Using q-tips and surgeon steady hands, Anika gathered up a small sample of his semen and sealed it off.

"You stupid fuck," she muttered to herself.

Satisfied with what she had, she set it aside and rummaged through her cleaning supplies. A cleaner with enzymes known to break down body fluids and a scrub brush should do the trick.

After scouring the basin for ten minutes straight, she was satisfied her bathroom was clean once more. All the toiletries and makeup brushes he'd ruined were in the trash, a list of what she'd lost cataloged in her phone.

Either he or Levi would be purchasing replacement items for her.

Scalding hot water reddening her skin and multiple pumps of soap finished off her cleaning routine. Wiping her hands on her pants, her towel also diseased, Anika slipped her phone from her pants pocket, needing a distraction.

Before she could consider *not* doing this, she typed out a quick text to Levi.

*Since you make big money and all...wanna spoil me this weekend? I need some new makeup to look pretty for you :**Anika***

His answer came back almost instantly.

Levi: *For once, I'm not the one arranging the date?*

Levi: *Consider it done, beautiful*

Anika huffed and merely shucked her clothes off and fell into bed.

28

Stalking

Unknown

He thought you didn't see him, *couldn't* see him, for everything that he was. But you knew when to let your guard down. Most of what you'd built around yourself was a facade—an illusion for others to drink up. And if he fell for it as well, all the better for you. You savored the attention, relished in the idea that he didn't know all your plans.

You had parked in the usual spot down the street from his house, content to lie in wait. The night was like any other, the leaves littering the sidewalk as the temperature dropped. The colors bled into rusty hues bathing the whole town in warm tangerines and vivid reds.

It reminded you of something else...

Movement caught the corner of your eye, the buildings you were watching suddenly coming alive with activity.

There you are, you little rat.

Swathed in shadow, you waited. This was another piece of the overall puzzle, and you'd be damned if it didn't fall into place just as you'd designed it. The man you'd been following was oblivious, unable to feel the telltale prickle on the back of his neck.

You loved when they made it easy for you. While your emotions were usually tucked neatly away, seeing his face incited an indescribable rage.

Later, you'd let it all out *later.*

Now, it was time to engage in a *delicate* dance.

Outwardly, you were normal. Another face blending in with the thousands roaming the city, but did anyone else see through the illusion? Even if someone did, it'd be too late, your gun silencing them.

Besides, you enjoyed the feeling of naivety that came with this persona, this *mask.*

Slipping from your car, you trailed after the man with your footsteps in time with his to avoid the echoing crunch beneath your boots. Subtly, you scanned the shadows making sure you were the only one with devious intentions. In the underbelly of the city, one could never be too cautious.

But nothing.

Adrenaline fluttered in your pulse, your body ready for whatever fight was about to come.

No, not adrenaline, excitement, a whisper said, brushing against your brain. It taunted a dangerous locked away portion of your head, coaxing it to come out and play. Tonight, that side would emerge, and everything you'd yearned for would be attainable under the cover of night.

The man you were following would discover this soon enough; he'd see what you were really made of. *All sharp edges.*

You weren't scared of the dark; you were the only thing mad and fearless enough to thrive in the night.

Time for him *to discover that too.*

"Hey," you stumbled out the shadows and the man startled slightly until he realized who you were, "I think I'm a little *lost*." He smiled at your slurred words and lilted laughter, his own barriers falling away. Such a shame...

29

The Spare Key

Anika

A week had passed since Mikko had showered in her house. He'd been eerily quiet since then, a fact she hardly found reassuring. If anything it meant he was plotting something nefarious. Levi had been his usual chattering self, excited to take her out and replace all the makeup she'd "dropped in the sink and ruined."

She'd sent a picture of her haul to Mikko as a big *"fuck you,"* but he'd left her on read. Boring.

Now, daylight streamed in across her work desk. The warmth of it made her tired, her sleeping patterns completely messed up. As much as her discretion mattered, Anika couldn't hold onto all the loose ends for much longer. Her body was giving out, and she needed to act soon. Levi and Mikko were closing in on her in their own way, and it made her skittish.

"Anika," a voice said from her doorway, "someone delivered flowers at the front desk for you." Looking up, Anika caught sight of their office manager walking away. She wasn't expecting flowers...

With wary footsteps and her heart in her throat, Anika made her way out to the front desk. Rounding the corner, the deep hue of violets popped against the white counter. Baby's Breath was tucked around the purple flowers, offsetting their vibrancy wonderfully.

But the hidden meaning behind these had Anika's movements faltering.

Watchfulness and everlasting love.

Two sides of a coin.

A crisp piece of folded cardstock with her name on it protruded above the flowers. Looking around to make sure no one was watching, Anika picked the whole arrangement up. She'd deal with this in the privacy of her office. It was either Levi buttering her up or Mikko taunting her. Both of which she didn't want her coworkers to see.

Gracefully sitting back down into her chair with her office door securely closed, she plucked the note from its holder.

We need to talk. Leave the spare key out for me.
—M

Anika snorted and pulled two small tubes that were nestled next to the note from the greenery as well.

What's this?

Perfume and lip gloss.

The fragrance brand he'd gotten her was one she'd been running low on and needed to buy. Her brow quirked.

She broke the seal of the lip gloss and opened it, the shade pale and creamy and—

Pulling up Mikko's number in her phone, she quickly typed up a response.

*Thanks for the flowers, still doesn't erase your intrusions :**Anika***

283

Also, wtf is the lip gloss about? :**Anika**

Despite him leaving her on read prior, he responded quickly this time.

Mikko: *The lip gloss is a shade that I think would look good on you...a color close to my heart, if you will*

You're disgusting :**Anika**

Mikko: *And here I thought my picture would sate you*

Levi does that all on his own :**Anika**

Mikko: *Suuure*

Mikko: *The toy in your nightstand says otherwise*

Anika's face reddened in anger.

Any updates on Ivan? I hear there has been some unrest within your company due to your lack of action :**Anika**

A terribly risky thing to say, but she couldn't help herself. Mikko answered shortly after, never one to be bested.

Mikko: *You're going to regret that*

Regret wasn't the word she'd use, but it didn't matter. She opened his message and didn't even bother to reply.

* * *

THE SOFT, BUTTERY light from the lamp next to her illuminated the pages of the book Anika flipped through. She wasn't sure what time it was, only that her back ached from the position she was in.

And she knew she should be in bed since it was a weeknight, but she didn't care, too engrossed in her book. Rain gently splashed against the window behind her, a gentle melody lulling her deeper into the pages. She'd vowed *multiple* chapters ago she'd stop for the night.

It hadn't worked.

After messaging Mikko earlier that day, his ominous last words had kept her on edge. She wasn't sure if he'd do anything, or let her believe he'd do something. How much of a coward was he? Only time would tell.

Memorizing the chapter number she was on, Anika set it on the side table next to the couch. Reaching over the armrest, she went to turn off the lamp since her mind was finally dulled enough for sleep when—

Blackness engulfed her.

But she hadn't even touched the switch.

Her mind was no longer walking the edge between consciousness and sleep; now she was wide awake.

Especially when she noticed her *whole* house was swathed in shadow. Outside, thunder rumbled closer than before.

Had the storm blown a power line down? Or is Mikko finally executing his threats?

Her conversation with him about coincidences floated back through her head.

On silent feet, she slunk toward the cased opening leading from her living room to the main hall of her house. If Mikko, or anyone for that matter, was breaking in, she'd be ready.

Peering down the corridor toward her kitchen, more darkness greeted her. Not even the light above her stove was on as it usually was. Nearby, she flipped a light switch, testing it for power. Nothing.

The rain outside pelted the windows as if it were clawing to get in. Something like excitement and dread ran through her, the telltale prickle of being watched returning. Someone was nearby even if she couldn't see them yet. But it didn't matter, she had an advantage here. Anika owned weapons and was in a space she knew well. An intruder wouldn't know the layout of her home like she did.

Unless it's Mikko...

Even then, his numerous visits didn't give him the same edge. Out of spite, Anika had rearranged her furniture slightly since he'd showered here to throw him off.

Padding into the foyer, she aimed to slink up the stairs so she could retrieve her gun tucked inside the safe near her bed. But something stopped her. The windows outlining her front door glowed.

Anika's brows rose.

Pressing her back to the wall, she inched closer, careful not to trip on a pair of shoes placed in the entry. Her movements were sure and soundless, eyes catching on the street lamp across the way from her house. Within the shadowed recesses of her home, the defiant source of light made her realize *her* power outage was an isolated event. If the storm was the cause of this, the whole street would be out.

"I swear to—" The sound of a door creaking open across her house halted her frustrated curses. Frozen, Anika flicked her gaze back down the hall in front of her, breath shallow as she listened.

A footstep.

The sound of her backdoor *snicking* shut.

Another footstep.

It *had* to be Mikko. No one else would be bold enough to cut her power and slip inside the privacy of her home. His message on her flowers was clear.

Moving about a foot to the right, Anika pressed herself up against the solid wood of the door lest her silhouette be seen against the windows. The ridges of her spine notched against the molding as she leaned into it, cloaked by its shadowed frame. Her mind calculated how long it would take for her to dash up the steps nearby, grab her gun, and meet the intruder with her weapon.

Anika's throat tightened, brain trying to stay calm and logical. She'd had plenty of years to practice—to hone her emotions into what she needed to survive—but there was still a small piece of her that remembered what happened when she was thirteen.

That home invasion had been one that had changed the trajectory of her life. Only this time she could fight and claw and scream. She had nothing to lose now.

More footsteps faintly echoed through her house, their origin on the opposite end and ascending the small set of steps leading into her kitchen. Without wasting another second, she dashed upstairs, avoiding all the creaking planks as she went. Her bare feet were nearly silent on the hardwoods, her gun safe greeting her as soon as she entered her room. Typing in the code, Anika's thoughts only calmed when the cool kiss of the gun was securely in her hand.

Would she now meet him on the stairs?

Only one way to find out.

Against her better judgment, she walked back the way she came, waiting to see his silhouette composed of shadow and molten viridescent eyes. Her breaths shortened, her eyes focusing on the stretch of steps leading down and to the front door she'd been pressed against. Slowly, she descended. There was no escaping Mikko, so she might as well meet him head on.

Step by step she made progress, expecting his head to appear between the wooden balusters at any minute. Her gun was pointed down, but both hands gripped it, her body ready to aim and shoot when the time came.

Down, down, down she went until finally her foot touched the wooden floor of the foyer once more.

A scuff of a boot on her floor had her eyes snapping up toward the hall, her gun following in suit. Mikko's frame filled the doorway before her, the image uncannily similar to the one he'd sent her a week ago. He lurked inside the short hall, about ten feet separating them still.

Come on, she taunted internally.

As if hearing her silent mocking, his boot crossed over and into the dim light. The windows surrounding her door provided enough to see by, her eyes already adjusted courtesy of her cut power.

Recklessness flowed through her veins, the promise of a game whispering in the back of her mind. She could pop off a shot and wound Mikko, which would give her enough time to fling herself through the front door. She didn't want to take her chances with someone twice her size even if he deserved it.

"Are you sure you're ready to put our lessons to the test?" Mikko's voice cut through the tension.

"You're the one who broke in," she countered, "seems like you have a death wish."

"We have unfinished business."

"I like to let my gun do the—"

In the amount of time it'd taken her to utter the words, Mikko crossed the foyer, his black jean clad legs eating up the distance. The air was sucked out of her lungs, his presence both frightening and overwhelming. Her finger barely pressed on the trigger, but she was too slow and he was too fast.

"Ow—what the fuck!" Before she could get a shot off, the barrel was securely in his hand, her wrists aching from where he'd squeezed hard enough to force her to release.

"That can be our next lesson, *malyshka*," he damn near gloated all while tucking her gun into the waistband of his pants at his back. There was that word again, only this time she knew the meaning: baby.

"I don't think I want any more lessons from you—"

A gloved hand wrapped itself around the expanse of her neck, squeezing the rest of her sentence out. His muscular body pressed itself against hers, her sleep clothes making sure she felt *everything*, and the scent of rain had followed him in. The fragrance of petrichor clung to his damp clothing, wafting into her nose as she huffed in irritation.

"That's too bad because I'm about to teach you one *right now*," he spoke again, fingers tightened in warning.

Although it was dark, Anika glared up at him as her teeth clenched in silent anger. She observed the dark shirt covering his skin, hiding the telltale tattoos she knew lingered underneath. And that wasn't accounting for the black balaclava pulled over his head, concealing his face from her. But not his identity…

Only a sliver of his countenance was on display. His eyes.

And it was like her nightmares—her body frozen in time, her own gaze locked with his.

A flash of lightning swept across the sky outside, painting her foyer in bright, white light. It disappeared as quickly as it came, but she saw all she needed to.

Sun dappled forest floors.

Frost covered blades of grass.

Will I die with each of his fickle moods painted in the back of my skull in the form of his ever changing eyes?

"And if I refuse," she finally managed, his hand still allowing room for her to speak.

"*Anika,*" his voice was deep, conveying authority, "this isn't negotiable."

"Why wear the mask?" His free hand came up and rested on the door next to her head, caging her in. "I already know who you are."

"Is that so?" A smile was evident in his words even though she couldn't see his mouth. "Is that why you didn't run? Thought you could talk me out of it?"

"Talk you out of what?"

A clothed thumb ran over her bottom lip. "Getting what I want."

She gritted her teeth. "I'm not following."

"Don't tell me your cleverness is slipping, *malyshka.*"

"*YA nachinayu dumat', chto tvoy,*" she sneered. *I'm starting to think yours is.* "Pretty bold of you to come back here."

A soft chuckle filled the space as he bridged the remaining gap between them. If her fluent use of Russian surprised him, he hid it. Her rage burned even hotter. A few stray raindrops dripped off his clothes, splattering onto her exposed skin.

"What can I say, something about this place feels like *home.*"

"If you don't get out, you're going to *wish* I shot you." She reached for where he'd tucked her gun away.

The hand by her head snatched her wrist, halting her movements. "Not so fast, Anika. At least ask for my consent first."

"You're infuriating."

Boots met the tips of her socks as he leaned in, unable to be close enough to her. Underneath the rain's musk, she smelled his cologne—a wash of bergamot layered in smoke, leaving her feeling lightheaded. "Watching you press your thighs together at the gun range was infuriating. This tiny sleep set is *infuriating.*"

Heat rushed over the surface of her skin, every exposed inch suddenly feeling vulnerable to his blatant perusal.

So he'd noticed that. Fuck. "Tiny is...subjective."

"And so is obsession, yet here we are."

"I don't know what the fuck you're talking about," she said, her body wiggling against his in search for space to slip through and run away. His muffled groan had her pausing, the movements way too close to something else. "But I *do* think you're losing it."

His laugh cemented her words. "Is that what you're going to tell everyone when the details of Ivan's death come to light?"

Her throat bobbed, his hands unmoving. "What? Maybe if you weren't so busy obsessing over me, you could've found the actual perpetrator."

"I tried, Anika, I really did. This all started as a precaution, but now..." Mikko's voice trailed off, "now, it's spiraling out of control."

Another shiver threatened to overtake her as Mikko's body heat mingled with her own, her skin prickling with goosebumps. She fought against his hold if only to prove her point. "And who's in control right now?" She pointedly looked at his hands and body compared to hers, but he shook his head.

"No," he huffed, his fingers trembling against her neck. "Not when you're in my *head*"—Mikko rested his forehead against her own—"not when I can't get you out."

"Not. My. Problem." Her voice was stern, but she didn't dare move, his own body way too close. And the same feeling that had woven itself beneath her skin at the range had returned. Tenfold. The heat of his gaze was unbearable in this small of a space.

"It *is* your problem because you *started* this."

Anika tugged her arm from his grasp. "You're crazy."

"Should've done better research on me." Mikko's hand released her throat, slipping down, down, content to trace the line of her collarbone. "You should've known that I can't just 'move on.' I get too...attached."

"Stop touching me."

"You didn't care when we met all those weeks ago." Her lips pressed into a thin line. She wouldn't rise to the bait; instead her hand inched back toward the door knob. "You didn't care when you walked up and touched *me*."

"Is that what this is all about?" She tried to lean away from him but there was nowhere to go.

"Depends...why are my men going missing?" His hands wandered back up, trailing up the side of her face, outlining her lips. "And don't lie. It only started happening after we met. I'm not stupid like Levi."

A fire erupted in her chest, chasing away the ice gathering there. She stayed quiet, hoping he'd take her silence for an answer all on its own.

"Oh, don't be shy now, *malyshka,* I know how much you like to tease."

"You know nothing," she spat.

"I *know* it was your DNA on the piece of gum securing the note to my bike's windshield." His hands planted themselves back on the door, bookending her head between them. "I *know* you singled me out in the club. I *know* you've been taunting me because I'm a Romanov."

"You're going to have to try harder than this to get answers from me, Mikko," Anika countered, fingers closing around the door knob.

"You think I won't do what it takes to protect what's mine?"

"Is this what you call protecting? Storming into a random person's house and demanding answers when you don't even know the whole story." Her words were dripping in venom.

A gust of wind rushed through the trees outside while she stood there, trapped, waiting for him to reply.

"If you were anyone else, my methods would be...*different.*"

"Is it because I'm a woman? Are you scared to hurt me? Finally find someone you can't beat answers out of?" Anika laughed, the sound bright and loud despite the gloomy atmosphere. "Or is it because you're a fucking *mutt* of a man and can't control the urge to stroke and shove you measly little cock into—"

"*Shut up.*"

"Looks like your father's habits really *did* rub off on you," Anika sneered.

Something in the air shifted. Mikko's desperate mood evaporated, replaced with a more palpable anger.

"You don't know what you're saying...who you're talking about." His voice was strained, the leash on his emotions barely keeping everything in check.

Anika yearned to push him a little more wanting to see what happened when he *broke.* "Oh, but I do. Alek would be *so proud—*"

Mikko caught her jaw between his fingers, squeezing painfully tight. The rest of the words died on her tongue, adrenaline freely flowing through her veins. Her stomach tightened in anticipation. Teeth cut into soft tissue, but she refused to yield even when rusted copper coated her tongue.

"*Wrong thing to say, little moon,*" the words were spoken through his teeth. "Now, I consider myself a patient man, one who is willing to wait for something they want—investigate those who are behaving suspiciously—but you–you've been a persistent, little problem." His shaky inhale set her teeth on edge. "But I intend to rectify—"

Anika's knee wrenched up, connecting with his groin, cutting his speech short.

"*Ungh!*"

Mikko folded, his hands finally free of her body. Shoving him back, she used the distraction and distance to yank the door open. It opened a couple inches, the feeling of victory swelling in her chest. Rain splashed on the concrete sidewalk right outside, beckoning to her slip out. She needed to feel the fresh air on her skin and in her lungs. She couldn't think with him that close.

Slam!

The door closed within inches of her nose and foot, her thoughts of escaping him dashed. A prickling heat pressed against her back, shoving her into the now closed door. Her cheek smashed against the wood, blood freely flowing across her taste buds.

"Now why would you try that?" he growled in her ear.

The lump forming in her throat now sunk to the pit of her stomach. *Fuck.*

30

Late Night Confessions

Anika

Wrapping the length of her hair around his fist, he pulled her head back, straining her neck with the harsh angle. While her body should be scared, arousal pooled between her legs. Towering above her, his cloaked face staring down, she saw the anger there as the lightning outside flashed again. Thunder rumbled across the sky in pursuit. She feared a whole other storm was brewing inside her house.

There was also something else present amongst his fury.

Want? Desire?

Anika couldn't be sure, and she tried to ignore the way it made her skin hum. Goading him was becoming a task she enjoyed. In public, he always made sure to keep himself put together, an unreadable force, but now…

Now, she could read everything hidden beneath his mask.

"Everything you do, Anika," his breath tickled her cheek, the thinness of his balaclava barely shielding it from her face, "always gets under my skin. Somehow, someway."

She smiled despite the strands of hair Mikko had pulled free, her scalp burning from his harsh grip.

Before she could tell him to "*fuck off*," he pulled away from her body. Using her hair as a leash, he dragged her back forcing her body to bump roughly into his. Spinning, he forced toward the kitchen.

"What are you—"

"Ah, ah, ah," he hushed, boots kicking the back of her heels as he continued to usher her farther in. Neck still cranked back against his shoulder, her feet stumbling multiple times as they caught on the edges of her rugs. He prodded her onward regardless.

The darkness was thicker back here, the street lights unable to penetrate this deep into her house, so she was at the mercy of Mikko's whims. Her brain didn't miss the way he navigated her house, his feet knowing every creaky board and slant of the floor.

"Now, I'm going to ask nicely, *once*," he spoke against the side of her temple, his covered nose dragging through her silky strands of hair, "please sit in that chair."

Anika bucked against him, wishing for something sharp to stab him with.

"If you keep moving like that, we're going to have *other* problems," he continued before shoving her away. His words implied things she couldn't afford to think about right now. Especially when her own lust was building.

What will he do if I keep resisting, if I purposefully disobey.

All the sounds he'd make—

Anika shuffled over to the nearest chair in her kitchen. Carefully sitting, she watched as he approached her. Like a moth to flame...

"Imagine my surprise when I discovered your surname," he began, standing in front of her, his legs almost touching her knees as he braced his large hands against the back of her chair caging her in again. "Your *real* one."

"So when any other woman changes her last name, no one blinks an eye. But when *I* do it, it's an issue?"

One of his hands reached behind his back and for a moment Anika pictured her life ending right here, her promises unfilled. All it would take was one bullet to her head—or her heart—and it'd all be over.

Cool metal pressing against her arm had her thoughts clearing. Her gaze flicked down, already knowing what it was. Her gun. Its weight sunk into her flesh, the round tip of the barrel sure to leave an indent on her skin, but his finger wasn't over the trigger. He was getting off on this power trip, curious to see how far she would let him go in her own house. Too bad Anika was all too willing to give up everything for her own vendetta.

"Changing your name certainly didn't erase your smart mouth."

"And your last name didn't give you any IQ points," she shot back.

The gun slipped further up her arm, goosebumps rising in its wake. "My men and I don't take lightly to threats."

"Obviously," she muttered, if only to intensify his glare in the shadows.

"Are you the one killing them, Anika?"

"You're such a well-rounded guy, Mikko," she threw his name back at him, "an entrepreneur, a scammer, a stalker, *and* an investigator. Do you do time at the police station on the weekends? Volunteer work? I'm sure they *love* you there—"

"*Zamolchi.*" Be quiet.

"Oh, and bilingual, how could I forget."

"Answer. The. Question." She couldn't see his jaw, but she'd bet money it was clenched, his words tight.

She huffed. "No."

"No, as in 'no, I didn't kill your men,' or 'no, I'm not answering?'"

"I'll let you guess."

"And I'll let you guess if this gun is really loaded." He nudged it harder against her bare skin.

"I always keep one in the chamber. But you won't do it, you value this too much." Her hand gestured between them, and she knew the insinuation would rile him up. Anika pressed her lips together to keep the smug grin off her face.

"I wouldn't be so sure," his hulking frame was hard to discern against the shadows ensconcing him. "I can still get what I want from you if you're wounded."

"Seems like you got a type: wounded women so they can't run from you."

He removed the gun from her arm before backing away. Despite the lack of light, she could see the slight shake in his hands. She'd hit a nerve.

Tucking it back where he'd had it before, Mikko strode a couple feet away before bending down. There, in the darkness, he'd dropped a duffel bag.

"Aren't you just a little planner," she taunted, squinting in an attempt to see what he was rummaging for. She could've used the time to run—to escape past him and back through her house, but a small part of her knew he could shoot her without killing her, and she *really* didn't want to know what that felt like.

The thought alone drudged up memories she longed to keep buried. Images of blood splattered carpet flashed across her mind, taking her to a place far away—a place where her parents' memory lived. A piece of her heart withered away, but if this is what she needed to do to avenge her parents, then she would do it.

Shaking her head, she decided to remain seated. Maybe if she cooperated, he'd think she was complacent and docile. Anika stifled a snort.

"My father was good for some things." Bitterness coated his words.

He straightened, items dangling from his gloved hands. Tucking them beneath his arm, he ducked farther into the inky depths of the doorway leading down to her basement.

Anika sighed. "Can you at least turn the power back on so I can see you as you antagonize me?"

His words were almost lost to the sound of the rain pelting against the glass windows and surrounding vegetation outside. "Could've been the storm."

"And the street light that's still on outside?"

"An anomaly."

"More like a giveaway of your desperation," Anika said, words dark and bitter.

"Maybe, but by then, it was too late, wasn't it?"

A soft *click* was audible before all the lights that had been on in her house previously flashed back on. The harshness of it cut through her brain, her eyes watering at the visual intrusion. Spots swam across her eyesight, blurring the man before her.

Risking a bullet to her body, Anika's arm instinctively came up and sheltered her eyes from the brightness. "Damn, warn a girl first."

"And miss out on seeing you like this." His footsteps plodded closer, her eyes still adjusting. Lowering her arm, Mikko's masked face was unbothered by the change in light.

Bastard.

"Piss off."

Setting his supplies down on her small breakfast table nearby, Mikko slowly unraveled a length of rope. "I hate for it to be this way, but you always have to be so *difficult.*" She rolled her eyes. "Arms on the armrests of the chair...*please.*"

Because she wanted to see his knot tying skills, she listened.

Kneeling before her, rope in hand, he grasped her ankle instead. The touch seared her bare skin and had her nearly gasping. The wetness in her underwear was growing more noticeable. Gritting her teeth, her hands and feet ached to fidget while he touched her. The invasion of personal space was killing her while simultaneously setting her skin ablaze.

It reminded her of the gun range; his touches were semi-professional and fleeting, but still invoking something deep within her. It had to be her hatred morphing into its own entity, a feeling she was unaccustomed to experiencing so thoroughly.

"Sit still, little moon, I'll be quick."

The nickname had her freezing in place as she let him bind her legs—one to each leg of the chair. The sound of a knife sawing through the threads of rope occupied the tense silence between them. He read her hesitance as fear. Most women would be alarmed by such an intrusion—Anika was too if she really examined herself—but she was prepared, ready to look into the jaws of the beast she'd taunted.

Mikko used his height and stature to get what he wanted, imposing himself on her and threatening her without using as many words as he could. But Anika had been around men like him before, maybe even worse ones, and made it out alive. This time wasn't any different. Her discomfort came from security, or lack thereof, but that could be rebuilt.

Still kneeling, he used his torso to pry her legs the rest of the way open, determined to press his heated flesh against hers. The rainwater on him was drying, but a dampness clung to his clothes. She fought to not clamp her thighs around him.

"Why do you keep calling me that?" Anika suddenly asked.

Mikko laughed humorlessly, his eyes darker than before when he glanced up at her. "Your hair."

Two words, but still Anika's breath left her lungs. "What?"

He reached out and touched it with his free hand. "It was the first thing I noticed about you that day at *Bubblegum*. You were standing in line, glaring, and I caught sight of this…" he twirled a strand around his gloved finger. "It reminds me of a crescent moon, only a sliver of light left to keep you company on long nights." His voice softened, eyes unfocused as if he was reminiscing something else. "And there are *many* nights where most of you is hidden. Untrustworthy."

"Some might see that as a warning."

"I should've…"

"Your father teach you to nurture that kind of negligence?" she asked, fire in her eyes and in her heart.

Mikko huffed. "He taught me to be unwavering. Although I might've misconstrued his teachings when I channeled it into going after the things I wanted."

"Which is?"

"*You.*"

She swallowed, speechless. Pressed to her very center, he tied each wrist to an arm of the chair. Every movement had her skin tingling. She was painfully aware of every inch where they touched. Warmth rushed to her cheeks, anger blossoming in her face. But beneath that, there was something else. An edge she'd refused to examine—a void that was sick and twisted.

"That's a weak explanation," she countered breathily, unwilling to acknowledge what he'd said fully.

"When you start cooperating, I'll give you a better o—"

"Wha–I *am*. I'm in this damn chair, aren't I?"

"Small wins."

Anika clamped her jaw tight, tipped her head back, and focused on breathing through her nose. The small breaths she expelled only semi-distracted her. If she started ruminating on the fact that her body was reacting differently than what she wanted, she wouldn't make it out of this whole.

Satisfied with his work, he leaned back

"If you wanted to tie me up, you could've asked," Anika said, needing to break the silence. "I'll try anything once."

He chuckled, the noise slightly muffled from his mask. "I thought Levi did that 'all on his own.'"

"He does." She cocked her head. "Do you want all the explicit details?"

The corners of Mikko's eyes crinkled in distaste. "There's nothing to tell."

"And how would you know?"

His fingers tightened around her legs as his eyes glinted with mischievousness. "There's *nothing* I don't know about you."

"Lies." The heat of him between her legs was distracting. "If you truly knew, you would've killed me already."

"I have better uses for you than death, *malyshka*. Don't play coy with me," he gritted out.

"And here I thought you'd figured it out by yourself, you smart, little daddy's boy."

Lie. Lie. Lie.

"Where did you put Ivan's eyes?"

"This again?" she scoffed, narrowing her eyes up at him. *"Nowhere."*

"Stop lying to me!" He abruptly stood, hands in her hair before she could even attempt to fend him off. Sparks of pain tingled across her scalp, a yelp echoing out of her throat as he bent her head back. Again.

Squinting up at him, Anika sneered. "It's not a lie," he pulled harder, tears pricking the corners of her eyes, "it's an *omission*. Maybe if you actually *read* the file your friend pulled on me, you wouldn't be so daft. No wonder Alek—"

"You think you're so smart, don't you?" he snarled, but his grip loosened. She'd surprised him with that little piece of intel. "But I see right through you."

"You see what I want you to see, but you're too dense to realize that," Anika spat back at him. "Why do you think it took so long for us to end up here? Because that's what I *wanted*."

"Shut up—"

"Ask your friend, the one with the different hair color every other week," she continued, "I'm sure he'll tell you."

"Don't bring him into this, I *swear...*"

"*My* house, *my* rules."

Releasing her, he stepped back. He was fuming, and she could feel the anger coming off him in waves, but she didn't care. It felt good to get under his skin and make him uncomfortable in return.

Finally able to take a deep breath, she choked down air still tainted with his cologne.

"I know you left your spare key out for me," he countered.

"I-*what?*"

Mikko kept talking, anger making his tongue loose. "You invited me in, targeted me first—don't forget that."

"I did no such thing," she lied.

"Shut up."

"*No.*"

Slipping the gun from his waistband, he aimed it at her again. "Maybe I don't have a better use for you...maybe I *should* shoot you right now."

Anika cocked her head. "Go on—kill me." His silence made her smile. "You seem to crave violence so much, yearn to see me dead, then do it. *Give in. Be just like daddy dearest.*"

His jaw ticked. "Only after you tell me where Ivan's eyes are. Where Dimitri is."

She laughed manically.

"You might fight it now, Anika, but I can be patient. I'll wait for you to come around."

She composed herself enough to respond. "I won't."

Stooping to her level, he wedged himself between her bound legs once more, the action mimicking vulnerability, but she didn't fall for it. Bringing the gun in close, Mikko pushed it into her sternum. "You're a bad habit." She swallowed thickly. "And you know what I do to bad habits?" Mikko asked, his other hand dragging down her thigh toward her knee, "I *break* them."

Anika shook her head. "Is that what happened to Samantha? Did you break her?"

His body stiffened at the mention of his high school girlfriend's name. "My father did that for me."

"Of course, he did *everything* for you. What about Ellie?"

He laughed, the sound more relaxed than moments before, his emotions were a rollercoaster that Anika was finding hard to follow. His gloved hand traced a lazy circle around her kneecap while she clenched her teeth, fighting the urge to gasp.

Damn this toxic connection.

His closeness, her anger, and the adrenaline coursing through her was doing weird things to her brain and body. Heat blazed across her skin making her mind dizzy.

"She decided I was…too much for her tastes," he finally answered.

"You make it sound so simple. So innocent."

"It was. She left quietly."

"How much did you pay her? Did you steal her clothes too? Break into her house?" Anika's words were steady despite the fury building inside her. Along with something else…

"You'd be surprised what I can convince people to do." His hand was still leisurely touching her.

"I'm not like the people you deal with."

"No?" A tense pause, then, "Maybe you're right, maybe you're worse."

Anika scoffed. "How has no one shot you yet?"

"Oh, they have, but they haven't been successful beyond anything merely superficial."

"Let me try then, *professor*," she murmured.

His breathy chuckle at the nickname made her gaze cut up to his awaiting one. "Maybe one day I'll let you."

Anika's lips pressed together tightly, everything leading her to this moment threatening to spill out.

With that, he reached back over to the table, setting the gun down and grabbing a roll of duct tape. "But now that you've gotten all that out of your system, I think"—the sound of tape ripping free of its backing echoed in her kitchen—"it's time for *this*."

Anika's spine stiffened against the chair. "I thought this was an interrogation...which involves *talking?*"

"I can't have you screaming and alerting all your neighbors now, can I?" The sticky piece of tape he held plastered itself over her mouth before she could spit at him. Her mumbled curses were trapped behind the tape.

What a dick.

"Did you ever ask Ivan how he felt when he was in this position weeks ago?" Silenced, Anika sat there, waiting. His green eyes roved over her, the feeling burning her skin as if he was physically still touching her. "Last time I saw him, this was how he looked."

"I didn't kill him," but the words were muffled, indiscernible.

"I'm going to ask you again, Ms. Naidu—a yes or no question—if you killed Ivan." He caressed the rope binding her wrists as if to remind her she was at his mercy.

She shook her head.

"Really?" Her brow raised in question, mute while he continued. "Because when I ran a background check on you it came back clean. Too clean if you ask me, but Cristiano has called me paranoid before, so I ignored it…for a while.

"Until the other morning. I was lying awake in bed when it hit me. Why is a seemingly nice young woman like you in all the places I'm at? Why would someone with a squeaky clean background, such as yours, wander into *my* club, tour one of *my* warehouses, date one of *my* men?"

Anika could feel the angst rolling off him in waves. Muttering incoherent sentences against the tape, she tried to wordlessly explain herself. His head cocked, a wicked glint evident in his eyes. While every other piece of him was covered, all she needed was this—eyes told everything.

"No one with a decent personal history, or self respect for that matter, would date Levi—would come around someone like me. So, what are you hiding, Anika? What plans are you brewing up in this pretty little head?" A gloved fingertip tapped her temple. "I'm feeling nice and want to give you this moment to come clean *before* I read your file myself. A little test to determine your trustworthiness, if you will."

Wiggling in the chair, she wrenched her eyes shut, desperately wishing to speak, to curse, to *attack.* But nothing. Mikko watched her struggle as if this was comical to him. Maybe it was, and that made Anika's blood run hot.

"Did someone put you up to this?" he placed his hands on top of her forearms, pinning her in place even more than she already was. "One of my own men?"

With a furrowed brow, Anika shook her head. She would not allow for a *man* to take credit for her work.

"Persistence is as much a virtue as patience, Anika. And I will find out why you singled me out; it's only a matter of time."

"Time you don't have," she mumbled behind the tape.

Despite her wrists being leashed to the chair, she managed to flip him off with vigor.

Leaning in, she had no choice but to stare into his emerald eyes, the irises glimmering in the light. His finger traced the outline of the tape on her skin, mocking her. His eyes dipped down to her covered lips, then back up. "I'm sorry, I didn't catch that." His sarcasm made her grit her teeth. Her nails dug into the arm of the chair, leaving little marks. Her mind tried to focus on that—the wood grain beneath her hands, and not the hate she concealed behind her teeth. Her throat ached as a scream built.

"Care to try and repeat it?" he pressed, his covered face impossibly close.

Anika mumbled, *"fuck you,"* this time knowing he wouldn't understand. Nonetheless, it made her feel slightly better, and he inclined his head farther.

"How badly do you want me to—"

Crack!

Anika knocked her head into his, their closeness making it easy. Pain radiated out from her forehead, her skull aching from the hardness of his own head. But his surprise made it worth it.

"Fuck!" Mikko backed away, gloved hand clutching his forehead. Hers currently pounded from the harsh contact. Despite the pain, she was relatively unscathed; Anika had a hard head in more ways than one.

"Why the *fuck* did you do that?"

Smiling beneath the tape, Anika shrugged, cocking her head to the side as if to say, *"no reason."*

As he turned away from her, his back was on display, and Anika wondered briefly if he had tattoos there as well.

Dangerous train of thought, she internally chided.

He gripped his head while trying to think of ways to torture her most likely. Anika squirmed in her chair. The ropes were tight, but if she could begin loosening them now, she'd be ahead of his own schemes.

Whipping back around as if remembering himself—and his *captive*—Mikko's hand lashed out. Anika was *sure* his palm would connect with her cheek, a punishment for her own retaliation. But she was surprised when he ripped the tape free from her mouth.

A gasp flew out of her, the freedom tangible—the cool air brushing across her mouth ushering in a sense of relief. She could finally speak. "Ow."

"Let's try this again," Mikko began, wadding up the tape and tossing it out of sight. His blatant disregard to her house pissed her off, but she kept her eyes trained on him. "I'm tired of playing these games with you, Anika. Why did you leave me the note?"

"If you're tired of playing games, why do this?" She looked down at her body as rope rubbed against her flesh.

He sighed as if she exhausted him. "Don't question me."

"And if that's *exactly* what I'm doing, what then? How far would you go for revenge?"

His eyes hardened, mind trying to unravel her so he could study her, but he'd find nothing. Anika was introspective, keeping everything to herself until she'd figured out what needed to be done. *Then*, she acted.

Until then, her secrets were just that.

Fire licked in her veins.

Desire darkened his eyes.

And the world stopped.

He was purposefully playing with her, drawing out her torture, trying to get her to crack.

And they were both feeding off the euphoric feeling.

"Then this is going to be a long, grueling process," he finally said.

"Someone is going to have to give," she started, "and it *isn't* going to be me."

"Oh, is that right?" His hand snaked up the front of her neck, gripping the delicate column of her throat. "Didn't I just tell you how patient I could be, little moon?"

He restricted her blood flow, squeezing tightly. "Those who are truly patient don't have to reassure those around them—"

Before she could even finish her sentence, the softness of his black balaclava brushed against her lips. Even though there was material still between them, shock sparked throughout her body, shivers zipping down her spine at the sudden contact. And as much as she wanted to shy away from him, she couldn't.

It felt dirty to kiss him. And she liked it.

The warmth leaching through the fabric had her tugging uselessly against her restraints. His lips pressed against hers, eager to touch her even if there was a barrier between them. Despite their argument, their overall situation, there was a hunger in Mikko—one Anika wanted to tear out of him. He always kept it locked behind his stoic facade unless he was around her. Then, all hell broke loose.

Everything sparking between them conveyed what they couldn't say: desire and unadulterated lust. Anika knew she shouldn't want it, knew they were always at each other's throats, but this felt so good. *He* felt so good. Curse the threads of hate tying them together. Those emotions were beginning to suspiciously feel similar.

If only he wasn't Alek's son...

Mikko groaned against her lips, the sound vibrating across her sensitive skin. It was at such odds from the ripping sensation of the tape moments before.

If she'd have guessed confessing partially to Mikko would encourage him to break in and kiss her, she might've gone about this differently. But now, she didn't want him to stop. He was in the palm of her hand, and it was the most exhilarating feeling in the world.

Pulling away, Mikko's breath slightly labored, had her wishing his mask was gone—that she could feel him against her skin unhindered. So she could sink her fucking teeth into him.

No, no, no.

Meeting his gaze head on, mostly unashamed of what had happened, she was surprised to see pain blatantly displayed in his eyes.

"Fuck," he whispered.

Heat pooled between her thighs, her ability to clench them together mostly prohibited from his expert knots. She swallowed audibly, trying to school her features and tamp down her vile thoughts.

"You shouldn't have done that." Anika's voice was quiet but strong. "Untie me and see how things go for you then."

Backing away, he put more distance between them as if he didn't trust himself.

Good.

"What and take the fun out of this?" His words were light but there was a fire blazing in his eyes.

"What? You don't want me to touch you?" she said, a sweet smile forming on her face as she teased him. "You showering and coming all over my things has me thinking differently. You don't want to know what it feels like for me to kiss and lick and suck—"

"I don't think you'd want to see the man I become..." he trailed off, emotions back to cool and collected.

If her hands had been free, she would've wiped her mouth. "I think you're using that excuse as a crutch."

She'd learned long ago that even though humans were complex, they could be boiled down into attributes. And she was figuring Mikko out piece by piece. He was ruled by his emotions, but did everything in his power to remain emotionless in front of others. Anika wanted to see him crack—knew he already had. Him breaking in and cornering her was an action so full of feeling that it was amazing he couldn't see it himself.

But Anika had no intention of giving the reins back to the man in front of her.

No, not until I get what I want.

"Besides, I've encountered people worse than you and made it out. I won't be intimidated in my own home."

Running his hands over the top of his head, forgetting his hair was protected by the balaclava, he tugged futilely on the fabric in frustration. "Intimidation is *not* the word I think of when I think of this." His hands motioned between them and the distance he purposefully put there.

Anika smiled, words full of venom to hide her underlying emotions. "At least this time I know you'll go home and have a great time with your hand..."

"That's low, even for you."

"Get out."

He gathered his things and slung the duffel bag over his back. "When you decide to play nice, *malyshka,* you know where to find me."

Her blood ignited farther. "Says the stalker."

"Takes one to know one, little moon," he started, a humorless smirk evident in his words, "but I believe our business here is finished. For now."

Backing away, he looked at her one more time, the intensity in his gaze crippling. "I trust you can weasel your way out," he said, nodding to her restraints.

"Wait—" she squirmed, trying to loosen the knots he'd created. She could, but it'd take her longer than she'd like.

"I'll see you around." With that he exited as quietly as he'd entered, leaving her too stunned to move. Glancing over to her table, she saw he'd left her gun there.

How generous, she inwardly scoffed.

The sound of the rain died down in his absence, leaving Anika feeling empty, anxious, and guilty. All emotions she hated more than anything else.

31

Lens

Mikko

Have I pushed too far? Crossed too many boundaries?

Mikko found himself not caring. Breaking into her house while she was there was risky—an idea that may come back and bite him—but he hadn't been able to help himself.

And their *kiss...*

He could still smell her on his balaclava; he could still feel her soft lips pressed against his. Shivering, he remembered the way her warm skin seared through his street clothes, making all his reasonable thoughts scatter. His dick had been too hard the whole way home, and even though he could relieve some of the pressure with his hands, it'd never fully work.

With a sigh, Mikko unlocked the door to his penthouse, eager to disappear and have a moment to think. His mind needed a quiet place to gather his disarrayed thoughts. Even though she'd told him she had nothing to do with Ivan, he didn't believe a single word that came out of her mouth. Even though he *really* wanted to.

"And if that's exactly what I'm doing, what then? How far would you go for revenge?"

Her words haunted him. All this time, while he'd been trying to protect his own business and friends, maybe she was also doing the same? The unopened manila folder with her background, her true background and not the fake one she put up, sat untouched on his kitchen island. After everything, doubt had crept in. Stopping by the office on the way home had been easy, carrying it with him in the elevator had been easy, but now as it stared at him...

He suddenly didn't want to know. Mikko had a sinking feeling that whatever he was about to find would shatter the illusion he formed around himself. Anika would no longer be an escape but a threat. She'd be someone he needed to eliminate.

The mere thought had anxiety crawling up the back of his throat. His mind pored over other avenues they could take that didn't involve bloodshed—that didn't involve Mikko becoming like Alek. His father had no problem eliminating threats, barely needed any information to come to a decision. Violence had always been the answer for him.

But for Mikko...

Her skin had been oh, so warm and soft against his, her compliance admirable even when he could see how much fire was in her eyes, but it was also alarming. She was too wild to not go without a fight, so what angle was she working tonight?

Why let me win? Why let me kiss her?

He didn't regret it. If anything he was disappointed that he hadn't continued. It'd taken everything in him not to rip the binds from her wrists and ankles and lay her out on her own kitchen floor, fingers and tongue eager to memorize the planes of her skin—

His body reacted, semi-hard cock already stiffening beneath his pants. He could take care of his lust, this physical issue, but there was something deeper that couldn't be satiated.

Another sigh filled the empty space around him, the city lights glimmering beyond the panes of glass. As he laid on his couch, eyes tracing the skyline's silhouette, he thought about all the decisions leading him here—leading him so far from where he originally wanted to go.

What had begun as a random interaction had quickly turned into a dirty investigation. One that had transformed into him feeling things he shouldn't toward a woman who was out for blood. *His* blood. But he'd always wanted to escape Romanov Real Estate, his burn out so far gone that he felt *nothing* when his men and business started crumbling all around him.

Instead, he only felt alive when Anika was near.

He needed to get some rest, but the adrenaline coursing through his veins made it hard. Many nights he fell into bed, drained and letting sleep claim him before the incessant thoughts did, but tonight proved harder. After many minutes of laying there, waiting for his mind to go blank and for the ever elusive pull of sleep to find him, Mikko gave up.

Standing, his sock clad feet carried him to the sleek stairs leading up to the loft of his residence. It was an open space overlooking his living room below. It was too small for his tastes for a bedroom, but it was perfect for one of his many hobbies. Photography.

The glass paneled railing allowed for unimpeded views while he sat at his L-shaped work desk. Papers and crafts and models littered the surface. It was the one area he allowed himself to be free and messy—no rules. Minimal wall space forced him to only hang art he deemed unparalleled: pieces of his mom's collection. The brush strokes were sure, the whispering and soft landscapes wholly her. Every time he saw them, he smiled. It'd been a pain in the ass to track them down after his father had sold them off nearly two decades ago, but now Mikko had limitless money and power.

When he wasn't consumed with the mafia or his father's incessant teachings, he let his mind wander to the aesthetics and the beauty of the surrounding world.

Painting with his mom had been one outlet, but now he enjoyed capturing people's essence through photos. There were binders on his desk that were filled with compositions and experimental shots. Pictures of places he'd visited abroad. Anything that captivated him, he had a photo of.

As his finger trailed over the edge of a model he'd made, he knew he was avoiding the inevitable—drawing out his fate. He should be opening Anika's folder instead, sifting through everything it contained like his life depended on it—because it did—but one last night of daydreaming wouldn't hurt, right?

How many times are you going to tell yourself that? he thought miserably. Other than vodka, avoidance was his coping method of choice.

Mikko was softer than most, a fact his father had drilled into him, but he shook the thoughts away. Running his hands through his hair, the strands wild and in need of a comb, Mikko moved over to gaze at the messy pile of photos on his desk—some ranging from sunsets and landscapes, to unassuming people he'd captured on the city streets.

And beneath those, lurked ones giving physical form to the muse of his mind. *Anika.*

Eyes full of anger and mischief, the color of melted caramel, liquid under the heat and sure to eviscerate anyone who got too close.

Dark hair enticed him to come closer despite her poisonous bite. Anika. Anika. Anika.

He made sure to hide them beneath the other photos, desperately trying to convince himself they were only here because of his personal investigation. And the hidden album of more photos on his phone? Same explanation. But now, after the night he'd spent pressed close to her—kissing her—he was starting to question it.

How bad can it be?

A dangerous thought.

As his mom always said, *"Beautiful things enrapture people like us, Mikko. Others often won't understand, but that's okay."*

He gritted his teeth, the pit in his stomach yawning, threatening to consume every bright spot he'd held close in his heart. He wondered who he would have become had his mom managed to stay beside him. It was a haunting question keeping him up on nights like these.

And with no one to tell, Mikko often slipped into bad coping methods.

Another one being Anika.

* * *

Mikko - 24 Years Ago

"—he's coming with me regardless if you think it's a waste of time," Mikko's mom whispered from around the corner. Her voice was strong and defiant in the face of his father even as she desperately tried to keep Mikko from overhearing the conversation.

Eavesdropping was becoming one of his favorite pastimes, his ability to creep through the halls of their house and gather information slightly addicting to his childlike brain.

"He needs to be here, with me, learning the business," Alek responded. "How else will he learn?"

"He has his whole life ahead of him, don't rush him. He's too young. What could you possibly have him do?"

Mikko softly smiled, forever grateful his mom spoke when he could not. Recently, tensions had been running high, the real estate business taking off and keeping Alek busy. Despite the success, his father was tense, looking for someone to take his frustrations out on, and Mikko always wound up being his scapegoat.

"Kids grow up fast, Eleanor. He'll be a spiteful teen who wants nothing to do with us soon enough. And by that time, it'll be too late."

"You're so dramatic. He'll come around when he's ready."

"He's ready *now*."

His mom ignored him. "We'll talk about this more later; you're going to make us late to our class."

At the sound of a faint kiss, Mikko knew he needed to put some distance between himself and his parent's private conversation.

Quickly, his feet were soundless as he ran back the way he'd come from. The corridor of their house was opulent and cold. Art his mom had curated and collected from art directors and galleries across the world hung on the walls, their colors bleeding together as he dashed past. Skidding around a corner, out of sight, he bent over to catch his breath.

"Mikko!" she called out not knowing he was closer than she thought, "You ready to head out to our painting class?"

Straightening his clothes, he schooled his features into something unsuspecting and rounded the corner. "Hi mom, I'm ready."

Her hair was dark and pulled back into a messy bun. Her clothes were casual, something she could get paint on and not care about. While she looked carefree—an artist's spirit embodied—he didn't miss the dark circles forming under her eyes and the shine dulling from her hair. Mikko was beginning to wonder if his father's money was taking a mental toll on her too. She'd never approved of the way he'd earned it or spent his time, but he bought her whatever she wanted, especially art.

Maybe it would be enough to keep them quiet—happy.

Despite the tired look in her eyes, her features brightened when she saw him. "Perfect, we have blank canvases awaiting us. I can only imagine what my little daydreamer will create today."

Her words erased the intuition that'd been niggling in his gut moments before.

AN HOUR LATER they sat at easels. His mom's fine brush strokes were enviable.

"How do you make it look so easy?" he asked, tongue poking out from the corner of his mouth in concentration.

She smiled, pausing briefly to glance over at him. "Years of practice."

"But I'm nine, that's plenty old enough to be good at this."

His mom's lilting laughter warmed his heart, canceling out the frustrations lingering there. "Hardly, you've got so much time left ahead of you, Mikko. Don't rush perfection." She wiped the color smeared on her fingers onto her apron.

"But I want to be like you." A protest from his lips.

"And you will, give it time." It was a promise from hers.

The conversation he'd overheard earlier lingered in his mind. What if he didn't learn fast enough? What if he couldn't prove to his father that he was meant for more than real estate and scams? What if he was roped into the family business instead?

Even as a young kid, Mikko knew that was the *last* thing he wanted.

"Besides, you have an eye for this. It's only a matter of time before it *clicks*." Turning back to her canvas, his mom continued. It was a sunset, the orange color blazing across the horizon defiantly. Everyone in the room was painting some version of it, the instructor at the front of the class helping lead some parts of the painting, but to him, his mom's was the best.

She always soared above the rest.

Unable to help himself, the words burst free. "What if dad is right?"

Her spine stiffened slightly. "What do you mean, dear?"

"That I should be focusing on learning all that I can from him about the business."

A moment of silence as she feathered in a rich pink color onto her piece. "Someone's been eavesdropping I see." She glanced over at him knowingly.

"I know...I shouldn't have, but dad's always arguing."

"He's going through a rough patch right now. Stress impacts everyone differently, and for your father...well, he has a tendency to expect everyone to play pretend like him."

Reaching over, her paint flecked hand squeezed Mikko's shoulder. "Besides, you know how he is, he's never been able to understand the world like us, dear. We see it from a different lens—as a place to be explored and revered. But your father," she sighed, and Mikko couldn't tell if it was in exhaustion or remembrance, "he sees the world in black and white, logic overruling everything else. He forgets the small things that make up life—make it beautiful.

"Never lose that, Mikko. It's what makes you special."

"I won't." He picked up his brush again, motivation reinvigorated.

Little did he know that would become a lie, that his promise would falter in the face of his father's anger. Everything his mom worked for would crumble, the city forgetting what kind of woman she'd been.

And never would he have guessed the same hands she painted with would wither away to bone, motor skills gone from the chemotherapy, and her brilliant shining light snuffed out like a candle blown out from a cold wind.

32

Masks

Mikko

Halloween.

The city was crawling with ghosts and ghouls wandering the streets in search of treats, and for the adults, alcohol to encourage the frivolity of the holiday.

Despite his best efforts, Mikko was among them, being pulled along by Cristiano—his hair currently orange with a jack'o lantern design etched into the short hairs.

"Keep up," he encouraged, throwing a glance over his shoulder. "We're going to miss the costume contest."

Mikko huffed. "I don't think I'm winning it regardless."

Cristiano socked him in the shoulder. "That's what a sore loser would say."

The historic neighborhood they wove through boasted small corner shops currently either selling wares for Halloween or they were reconfigured to entice people to enter into their "haunted" depths. After parking down the block, the place they headed toward was one Cristiano's friend owned. Mikko had only been convinced to come out because for one, Cristiano was too sweet to say no to, and two, because he promised the venue was quaint and cozy. No large, distracting crowds for either of them to become potential targets in.

Hopefully.

It still didn't prevent Mikko from looking over his shoulder and noting every face passing by him. Even if he was mainly doing that to see if he'd catch a glimpse of Anika. He'd finally opened her file late last night. Anika Naidu's past was much different than Anika Simmons. Petty crime including theft, hacking, and physical assault littered her teenage years until she went to a local college for data analytics. After that, her life seemed to straighten up, her appearances aligning with the young business woman she was today.

But none of that was what made him pause.

It was her parents instead.

Khalid and Ira Naidu. He was dead, and she was currently living in an assisted living facility. The last name seemed familiar, and upon further investigating, Mikko found out one of their properties was acquired mere weeks after Khalid's death. By Romanov Real Estate.

His blood had run cold, his father's signature smattered across the scanned in paperwork. That could only mean one thing. Anika's father had paid in blood, and now she was hellbent on forcing Mikko to do the same thing.

Revenge brought them together.

Even though his brain tried to deny it, Anika was the one behind his men's deaths, picking them off in order to get closer to him—to incite fear.

Clever, *clever* woman.

And that should've sent him running right there, but a more twisted realization formed in his head. They shared the same enemy: a dead man.

Then, there was the more complicated matter of their kiss. It still seared against his lips, the same balaclava he'd worn last night adorning his face now. He could faintly smell her perfume on it, and he'd be damned if he washed it.

While Mikko had chosen an unremarkable costume—he'd thrown his balaclava, helmet, and hoodie on to emulate a biker—Cristiano's getup was the complete opposite.

The Headless Horseman.

Cheesy eighteenth century garb cloaked Cristiano's frame. An inky frock coat with gold buttons glinting in the streetlamps was perched on his shoulders, a white and wrinkled waistcoat beneath it. Dark breeches with tall socks and silly buckle shoes at his feet completed his outfit. He'd be lucky if those lasted the night with how cheap they were. A long cloak was draped over his arm, a necessary accessory he'd mentioned on the way over, but he kept it off so people didn't "step all over it."

But the final piece was his hair. The Headless Horseman's signature pumpkin head colored into his buzz cut. It was clever, and Mikko knew there would be endless praise coming his friend's way.

Mikko's armored hoodie and pants kept the chilly wind at bay, but once they reached their destination, it may bite him in the ass.

Oh, well.

The price he'd pay for being lazy and wanting to keep his face and skin covered.

"How much longer?" Mikko asked, tired of bumping shoulders with everyone on the sidewalk.

"Why? Second guessing this already?"

"No…maybe."

Cristiano laughed.

"What? These boots are meant for riding not walking," Mikko added defensively.

"And who's idea was that?"

"*Mine,*" he grumbled. "But you encouraged it, saying something like 'it's Halloween, Mikko, live it up.'"

"Fair, but when I'm right and the ladies are hanging off your arms by the end of the night, I expect a thank you."

There was only one woman he wanted hanging on his arm. "Sounds exhausting."

"Suit yourself." Cristiano grinned, before pointing up ahead. The brownstones had thinned out, a large swatch of grassy lawn—its green dulling with the frigid air—spread out before them. "But here we are."

Faux tombstones lined the tall wrought iron fence edging the sidewalk from the manicured landscaping. Fallen leaves filled the spaces between the decorations. Twinkling lights and skeletons littered the lawn, the voids between them creating walking paths. A few mature trees stood stoically, sheltering the "quaint" house they were going to.

"You said this was a *small* party," Mikko commented as people filed up the drive and into the ornate, Romanesque house. It felt rude to only call it a house; its grandeur deserving more. It was reminiscent of a castle.

And he was going to laugh his ass off if Cristiano's friend was dressed as Dracula.

People dressed up for the occasion mingled on the lawn, either surrounding a couple of the small fire pits or wandering through the maze of decorations expertly set up.

"It *is* a small party…for us." Cristiano wasn't technically wrong, but—

"You're lucky your pumpkin head is truly attached, or else I'd swat it off your damn shoulders." Mikko rumbled darkly, though his words lacked any true malicious intent.

His friend's laughter warmed something deep inside his chest as they headed toward the entrance.

As soon as they'd stepped inside the time capsule of a mansion currently draped in cheap Halloween decor, Mikko had flipped his helmet's visor down. The dark tint of it made it hard to navigate parts of the house, the wall sconces dimmed to set the mood, but it also allowed him to remain anonymous.

Rugs softened his footsteps as he followed Cristiano toward the kitchen where the drinks were being served. Apparently, the friend who set up this "quaint" party could be found there. Brushing past the shoulders of other partygoers, Mikko trailed behind, his sharp eyes cataloging his surroundings. It was a habit he found hard to break, even when he was somewhere non-work related.

Polished woodwork lined the halls before opening up to a bright kitchen, its tiles spotless. Everything had a place and purpose, an idea he could personally get behind, but something about the coldness of it had his mind pausing. Honestly, he wouldn't be surprised if this room was even used by the family who owned the mansion. More cheesy decor was scattered about, flickering faux candles and black glittery skulls lined every flat surface.

There were two large islands amidst the sprawling white marble. The first one was where a group of people gathered to talk, and the other had a man dressed up as a werewolf serving drinks to whoever wandered up. It was trendy and gaudy, but he had little time to formulate a retort to Cristiano about how their definitions of small were vastly different when his friend was already making a bee-line for the bartender.

Be ready to socialize, he thought.

"Weston!" Cristiano called out, rounding the island and clapping the other man on his back. Most of his costume had been shucked off, claw gloves and mask sitting on the counter, to give him the ability to play bartender. Weston's light eyes lit up when he spotted Cristiano, quickly setting a bottle of liquor down so he could embrace the other man.

"Cris, glad to see you"—a lifted brow as he took in his costume—"and I see you've outdone yourself. As usual."

Cristiano spun playfully to show off his outfit and hair.

"Every year has to be better than the last. I'm the Headless Horseman," Cristiano said before gesturing to Mikko. He opened his mouth to follow in suit, but his friend beat him to it. "And this is my steel horse also known as my getaway method, Mikko."

Weston chuckled and reached out to shake his hand. Quickly, the other man grasped his fingers, and Mikko was grateful for his gloves. Mikko nodded before flipping his visor up to appear less closed off and more personable for the benefit of his friend. He added, "More like I'm the only one who can drive us home after these kinds of parties."

"Ha! You're just jealous I know how to let loose," Cristiano jabbed.

"Sure, something like that."

"Let's get Mikko here a drink, what do ya say?" Weston nodded along with Cristiano. "Somethin' to loosen up his jaw."

Mumbling phrases that would warrant soap in his mouth, he told Weston he'd take anything as long as it was a vodka neat.

DRINKING WAS MORE of a challenge than he'd anticipated. While his helmet kept him tucked away like a piece of armor, it prevented him from accessing fluids easily. Cristiano noticed a few minutes into their evening and promptly got him a straw, but he was still apprehensive. While drinking may be one of his questionable outlets, he wasn't one for getting intoxicated at a stranger's house.

And he wasn't lying entirely when he told Weston someone had to get both him and Cristiano home. He wanted his friend to have a good time, so he'd be their designated driver.

His vodka was getting warmer by the minute, but he didn't mind. The thought of alcohol didn't sit right with him anyway tonight, Anika still lingering in the back of his mind. Cristiano had slipped off with a couple of other friends, and if he had to guess, they were playing drinking games out in the elaborate sunroom.

While wandering through the house, Mikko took his time looking past the Halloween decor and digesting the curated art hanging on the walls. Many were one of a kind pieces speaking to Weston's taste and bank account. Beyond that there were sculptures and statues decorating the halls, some made of marble, others made of bronze. He'd even stumbled across a couple of knights' armor, their pieces and parts polished in the candlelight. It was a beautiful distraction from the loud music and rowdy crowd downstairs.

And it was a collection his mom would've loved.

Brushing a gloved finger over the marble forearm of a statue in one of the many halls currently strung with orange and purple lights, Mikko admired the craftsmanship.

"Please tell me this city is bigger than I think it is," a feminine voice spoke from behind him. His hair prickled, her proximity undeniable.

Turning slowly, Mikko faced Anika with his helmet cocked in curiosity.

As soon as his eyes landed on her, his chest clenched. Every thought that had her in it, came rushing to the forefront of his mind. His mind whirred, stuttering like a bike chain seconds away from derailing itself. He swallowed.

And her Halloween costume didn't help.

A navy jumpsuit clung to her figure, the zipper running up the front showing ample cleavage that had Mikko clutching his plastic cup tighter.

Fuck.

Leather fingerless gloves covered her hands and ended below her elbow. Cheap silver grommets and buckles decorated them. A flimsy belt modeled from similar material slung low on Anika's hips, a baton and handcuffs holstered there.

His dick was paying attention, more than he'd fucking like.

A black garter gripped her thigh, its purpose for a toy gun, but all it did was squeeze the lush meat of her thigh, making his mind wander while he stared, imagining sinking his teeth there. Knee high boots and a police hat sitting crooked on her head in a maddeningly cute way completed the outfit.

"No real gun?" he asked, words finally forming on his tongue. "I'm disappointed."

"Consider yourself lucky."

"Oh?" he set his nearly full drink down on the plinth of the statue hovering above him before stepping closer with his hands raised in mock surrender. "You're saying you'd shoot poor, lil' 'ole me?"

"Wouldn't think twice, actually."

"Has anyone told you that you don't think at *all?*" He said it to piss her off knowing the opposite was true. Her fingers played absentmindedly with the handcuffs at her waist, annoyance swirling in her eyes.

God, what I'd do to have those cuffs bite into my skin right now...

"Then you'd be appalled to hear I've been thinking about you," Anika muttered dryly.

He cracked a smile she couldn't see behind his helmet. "Sounds scandalous. Do tell me more."

Click.

She unhooked the handcuffs and his heart thrashed in his chest. "Seems like police brutality always works in *your* favor, so why don't I give it a try."

"A typical Friday night for me, *malyshka*." Mikko didn't make a move to step away, sharp eyes tracking her every movement from behind his visor.

"Is coming all over someone's things a part of that routine too?" She stopped an arms length away, smiling with faux saccharine sweetness. "Although *Levi* bought me a whole new collection of cosmetics to make up for it." His gloved fist flexed. "And since *you* sign off on his paychecks, should I also be thanking you for the eight hundred dollars worth of items he bought?"

"Oh? I suppose my gifts aren't even worthy of being mentioned?" She sneered at his words. "I guess it's good to know he's putting *my* money to use." His eyes hardened. "Goes to show he'd be nothing without me."

"Daddy Alek's ideals really have been ingrained into your pea brain, haven't they? But that can be fixed with *training*."

Mikko scoffed, his brain fixating on the word *daddy* and how it sounded coming from her lips despite his best efforts. "This outfit is giving me other ideas."

Rolling her eyes, she let him visually drink in his fill before talking again. "Took a page out of your book," she taunted, "and decided to play cop for a night. You can ask Ivan how well that went for him…"

It was the first time she'd admitted to it, even slightly. Mikko pushed on. "The city is the safest it's ever been," he mocked. "Especially without Ivan."

"That's cold." She twirled the fake handcuffs around her pointer finger while he shrugged. "But it'll be even more safe once I put *you* away too." Her glare was obvious, dark makeup allowing her molten eyes to flash in the light.

"And just *where* do you keep your prisoners, miss officer?"

"My basement."

God, I'm gonna lose it.

329

He'd go with her willingly, let her tie him up and do whatever as long as she was there to accompany him.

With his helmet in place, he was able to trace the outline of her figure as she stood there unaware of his stare. Images flooded his mind, his fingertips grazing her warm skin, goosebumps rising to meet his touch. The scent of her soap clinging to him for days. The way she'd moan under his to—

"There you are," Levi said, appearing from behind her, his breaths slightly short as if he'd searched everywhere for her. "I was looking..." he met Mikko's menacing gaze beyond the tinted panel of his visor and trailed off. *"Oh."*

Mikko waved his fingers coyly in hello, but his jaw was tight with annoyance. An orange jumpsuit covered Levi's body, the word "prisoner" stamped across his chest.

Classy.

"Care to introduce me to your friend," Levi spoke first.

"Oh? You don't recognize your own boss, Mikko?" Anika asked. Her knowing smile made it feel like she was toying with them.

"Uh, I—" Levi stumbled as Mikko's blood pressure skyrocketed. "Of course, I guess, it's just, erm, been a while since I've seen him in his helmet," Levi rested his hands on Anika's shoulders, trying to turn her away from him and his monumental disaster of a conversation. "But we're gonna head back downstairs, yeah?" The last part was aimed at her, his eyes conveying discomfort.

"Yeah, sure. You both are acting weird anyway," she retorted.

Relenting, they both turned, cordial nods exchanged before they walked away. Mikko watched as Levi's mouth brushed along the side of her temple, his lips mumbling something to her. A soft smile edged across her face when she looked up at him.

Red dimmed along the edges of Mikko's vision.

As soon as they disappeared around the corner, Mikko slipped his helmet and balaclava off over his head, the accessories suddenly too tight and claustrophobic. Running his free hand through his hair, he tried and failed to tame it.

It was time to find Cristiano since this party was boring him.

Walking down the hall, trailing after Anika and Levi, Mikko found himself scenting her perfume lingering in the air. He needed to find his friend and fast, or else he was going to do something he'd regret— or worse, that he *wouldn't* regret.

Slipping past costumed bodies dancing and talking in various parlors and living rooms, Mikko wasn't immune to the stares he was getting. Now that his helmet and balaclava had been torn off, people started realizing he was a Romanov.

Ugh.

A group of young women turned to look and kept staring unabashedly. He wasn't in his usual polished suit, but he found that the helmet and riding gear always caught the attention of women—and men.

"Nice costume," one of the women commented, dark hair making him think of Anika. He smiled tightly, nodding once at them, but broke eye contact.

Only one woman occupied his mind.

A woman who couldn't even stand to be in his presence for long.

A woman who prefers that sleazy bastard Levi over me.

Preposterous.

Quickly striding down the main staircase, Mikko was deposited into the lavish foyer. A fog machine kept the space on theme. Only a few people loitered there and none of them were Cristiano. Pushing on, Mikko checked every damn corner in the large house before finally deciding his friend must have wandered farther out into the manicured lawn.

Slipping his balaclava back on, Mikko was careful not to step on anything or *anyone* littering the yard. Weaving between trees, props, and clusters of people laughing and drinking, he started slowing down.

I'm going to make this man swallow an Airtag next time.

With his patience running thin, Mikko began to ask around. His friend's laughter could usually be heard above the din of a party, but this time, Mikko heard nothing. It made his blood freeze.

It's fine, Anika just set you on edge.

When Mikko's eyes caught on the makeshift maze toward the back of the property, his mind clicked. Cristiano had to be in there; there was no other option. Hand painted signs splattered in red paint mimicking blood pointed toward the haunted hedges.

Great.

He could hear a fountain bubbling nearby and excited squeals of laughter coming from inside.

"Klyanus' Bogom..." Mikko muttered before stepping in. *I swear to God...*

33

Search Party

Mikko

S weat glistened across his skin as he painstakingly searched for Cristiano. He tried calling his friend multiple times and texting him, but no response. In all honesty, he was beginning to worry.

That elusive, pumpkin headed bastard...

The *only* thing Mikko was grateful for was the fact that October meant most of the bugs and mosquitoes had died, or else he would've been covered in bites from wandering around.

Striding past couples making the most of the darkened maze corners, Mikko had one goal on his mind: find Cristiano. And then he'd berate him for having a phone that *apparently* didn't work.

After a couple more turns, the bubbling fountain sounded closer. Was he nearing the middle? Dew clung to his shoes and the hem of his jeans, the sensation annoying. But above the scent of fall and crisp foliage, Mikko smelled something else.

Vanilla musk and sharp hints of pink pepper.

Anika.

It was as if fate was drawing them together. Again.

Or I'm hallucinating.

Rough hedges scratched against his bare hands, gloves abandoned long ago and stuffed into his pockets, as he continued onward. A feeling in his gut propelled him to creep down a darkened branch of the maze. Every now and then, a soft grouping of fairy lights lit the way, but now it was dark. Only the moon overhead provided him with enough light to navigate by.

One foot in front of the other—

Passionate sighs and soft kisses could be heard from around the corner.

And Anika's perfume grew stronger.

I swear to God if...

Peeking around the flora, Mikko was surprised at the sight unfolding before him.

A statue loomed in the clearing, water bubbling from its upturned palms—the source of the noise he'd been following—but that wasn't what he focused on. Instead, his gaze latched onto Levi who was pressed back against the base of the statue, uncaring for the water splashing around and against him. Anika's back faced Mikko, her handcuffs glinting in the light as she pinned Levi against the art piece, their fervent embrace hard to miss.

Levi's hands tangled in her hair and roamed the silhouette of her body in a way Mikko wanted to.

He grit his teeth.

Apparently, Levi was growing on her.

He wasn't sure if he was surprised or concerned by this realization. While at the beginning he'd hoped their personalities meshed well enough to have Anika grow comfortable around them, Mikko had been certain Levi's arrogance would eventually annoy her.

He appeared to be wrong, and he *hated* being wrong.

Standing amongst the shadows, he had the perfect view of them. A front row seat as they shared whispers and gentle, imploring kisses. With each touch, Mikko unraveled.

His left hand throbbed, the chilly evening air irritating the scars there. He couldn't discern if clouds had moved across the moon, blocking out a portion of the light or if his fury was clouding everything else in his vision.

Go out there, his brain demanded. *Make them stop.*

But he couldn't.

His fury had him rooted to the spot, sharp eyes counting every single time they touched and kissed. He tried to focus on his breathing, but with every inhale, her scent was there along with a rage-filled haze descending over him. He'd ventured out here to find his friend and *this* was what he stumbled upon instead?

Disgust crawled up the back of his throat, his annoyance increasing until—

A soft gasp resonated out of her mouth.

He *knew* it was Anika's, his own body reacting. He'd studied her for too long to *not* know every little sound she made.

And if he'd been a rubber band, he would've snapped right fucking then.

Despite his revulsion at the man eliciting these noises from her his cock still hardened at her quiet moans. Mikko hadn't been this weak in a long time. Now, he felt helpless and at her mercy.

Cursing under his breath, his body went rigid. Blood rushed in his ears, and he was surprised to know not all of it was in his dick. Time slowed as he listened to her, enraptured but also vexed beyond measure. Forget pain and pleasure, this was another level of psychological torture.

Fuck.

He discreetly shifted where he stood, cock aching and pressing painfully against his zipper. He'd have to use his helmet to cover up the tent in his fucking pants. Forget the idea of making Anika his; how was he going to kill this bastard for touching his salvation? No, his *ruination*.

Creative ideas flashed in his mind in a perverse slideshow, fueling his rage, each more vile than the last. He landed on one involving blood, so much that the tang of copper permanently coated the air. And Anika's skin was painted in it—smeared in Levi's gore, poetically marking the last time *he* would ever touch her skin again. His typical aversion to blood was erased when it involved Anika. Mikko's hand skimmed across her bare body, crimson clinging to both their flesh as he coaxed those same noises out of her, but this time it was wilder. *Hungrier.*

And Mikko was finally doing what he wanted all along—he was claiming her, fucking her until there was nothing outside of them. Gone were the thoughts of her getting even with him; gone was the apprehension he usually carried. Now, in its place, was a certainty like no other. *She's* mine, *fuck* everyone else.

A growl escaped his throat.

He'd stepped out from the shadows before his logic could stop him. Words rolled off his tongue, "The system really is corrupt."

Breaking away, Anika turned toward Mikko's voice. He wanted her to be panicked, embarrassed, ashamed, but she conveyed none of that. As always she was calm and collected. A hand propped itself on her hip as Levi followed her gaze to Mikko.

"As much as you might enjoy cuckolding, this isn't what I had in mind, Mikko," Levi said, a stupid grin plastered across his lips. Mikko noted they were smeared with Anika's lipstick.

His jaw twitched. "You shouldn't be here," he started, "with her."

Levi stood to his full height, straightening his jumpsuit. "And why's that? You asked me to do this."

Anika said nothing, content to watch. She most likely had already figured them out anyway.

"That was before I knew her background." Mikko stepped closer. He should've turned away, left this maze before speaking if only to avoid the bloodshed that was sure to happen if things progressed negatively.

Anika spoke now, "And just what did you learn?"

Heat rushed his cheeks, both from anger and from her unapologetic demeanor. His balaclava still obscured his face, but his tense stance spoke of his inner turmoil.

"As if I'd tell you," Mikko scoffed.

Levi opened his mouth to demand answers, but Anika cut him off. "Leave."

Mikko's hidden brow rose, the taste of defeat sure to melt on his taste buds, but—

"Levi, I won't ask again. Leave us."

"I'm not going to leave you here with him," Levi argued. "You don't even know how dangerous he is."

"And you don't know me either" Her rebuttal had his jaw snapping shut, uncertainty evident in his light eyes.

"She's right, Levi. This is bigger than us now." Mikko's voice was steady despite the adrenaline pumping through his body.

"I'm not going. You expect me to leave without an explanation—"

"Yes," Anika and Mikko both said in unison. Were they suddenly in agreement about something?

Oh, the things we could do together if you let me, Mikko thought. His business driven mind was already formulating ideas based on his new knowledge of her. Even if it was stupid and risky.

With a loud, petulant sigh, Levi conceded. "Fine, but I better get debriefed on this later," he glared at Mikko before pointing to Anika, "and you better find another ride home." Mikko's fists clenched, one at his side and the other gripping his helmet. Firing Levi sounded way too appealing at the moment.

It was only after Levi's footfalls had faded when Mikko lunged toward Anika. "For not liking him you sure were enjoying yourself," he seethed.

Anika sidestepped his attack, brandishing her faux baton. "Mmm I kinda like jealous Mikko." She jabbed him in the chest with it for added measure. The fire in his heart blazed hotter at her words. She had no idea the things he'd do out of envy.

It was just their two silhouettes beneath the light of the moon.

"I read your file, the one containing all the information about Anika Naidu. Not Simmons."

If he'd wanted to see fear in her eyes, he was greatly disappointed when she'd met his gaze with a sharp smile. "Took you long enough."

"Send my condolences to your mom." Her presence crowded in on him, but he wielded his words against her.

"I swear to—" She didn't have a chance to finish the sentence before Mikko's hand closed around her throat. Pushing against her, they fell into the foliage of the maze. In his haste, his motorcycle helmet fell from his hand before rolling over the dew-covered grass. Both of her hands came up, clutching at his arm, short black nails digging into his jacket's fabric. She looked deadly—rage embodied.

Mikko smiled at his own fury reflected in her.

"Let...me...go," she rasped against his hold. He shook his head, the scent of her catching up with their movements, freezing him in place. *Dark, sugared vanilla musk.*

He abstained from pressing the rest of his body into hers.

"Care to explain why you were...hovering?" she asked, voice tight from his hand.

He chuckled darkly. "It's a public maze, darling. If you wanted

338

privacy, you should've picked a different setting."

"Jealous that no women wanted to kiss you?"

"I don't have that problem."

"Sure," she wiggled under his hand.

"I think you're forgetting who's got who pinned here."

She coughed. "Squeeze any tighter…and I won't be…conscious to annoy you."

Mikko loosened his grip slightly, still holding her in place, but releasing the pressure off her throat. He didn't want to stop touching her now that he'd started. "Better?"

Clearing her throat, she nodded. "Although I still have a *burning* desire to know what you read about me." She released her hold on him just to twirl a strand of her hair.

"I wouldn't want to inflate your ego more than I already have."

"Of course," she crooned, "you'd much rather seduce me with your nonexistent stealth."

"I made myself known," he countered.

"And I knew you were watching us moments before you announced yourself. Anger really does suit you, *malysh*." His heart stopped. She'd echoed his term of endearment. "I just like to let you believe you're in control. Gets me off in a way."

Now he pressed into her, enjoying the way her breath stuttered from his body heat and the way the shrubs had to be poking into her delicate skin.

She continued to taunt him. "Not to mention, your big ass frame couldn't hide in this maze even if you wanted to."

He looked down at his *frame* between them, inspecting his height compared to her. "That's cute coming from you," he remarked. If her glare could cut him, he'd be in pieces.

"Imagine how tall I'd be if you were on your knees?" Somehow Mikko held in the cough threatening to slip from his mouth. Thank

God for his balaclava.

But her honeyed eyes caught everything. Despite the inky darkness surrounding them, his own eyes had adjusted. Anika's face was calculating, her anger honed the features of her face into something deadly. The fake buckle of her police outfit dug into his lower abdomen as she pressed back against his ironclad hold. He hoped it left an impression on his skin.

The scent of her overwhelmed his senses and the smeared dark lipstick around her mouth painted Anika as a temptress. One he wanted to give into, desperately. Even knowing that it was Levi who had smeared her makeup…

"While enticing, I'd like to know why you're killing my men before offering you my neck." His tone was stern.

Her teeth flashed. "Is it really murder if it's so therapeutic?"

"Answer me, Anika."

"Imagine what you'll feel like when more of your men start dropping like flies around you," she drawled. "The feeling of finally being chosen as you're the last one standing."

"If you think I killed your dad—"

She swiftly cut him off. "I know you didn't, but *your* daddy isn't around to pay for his actions," her eyes darkened and a mischievous grin appeared, "but you know who is?"

Mikko didn't answer, didn't want to give her any more diabolical ideas. She could do that all on her own.

Her finger trailed up his abdomen, his muscles clenching in her wake. "What about Cristiano, hmm? Do you think he would suffice as a sacrifice?"

"Don't you dare even say his name—"

"Or *you*," she spoke over him as her nail dug into the hollow of his throat. Only the thin layer of his mask protected him.

"Those are dangerous words to say to someone you hardly know," he said, throat tight with unspoken emotions.

"You're hardly a stranger to me, Mikko," she replied. "In fact, there's not much I *don't* know about you."

"Meeting a couple of times makes us acquaintances?" he asked.

"You tell me, you jerked off on my things."

"Khoroshiy moment." Good point.

She leaned in, pushing against his hand still resting upon her throat. "You'd be wise to *not* underestimate me."

Using his knee, he pushed her legs apart, leaning in to intimidate her. It didn't work. In fact, she opened her legs wider, beckoning him in. The heat of her cunt pressed against his thigh. His mind shorted. She met his gaze with fire, challenging him with every passing second. "So, give me one good reason why I—"

Click.

Her costume handcuff snapped into place over his wrist holding her. Panic and lust intertwined in his stomach, a mix of emotions he was growing to hate. Part of him wanted her to make good on her threats, to torture and confine him, but another part of him was nervous. His men were expendable, but she'd mentioned Cristiano. He was *not.*

Her dark brow lifted in question. "What was that?"

"Take it off me."

"Give me one good reason why I should," she mocked.

"So I don't do something I regret."

She licked her lips. "Like what?"

Mikko didn't answer, he couldn't. His mouth couldn't be trusted when it came to her.

Yanking on the cuff, she taunted him further. "What? Shy all of a sudden?" Shoving against him, he stepped back an inch, relenting to her. "Scared I'll see who you truly are." He counted his breaths, struggling to keep his emotions locked away. They thrummed in his blood, clawed out from beneath his skin, yet... "Mikko."

All it took was one word, and he shattered.

Before she could stop him, Mikko lifted the hem of his mask up, exposing his mouth to the cool night air. Anika's gaze tracked his movements, pupils blown wide in disbelief. Her mouth popped open in question, but nothing came out. His lips slanted over hers, silencing whatever smartass remark she'd been formulating. Levi's cologne swirled between them, his presence tainting her clothing, but Mikko didn't care.

She might've let Levi in, allowed him to have a taste, but Mikko would be sure to savor her too. He was a jealous man, but he'd play the game; he'd wait to see who she truly resonated with.

Me, me, me.

Her lips were soft against his, supple and plush as he devoured her. A quiet moan slipped free from her lips, or maybe he was delusional and imagining things again, but he didn't stop to analyze. For once, he went with it. Lived in the moment. And it felt *right*. Anika was something to be revered. Cherished.

His tongue traced the seam of her mouth, her lipstick sweet, or maybe that was just *her*, as it blossomed across his taste buds. A roaring built in his ears, the nighttime din and party around them fading away. Stars sparked behind his eyes as her hand grazed up along his arm. Instantly, he was transported back to the night they met, her incessant touch unable to deviate from his skin.

Now, he wanted it—

Anika shoved him away, breathless gasps filling the space between them. He couldn't go far, her stupid little handcuff still clasped in her hand. His balaclava fell back over his mouth, her lipstick surely smeared there.

"What the fuck are you doing?"

"Anika, I—"

342

Reaching out, she ripped his mask off. "You're pathetic."

"Seems like you have a type."

"I do," she quipped, "And that's why you're right where I want you."

His jaw ticked. "I beg to differ."

"I prefer it when you just *beg*." A soft breath was the only audible noise in the edgy silence between his words. Her eyes narrowed, a deep whiskey color now in the low light. "You're just like your father."

Her words physically scalded him. Backing away, he shook his head. "You may think you know him, know me, but you don't."

Anika grabbed his wrist, warmth searing through his sleeve, "Mark my words, Mikko. We *will* meet again, and it'll be on *my* terms."

"Sounds like a poor excuse for when you come track me down." He ripped his arm out of her grasp, plastic handcuff digging painfully into his wrist.

Anika said nothing, letting him back away, eyes tracking his every movement. Walking backwards, not trusting her, he made his way down the length of the maze.

As he was about to turn the corner, her voice echoed down the grassy expanse. "Don't forget, I always remember a face. And I've seen yours enough that it *haunts* me."

With a cold sweat breaking out over his skin and his mind spinning, he stumbled out of the maze. After cracking the plastic, he finally got Anika's prop off of him before resuming his search for Cristiano. Thunder rumbled in the distance, a sharp crack of lightning zipping across the sky a couple miles away.

Things were going to get much worse before they got better.

34

Come In With the Rain

Anika

A gaze reminiscent of frost covered blades of grass pinned her to the spot. His heat encompassed every exposed plane of her skin. Unable to speak the words caught in the back of her throat, Anika let Mikko's faint touch graze along her skin.

And it felt so, *so good.*

His fingers danced across her forearms and shoulders. Lingered on her collar bones and skipped over the fluttering pulse in her neck. Her nerves had her knees trembling, a feeling she hadn't experienced in years—since one night long ago.

What was happening to her?

"Oh, *malyshka,* you have no idea what you do to me." His voice was smooth and deep, a hint of his Russian accent evident. He usually curbed it, unwilling to let people associate him with his father's homeland, but right now, he didn't seem to mind.

A single fingertip trailed along the edge of her jaw, the pad memorizing her bone structure.

"You should hate me," she said, tongue coming unstuck from the roof of her mouth.

"I could never hate you." Another touch. "It would be like hating myself."

Anika was quick to retort. "Liar."

"Look deeper, *malyshka*. We're more alike than you'd like to admit."

The intensity in his gaze was too much to look at, her mind struggling to stay put and not spiral. Flicking her eyes up, she focused on a single dark strand of hair hanging over his forehead. Why did he have to be so devastating? That was the only word she could think of when she saw him. And untouchable. Certainly not someone *she* should be lusting after.

Mikko's thumb pulled on her bottom lip. "This mouth," her skin heated as he spoke, "it says things I wish I was bold enough to say."

"You don't mean that."

"I do. And this heart..." his fingers settled over its rapid beating, "it's wicked and corrupt. A mirror of mine."

"No."

Leaning down, he ignored her and planted a kiss right where his hand had been. The thin material of her sleepwear did little to mitigate the heat of his lips. And it hardly hid her nipples. Looking back up at her, Mikko grinned. He'd noticed. Before she could protest or voice her embarrassment, his mouth closed over one of the hardened peaks. The warmth of his mouth had her shuddering as he sucked, desire coiling low within her stomach. A moan tore from her mouth as he pinched her other nipple.

Pulling away, the now cooling wet spot on her shirt was vastly at odds with the heat of his mouth. The difference had her mind stuttering. Kneeling, Mikko's touch slipped beneath the elastic waistband of her sleep shorts. Anika's spine was ramrod straight even as her muscles threatened to turn to liquid. She was pulled between desire and guilt. Either way, her body was on the edge of combusting.

"What are you doing?" she gasped.

In a wordless response, he leisurely pulled her shorts down. She knew she should've stopped him, yanked his hands away, but she did nothing. Anika was too entranced by him, his reverent position altering her brain chemistry.

Mikko kept her sleep shorts wrapped around her thighs, his hands clutching the delicate fabric as if he was sure she'd slip through his fingers. Maybe she would; her head was filled with buzzing, and a dizziness threatened to overtake her.

"Let me worship you." His lips skimmed across her hip bone. "Let me make it up to you." A soft kiss planted right atop her landing strip. "Let me *beg*."

With a hand clasped over her mouth in an attempt to stifle the sounds she made—not that it mattered—Anika watched as the man she'd vowed to hate dipped his tongue between her legs. At first, he was gentlemanly, a patient man who was waiting for the signal to *feast*. For a moment, he was content to let her quiver above him at the behest of his damn mouth.

A flutter of dark lashes and sinful glimmer in his eyes was the only image she needed to fall off the edge she'd been hanging onto. The pillowy softness embracing her heart as blood hummed in her ears and dampened the logic rattling around in her head.

Why had she held back for this long?

Her mind couldn't remember, couldn't find a reason to care.

One long lick of his tongue against her clit had the tensions holding her body together bursting free. Anika felt too big for her skin, the sensation tight all while another feeling coiled low in her stomach.

It was all too easy to fall into his touch, his lips expertly sucking at her clit while his tongue tasted honeyed ichor dripping from between her thighs. She ached to weave her fingers into his hair and pull him close and thrust her wet cunt onto his face as punishment, but she had the feeling he'd like it.

Fuck.

Pulling back, his pale skin glistening with her arousal, Mikko grinned up at her. He was a madman finally given a taste of his cure. "You positively melt on my tongue, *malyshka*." His fingers gripped her thighs tighter. "A sweetened essence I've been craving for far too long."

It was as if cotton had been stuffed into her ears and mouth; her words were nonexistent as the world dimmed. She nodded along with his praise. It'd been too long since a man had made her feel this way.

Mikko had a habit of stealing everything from her, and she internally cursed his ability to do that. Relenting as her body trembled, her hand finally slipped into his midnight hair. Pulling him closer, his warm breath washed over her throbbing pussy. Her muscles tightened, pleasure lapping at her insides just as he was licking at her most intimate parts. Deep down, a darkness slithered free, her body ravenous—craving carnal desires she'd long since locked away.

Too late to stop it now...

A LARGE GUST of wind shook Anika's house, and the sound of rain pitting against the panes accompanied it. The storm raged on outside, the clamoring of nearby tree branches startling her awake though her eyes remained closed. Her mind slowly surfaced from the depths of sleep, groggy and reluctant to relinquish the slumber she'd succumbed to.

Or maybe more so the dream she'd been having, desperately

clinging to the fading memories she'd awoken from.

Fingertips skimming the surface of her skin.

Stolen kisses and breathless sighs.

Cool air brushed across her bare shoulder, her blanket tossed aside mindlessly in her sleep. While she'd been warm inside the recesses of her mind, the air shifted as she continued to wake, goosebumps erupting over her skin. Reluctant to move too much, Anika curled into herself, searching for warmth.

The storm outside rumbled, lightning flashing across her room.

What time was it?

She cracked open one eye, assessing the amount of light streaming in through her open curtains. It was almost completely dark, a hint of soft glow from the muted street lamps outside the only thing making its way into her bedroom. Dawn was still a couple hours away, if she had to guess.

Remaining relatively still, she burrowed down into her pillow, closing her eyes and hoping to slip back into sleep before the sun rose, but a noise echoed throughout her house.

Not a noise, but a creak.

Her muscles tensed.

The stairs.

Her old house made specific noises, settling and groaning under the touch of gravity and weather, but this was inconsistent. The stairs *only* creaked like that when she stepped on them. Which meant—

Someone was in her house.

Ice filled her veins, and a cold sweat collected on her skin.

Reaching across the remainder of her bed, her fingers brushed across the outline of her small gun safe. Quickly, she unlocked it, and only once the weapon was clutched in her grasp did her heart slow.

As quietly as she could she crawled across her mattress, angling herself toward the entrance into her room. With one hand keeping the gun pointed at the closed door, the other kept her balance as she maneuvered over rumpled sheets. Nearing the edge of her mattress, her mind prepped to face whatever was on the other side of her bedroom door—whoever dared to break in. If it was Mikko again, she really was going to shoot him.

It's what he gets for kissing me...again. And haunting my dreams.

All thoughts of violence in her head drained away as her free hand brushed across damp coldness on her mattress. Her pulse spiked.

"What the fuck," she whispered, voice laced with uncertainty.

Eyes flicking between the door and the wet spot she'd stumbled across on her bed, her hand traced the indent of what had been a person. Anika's eyes pricked with tears, her lids unblinking because of adrenaline all while her heart galloped in her chest so forcefully she was sure it was going to burst through flesh.

Despite her dreams, she'd woken up dry. As if reaffirming her thoughts, the smell of wet earth assaulted her nose. *Rainwater.* And her mind instantly pictured a certain someone.

Emerald hued eyes and an incessant need to be right.

Sleep no longer clinging to her bones, she quietly slipped from her bed in hopes of catching him and showing him how good her aim had gotten. Lightning flashed, the harsh light slanting across her wood floors. The relief she should've felt at not seeing any silhouettes during that flicker was erased by a new discovery.

A more chilling one.

A puddle of rainwater had accumulated at her door along with stray droplets. It looked as if someone had come in from outside to stand there and watch her sleep. Anika shivered again, her tank top and shorts unable to keep the chill from her skin.

Not only had Mikko stood and watched her sleep, but he'd also been in her bed.

Anika's eyes shifted from the puddle—one she could no longer see since the darkness had taken over again—and the wet spot on her bed.

How long had I slept with him watching me?

Suddenly, the dream-like caresses she'd experienced right before she'd woken up made more sense. They hadn't been phantom touches, but real fingertips tracing her body's side profile. Fear and anger pulsed within her, banishing the desire she'd felt upon waking.

Each interaction he had with her was like he was trying to prove what he could do and get away with. The feeling of Mikko's lips pressed to hers on Halloween hadn't vanished from her mind. He was everywhere, a fact that made her thirty-one year old self smile, but her thirteen year old self shudder.

Emotion curled in her throat making it hard to swallow, and everything that had led Anika to this moment was starting to feel like it was going to explode. The pieces of her puzzle were simultaneously falling into place while also fragmenting in others.

It was now or never.

After clearing her entire house, Mikko nowhere to be found, Anika vowed that all this had to come to an end.

And soon.

* * *

Mikko - A Few Moments Before

He knew he was pushing his luck, but he couldn't stay away. After he'd found Cristiano at the party and returned him home safely, albeit slightly drunk, he'd changed out of his costume and went for a drive. The storm that had been brewing unleashed itself on him, but he stayed out, content to let the precipitation wash away his thoughts.

And somewhere along the way, Anika's house had materialized before him.

Mark my words, we will meet again, and it'll be on my terms.

Mikko disagreed, and that was why he was here.

Rain dripped off his clothes, trailing down his skin causing goosebumps to pop up in their wake. The droplets that had collected on him during his trek to her house now puddled beneath him as he stood at the top of the steps leading into her kitchen.

He was here so much that it was beginning to feel like his own home.

Maskless and emboldened from the kiss he'd shared with Anika in the maze, Mikko had decided to pay her a visit again. He was hellbent on proving her wrong. Inhaling, the deep breath bringing reassurance and balance back into his body, Mikko noted the ever-present fragrance of her. While he might feel like it was his house through association, her scent was everywhere, reminding him of the opposite.

It was all he'd been thinking about since he'd stumbled out of the maze practically drunk on her touch and promptly found Cristiano. After a soft scolding—Cristiano told him he'd been around one of the fire pits close to the sunroom—both men had left. His friend had tried to ask what had Mikko so riled up, where his helmet had gone, and if he was on drugs. But he quickly shut those questions down.

Now, he was silently slipping his boots off in the house of a woman who'd plagued him endlessly. The light above the stove was on as always, lighting his way and inviting him in farther. But at this point, he was able to walk her house from memory, even if she'd tried to shift her furniture slightly every couple weeks.

The stove clock had indicated it was a little past two-thirty in the morning and a certain kind of quietness blanketed the house. It was Mikko's favorite time of night since he felt the whole world lay vulnerable at his feet while he crept through the shadows, not disturbing a soul.

And tonight, his world was Anika.

In the dim light, he sought out her sleeping form on the bed in front of him.

There.

Her thick covers were thrown off her body, bunched up under her legs as she lay on her side. An extra pillow was clutched to her chest and the sight made his heart lurch. Suddenly he was wishing to replace the pillow with himself.

Pitiful.

A flash of lightning outside lit her room up momentarily and Mikko gathered more details in that short span of time. Her shorts barely covered her upper thighs, and the tank top adorning her chest left little to the imagination. So many of her tattoos were on display.

He longed to walk over and run his fingertips across her silky skin, but he remained rooted to his spot near the door. Her soft breaths calmed the inner turmoil wanting to rise up in his throat. Raindrops splashing onto the floor sounded occasionally, reminding him that he was dripping all over.

His mind thought back to another time he'd been in here, *dripping* all over everything.

He smiled.

Another flash. Her hair, colored to represent the night, was carelessly thrown over her pillow as her green sheets swathed her.

Each time the storm showed Mikko her room, the harder it became for him to remain where he was. He yearned to touch her—to caress her skin and risk her sensing he was there. Despite knowing she wanted to kill him, that she was coming for him or Cristiano, Mikko's lust was undeniable. Maybe he could blame it on his childhood, so riddled with pain and loss that when faced with it now, it turned him on. His body was confused—unregulated. He yearned to push past the boundaries she'd erected, and if she didn't wake up, maybe he'd visit her in her dreams.

With the continual flashes of lightning to hide it, Mikko slipped his phone from his pocket, needing to solidify this moment. His camera clicked, the flash blending in with the storm. Anika barely stirred. These photos would join the rest of them.

A soft sound came from her silhouette along with the shifting of the sheets. Mikko froze, barely breathing. After a few seconds, Mikko was confident she was still asleep—unaware of the predator lurking in her room. But *he* was well aware of the predator prowling beneath her skin.

Anika had shifted more to her stomach, leg hiked up, and hugging that damn pillow. In a short burst of light, like the flash of a camera, he committed the image to his mind. Her sleep shirt had ridden up dangerously, hem barely covering her stomach. Floral ink trailed up her legs and arms.

"Fuck it," he whispered, rain pounding against the window, drowning out his words.

As if a spell had been broken, Mikko stalked to her bedside. His clothes smelled of petrichor which made him hesitate briefly. Her sheets were dry and warm and smelling of her in a way he knew intimately. It drove him insane. Need made him abandon all reasonable thought and without another second to waste, he silently crawled into bed with her. He expected her to wake under the shifting mattress, but she didn't, deep in sleep and ignorant of the beast crawling into her sheets.

Mikko laid down on his side, his front facing her back, about a foot separating them. Feeling her body heat pouring off her in waves, he was tempted to close the distance, but he didn't. He was careful not to lay on her hair fanned out behind her, threatening to tickle his skin.

"Looks like we're meeting on *my* terms," he whispered, voice lost in the inky darkness and raging storm.

Mikko wasn't sure how long he laid there, ruminating in Anika's presence. When she was asleep like this, it was easy to see her as she truly was. There weren't any walls in his way to block her true emotions. Now, in the soft caress of sleep, he could feel the solitude she ensconced herself in. It sounded silly to think, but his emotions had always ruled him, and so, he'd learned to also read others so he could rule *them*.

As the storm died down, Mikko resigned himself to leaving. He needed to go home to change and ask Cristiano for any more leads on Dimitri. They'd reported him as missing, unable to find him or any trace of him after Cristiano announced his absence.

Worry threaded itself through his heart along with whatever else consumed him when he looked at Anika. While there were no tangible leads, he knew who'd done it. All he had to do now was wait for the evidence to show itself.

Sliding soundlessly from her bed, Mikko crept back toward her door, but something glimmered out of the corner of his eye.

A necklace on her nightstand.

He hadn't seen it at first, too consumed with her when he'd first arrived, but now...

Now, his eyes couldn't stop staring at it. Stepping closer, mind trying to keep up with what his eyes were seeing, Mikko realized why it caught him off guard.

He recognized it.

And it wasn't because he'd seen it around Anika's neck.

It was because it was Dimitri's.

35

Threaded

Mikko

Mikko's vision blurred, the streets dark and indiscernible, but he couldn't stop.

Ever since he'd left Anika's house, he hadn't been able to slow down, his Audi speeding along the interstate. His discovery shouldn't have come as a surprise, her guilty actions and words clearly laying out her plans before him. But finding something as concrete as Dimitri's necklace? It was everything he'd been looking for weeks ago.

The metaphorical blindfold had been ripped from his eyes. And what had she done to him to warrant his necklace being at her house? A wave of jealousy flooded him.

He'd been too consumed with seeing her as someone he couldn't get out of his head—a beautiful entity ensnaring its prey. Only after it was too late to escape did he see the monster before him.

Fingers shaky, Mikko dialed Cristiano, needing to talk to someone else. He hoped his friend had sobered up enough to be able to tell him he was being dramatic and misreading the evidence. *Anything* to prove him wrong.

The ringing was loud in his car's Bluetooth while he waited for Cristiano to pick up. His fingertips drummed the steering wheel, breathing becoming more erratic.

"Hey, what's up?" Cristiano's sleepy voice came through the car speakers. He sounded sober enough, and Mikko's breath of relief was audible. "Everything okay?"

"I—" Mikko's voice cracked, so he cleared his throat and tried again. "It's Anika."

"What?"

"Anika is the one killing our men." Mikko's car shifted with a rumble as the dashed lines of the highway blurred. "Dimitri included even though we haven't found his body yet."

"I—wow, okay…" he trailed off, the sleepy tone in his voice completely gone now.

Mikko's hands gripped the steering wheel, the leather creaking beneath his fingers. "I found Dimitri's necklace. *In* her house."

Silence greeted Mikko after his words were out there. Only the dimmed sound of the road beneath his tires kept him company.

"*Oh.* Oh, that doesn't look good." There was rustling as Cristiano sat up in bed and the crinkle of a water bottle as he drank. "Let me get dressed, and I'll meet you over at your penthouse."

"No." The word was sharp, quick. "No, she's been there and who knows what she did to the place. We cannot trust her." Mikko took a deep breath, exiting from the highway, needing to find a dark street corner to sit in. Driving while the pieces were falling into place was a dangerous idea.

Cristiano's voice broke him out of his brief mental fog. "Okay, come over, and we will figure out what to do next, yeah?"

Mikko nodded, then realized his friend couldn't see him. "Yeah.

Yeah, I'll be there in ten minutes."

* * *

CRISTIANO'S APARTMENT OVERLOOKED a different portion of the city than Mikko's, a fact he used to distract his mind as his friend poured him both a glass of ice water and a generous amount of vodka.

"Here you go," Cristiano handed him both glasses, motioning for him to drink some of the water first. They sat on Cristiano's couch, his living room masculine but more plush than Mikko's. His friend enjoyed colorful accents and unique patterns lending themselves to his laid back personality and adventurous side.

Prints hung from the walls and curated abstract art lined every surface his friend could place something. It was a nice change from Mikko's own stark penthouse.

And it was a space that *hadn't* been tainted by Anika.

"Does Levi know?" Cristiano asked as soon as Mikko finished his water, setting the glass onto a nearby coaster.

Mikko scrubbed his face with his hands. "If he does, it's not because I told him."

"Do we use him as a pawn against her?" Cristiano took a sip of his drink—a steaming cup of tea to most likely ease his headache from earlier.

"Potentially, unless she has the ability to turn him against us."

"It is known he favored Alek and his methods," Cristiano started. "Always preaching to anyone who'd listen that you'd eventually run this business into the ground with your," he gestured vaguely in the air, "ways."

Rage flowed through Mikko's veins at his friend's words. Cristiano

357

was right. Levi, while working for Mikko for years now, had never been shy about his beliefs and feelings toward the newest Romanov. It was a topic they'd butted heads about, but in the end Mikko hadn't cared enough to fully take care of the man. Knowing the enemy was imperative, and killing him reminded Mikko of something his father would do, so he let him live.

It was a thought that made the words Levi had whispered to him at a work event years ago flash across his mind. *You rule with a soft hand, one that isn't meant for this city.*

"She could be keeping him around to annoy me too," Mikko mused, a short, sarcastic huff breaking the tension.

Cristiano's eyebrows furrowed. "Or he's next."

Mikko pondered that before a more devastating thought formed. "One way to find out."

"I know that look."

"Let's see if he still thinks he can snatch the metaphorical crown from my head," Mikko took another sip. "If he thinks he can run the city better than me—do work dirtier than me so people fear him—let's see how he handles Anika."

"And maybe she won't see it coming from him until it's too late."

36

Vendettas

Unknown - Almost Two Months Ago

L icking the front of your teeth, you stepped outside, leaving the thudding music behind. Evening air traced the exposed planes of your skin, thick with the promise of a storm. The ever present noise of the city surrounded you, but it was a commotion you were content with. It made your muscles relax, relishing in the thought that you were right where you needed to be. Had met who you needed to.

Mikko Romanov.

A man who was considered immortal and utterly untouchable. An heir to this city essentially, his real estate business carried him farther than anything else his father Alek could've left him.

And it made your blood boil.

As did the view of his motorcycle next to the curb in front of you. Its sleek, black silhouette made the corners of your lips tip up as another gust of wind brought the scent of incoming rain to your nose. Portland was never dry for long, and you hoped Mikko would get rained on on his way home.

Honestly, you were surprised he was still there, his usual media presence portrayed him as someone who kept to himself, only attending certain events that would make or break his company. His secluded lifestyle was a side effect of carrying the weight of everyone's blood on his hands. Hiding from the inevitable was a worthless coping mechanism.

You would know.

Slipping a piece of gum from your small clutch, you leaned against the exterior wall of the club, its rough surface catching on your soft dress. As you chewed, you contemplated how someone could be so despicable, but the answer was one you were already familiar with.

Sighing, you considered going home, satisfied with your impromptu meeting with Mikko, but still you lingered. People passed you, on their way to an unknown location, oblivious to the vileness happening within the building behind you.

And within your own heart.

Everyone had done deplorable things to survive; you were no different.

Your long hair tickled your arms as it billowed in the breeze. While Mikko had been seemingly unaffected by your advances in the bar, you knew his mind had to be spinning with your words. Men were all the same, visual creatures with a specific kind of desperation. Something you had no qualms stoking like the embers of a fire.

He might play the unattainable bachelor, but you knew he was more like a fragile bomb. Any wrong movements and his exterior would implode into a million pieces.

Let's see how long it takes for me to accomplish that, you thought darkly.

Drawing a gas station receipt from your purse, you scrawled a hasty note on it, your grin widening all the while. Once you were satisfied, the click of your heels accompanied you as you walked toward his motorcycle. Quickly, before you could get caught by whatever unlucky bastard Mikko paid to watch his precious possessions, you pulled the chewed piece of peppermint gum from your mouth, stuck it to his windshield, and placed your note on top.

Perfect.

After the research you'd done, you knew he liked his things clean and tidy—untouched by those outside of his friend circle. So this, this was a retaliation; the first chip in his facade.

Well, maybe the second...

The small touches you'd shared with him earlier proved to wind him up even tighter than anticipated. His lackluster dating life was evident in the way he responded to physical touch.

Throwing one last glance over your shoulder to make sure no one was watching, you walked away. Your own car was parked down the block, inconspicuous. Halfway there, the clouds that'd gathered above and thickened with the scent of rain whispered through your hair. The foreboding sense of anticipation reminded you of another time, long ago.

But your fate was all but signed and sealed when the first fat drop of rain splattered against your cheek as the heavens opened up and a flood came rushing forth.

37

Flora and Fauna

Anika

Almost a week had gone by since Mikko's water logged break in, and despite leaving Dimitri's necklace out for him to see, nothing had happened. In reality, she was a bit disappointed. A man of his status and upbringing should be able to catch the small details—to not be afraid to dole out punishment where it was due.

And yet, Anika remained unharmed, unthreatened.

How boring.

Except, that wasn't entirely true. Two days ago, Levi had reached out, promising a relaxing date at his apartment again. It was all too close in timing to be a coincidence. Testing the waters, she declined, curious to see how far he would push her. If he was up to something suspicious, he wouldn't let her denial drop.

And he didn't.

"Your place, then?" he'd asked through text.

A devious grin had graced her countenance as she replied with, *"Perfect!"*

He may be more forward than Mikko, but he was twice as dumb. His own desperation and bullheadedness would work in her favor.

Now, she stood in her kitchen, the soft din of the movie they'd chosen playing on the TV in her living room. The carefree rom-com echoed down the hall, a terrible backdrop for Levi's soon-to-be downfall. In front of her, she mixed two cocktails. Levi's consisted of a large square ice cube, a generous splash of vodka, and a finishing touch Anika was fiercely proud of. Her own homemade violet liqueur made from ingredients she'd grown herself in her backyard.

It was a potent batch, a few drinks containing the liquid sure to put the drinker to sleep. Most people used these flowers for insomnia and anxiety, but Anika had gotten *creative*. A fact she'd tested with Ivan and perfected with Dimitri.

Defeating men at their own game was easy when it came to mental challenges, but physical ones proved to be slightly more difficult. This drink leveled the playing field, especially since she discovered Levi had shown up to her house armed.

When he'd given her an enthusiastic hug right inside the front door, he'd made a fatal mistake. Well, *two*, but who was counting? The first was coming to her house, her domain. And the second was embracing her tightly, the unmistakable press of his gun poking into her abdomen. They'd made out enough on her couch for her to know what his erection felt like, and it was *nothing* like that.

Mikko had warned him, and now Levi had a dark plan unfolding in his mind.

But so did she.

Her drink looked similar to his, but the ingredients were vastly different. Instead of vodka, she'd substituted it with soda water with a dash of food coloring to give it the same ethereal lavender hue as his. If he looked closely, he might be able to tell the difference, but he was too dimwitted to do so. This secret would be one for her and her alone.

Satisfied with the results, she gripped both glasses and returned to the living room. Levi sat there, his body positioned to look like he was lounging, but his muscles were wound tight. His hand rested on his upper thigh, close to the concealed gun he carried in the front of his jeans.

"I'm so glad you like these," Anika said before plopping down on the couch next to him. He'd already had two thirty minutes prior, the flavor too good for him to resist. The idea of liquid courage was an added benefit.

"Never had anything like it," he grinned while taking his glass from her.

"It's a similar recipe to a drink I had while traveling on the east coast." Her eyes hungrily watched him take a sip. Men had such privilege. It infuriated her. All her life she'd been raised to be aware of men, to cover her drink while out with friends, and to *never* accept drinks that weren't capped or hadn't been made in front of her. Yet, Levi missed that lesson.

A fatal flaw.

Holding in a scoff, she leaned in. It was time to play a loving and supportive girlfriend until his eyelids drooped. If he kept going at this rate, it wouldn't be long.

"I didn't know you traveled that far," he responded, keeping his drink in his clutch. As if it'd help; she'd already tampered with it.

"I've been known to be full of surprises."

"Something I'm coming to realize." His pupils dilated and the tension seeped from his shoulders as he took another swig. "It's why the nickname *firecracker* fits you so well."

She hardly reigned in her grimace.

To keep up appearances, she drained half her drink in one go. Long ago, Anika had realized people tended to follow in suit if their friends' inhibitions were equally impaired. Too bad she couldn't get drunk on soda water.

"Nervous?" he asked, falling into her trap.

With a timid giggle, Anika said, "A little, I feel like I haven't seen you in forever." Lies, but Levi would misconstrue her faux drunkenness as a sign she wouldn't even fight back against whatever he was planning. *Ha.*

"No need to be nervous," he reached out to tuck a hair behind her ear, but his movements were sloppy. "You know me."

All too well. "I do. Thank you for coming over tonight."

Levi took another large gulp. His body slouched. "Of...course."

"Are you okay?"

"Y-yeah...just got really tired out of...nowhere."

Anika stifled her smile. "We can turn off the movie and go to bed if you'd like?"

"I don't think–really?"

"You're in no state to drive home."

"But you've never let...me stay before..."

"I think now is as good of a time as any." Standing, she set her own glass down before turning to help him stand.

Facing him once more, her smile turned sinful. Levi had sloppily drawn his gun, elbow resting on his thigh as if his own arm was too heavy to endure holding it up and aiming it at her completely.

Feigning surprise, Anika held up her hands. "Well, well, well, someone is happy to see me."

"Wha–what did you put...in m-my drink?" Levi slurred, his words taking a painfully long time to leave his mouth, but she waited all the same.

"I don't know what you're—"

"*Bullshit.*"

Her mouth popped open, his anger hardly veiled now. It was only dimmed because of the violets coursing through his body. Before she could call him all the filthy words in the book, his hold on his glass slipped.

Crash!

The delicate cup shattered as soon as it hit her wood floors, splinters of glass flying across the space and littering the hardwoods. The last swig of the drink that he'd been saving now leaked out from the broken vessel.

Anika didn't flinch. "Shame, that was a family heirloom." Another lie. "And now I'm going to have to punish you for it."

"Oops."

She knew her eyes must be damn near glowing with her fury. "Give me your gun."

"No."

"I'm trying to be nice here and allow you to cooperate, but I won't hesitate to take it myself."

"You won't–can't."

"Want to bet?"

"Ye—"

Before the rest of the word left his foul mouth, Anika leapt at him. His motor skills were slow and before he could even move his finger to touch the trigger, she was in his lap. With practiced motions, she had the gun unloaded and tossed aside.

"Can't have you figuring out how to use that, now can we?" she taunted.

Levi's stunned look, although clouded with the violet haze, made her black heart soar.

"W-who are *you?*"

"A nobody really," she replied, gripping his face in her hand before squeezing. Any pain she could cause him before his death was a win. "But you still should've been more careful. Didn't anyone teach you not to take open drinks from strangers?"

"What was...in that...what did you..." his voice trailed off, his tongue damn near worthless inside his mouth. She hoped he'd bite it off in his own blabbering stupor.

"What did I put in it?" she repeated. "Honestly, you're lucky. I could've slipped you something nasty, something that could've really altered your brain, but I prefer organic solutions to my problems. Mother nature gives, but she can also *take*."

Levi gurgled on his accumulating spit.

"My *special* drink is made from violets." Levi's brows furrowed. Anika rolled her eyes before continuing. "Which makes you sleepy, especially when highly concentrated and paired with vodka."

"Y-you drugged *me?*"

"And you came here to kill me. Call us even, yeah?" She nodded to the dismantled gun lying on the floor a couple feet away. "I must say, though, you and your friends took way too long to figure this out. To figure *me* out."

"Figure what out?"

"Aw, don't play dumb now. I'll start to actually believe it." His hands came up to swat at hers currently still gripping his face. She brushed them off, his weakened state making it easy. "I had so much fun with Ivan; he begged up until the very end. I tried to warn him, but before I started firing off shots he'd laughed in my face," she paused in thought, "so I plucked his eyes out."

Levi's eyes widened, either in surprise or confirmation, she wasn't sure. Semantics didn't matter.

"And Dimitri...well, we had some fun before I did the same thing to him," she continued. "I'm sure his bloated body will turn up soon. Both pairs of their eyes fetched me a large sum of money and information. No one is tight lipped when you name their price.

"And then there's you," she drawled. "I was going to wait a little longer before killing you, but…I was rushed."

Levi swallowed audibly. "You won't."

"I'm afraid I *will*. You won't be my first kill, *milyy*. Nor my last."

Shaking his head feebly in her hands, he tried to break free, hips bucking up against her, but she gripped him tighter. Her center of gravity was low, it would take much more to dislodge her, and he was too weak.

"Drinking three of my concoctions was a bad choice now, wasn't it?"

His mouth opened and closed like a fish out of water, but she leaned in and waited. "Bitch."

"Such a dirty little mouth"—she slapped him—"but that can be fixed."

Opening his mouth, to scream no doubt, Anika clapped her hand over it. Silencing whatever words or noises he'd been about to unleash, she whispered in his ear. "No need to scream; we're going to have some fun you and I." Mumbled yelling vibrated against her hand. "Maybe I'll even let you keep your eyes."

38

Saving the Best for Last

Mikko

Levi's muffled scream rent the air.

Mikko had been content to watch from afar as the man had slipped into Anika's house, gun tucked in his waistband. Cristiano had thought it wise to share their findings with Levi, but Mikko decided to lay low, to see if he could catch Anika in the act.

And he didn't have to wait long from the sounds of it.

With Cristiano stationed down the road in his Mercedes, Mikko lurked in the shrubbery outside of Anika's house.

Like always.

A few tense moments passed while Mikko waited to hear Levi again. Anxiety wove itself into his muscles and viscera until he felt numb, powerless. A part of him wasn't entirely partial to his employee, but the chaos that would ensue if another one of his men wound up dead made Mikko's feet move. Well, that, and the hope of seeing Anika.

Muscle memory guided the hidden key into the lock of her side door, the mechanism *clicking* free easily. Stepping inside, he closed the door behind him. The familiar scent of her house and the space around him calmed some of his worries. But beyond that, there was the notion of the truth escaping. It was bound to come out whether they were ready or not. Anika had chosen her actions carefully, their game coming to light as each layer of armor was peeled away. Soon, the raw fragmented pieces of his heart—his obsession—would be exposed for the world to see.

"Good things never last, son." With a tired sigh, Mikko shook Alek's voice from his head as he stepped out of the darkened stairwell and into her kitchen. His gun was drawn, posture practiced and ready to wound if necessary.

The plants and moody surfaces were awash with warm light. His eyes caught on the liquor bottles sitting out on the countertop. Creeping closer, he read the labels, curiosity getting the better of him. Vodka, soda water, food coloring, and…a lavender liquid in an unmarked mason jar.

Even though he had on his balaclava, he sniffed the loosely capped jar, and it smelled of sugared flowers and alcohol. He stifled a cough, the fabric of his mask not enough to block the scent.

Using his shoulder to scratch his nose since the scent lingered, Mikko listened for voices. Hushed mumbling could be heard from what he assumed was her living room. It was the only light on in the house, but the curtains were drawn so when he'd been outside he couldn't see anything.

With his back pressed against the cool hallway wall, he was careful to avoid her frames as he slunk closer. His hands sweated, but his grip on his gun never faltered, the weight of it grounding and familiar. He'd done this before, too many times despite his hatred for it. The accompanying cold that came with the adrenaline settled into his chest, cloaking the rapid beat of his heart. He'd done worse for less, but he never lost the feeling of a thousand insects skittering across his skin right before he needed to strike. Tonight was no different. Even if it did involve someone he found himself caring about.

Pushing that aside, he vowed to force Anika to failure. It was time to see what happened when one predator confronted another. And a path forged in bloodshed was the only way. Mikko didn't *want* to be like his father, solving his problems with more agony, but Anika had left him no other choice.

Glass crunched under a boot that wasn't his.

And Mikko stiffened.

A whisper followed by a smack, and then...

Gurgling.

Three strides was all it took for him to clear the rest of the hallway and position himself in the doorway of Anika's living room.

There, at the end of his gun's barrel, was a scene he should've known was coming.

Levi was slouched on the couch, his face red and movements jerky as he tried to fight off Anika. It was *his* boot kicking and stepping over broken glass littering the floor around where he sat. His mouth opened and closed, no words coming out, just a pleading look in his pale eyes as Anika's pretty little hands wrapped tighter around his throat.

She straddled his lap, her pale blue nightgown at odds with the violence she bestowed. Veins bulged in Levi's face, but he could also see the corded muscle in Anika's arms as she wrestled with the man below her. Sweat glistened on her tan skin, and her hair fell loose over her shoulder.

Mikko's jaw clenched and his finger poised on the trigger.

Shoot, his mind urged. And yet...

Time passed slowly, Levi's consciousness fading.

He knew he should be angry at Anika, at Levi even, for putting him in this situation, but all he felt was guilt. Maybe this was his retribution; the universe was punishing him for everything he'd done in the past while simultaneously giving him a chance to fix it—to end it all.

Suddenly, his escape from reality needed to be put down, but he wasn't sure if he could shoot Anika. He wasn't ready for their game of cat and mouse to end. An emotion he vowed to ignore still swirled in his chest. Anika was everything a man could want—sharp and witty with a lethal innocence striking when one least expected it. A weapon all on her own that she'd honed and used against him.

And he *fucking* fell for it.

The universe was a dark, twisted place, and it was throwing his obsession, his *mistakes*, back in his face. He wished he could've crumbled to his knees, begging at Anika's feet for an explanation to make all this go away. Pleading with her to stop might've been his solution if he didn't have a business to uphold.

And a reputation.

You deserve this, a small voice whispered in his head. *Happiness isn't attainable for someone like you.*

Do it. Do it. Do it.

Mikko's mind warred between retribution, gaining the answers he desperately needed to protect his empire, and yearning for her to touch him instead.

Oh, to be tortured by her hands...

Mikko held the gun tighter.

One bullet...it would end it all

Something in him pulled taut—he struggled to keep from coming undone—before snapping. There were no spots blocking his vision like there had been in the past when rage fueled his actions.

No.

This time everything was crystal clear, vision sharpening.

He *knew* what he had to do—

"I wish I could say I was surprised," Anika gritted out, her grip unrelenting against Levi's neck. "But I'm almost disappointed you haven't shot me yet."

"Let. Him. Go," Mikko responded, spine ramrod straight. Levi's eyes rolled into the back of his head. "I won't ask again."

He counted four heartbeats and shifted his gun slightly to the left of Anika's form. All his life, he'd been underestimated, abused, and thought a fool. But now—

Molten honeyed eyes met his, her confidence at Levi's now limp body evident on her face. The other man's chest still rose and fell indicating he was alive. For now. Mikko's hand lowered infinitesimally, her gaze breaking through his haze. A sweat broke out on his brow, but he pushed on.

"Always a couple steps behind," she taunted. Bruises marred Levi's throat as she pulled away. "But if you expect me to apologize for this"—her eyes flicked back to Levi—"I'm afraid that's a promise I can't keep."

"Promises aren't your strong suit."

Her eyes darkened. "If you shoot me, you risk harming him." Her fingers carded through Levi's hair before yanking the man's head back.

"Get up."

"I'd like to see you make me."

Bang!

Mikko sent a shot off into the couch cushion to the left of her. A fluff of feathers and a small hole was the only evidence of his assault. The noise was loud, his ears ringing painfully. Cristiano would have to pay off every single fucking cop who showed up to this scene from the neighbors complaining, but it was worth seeing her flinch. *Slightly.*

"Oops," he grinned, his rage boiling up beneath his skin. "I forgot how sensitive this trigger is."

Anika's unwavering hate met him head on. And he suddenly had the terrible thought of not having enough bullets to kill her if he needed to. Mikko had seen what spite could do to desperate men—what it'd done for him when he needed it. It could be like taking a bear down with a pellet gun.

"That's not very teacher-like of you," Anika pouted. "And here I thought I had a well reviewed shooting instructor a couple weeks ago."

"What did you give him?" Mikko questioned, stepping closer.

She lifted her hands in surrender, unfazed that an unconscious man was between her legs. "Nothing, he just had too much to drink. An honest mistake if you ask me...something the coroner won't even question, yeah?"

"Bullshit." Mikko's bones grated together, muscles tense at the force of keeping him in place. "Your finger prints are all over his neck."

"I'm not really worried about it." She shrugged like it wasn't attempted murder they were discussing. "You won't let me go to jail."

"You don't know that."

"Oh, but I do." Her grin was playful all while her eyes conveyed malicious intent. "You'll pay off whoever you need to to keep me free. Just so you can have me all to yourself."

Mikko scoffed, but said nothing because as much as he hated to admit it, she was right.

She smugly continued. "Fate has always been a tricky little thing. Wouldn't you agree?"

"I don't believe in fate."

"Of course, how could I forget." She tapped the side of her head as if hit with a new thought. "Daddy's little plaything thinks he can construct the world exactly as he sees fit so he can control how each piece is then destroyed."

"Like you're playing God?" he countered.

A sinful glint flashed across her eyes before, "If you bow down now, I might spare you."

"Liar," he said aloud, but deep down something sinister stirred in his gut.

"Although," she continued, "I prefer my offerings covered in blood."

Before Mikko could form a rebuttal, silver flashed in the light as a small knife bit into Levi's tender skin. Anika wielded it, her intentions clear. A little more pressure to the hollow of his throat would surely produce blood. She'd slipped it free from Levi's pocket, a smile gleaming on her face.

"Maybe I'll *cut* my fingerprints off him," she said, waiting for Mikko to move.

But once again, he felt out of control. He suddenly felt like his eleven year old self, powerless.

A flick of her wrist; a flash of crimson as a small rivulet streaked down Levi's neck. It was shallow, not large or deep enough for him to bleed out from, but the sight of it infuriated Mikko.

Mine, he brain shouted, *mine to torture and torment and kill.*

He was devoid of anything else, of any other thoughts. This had to end. He was prepared to yank her off his worthless employee by her hair, but the sickening *squelch* of her knife slipping into Levi's soft tissue finally made him lunge.

Mikko's shoulder collided with Anika's warmth. Her body gave easily beneath his strength, the softness of her cushioning his own fall. Tumbling to the floor, her knife skittered out of her hand and out of reach as Mikko used the moment to straddle her torso. The shards of glass nearby embedded themselves into Anika's back and Mikko's knees. Still, she fought him with everything she had, desperately trying to wrestle herself out from under him all while narrowly missing the swing of his gun.

Bang!

It went off in their scuffle, the bullet ripping through the outer edge of Anika's arm. It was a flesh wound, but it bled profusely regardless.

"You bitch," she seethed.

Blood splattered across nearby surfaces making everything slippery, both of their hands struggling to find purchase on the gun and each other's skin. She was strong, but Mikko spent hours in the gym preparing for moments like these—had trained to be the best. He focused on his physique, determined to be the strongest version of himself, honing his body into a lethal weapon.

His father had always used his height and weight against Mikko— no one else would.

Bucking and screaming, her teeth gnashed at him, fingers clawing and searching for flesh to shred. Her hair spread out in a wild halo around her head. Tangled and bloody, they fought. Unable to hang onto his gun, it fell from his hand as he attempted to control the woman below him.

If it hadn't been for her scheming—her elusive nature—he would've found the chase enticing, adrenaline racing and fingers aching to dip themselves into the crimson splattered around them.

But he was too pissed.

With her arms beneath his legs and his hands around her neck in warning, he finally asked, "What's in the mason jar?"

"You're the alcoholic," she gasped, words still steeped in venom, "take a guess."

Mikko's hands tightened around her throat in an effort to tame her. As much as it pained him, he *needed* answers, and she was making it really damn difficult to hang on.

Red encroached the corners of Mikko's vision, his own obsession getting in the way of his success once again. And this time, it cost him more than himself—it involved Levi.

Stupid, stupid, *stupid*.

Mikko acquiesced. "Vodka sodas don't impair men of his size that quickly."

"He had a few…"

"Bullshit!" His muscles ached and sweat gathered beneath his clothes.

"I put…" she spit past Mikko's harsh grip, "violets in…his *drink*."

"What?"

Squirming, she flashed bloody teeth at him. Somewhere along the way, she'd bit her tongue or lip in their scuffle. "They make you…drowsy."

She's good. "That was stupid of you," he threatened aloud.

Instead of cowering in fear like he wanted her too, she laughed, the sound manic and raspy from his ever tightening hold around her neck. He felt the vibrations of it against his palms. Fury mounted in the back of his throat, a feeling he'd always held dear to his heart—an emotion that never let him down.

All the others got him in trouble, but this one…

"You're gonna be next if…you don't let me go."

His harsh laugh echoed around them. "As if I'd accept a drink from *your* tainted fingertips."

"You already have…when we first met." Blood splatter stained her skin, her eyes glinting with malicious intent. The light colored strands of her hair surrounding her face were also stained with crimson flecks. It was an obvious taunt, one he tried to ignore. He could finish this, even if she'd fucked everything up.

Despite Anika's skin being on display, the warmth of her body pressed against his as he held her down, Mikko stayed focused. Now was not the time to be thinking of all the things he'd done in her house, or the way she occupied his mind when he relieved his body of all the tension late at night when no one was watching.

All of that had to disappear; he had to start over.

And inside his head, his father's voice echoed above them all. *"Kill her. Be done with it."*

But he couldn't, even as his fury increased; something stopped him. If only he could get past his *fucking* emotions—

Whack!

Hot pain flashed across his jaw. Looking down, a smear of blood marred Anika's forehead. She'd headbutted him. *Again.* Last time she'd done it, he swore he'd lost brain cells.

The pain distracted him, his limbs loosening their hold around her, which she took immediate advantage of. Dislodging him, she turned onto her stomach and crawled toward her knife, her fingers reached out, *almost* touching what she desired.

Leaping onto her, Mikko tried pulling her away, back toward himself in an effort to dissuade her from grabbing the weapon.

And when he thought he had—

Whipping around, eyes flashing with vengeance, Anika swung at him.

A stinging sensation seared through him, slicing through the fabric of his balaclava. Warm liquid dripped down his cheek as he looked down at Anika, droplets of blood splattering onto her chest. Her armed hand was raised, ready to strike again if she needed to, but Mikko could only laugh.

"Damn, not my pretty face," he drawled. "Now you *really* won't want to date me."

"As if I ever did before."

"True, you did pick Levi even after meeting me."

"Second time's a," she swung her blade at him, but he blocked it, *"charm."*

"You think you're going to make it outta here alive?" he murmured, voice deadly calm as the rage took over.

"You could *never* kill me, *malysh*." Her chest heaved, body bruised and battered from their scramble, but her words were sure.

His hand brushed against the cut on his cheek, teeth clenching at the burn of it. His fingers came back wet and *red*. Too bad that was his favorite fucking color. He saw his own blood drip down the edge of the knife Anika still clung to. It gleamed, thirsty for more—for another taste of his tangible sacrifice.

It took more than this to deter him.

Harshly, he swiped his bloodied fingers across Anika's mouth, fingers pushing past her parted lips, needing to mark her—yearning to make her taste her own consequences. The wet heat of her mouth enveloped his two digits, her surprised gasp quickly muffled by his intrusion. Farther than he should've gone, he pushed, determined to make her gag and heave and regret every *single* decision leading her here.

And he'd enjoy torturing her along the way.

His other hand grasped hers, her grip slipping but she held tight even as the sharp edge bit into her hand. He didn't stop until the blade cut through her skin, more crimson bubbling up and dripping across their knuckles.

"You forget," he started, "I grew up with a father who did this for a *living*."

A flash of pain radiated over his fingers as Anika bit down on his digits still partially lodged in her mouth. Her teeth sank into his knuckles before he quickly yanked his hand back. Skin sloughed off, her teeth scraping the top layer off.

"Fuck!"

She spat out the gore gathering in her mouth. "You taste like shit."

Somewhere in the corner of his mind, he knew he should stop. The plan—despite his fluctuating emotions—wasn't to kill Anika, just debilitate her until he came up with a way to convince her to work for *him*. With burning muscles, Mikko held her down, fingers slipping in the blood pooling between them. Every action became increasingly more difficult, their bodies tired and slick.

The metallic tang coating the air had Mikko's mouth watering as he fought for a hold on Anika. She would *not* win this fight. He remained solid even though his body screamed in defiance. Muscles ached, begging for release, but he pressed on.

Her cheeks were flushed from the adrenaline, eyes wide, taking in the scene before her. Mikko knew his own masked face was splattered in crimson, emerald eyes contrasting with it, but he didn't care. This was him; she had to realize that sooner rather than later.

This is us.

The clothes he wore were soaked, both his Anika's and growing heavy with sweat—

Defying all odds, Anika let out a primal screech, her other hand ripping free from beneath his leg. Coated in blood, it allowed her to wiggle free and supplement her other hand currently holding the knife.

Thrusting up, blade gripped by the other of them, she impaled him with it. It was a shallow stab, but the pain radiating out from the wound hurt nonetheless. A wheeze fell from his lips as annoyance faded to shock.

Fuck this, he thought dismally.

He fell off her writhing body, her fury untamable, and she scrambled back, soiled knife still clutched in her bleeding and cut hands. Glancing over at Levi, his chest was rising and falling, but his eyes were closed, the flower's properties in full effect now.

Fuck.

Flicking his gaze back to Anika, he saw she'd stood on wobbly legs, defiant look evident in her golden eyes.

A stillness fell over the room. The calm before a storm.

Mirroring her, he stood, body aching in places he hadn't felt in *years*, but he was dead set on catching her. His stance turned predatory, eyes honing in on her weaknesses. She was half naked—her nightgown splattered with blood and torn—and smaller than he was. Unlike Levi, he hadn't been drugged; she couldn't overpower him.

Tensing, she sensed the impending doom—the tranquil resolution settling into Mikko's bones.

He stalked toward her, slowly.

"It's too late," she breathed, "you'll either have to kill me, or I'll kill you."

"You could never kill me," he mocked. "I think you get off on the idea of me being your last victim. The final piece to your twisted puzzle."

Adrenaline coursed through his veins, and he could practically taste hers. It took everything in him to relish the moment, to not to rush it. He wanted to savor the closeness of her before he took her within his palm and *crushed* her.

"Maybe I *am* saving the best for last." Her words were haunting, a horrid promise he found himself wanting to test. He'd been begging for people to kill him for as long as he could remember. If someone finally succeeded, he might thank them.

"You're stroking my ego, *malyshka*," he said sarcastically, a grin spreading across his face.

Shifting around the coffee table, her feet stepping through glass if only to put distance between them, she hovered in the doorway. "Just what you need."

He stepped toward her, intent on turning her dreams into nightmares, but she turned and vanished into the darkness of her own house. And he let her go.

With a devious smile still adorning his face, he called out after her,

"I forgot to mention, Anika...I *like* the chase."

39

Violets

Anika

Battered and bleeding, Anika scrambled up the stairs toward her bedroom. While she'd dismantled Levi's gun, hers was still in working order next to her bed. All she had to do was get there.

Mikko's chuckle followed her up the steps, a terrible promise if he caught her. Glass shards dug into the bottom of her feet, each step burning and leaving a trail of her blood. Her back burned equally, more pieces embedded there. Once she had her weapon, it wouldn't matter; Anika wasn't a little girl anymore, and she could hold her own. She'd shown as much with Ivan and Dimitri and now Levi. Men always had a way of succumbing to her.

Mikko wouldn't be any different.

He may think he had the upper hand, his knowledge of her encompassing all the variables at play, but they still wouldn't help him in the end. Her sweaty palms gripped the door frame of her bedroom as she flung herself through. Behind her, she heard the *thud* of his boots on the steps, his stealth abandoned in hopes of exacerbating her fear.

But she wasn't scared, she was angry.

All her life had consisted of moments like this: constantly proving herself and fighting for what was right until she'd relinquished her morals in favor of winning.

Sometimes to tame the monster, you had to become it.

There, in the dark, she saw the glint of her safe, her salvation within reach—

Sharp pain erupted across her scalp as fingers tangled within her midnight strands and *pulled.* The momentum she'd built immediately shifted, the floor rushing up to meet her as Mikko threw his weight into her.

Thud!

Together they fell to the floor, the rug barely cushioning the impact. The wind whooshed out of her lungs and for a moment, Anika contemplated if she'd be able to walk without a limp tomorrow. That was if she made it out. With a grunt, Anika clawed at the rug, desperately trying to pull herself free of Mikko's ironclad hold.

"Not so easy now, is it?" he breathed into her temple.

She wriggled and swung her elbows, eager to feel one of them dig into his ribs or the wound on his side. "I don't know...what you mean," she gasped. He swatted her arms away, treating them like more of a nuisance than a threat as he pressed her harder into the floor.

"No violets," he flipped her around, strong legs straddling her torso, "no advantage."

"Tell that to the blood collecting on your clothes," she spat. While he was swathed in shadow, she could feel the wetness clinging to his clothing and see the darker stains of his blood. Anika remembered the way it felt when her knife had cut him, punctured his skin, and while it wouldn't kill him, it'd make his healing process *that* much worse.

Her fingers curled into claws, honing them into something to be feared. She aimed for his exposed flesh, eager to rend it from his bones. If she could bury a digit in any of his orifices or wounds, she'd be happy. While he may have brute force, she had pure rage. Currently riding the high of Levi being unconscious downstairs, she vowed none of her actions would be in vain.

Not for her.

Not for her parents.

"There's going to be more once I get done with you," Mikko said, his eyes flashing in the low moonlight streaming in through her bedroom windows. He caught her flailing wrists before squeezing hard to try and prevent her from continuing to attack him, but it had the opposite effect. Anika's adrenaline dumped into her veins with a renewed vigor.

"I hope you bleed out on these floors," she declared between grunts.

Mikko chuckled darkly. "You and me both, *malyshka.*"

The scent of him this close, the notes of patchouli and oiled leather, was something she hadn't mentally prepared for. The last time they'd been this close he'd caught her making out with Levi.

Not counting the night he'd snuck in and watched her sleep...

Her secrets were unraveling, the plans she'd curated the past couple years coming to fruition. And she was drunk on it all.

"I should've killed you when I had the chance," she hissed.

"A shame honestly," he said, releasing her wrists only to slam her against the floor. Her head cracked against it and all the air in her lungs rushed out, leaving her gasping. Reaching out, he clutched her jaw in his bloody grip.

"Look at me," he demanded. Her mouth popped open in a small *o* in his clenched fingers as her cheeks squished under his strength.

"You." A gasp. *"Fucker."* A wheeze.

Blood dripped from the laceration on his cheek, a droplet of crimson splattered on her bare face. He smiled as if the sight of his blood on her skin was intoxicating to him.

Bastard.

Mikko enjoyed making others suffer no matter what lies he tried to tell himself. He was exactly like Alek.

The cool kiss of his gun beneath her chin proved her point and stilled her movements. Desperation crept into the edges of her brain, warning sounds damn near blaring but she shoved it down. She wasn't thirteen anymore; she could survive this. Resiliency was in her blood. Mikko wasn't going to get away with this. She wouldn't let him.

A taunt rolled off his tongue. "Fighting me only proves my point."

"Typical that a man of your status would need such reassurances," she fumed, whipping her head back and forth to try and break the hold he had on her face.

"The moment I walked in on you strangling Levi, I knew all I needed to."

"And yet here I am, still breathing." Her lips pressed into a firm line.

His muscles tensed at the insinuation, but he kept his mouth shut, content to prod her with the barrel of his gun. In his attempt to intimidate her, he'd loosened his hold, her arms wiggling free from between his thighs.

"Don't make me regret sparing you," Mikko murmured, the sound almost too silent for her to hear. She should've paused and asked what the hell he meant, but her brain was already in motion, her elbows swinging down, hard.

"Oof!" Air wheezed out of Mikko as Anika's arm connected with his crotch. It served him right when he'd been too busy talking instead

386

of securing her. The wound in her arm pulsed with every beat of her heart, but she pushed on.

Bucking her hips up violently, she unseated him from around her waist. Knocking the gun from his grasp, she felt like she could breathe easier when it slid across the floor. In one final moment of retribution, she tugged at his mask. The eye portion was askew, momentarily blinding Mikko as she scooted away and got back to her feet. She only needed a few extra seconds to type in the code of her safe and she'd be free.

She could end it all.

Even if that wasn't the original plan, but she'd acclimate—

Tendrils of her hair caught on his outstretched hands again as his fingertips ripped some of the strands free. She yelped, her thoughts of freedom and retribution cut short by his relentless grip. Mikko reeled her back, using her hair like a leash and she was a disobedient mutt, until her back collided with his chest.

His skin was hot against her sweat-soaked sleepwear, his chest heaving from the exertion. It reminded her of the night in the maze and the one in her house where he'd tied her up: the feel of him both infuriating and intoxicating. Even now, she couldn't follow her brain when her heart refused to see this man as disposable.

Their ragged breaths filled the silence with his whispering against the top of her head. A shudder wove through her, her muscles tired and sore even though this was nowhere near finished. Drawing on her cardio and endurance training, Anika squirmed against his arms wrapped tightly around her.

But it didn't matter, he drank in the fear pouring off her like an elixir.

Before she could brace, Mikko slammed both of their bodies into the nearest wall, preventing her from reaching her safe. Her teeth rattled in her skull and her body vibrated with the impact. His weight pushed against her, keeping her immobile to the best of his ability, but she still fought, her head lashing backward in hopes of cracking his nose and her feet kicking and swinging at his shins. Mikko remained firm, hardly giving her an inch.

Clamping his hand onto her face, Mikko's blood—along with Levi's and hers—smeared onto her skin. He forcefully brought her face inches from his, their breath mingling. It was only then she realized he'd shed his balaclava completely. His bare face, the cut on his cheek red and angry even in the dim light, haunted her.

"You can't escape me, *stop* fighting it."

Her brows furrowed, eyes cloaked in shadow as her mind remembered a time when blood had coated her skin; there had been a time when she grasped her mom's face to—

Stomp!

She stamped her heel down onto his foot. The pain made him loosen his grip and she took the moment to break free again. Drying remnants of blood smudged across her face, her mind oscillating between the past and present as she landed a blow to his stab wound.

"Fuck," he swore, leaning against the nearest wall momentarily, "that was *rude*." Mikko's growl resonated in his chest as he watched her put distance between them, too stunned to catch her again. She flipped him off before hurriedly rushing to her gun safe.

"*That* was even more rude," he added as she input the code into her safe.

It beeped and flashed red.

Fuck, wrong password.

In her haste, she must've mistyped.

Copper bloomed along her taste buds and bile rose in the back of her throat as she caught sight of Mikko striding across the bedroom. At first, she would've thought he'd come for her, but he made his way to where his gun had been discarded.

Fuck, fuck!

Red flashed again.

Inhale.

Exhale.

Anika's fingers shook and bloody fingerprints smeared onto her gun safe, but she forced herself to reign in her adrenaline and her fears.

You can do this.

While her kills before this had gone according to plan, she would *not* be outsmarted by a man.

Bang!

Mikko's firearm erupted in the stillness.

The bullet ripped past Anika, her safe still flashing red, and buried itself into the plaster a couple inches from her head. Debris and dust settled to the floor as they both stood there frozen.

"Relent," he commanded, hands steady and form unwavering. A true predator on the hunt.

Four strides separated them.

It felt monumental and suffocating all at once.

Anika was a grown woman still tormented by her thirteen year old self's trauma.

Gunshots still made her flinch despite her training. Blood marring her hands reminded her of her mother. And the panic settling inside her chest...well, that had been a long time companion right alongside of rage.

She'd tried to overwrite it all with new memories, empowering actions, but some wounds took too long to fucking heal.

"It's useless, Anika, I changed the passcode," Mikko's voice rang out above the eerie quiet. It'd only be a matter of time before one of her neighbors called the police to report a disturbance.

"What?"

"Your gun safe."

"How the fuck did you do that?"

"My obsessive tendencies eventually pay off." A glimmer of something else flashed across his eyes, his hair tousled and his chest heaving. It was almost as if he was vouching for a younger version of himself too.

"Shoot me then, " she crossed her arms, "get it over with."

"I have a better idea, *malyshka*." He waved the gun, motioning for her to walk. "Let's take this back downstairs, shall we?"

Her spine was ramrod straight, her senses on high alert, but there was nothing she could do at this very moment.

Cooperate, assess, then act, her brain chanted.

"Eager to check back in on Levi?" she goaded. The soles of her feet stung with each step, her arm felt inflamed from the flesh wound, and her brain felt swollen inside her skull. Shock was the only thing keeping her pain at bay and her body in motion.

"Despite his shortcomings, he's more helpful to me alive than dead," Mikko said, falling into step behind her. The press of his gun to her back had her thoughts scattering.

"Makes one of us," she muttered dryly.

"Even after all this, you cling to your sarcasm. How cute." He prodded her when she hesitated at the top of the steps.

Inhale.

Exhale.

Her feet touched the first tread and within a few short seconds she stood in her dark foyer.

"Cristiano visited your mom," Mikko said, the words sitting like a rock in her gut. "She was all too eager to welcome a new face. Barbara too." They walked past the living room, Levi's sleeping form still sprawled out where they left it. The small victory of it all was overshadowed by Mikko's presence at her back and his filthy words.

390

"Seems like they need to up their security measures, wouldn't you say?"

"Fuck off," Anika snapped, the frames in her hallway the only witness to her humiliation.

"Imagine my surprise when I learned who your parents are...or were." He continued, uncaring for whatever she had to say. Shuffling into the kitchen, she tried to stay silent, not wanting to fall into his poorly set traps. She failed.

"You know nothing of them—"

"You know, I'd agree, except I can guarantee your father would be disappointed in you for throwing a brick through someone's window, Anika."

"Don't you even *think* about him—"

"Do you really think killing me will make you feel better? That it'll erase what my father did?" Mikko interrupted again.

"Killing Alek would've made everything better, but he had to go and die before I could draw out his torture." Venom dripped from her words. "You're the next best thing, *malysh*."

"Seems like we're perfect for each other then, one hunting the other in an endless cycle."

"You're a freak. Comparing us to each other demeans my work." Anika picked at the dark nail polish on her fingers, flakes of dried blood coming off with it.

Mikko huffed, pushing her toward the kitchen counter with the alcoholic concoctions. "You mean murder? It demeans your murders?"

"*Semantics.*"

"So pouring yourself a drink from these ingredients here won't be a problem? I mean, it's just semantics after all. Anyone could accidentally overdose on violets."

"What are you getting at, Mikko?" The countertop was cold beneath her dirty hands. "Spit it out."

"The same dose you gave Levi, I want you to make it for yourself."

"No."

He cocked his head, emerald eyes alight with the promise of torture. "It's either that, or I'll tell Cristiano to pay your mom another visit... only this time he won't be so friendly."

Anika's jaw tightened. He was never supposed to find out about her, let alone visit her and use her existence as blackmail. She'd been careful, but her safety nets had been yanked out from under her. In reality, she knew the moment she'd talked to Mikko at *Bubblegum* she was playing with fire, bound to get burned, but Anika could only hope it was worth it.

"Fine," she relented, "but the same dose I gave him would kill me."

"How much will it take to make you go to sleep?"

Instead of answering, she opened the nearby cupboard and procured a clean glass. Mikko set his gun on the counter, but it never strayed far from his fingers. One wrong move and he'd aim to wound. He'd perfected hers after all; his misses were intentional, and his hits...

Anika didn't want to find out. A cold sweat broke out across her forehead, the memory of her mom in pain from multiple bullet wounds flashing across her mind.

Clear vodka splashed into the glass and like a wave cleansing her, Anika banished her thoughts along with it. Muscle memory took over as she added a large rectangular ice cube. Her movements were watched by Mikko, his keen eyes never leaving her figure.

"Want some?" she asked, holding out the vodka bottle. His jaw twitched, but he shook his head.

"How long will Levi be out?" he asked instead as she started pouring the violet liqueur into her glass.

"For a man of his size, about forty-five minutes." She capped her homemade concoction and set it aside. With her index finger, she stirred her drink. Pink swirled among the liquid, faint traces of blood washing away with the motion.

"And you?"

"About the same, if not an hour." She held eye contact with him as she slipped her wet finger into her mouth and sucked it clean. *Use it wisely.*

Before she could change her mind, she gripped the cup and knocked the mixed drink back. The alcohol burned her throat and another flash of panic erupted in her gut. Anika was willing to put herself under and leave herself vulnerable in the presence of a man she didn't trust. But to build his trust, she'd have to sacrifice this moment of control.

She took another deep breath.

Inhale.

Exhale.

Quickly, she repeated the motions and downed a second drink before sitting at her breakfast nook. "Have fun carrying us," she quipped.

Her body was warm, the vodka already loosening her muscles. The tension between her brows faded and her thoughts grew soft around the edges. Anika preferred to refrain from drinking, especially recently since she had much to accomplish, so her tolerance had dwindled. That, and she'd learned to not eat before a kill. Sometimes what the mind could handle, the stomach could not...

He tucked his gun back into his waistband before striding over and taking a seat opposite of her. It was uncanny and way too domestic for what their current relationship warranted, but her tongue felt swollen. Her words could wait.

Anika's eyes traced over Mikko's strong jaw and piercing eyes. Blood was crusted on his pale skin, his cut scabbed over along his cheekbone, and sweat also coated his forehead. Again, she was struck by his beauty. She hated herself for thinking it, but maybe for now she'd let herself feel. It didn't matter anyway. Once the blur of the violet haze cleared, she'd be back on track.

Then, it would be time to burn everything from the inside out.

40

Waves

Mikko

For once Mikko's left hand didn't ache while he drove, his destination visible in his mind.

Maybe it was the adrenaline, or the fact he'd texted Cristiano as soon as Anika had finished her second violet drink, or that his muscles were screaming. The blood coating him had mostly dried or been rinsed away in her bathroom sink, but he still felt dirty.

After Anika had slipped unconscious, he'd let Cristiano into her house. Quickly, they worked in unison to clean up as necessary. It was like old times for a brief minute. While his teens and early twenties had been tumultuous because of Alek and his *lessons*, his best friend has always been there to help him clean up the aftermath.

This colossal shit show was no different. Except Cristiano wouldn't shut up about "Anika being his crush" and "this is a hell of a first date." Mikko could only shake his head while they worked.

"I'll pay them off," Cristiano had said as they'd tucked Levi into the

passenger seat of Cristiano's car. Although drugged, Levi's breathing was steady and his lashes fluttered against his cheeks. They'd found Anika's first aid kit and quickly tended to his wounds until Mikko could get him to an actual doctor. *"They won't want to deal with the extra paperwork and news attention this would bring."*

Mikko had only nodded, his body exhausted.

Now, glancing in the rearview mirror, he looked at Anika. Her face was calm and relaxed, so at odds with the way he usually saw her. Like a venomous snake lying in wait, he could've been fooled momentarily. She was no longer a woman trying to kill him while avenging her parents. She was just Anika. The fight, usually lining her body and burrowing itself in her bone marrow, had been sapped out.

Was this what she was like before all the trauma Alek had inflicted upon her? Would I be the same if my father had spared me his teachings?

Cristiano and him had also cleaned her up, dressing her flesh wounds. The glass pieces would be addressed later along with his. Mikko had a doctor he trusted on speed dial who wouldn't ask too many questions.

Soon, the landscape would change from the outer suburbs of Portland to lush pines creeping in alongside the margins of the two lane roads leading him to his secluded house. As always, he was running toward his refuge, praying to whoever or whatever that would listen that this would work. He needed time alone with Anika; he needed her to trust him. Especially if he was going to ask her to be his business partner.

A fact Cristiano didn't even know yet...

Mikko felt bad for keeping his idea to himself, but he didn't want to reveal his plans yet in case they failed.

In case I have to kill her, he thought darkly.

The idea made him shudder; the thought of her being gone forever was detrimental to his mental state. He should feel the opposite, her death relieving to him as it expunged his need for retribution and being her fucking clean up crew. He could pin Ivan and Dimitri's deaths on someone else and leave all this in the past.

But his damned heart didn't make it that simple. In a way, he felt bad for her, knew she'd also suffered at the hands of his father. It was a grief they shared in a not so different way.

The very breath in her lungs spoke to his weakness of killing her.

That and her name, her *real* name, had unlocked a memory. Alek mumbling in his study late one night about people unwilling to accept his offers—his generosity. Mikko had been young, unweathered in the sector of his father's dealings, but still he knew.

Khalid Naidu, current owner of Northeast Market.

As clear as if he'd been looking at the document now, Mikko recalled the name and place burned into his head. He'd seen it on paperwork on Alek's desk, a red asterisk on a map of land his father wanted to buy and redevelop. A sinking feeling wove itself into Mikko's gut.

Focusing on the road, he pressed the gas pedal a little harder, urging his Audi faster. There were still too many miles between him and his oceanside house for his comfort. The sun was rising slowly, its bright kiss barely visible above the tree-lined horizon before him.

I'm in control, I can do this, he internally chanted as the miles ticked away.

Cristiano would hold down the business while he was away, and many work items could still be done from Mikko's house. Although he'd have to be careful where he left his electronics lest Anika try to ruin his life. *Again.*

Foam capped waves peaked through ahead, the pieces of his plans falling into place.

I can do this, he repeated.

Soon, he'd be greeted by an ordinary wooden gate, one leading down a winding drive carved into a cliffside before a home sculpted into the rocks overlooking the ocean materialized.

Home sweet home.

41

Fractured Memories

Anika

Her body felt wrong.

Her skin was too tight and her bones brittle. Every muscle she could feel was bruised—torn and tattered. Her lashes fluttered against her cheek as she futilely tried to open her eyes. It was as if she was there, but her body couldn't keep up with brain's commands. She was a prisoner in her own skin, the sack of meat preventing her from waking up. From fighting whatever this feeling was off.

Flashes of light and warmth scattered across her battered skin, and she assumed daylight was streaming in. Pain radiated in her skull making the flashes of light excruciating even if the warmth was welcomed. A tentative swallow proved difficult, her tongue dry and her throat sore. If her muscles could cooperate, a cough would've spewed from her lips, but she was too tired.

Oh, so tired...

The steady thrum of a car moving beneath her aching head lulled her back to sleep, distracting her from the haze in her mind and the throbbing in her arm.

* * *

"I HEARD MR. Alek Romanov is interested in our store," her father, Khalid, informed before planting a soft kiss on her mother's cheek.

She huffed, her head tilting toward him to receive his affection. "Oh, and what is it he's interested in?" Excitement lined her words, Anika's sharp ears picking up on it even as she pretended to be engrossed in her homework. Her parents talked more that way.

"Nothing that I believe in."

Ira smacked her husband's arm as he strode past, making his way to Anika. "How pessimistic of you, at least tell me you listened to what he had to say?"

"I would've if it had been him who'd come to talk to me," her father called over his shoulder before mumbling a, "good evening, my dear," into the hair atop Anika's head. She smiled up at him in response before turning her attention back to her studies.

"What do you mean?" her mother questioned, hands busy with the last remaining steps of dinner prep.

Setting his items down on the table, he returned to his wife, his tone lowering. "I mean, he's interested, but not enough to come talk to me in person himself. He sent some"—her father's hand flourished in the air—"new guy instead."

"Well, still, that's not a bad sign, right?"

Anika pressed her lips together. Her mom always had a way of seeing the good in others, even if they were rotten to the core. It was what made her into the woman she was today, but it also made Anika and her father roll their eyes. While she was the kind-hearted giver of the family, Anika and *her father kept people at arm's length until they passed a series of...tests. It wasn't anything personal, just a logical approach when it came to making acquaintances.*

It was what made her father so successful in his business—he only trusted those who'd won it over. Anika saw the way people respected her father and wanted that for herself. Besides, there had been many times she'd overheard her parent's speaking in hushed tones, her mother's kindness always resulting in her feelings getting hurt.

"I didn't say it was a bad sign, just that we shouldn't get our hopes up."

* * *

THE SECOND TIME she awoke, her head felt slightly better, but ached nonetheless. She tried to open her eyes again, anxiety rushing through her blood at the idea of her vulnerability, but nothing. Even though her mind was awake, the rest of her body wasn't. No matter how hard she tried, she couldn't move a single extremity.

But she did notice another subtle difference.

This time, there was no car humming beneath her, only a steady warmth surrounding her and a hint of a man's cologne.

Levi?

Again, Anika tried to remember the last moments of her evening with him, but nothing came to the surface of her mind other than the last drink she'd poured for him. Sleepiness pulled at her restless mind, slowly chipping away at her resolve.

Or maybe it was the pleasant feel of strong arms around her.

She was being carried, a fact that should worry her, but after all this time, it felt good. She'd fought off the scum of the earth for long enough—denied herself happiness.

One little moment wouldn't hurt...

Even the wounds afflicting her previously were now muffled as if she was wrapped in cotton. Drowsiness took hold of her. It erased the caution usually living within her heart. Now, all she cared about was sleep and how it relentlessly called her name.

Anika, it crooned, *give in to me.*

So, she succumbed.

* * *

DESPITE HER FATHER'S reservations, Mr. Romanov had been persistent.

Anika had accompanied her father to the store, content to be in his presence while he restocked items during a slow period of the day. All had been quiet, the two of them chattering—Anika perched on empty crates while her father knelt nearby—about nonsense until it was interrupted.

The bell above the door dinged cheerily.

"Wait here, dear," her father said with a grunt as he pushed himself back up. He walked toward the front of the store to help whatever customer awaited while Anika stayed put. For now.

Shortly after, she heard his voice drifting through the shelves, but the words were indiscernible from this distance. It lasted for longer than she expected, the words fast and jovial. Mostly. Although something about the reserved tone in her dad's voice had her soundlessly slipping from the crates.

The soles of her shoes were soft rubber which silenced her steps as Anika snuck closer in hopes of catching the conversation taking up more time than a typical transaction.

"—understand your hesitation, but this could benefit the whole community," an unknown male voice said, his words accented and filled with persuasion. Anika's brow raised.

"In theory, yes, it's good for the neighborhood, but I don't want to sell." Her dad's voice was strong, his ever defiant attitude shining through.

"Well, this is the best offer you'll get I'm afraid."

"I know, and I'm still turning you down."

Anika stalked closer, a sliver of her face peeking out around the shelf.

"Please," the unknown man said, his side profile visible to Anika now, *"I want to help you out."*

His pressed suit and glinting gold watch spoke volumes. Anika's stomach clenched with apprehension. Dark hair was combed back stylishly from his face, the temples peppered with gray. He was mostly likely around her father's age, but had lived a much different lifestyle. Harsher.

The man's prominent nose and jaw caught her attention, his features brutal and unforgiving. In that moment, she had a feeling his temperament was as menacing as his face even though his words were coated in sticky honey.

Her dad spoke again, *"This store is my livelihood, you can help me, and the community, out by purchasing an item from it."*

The corners of the man's mouth tipped up, a game of who would give first ensuing. *"Of course."* Grabbing the closest item—a magazine with a man's portrait printed on it—he placed it on the counter for her father to ring up.

Tensions grew thick in the air, and Anika's heart pounded.

After a couple quiet seconds, the man took his purchase and nodded to her father. *"I'll see you around, sir."*

In response her dad plastered a smile across his face, the gesture genuine to an outsider, but Anika knew. She knew what it felt like to don a mask to keep others outside of her aching heart. She'd learned it from him, of course.

As the bell chimed again, she moved. Her father's attention snapped to her. His smile faded and his eyes shifted. *"Never trust men in suits, Anika."*

She nodded. *"Especially when they promise you the world."*

Now, in her closeness, the magazine the man had bought was one professing about the man's business success and real estate endeavors. His dark hair, defined nose, and sharp jaw all fell into place.

Alek Romanov.

The man who'd offered to buy her dad's store was Alek Romanov, and he hardly ever took no for an answer.

* * *

ANIKA AWOKE, UNSURE of how much time had passed since her last bout of consciousness, but her body felt like it'd been stuffed with lead, weighing down any effort she made to get up. But she could feel she'd been laid upon something soft, its cushiony shape molding to her body. And she could feel the brush of a soft blanket. The promise of her senses coming back excited Anika, and she pushed their limits.

With slow movements—ones exhausting her mind—she sent signals to her fingertips and toes, willing them to move. Even if it was just a fraction.

Nothing.

Nothing but darkness ensconced her, and she let it.

* * *

DROPPING HER BOOK bag onto the floor next to the dining room chair she usually did her homework in, Anika realized the table was set. For four.

"Mom?" she called out, the smell of food cooking on the stove permeating the air, but her mom was nowhere to be found.

"Coming dear," drifted down the hall followed by her mom's frame

whisking into the kitchen. An apron still adorned her front—if only to protect nicer clothes underneath—her hair pulled back into a tight, low bun.

"What's going on?" Anika pointed to the table.

"Oh, I meant to mention, your father and I are having a guest over for dinner."

"We are?" Both Anika and her father spoke at the same time. His face was unreadable as he entered the kitchen, home from work.

Looking back and forth from both her daughter and husband, she nodded. "Yes, a kind gentleman I spoke to over the phone said it'd be better."

"What gentleman?" Her father's voice was gentle, but Anika detected the underlying edge beneath it.

"Mr. Romanov."

Anika's teeth clenched, but her dad spoke the words she was thinking. "Love, there is no need for that man to come to this house. We already talked at the store, we don't need his money."

"Or his lies," Anika mumbled under her breath. Her parents heard, their faces different with their reactions. Her father grinned and her mother gave her a pointed look.

"The two of you aren't even giving the man a chance to explain himself. What if he's actually a great business partner?"

"What he's proposing isn't a partnership, jaanu, it's a transaction."

"I don't know—"

"Give me the phone, I'll call him, tell him we changed our mi—"

Ding!

The telltale sound of the door bell resonated through the house, halting everyone's words.

"That's probably him," her mom finally said, untying her apron and heading toward the entry of their home.

Anika and her father shared a knowing look, one that said, "humor your mom, but fall for nothing."

Nodding, they took their seats, waiting as Alek walked closer, her mom chattering with him innocently.

She's too good for this world, *Anika thought as she placed her hands in her lap as they reappeared.*

And Alek was as she remembered—warm with his words and smiles and gestures, but so, so cold with his eyes.

This was going to be the longest dinner of her life.

SOMETHING WOKE HER later that night, the blanket of darkness thick and stifling, but Anika's eyes opened regardless, sleep erased by something.

Turning over in her bed, she noticed the time was a little past midnight, but despite the late hour, she heard the whispered voices of her parents. The words were unintelligible, fragments of a private conversation, but a sense of dread filled her gut. It's cool clutch urging her to slip from the safety of her warm sheets.

Softly, her bare feet touched the carpet in her room, dampening her approach toward her cracked bedroom door. A slash of dim light cut across her room from it, but she stayed in the dark, unsure of how close her parents were.

"I'm not mad at you, dear," her father mumbled, his words clear despite the volume he spoke in. "I'm upset he got an answer from me he didn't like, so he targeted you instead."

"I know, people can see right through me." Anika could almost picture her mom, a gentle, sad smile adorning her face. "I always get us into trouble."

"No need to worry, I'll handle it. While Alek may not be a door-to-door salesman in need of shooing off our property, I'll make sure he gets the message all the same."

Her mom laughed. "I trust you. Whatever you need to do, I'll support you."

The faint sound of a kiss met Anika's ears. "I know. We can't let this man take away our livelihood all for the sake of revitalization. *We've seen what it's done to other neighborhoods..."*

* * *

CONSCIOUSNESS WAS FLEETING, but this time she was ready when it graced her, its touch soft against the wrinkles of her brain.

Again, she tried pouring every ounce of will into moving her extremities. And when she was about to give up, her mind spent and sweat somehow forming on her skin, she felt a fingertip move. Nervous excitement coursed through her and she tried again, but a noise caught her attention.

Begging her body to cooperate and open her eyes to see what had made the noise, she was disappointed when it refused. She was nothing more than a pile of bones; her eyelids were controlled by another entity, not listening to her own mind.

A scream clawed at the back of her throat.

Anika didn't stand a chance at protecting herself like this. Something was amiss, and she wasn't alone in the room. Intuition and the familiar prickle skittering across her skin told her this. Even in her debilitated state, she *knew* it was Mikko. She grappled against her mind even more fiercely.

As if sensing her trepidation, he spoke. His voice filled the space around her. "I can see you struggling to come to, *malyshka*, but I can't have that. Not *quite* yet."

Her tongue twitched in her mouth, choice words for him dancing behind her teeth, but silence was all she could manage. Rough bandages scraped along various areas of her skin, her wounds miraculously patched up although still sore.

Mikko continued, not needing her responses to carry on a conversation of his own. "But I'm going to give you more *medicine* so you can heal." He was closer now, the mattress dipping beneath his weight as he presumably sat next to her prone form. "If you're to be your best self when you come to, you'll need rest."

Moments from before flashed behind her closed eyes.

Levi's blank expression, the violets in his drink taking effect.

Her struggle in the dark to reach her gun.

And the taste of violets on her tongue as Mikko made her drink her own poison of choice.

"You'll wake when I want you to," his breath whispered across her face in the present. Internally she cringed, wishing she could headbutt him in retaliation. Again.

The pieces started falling into place as the feeling in her entire left arm started coming back. Excitement wiggled its way into her head; Mikko thought her weak and dull in comparison to him. All she had to do was act incapacitated—

Something poked her arm near the crook of her elbow. The pain was a blessing spreading across her skin as a reminder she was returning to this dimension, but that relief was soon erased.

A needle wormed its way beneath her flesh, the unknown liquid inside eager to make her forget—to make her weak. Anika tried to fight it, teeth gnashing together faintly behind her lips, but it was for nothing. She couldn't outrun the effects of whatever drugs Mikko deemed acceptable to pump through her veins.

And the blackness enveloped her, her childhood memories the only thing left to keep her company.

Acknowledgments

Thank you to my lovely husband who spent many nights either listening to me ramble on about this book and these characters, or he didn't see me for *hours* because I was typing away trying to get this story to where it is today. Regardless, this story wouldn't exist without your encouragement, patience, support, and love. Thank you, mi amor. There's a piece of you in every character I write because you endlessly inspire me.

Hugs and kisses to all the friends and family who I shared this with (even though they now know I write demented things). Your support and feedback means the world to me, and thank you for not institutionalizing me afterward.

To my Betas: Senna, Wren, Katia, Riri, and Sav. Thank you for seeing the vision and giving me the best suggestions to make this story more layered and impactful and *unhinged*. I couldn't have done it without you all; your comments were received at a much needed time.

Dave and Roberto, thank you for not only being wonderful and inspiring people to me in real life, but also when it came to running graphics and title ideas by you. This (soon-to-be) duet wouldn't have it's name without the two of you.

Thank you to Maria, who *repeatedly* told me this book wasn't a short story anymore, but a full blown novel (sometimes I still deny it). Our brainstorming sessions during lunch breaks got this story to where it needed to be. It's a fond memory I look back on and laugh at!

To my therapist who cheered me on despite everything and continuously asked how I was doing. Thank you for seeing my potential and skills before even *I* could.

And of course, thank you dear readers! Without you, this book would still be stuck in my head and unpublished if it wasn't for you guys (especially those of you who I met on ao3 and who read the first really, *really* rough draft of BTLOTM). Whether this story spoke to pieces of you or just offered you a necessary escape for a while, thank you for being here. I love you. Thank you for giving me the courage to do this and to pursue a dream I wasn't sure I could even have.

And until next time, make sure your doors are locked; Anika and Mikko always seem to find their way inside...

Coming Soon: Book II

Title to Be Revealed

Anika wakes to find herself closer to retribution, but when Mikko proposes a business deal to her, she has to decide if her previous vows or her life are more valuable...

About the Author

Lilliana Hazel is from a small town in Indiana and has always found her voice through storytelling. Anything dark, demented, and so very human is what she loves to explore. It's through words that people can find and express themselves, so delving into these emotions are close to her heart and healing. *Beneath the Light of the Moon* is her first novel, but she has others brewing in her head that she hopes she can share one day. When she isn't writing, she's usually reading, listening to eight hour rain audios, or at her day job—an architecture firm.

You can connect with me on:

🔗 http://instagram.com/authorlillianahazel

Subscribe to my newsletter:

✉️ https://lillianahazel.substack.com/subscribe?params=%5Bobject%20Object%5D

www.ingramcontent.com/pod-product-compliance
Lightning Source LLC
Chambersburg PA
CBHW020009120726
47903CB00004B/1206